the
Riverhouse

a novel by G. Norman Lippert

DEDICATION:

This one's just for me.

Contents

1972

Sometimes, when Marlena painted, she could hear the Riverhouse breathing.

She hated the sound of it. It reminded her of dead leaves blowing through a winter culvert, rasping with borrowed life. Often, she drowned out the sound by leaving the television on in the parlor, blaring and echoing throughout the empty rooms with its own borrowed life. She couldn't leave it on all the time, however. That would be crazy, and one thing Marlena Wilhelm certainly was *not* was crazy. She wasn't even slightly senile, even though there was a history of it in her family. Despite her advancing age, and despite what all the white trash hicks in nearby Bastion Falls thought, Marlena's mind was still as solid as cedar. This was what she told herself as she painted, sitting in the attic room near the round, leaded glass window. She was *not* crazy, despite the things that she heard and saw in the Riverhouse when no one else was around.

Which was most of the time, now.

A dull thump came from the floors below her.

"Mr. Stambaugh?" Marlena called out, her voice tremulous with age but just as commanding as it had always been, back in the years when the house had bustled with cooks and maids, workmen and groundskeepers. Now there was just Mr. Stambaugh, and he only came a few times a week. She knew he wasn't there now, but sometimes she thought she heard him anyway, clumping distantly on the kitchen stairs or rattling doorknobs in the locked back hallway. She paused in front of the canvas, her paintbrush raised in her right hand. Mr. Stambaugh didn't answer, and Marlena wasn't surprised. It had just been the Riverhouse. Or maybe it had been…

She stopped herself, shook herself. Not today. She wouldn't think about that.

"He's gone," she said to the canvas, not referring to Mr. Stambaugh.

The painting was finished, and yet she couldn't bring herself to put down her paintbrush. She'd been painting all of her life, and yet this painting felt different. It showed her and her son and husband, Hector and Gus. Gus's face was stern, immaculately shaven, as she always remembered him. Hector was smiling, pink-cheeked, balanced happily on his mother's lap. She'd almost been able to feel him there on her lap as she'd painted him, as if the painting had reconnected her to that time when he'd still been small and sweet, bubbling with that sort of tidal love that only toddlers know for their mothers. She didn't want the painting to be finished, not just because it had awakened the memory of that time in her heart, but because she knew, somehow, that this would be the last thing she would ever paint. Her vision blurred as she looked at it, and she sniffed wetly. Trembling, she set the paintbrush in the gutter at the bottom of the old easel and rubbed her eyes with her thumb and forefinger. There was nothing magical about the painting. It wouldn't bring them back.

Hector would be a grown man by now. She thought she saw him sometimes, walking on the street in downtown Bastion Falls, or even hiking along the Valley Road, a man with dark blond hair and his father's long gait. It was never really him, of course. She was suffering from the delusions of hope, that was all. She hoped for it so much that her mind couldn't help bringing those hopes fleetingly to life sometimes.

That wasn't *crazy*, though. It was only crazy if she forgot that the visions weren't real.

She got up and stretched her old back. It crackled faintly, sending sparks of numbness down to her toes and the tips of her fingers. All around her, the Riverhouse sighed, and in the floors below, something clanked and thumped. Marlena listened. The sound didn't repeat itself, but she knew she'd heard it.

"Gus?" she called, but not very loudly. There was no answer. A gust of wind shook the round window in its frame, and Marlena spun to look at it, her eyes widening. Outside, the sky was low and steely, moving with sluggish deliberation, as if it had a long way to go today, and wasn't looking forward to the journey.

Another thump, very faint and distant, emanated from far below. Marlena's breath caught in her throat. That sound hadn't come from the first floor; it had come from the basement. Her knees shook beneath her, and for a moment she didn't think she'd be able to hold herself up. Then, she remembered to breathe, and as the air filled her lungs, the strength returned to her body. She strode across the attic room, entered the dark hallway, and listened again.

The sound came once more, clearer than before: a shuffling and a tiny exclamation, a sort of whimper. That didn't make any sense, though, did it? The river behind the house was a little high in its banks, but it was nowhere near flood stage. Why would it happen now?

Even as she thought these things, she fled toward the stairs, lurching to grab the banister and steady herself as she descended first through one level, and then the next.

"It's a trick," she told herself, her breath coming in quick gasps. "It's just the Riverhouse playing a trick on me. Like every other time." She raised her voice and gritted her teeth. "It's a trick, damn you, and I won't fall for it!"

And yet, she couldn't keep herself from traversing the stairs, even as they turned and looped back up again, forming the new section that the workmen had added several years ago at her behest, the section that the locals referred to as the Insanity Stairs. This didn't bother Marlena. What did they know? They didn't live in the Riverhouse. They didn't know its secrets. *She* wasn't the one that was insane. It was the house itself that had gone crazy all around her, and all because of Gus. It was his fault. After all, it had been his choice to leave her and run off with the damned nursemaid, taking Hector with them. The Riverhouse had been his creation, and a part of him had stayed with it, driven mad and spiteful with isolation.

"God damn you, Gus!" she cried out, her heart pounding as she reached the base of the steps, stopping in front of the curtain that closed off the rest of the cellar. Her voice was thin, cracking with exertion. "Damn you! I hate you!"

She pulled the golden cord next to the curtains and they swept open, revealing the cellar beyond the thick glass window. Darkness filled the space, but not so much that she couldn't see the pit in the cellar floor, covered with its iron grate. Marlena threw

4

herself forward, cupping her hands to the side of her head to cut off the glare.

There was movement in the darkness of the pit. Shadows shifted, and then something white moved between the rungs of the grate, reaching and clutching slowly. Marlena gasped so hard that her chest hurt. She swayed slightly on her feet. It was finally happening, just as she'd always known it would.

"Don't go!" she screamed through the glass. "I'm coming! Don't go!"

She scrambled at the gold chain that hung around her neck, seeking the key that hung there, but even as her fingers closed on it, she heard another sound, one that came from all around. It was a low laugh, delighted and amused. Marlena startled at the sound, and then pressed her face to the glass again.

The grate was empty. There was nothing moving in the shadows of the pit beneath it.

"I'm not crazy," she whispered to herself, pleading with herself. She slumped against the glass as the strength leaked from her arms and legs. "I'm not... I saw this time... with my own eyes..."

The laughter was quieter now, satisfied. Every other time, Marlena had cried out in rage at the meanness of the Riverhouse. Now, she was simply too weak and emotionally exhausted. She had been prepared to do what would be necessary, even though it would be extremely difficult. Marlena had never been afraid of hard work. Hard work was, in fact, what she thrived on.

It was the waiting that was killing her.

She slumped to the floor and sat there, weeping helplessly, her legs tangled and her arms hanging listlessly at her sides. "I can't do it anymore!" she said suddenly, almost accusingly. "I can't live everyday with the weight of this hope hanging over me! Every day I pick it up, even though it's so very *heavy*! And every day *you* dash it from my hands again! And *laugh*!"

The Riverhouse was silent now, listening, drinking her anguish like wine.

"I hate you," Marlena said, quieter now. "I helped make you. I gave you life. But now I hate you."

The Riverhouse was still.

After some time, Marlena climbed to her feet again, clutching the banister for support. Slowly, she began to climb the stairs. It took her several minutes to reach the attic room again, not because she was old, but because she was used up. The Riverhouse had sapped her, taken everything from her except her life. The bitterness of her loss filled her like lead, forming a very nearly physical ache in her chest.

"I always thought you'd come back," she said, no longer speaking to the walls around her. "I was prepared. I loved you, Gus. Despite what you did and what you took from me. Why couldn't you come back, and bring everything back with you? How could you be so cruel?"

The sky had grown darker beyond the round window. A storm was coming in over the trees, carried on a stiff wind. The storm would bring rain, and the rain would probably swell the river, drive it to flood stage. Marlena didn't care anymore. The hope had been dashed from her hands, and this time she wasn't going to pick it up again.

"The definition of insanity," she whispered to herself, "is doing the same thing over and over... and expecting different results."

She'd been doing the same thing for decades now. Now, it was time to do something different.

She approached the painting on its easel. It was heartbreakingly beautiful, much like the one she had painted on the wall in the back hallway, the one with all the locked doors, except that this time she'd added the faces. It was complete. She smiled at it wistfully, and then picked it up in her hands. It was a small painting, but it seemed to have a sort of otherworldly weight as she held it.

Marlena carried the painting to the round window, leaned it against the wall, and then unlatched the window lock. The hinge squeaked as the window blew open in front of her, letting in the constant shush of the trees and the driving wind. It felt cool on Marlena's face and she breathed it in deeply. After a moment, she picked up the painting again and climbed through the window, out onto the ledge that overlooked the circle drive far below.

"I always thought you'd come back," she said to the painting, raising her voice against the stormy wind. "I was prepared. Maybe you knew that. Maybe that's why you stayed away."

She clutched the canvas to her chest then, heedless of the still-wet paint that smeared onto her blouse, distorting the image. It didn't matter now.

Before she stepped off the ledge, however, she looked out over the river valley.

A long time ago, back before Hector had been born, when Gustav Wilhelm had first brought her here with the idea of creating an idyllic home for them, Marlena had fallen in love with the valley. It was a boundary land, a line drawn between earth and water, making a sort of natural magic. That magic had captured Marlena and enthralled her. She'd thought to herself, *I could never leave this place. I could raise my children here, live here every day of my life, and die happy.*

But then, things had changed. Life had turned ugly all around her, and the Riverhouse had absorbed it, turned what she'd loved into a dagger, stabbing her with it every day.

Standing there now, on the ledge high over the brick driveway, Marlena looked again at the river valley, and loved it. It was a balm to her broken, pierced heart, and she realized something extraordinary, something that made her pause, frozen halfway between the window behind her and the yawning emptiness in front of her: *somewhere out there,* she mused tentatively, *there is still life to be had.*

Was it true? It seemed laughably ridiculous, and yet she wondered. She had stayed in the Riverhouse, despite its poisonous influence on her, because she believed that it held the only thread to her old life, the life she so desperately wanted back. If Gus and Hector were ever going to return to her, then this was where they would come. The Riverhouse was the key to everything. She *had* to stay, so that they could find her.

But what if they were never going to return? What if it was ridiculous of her to hope they would? What if such a hope was… crazy?

Then she could leave, couldn't she? She could run away, and leave the horrible walls of the Riverhouse behind her. No more pit in the cellar, no more Insanity Stairs. No more locked doors in the back hallway, leading to nowhere. She could leave the Riverhouse. She could escape!

The idea burst in her mind like a sunrise, and suddenly the drop before her seemed terrible rather than beautiful. There was another out. There were other ways to do something different. Marlena drew a sharp breath, as if awakening from a terrible dream, and reached out with both hands, grasping the angles of the roof that overhung the round window. The painting fell away from her chest, spinning as the wind buffeted it. A few seconds later, it clattered to the bricks of the driveway below, its frame breaking with a loud snap.

That had almost been me, she thought. She had almost jumped. She shook her head in wonderment. Slowly, shuffling her feet carefully on the ledge, she turned back to the round window that stood open behind her.

Gustav Wilhelm was standing in it, lit by the gray stormlight, a small smile on his face.

"Hello, Lena," he said kindly.

Marlena looked down at him, her eyes wide but not exactly surprised. "Gus," she said thinly.

He nodded. "You always knew I'd come back."

Marlena tried to respond, but her throat felt locked. He waited patiently, still standing framed in the round window, blocking it. Finally, in a dry whisper, she asked, "Where's Hector?"

"Around," he answered, his smile widening, turning into a grin.

Marlena's eyes blurred again with tears. "You—" she began, but her voice cracked and fled her. She swallowed thickly. "You aren't really here. You're in my mind. I'm... crazy. Aren't I?"

"Yes," Gus answered, nodding sadly. "Yes, dear. You are."

Marlena gripped the frame of the window. Tears ran down her wrinkled cheeks. The front of her blouse was smeared with the colors of her final painting. It had been one of the best things she'd ever made.

"You're in my head," she told the shape of her husband, nodding slowly, firming her voice. "You aren't real."

Gus nodded in agreement. "Yes, Lena. But I'm real enough to do this."

And he pushed her.

Part I: The Riverhouse

Chapter One

Shane Bellamy awoke with sunlight streaming in through the sheer curtains and needling at his eyes. He sat up, feeling groggy and thick-headed from sleeping in an unfamiliar bed, and realized, with a mixture of trepidation and excitement, that he was officially beginning the second chapter of his life.

Take two, he thought with some bemusement, squinting into the early rose sunlight. *Do-over*, like they used to say back when he was a kid on Brush Street, playing horse in Stevie Burkett's driveway with a beat up old Spalding basketball. It was as good a term for it as anything, even after the months of sessions with Dr. Taylor, who tended to dismiss easy answers as "mental red-herrings". Shane was getting a do-over, that's all. Not everybody did. It was a little frightening and totally unexpected, but it was also teasingly hopeful. Despite everything, despite all the ugliness that had led up to this moment, Shane decided to make the best of it. It wasn't like he had much of a choice, anyway. After all, there was no turning back, even if he wanted to; the one bridge he hadn't deliberately burned had ended up collapsing entirely on its own. *Structural failure*, he thought, and grinned bitterly to himself.

It was a morbid thought, and it pained his heart a little, but it also seemed like a good sign. *If you can grin about it*, he mused, *then maybe you're beginning to own it.* He knew he'd never look back on the previous year of his life and laugh, but a rueful grin was probably close enough. It was easy enough in the morning, with the dawn sunlight streaming in and the thought of percolator coffee rattling around all by itself in his head. Later, things might look a bit different. Shane decided to enjoy it while he could.

He started the water boiling on the little gas stove and showered quickly, wondering if he'd get dressed at all that day. Why should he? No one was going to see him. He was home alone in the small river cottage, completely hidden from sight within the dense trees of the bluff. In the past, he'd always been very jealous of the artists who worked from home, spending the entire day in their pajamas as they painted in their private studios. He'd never admitted it to the people in the office, of course. The staff at Tristan and Crane had maintained a sort of amused scorn for "starving artists", even though they contracted them regularly enough. Despite their nickname, the starving artists never actually seemed to be all that hungry. Granted, they were usually thin and squirrely-looking, but Shane was fairly certain that being thin was just part of the mystique. Whenever the contract artists showed up at the agency for client meetings, they invariably wore black and had some combination of creative facial hair, rimless glasses or indecipherable tattoos in interesting places. Compared to them, Shane barely qualified as an artist.

Not that he wasn't good. Shane was very good, and he knew it. It was just that, to him, the act of drawing and painting was like any other manual job; like laying bricks or digging a trench. He knew that art required skill and talent, but so did operating a bulldozer, and Shane approached it in much the same way. Like any other manual worker, he preferred to work a shift, putting in his time at the job site and then being done with it for the rest of the day. This meant that he'd never had to rely on the quirky vagaries of inspiration to get the job done.

Unlike the starving artists back at T and C, Shane preferred to bypass the legendary artist's muse, which could be fickle and temperamental and prone to long vacations. Instead, he relied on a sort of foreman in his head, one who had the blueprint for any given job and knew exactly where the marks needed to be. The foreman would call out the orders, and Shane's hand would simply obey. Shane himself barely had to pay attention. He may have been a teensy bit jealous of the starving artists, with their auras of quirky eccentricity (which the rest of the world seemed to think of as the mark of the "true artiste") but he didn't envy the way they worked. For Shane, sitting around and waiting for inspiration to strike was both silly and unnecessary; he had long ago learned the way down to the well of creativity, and figured out how to dip out whatever he needed all by himself. For him, waiting on the muse was a sucker's game.

While the coffee percolated, he went to get dressed. Starving artists might be the kind to lurk around their apartments all day in their underwear, but Shane was too used to the routine. This would be his first shift in the cottage, but there was no reason things should be any different. The movers had been very thorough and Shane had officially unpacked his studio yesterday afternoon, setting up his easel, art board and work table exactly as it had been at his apartment. He'd decided on the little upstairs room with the canted ceiling on one side and the single window on the end, positioning the canvas so as to take full advantage of the morning light. In many ways, the new studio was even better than the big studio back in New York. Maybe, he mused, he should have done this years ago. It had never crossed his mind, of course, and if it hadn't been for the lay-off, the divorce, and... well, everything else, it certainly never would have. As bad as all of that had been, at least it had led to this.

He looked at his watch as he climbed onto the stool before the huge canvas. It was two minutes before eight. He was a little early, but that was fine. He set his coffee mug on the side table, in the little cleared space on the corner that wasn't cluttered with paint tubes, brushes, magazines and CD cases, and looked up. The sign on the wall over his easel had come with him from his office back at Tristan and Crane. He'd hand-lettered it himself. It read:

"I often seem to have more in common with mathematicians than with my fellow artists." – M. C. Escher.

He read it as he rolled a brush head between his thumb and forefinger, absently shaping the bristles, and then he looked down at the canvas before him. It was only half finished. The top half showed a nearly photorealistic castle in the distance, blue with haze against an almost absurdly dramatic, stormy sky. There was supposed to be a forested foreground scene as well, full of huge, ancient trees—"loaded with personality" the art director had instructed—with a winding, curving path cutting through the middle. It was a matte painting, intended for use in a television movie that was currently being produced for TBS.

Despite his skills, Shane was not particularly creative. He couldn't invent. He could, however, mimic, and this had made him very good at finding resource material. There were magazine clippings and computer printouts taped all around the edge of the canvas, and dozens more tacked to the art board below the M. C. Escher quote. The images showed a dizzying variety of forest scenes, mountainous vistas, stormy clouds, tree close-ups, sprawling redwood canopies, and ancient castles. Shane had cobbled all of these elements together in the original sketch of the scene, and that sketch had been enough to get him the contract with the production studio in the first place—his first contract since being laid off from the agency early last year. Now, his original sketch was mounted on a smaller easel next to the canvas. Shane looked from the sketch to the various reference materials, connecting the elements in his head, and then began to paint.

It was better today, but not great. Progress has been slow lately, and this was slightly worrisome to Shane. The problem wasn't that the inspiration wasn't there, of course; that wasn't the kind of artist Shane was. Instead, the problem simply seemed to be one of focus. The foreman in his head still told his hand where the marks were supposed to go, filling up the white and bringing the image to life, but for some reason he had gotten a little lazy about the schedule. Shane would find himself getting bogged down in the details, spending far too much time on minutiae and forgetting the overall scene. He'd lean gradually closer and closer to the canvas until the brush was barely inches in front of his eyes, teasing out some tiny, insignificant detail that wouldn't even be visible in the final film.

He'd been working on the painting for almost two weeks, back in the old apartment, and it was due for delivery to the production studio in Los Angeles in four days. Normally, he'd have been easily finished by now, the painting leaning in the corner and drying while he milked the deadline, reading paperback novels and playing Sudoku on his computer. Instead, it looked like he'd barely be done in time, and he'd had to start mixing his oils with an alkyd gel so the paint would dry soon enough to ship. It worried him, partly because he needed this contract, needed to prove to himself and his clients that he could still produce, even outside of the world of Tristan and Crane. But it also worried him because it made him feel like he wasn't in control of the art anymore. After all, he wasn't like the starving artists, the ones who wore black and had coke for lunch and sat around moping while the muse flitted around like an unfaithful lover, refusing to land and put out. Shane was used to going down to the well of creativity and sending down his bucket all by himself, drawing up whatever he needed, dismissing the muse for the fickle whore that she is.

Now, for the first time in his adult life, Shane found himself nagging at the foreman in his mind, reminding him that there was a deadline to meet, and that he couldn't afford to fritter around on a tree root or a butterfly or some damned bluebird on a branch that no one was ever going to see. Maybe the foreman was just out of practice. If so, Shane couldn't blame him. Before this project, he hadn't painted anything for months. Probably, the foreman in his mind had been off on vacation during those months, getting tan and lazy somewhere, and was just now getting back into the swing of things. Shane hoped that was all there was to it. He strongly preferred the foreman in his mind to the muse. After all, anthropomorphic visualizations aside, the foreman in his mind was really just Shane himself. He could control the foreman, make him do the work. The muse, however, was different. She was her own, and she was capricious. *Screw her*, Shane thought as he painted, and not for the first time. *Screw the muse and the paintbrush she rode in on.*

Metaphorically, of course.

He caught himself focusing in on a boulder by the path, spending way too much time sponging on a layer of moss, dark forest green on the bottom, bright lime green on the top, where the sun was hitting it. He sat back, blinking and shaking his head. How much time had he wasted on that? He refused to look at his watch. Instead, he reached for his coffee, took a sip, and then grimaced. It was stone cold.

Damn.

Two o'clock came and Shane clumped downstairs for some late lunch. Steph had always told him that he needed to take a snack with him when he went to paint. "Take a banana or a muffin," she'd say. "Quit starving yourself. You're telling your body to pack on the fat, like a bear getting ready to hibernate." Sometimes Shane did bring a snack with him, but once the shift started, he'd forget all about it. For whatever reason, the foreman in his head allowed the occasional sip of coffee, but never any snack breaks. As a result, once the mental whistle blew promptly at two o'clock, Shane always found himself ravenously hungry, ready to eat whatever was in sight. Today was no different.

He slapped together a ham sandwich and ate it standing by the sliding back door, looking out over the patio and the river below.

It was a grand view indeed, even if the Missouri wasn't going to win any Most-Beautiful-River-of-the-Year awards. It was still swollen high in its banks, nearly opaque with mud. It looked thick enough to walk on, and the effect was only increased by the amount of flotsam slogging along on the slow current. Uprooted logs and broken branches of all sizes mingled with a colorful variety of trash and debris, all greedily collected by the river during its most recent flood.

It had been a big year for floods in the Missouri river valley, but the people who lived there had grown accustomed to just rolling with it. Shane had always marveled at the attitude of the locals toward the river, at their shrugging resilience in the face of such a huge and unpredictable neighbor. Much like them, though, he had recently endured his own fairly devastating flood, albeit a uniquely personal one. In the aftermath, just like everybody else, he'd simply had to suck it up, muck out all the stinking mud, decide what was salvageable from his old life, and try to move on.

Shane had contemplated suicide, and more than once. Not because he was depressed (or so he truly believed) but because he was just so tired. Dr. Taylor had helped—probably more than Shane was willing to admit—but it had been a near thing. Moving on was such damn hard work. He'd thought that he'd had his life all put together, patted down and comfortable by the ripe old age of thirty-three. It hadn't been a particularly exciting life, but it had been his, and it had looked more or less the way he'd always hoped it would. He'd had a decent job doing what he liked to do, a good-looking and fairly pleasant wife, a nice apartment just across the river in New Jersey, and a new Saab that was still, on the day that everything had begun to go neatly to hell, smelling a bit like it had just rolled off the lot.

Less than a year later, he had none of those things anymore, not even the Saab with its persistent new car smell. All he had left was the vacation cottage and his art, and even the art was, at the moment, a little shaky. It had been a long journey, a terrible, devastating flood, but Shane consoled himself in the knowledge that, at long last, the worst was finally over. Such things only happened once in a lifetime, and at least his was now behind him. By comparison, whatever rages the river below might have in store for him seemed fairly manageable.

He finished his sandwich and walked into the bedroom to change into shorts and a tee shirt. Now that his shift was over, he'd decided to go for a bike ride.

The sun was a high, bright diamond by the time Shane rolled his bike out of the little wooden shed attached to the side of the cottage. It was September, and even though there was a tang of autumn in the air, it was still almost stiflingly hot in the river valley. Tom, the cottage's big gray cat, jumped off the tiny front porch, tail up, and padded over toward Shane, purring audibly. Shane had never thought of Tom as his and Steph's cat, since they really didn't do much to take care of him. He'd always just show up when they came to stay, and they would occasionally feed him or put out a saucer of milk.

"Why do you want to call him Tom?" Steph had asked when they'd first encountered the big gray cat, as they'd sat petting him on the back patio.

Shane had shrugged. "It just fits him, don't you think? Tom-cat. Tom and Jerry."

"I'd give him a girl's name," she replied, watching the cat stretch and spread its claws. "I can't help it. When I was a little girl, I thought all dogs were boys and all cats were girls. Some things just stick."

Shane had thought it both silly and a little cute.

Shane squatted and petted Tom on his big, bullet-shaped head. In response, Tom pressed his head and back up into Shane's hand, rubbing against his leg and purring like an outboard motor. There were a few burs buried in the fur on Tom's flank. Steph used to brush them out when they'd come, and Tom would always patiently endure it, but it was a lost cause. He was an outdoor cat; for him, burs were a way of life. As Shane squatted, he glanced aside, into the tiny window that peeked into the cottage's cramped basement. There was only one light inside, a bare bulb hung from ancient black wiring, and it was on. Shane shook his head a little.

"Whaddaya say, Tom?" he said, still peering through the dirty basement window. "Looks like Smithy knows we're here, huh?"

Tom purred even louder and twined sinuously around Shane's legs, arching his back luxuriously. Smithy was a pet name that Steph had come up with, the first time they had vacationed in the cottage. The real estate agent, a woman in her fifties, with square eyeglasses and very short blonde hair, had told them that the cottage was rumored to be haunted. She'd apparently found the idea rather charming. It was Steph's idea to give the alleged ghost a name, and they had officially christened him "Smithy", after the man that had taken care of Steph's parents' summer home when she'd been a kid.

"If he's going to live here when we're gone, he can at least earn his keep," she'd said. "He can be the caretaker." Later, whenever something would go missing—a sock in the wash or a set of keys—or whenever one of them forgot to lock the cabin door, it would be blamed on the elusive Smithy. It wasn't until their second year vacationing in the cottage that Smithy had taken on any sort of reality. The cottage did indeed seem to have the sorts of quirks and idiosyncrasies that would lead people to call it haunted. The basement light would be found on more often than not, even when Shane knew he'd turned it off the night before. Same for the light in the upstairs bedroom, the room that was now his studio. The toilet would even flush sometimes, all by itself, although never while Stephanie or Shane were in the bathroom. "Smithy's using the john again," Steph would say, a little wigged out but not really frightened.

Once, according to the same real estate agent, a local radio station had held a Halloween contest nearby, getting people to stay in the old manor house next door, which was reputed to be even more haunted than the cottage. The truth was that both the cottage and the manor house had once been part of the same complex. There was a story connected to the property, but all Shane was able to remember of it was that the manor house and cottage had once belonged to a relatively famous artist and his wife. It had seemed comfortably fitting to him. After all, he was an artist, too, even if he wasn't particularly famous.

Thinking that, and dismissing the troublesome but harmless Smithy, Shane stood up, brushed gray cat hairs off his hands, and straddled his bike. If Steph had been there, she'd have told him to remember his helmet. He hated wearing a bike helmet, but he usually would when she asked him to. It always annoyed him a little when she nagged him about it, but he sort of missed it now, nonetheless. Her nagging had meant she cared. He considered wearing the bike helmet this time, for old time's sake, but decided against it. This was a do-over. Steph was gone, and nobody cared if he wore his bike helmet or not, least of all him. He sighed and paused, looking over the cottage that was now, at least for the foreseeable future, his permanent home.

Everything about the cottage was sort of pleasantly miniature. There was a miniature porch that wrapped around the northwest corner, facing the driveway, a miniature flagstone patio in the back that overlooked the river far below, and even a miniature crooked chimney that climbed up the north side, in the shade of an elderly eighty-foot pine. The cottage itself was mostly made of stone with a cedar shingled roof, thick with moss. It had always looked to Shane like something a Hobbit might live in, sans the round door. It was perched on a rocky bluff that brooded over a bend in the river, surrounded on three sides by trees, and accessed only by a long gravel driveway. As Shane began his ride, pedaling down into the shaded valley of the driveway, he saw mud caked onto the weeds on both sides, dulling it and matting it down. It was possible that he could get stuck here sometime, he thought, hemmed in by floodwaters even if his cottage remained high and dry. It was something to keep in mind for next year, when the spring rains started up again.

Trees crowded the driveway on both sides, still and limp in the humidity. Shane was sweating freely by the time he came to the paved bike trail that crossed his driveway, almost in sight of Valley Road. He slowed and turned left, heading away from Simpson Park and in the general direction of Bastion Falls. He'd probably not ride all the way into town today, but he could if he wanted to. The bike path meandered and wove through the woods, curving back and forth between the river and Valley Road, and eventually merging with the road where it entered the town, at the gate of the floodwall.

Riding bike was the only form of exercise Shane enjoyed. Stephanie had loved to exercise. She had been a runner and a swimmer. She had been into yoga and Pilates and whatever else new work-out was being offered at the YMCA three times a week. She had been addicted to endorphins. As a joke, Shane had even had that phrase printed on a tee shirt for her—ADDICTED TO ENDORPHINS!—in huge block letters on a blue background, and had given the shirt to her for Christmas five years ago. She'd laughed out loud, because she'd known it was true, and had worn the shirt regularly to her workouts. Shane had been absurdly proud of that. The tee shirt had been meant as a joke, a sort of a booby prize (so to speak, hah-hah), but she had truly loved it, wearing it until it had gotten thin and faded, finally relegated to nightshirt status.

When she divorced him and moved out, she'd left the tee shirt. Shane had found it neatly folded in the bottom drawer of her old dresser, sitting all by itself in the back corner, like a forgotten relic. He'd taken it out and sat on the edge of the bed, staring down at it on his lap. The letters were still perfectly legible, even though he couldn't see all of them because of how it was folded. It read: ICTED TO END. It didn't make any sense, but then again, maybe it did. Maybe it made all the sense in the world.

Shane pedaled hard. He pumped until his thighs began to sing with the exertion, and then he stood on the pedals, coasting and letting the hot air stream through his hair. Like the trail, his thoughts meandered. As he rode, the events of the past year unwound in his head like the carcass of a dead snake, one that had bitten, but could bite no more. Shane let it. It seemed safe to look at when he was riding, when his body was occupied and his brain was free to relax, to begin the long, possibly permanent work of resolution.

The first part was hard but relatively simple. It had begun with the lay-off. It would have been easier if all the staff artists had gotten the axe, but they hadn't. Tristan and Crane had let Shane and Rafael go, but they had kept Stuart and Monica. Shane had understood. At least, that's what he'd told Harvey Crane when he'd called Shane into his office. Tough times called for hard choices. He'd be fine. He'd always done well as a freelancer (not as a starving artist, of course, but as a *freelancer*; Shane just wasn't that kind of artist) and it would probably be nice to explore some new mediums and themes.

This had been bullshit, of course, from start to finish. Shane wasn't at all looking forward to going freelance again. It had been almost eight years since he had done contract work. All of his old industry contacts were surely by now either stale or nonexistent. Nor was Shane particularly interested in exploring any new mediums. It had just popped out of his mouth, sounding like an artsy thing to say, but Shane was an oil painter, pure and simple. He could draw, of course, and always sketched his paintings first, but when it came time to make the final product, when it came time to put in his shift, it was oils and sable hair brushes, period. Harvey Crane had nodded, his lips pressed together, and told Shane to let him know if he needed anything, anything at all: contacts, references, anything. Shane had assured him he would, but he hadn't. He'd not spoken to Harvey

Crane at all since his last day. By the time he'd gotten home that afternoon, contacts and references had been the last thing on his mind.

Stephanie wanted a divorce. At first, wildly, Shane thought she had announced this because he'd lost his job. That certainly didn't seem like something she would do. After all, she had married him back before he had landed his job at T and C, when he was still eking out a living on Hallmark greeting card illustrations and the occasional magazine cover. Then, slowly and with a sort of dazed wonder, Shane realized she'd been gearing up for this for some time. Some cosmic bad omen had simply arranged for it all to happen on the same day. It was like he'd won a sort of bad luck Powerball jackpot. "I'm sorry, Shane," she'd said, not meeting his eyes as they stood in the kitchen of their apartment, standing with the butcher block between them, like a stubby referee. "It's rotten timing, I know. Obviously I didn't plan it this way. But I can't pretend anymore. This has been coming for a long time now. I'm sorry. I really am."

When Harvey Crane had called Shane into his office, Shane had been disappointed, but not particularly surprised. In this economy, everyone was watching their backs, counting their eggs, waiting for the other shoe to drop. But for Stephanie to leave him? That had come entirely out of the blue, like an asteroid in a disaster movie. He had been knocked completely speechless. When he could finally form words, he had simply asked her why. What had brought it on? His greatest fear was that she had been having an affair. He'd never even considered the idea before that day, but now, suddenly, the possibility of it loomed over his world, darkening everything in its awful shadow. It hadn't been an affair, though.

"Not yet," Stephanie had said, enigmatically. She claimed that he had been growing less and less available to her for years. He'd become too engrossed in his work, too disinterested in her and her world. It had happened so slowly, so gradually, that it had been almost impossible to notice, "like the frog in the pot", she'd explained. But she was no frog, and she *had* noticed. At first, she explained, she had felt hurt, but then, later (and far worse) she'd just gotten bored; bored with him, bored with their marriage, and bored with life. At the same time that Shane had come to believe that he had finally settled down into the kind of life he'd always expected, Stephanie had begun to feel disillusioned and restless, depressed and alone.

And was it true? At first, Shane suspected that it probably was. Maybe he *had* gotten a little complacent. Maybe he had stopped pursuing her. But she'd never said anything, not until now. He loved her, and even if their life wasn't exactly a storybook romance, it was pretty good, wasn't it? And damn it, he was willing to work at it, if it would help. He'd asked her if it was too late to make a change, and even as he'd said it, he'd hated the way he sounded, like he was the bad guy, begging for a second chance. He had just been fired that day, and now here she was, pouring insult onto injury, and adding a good bit more injury as well. This wasn't the way it was supposed to be. She was supposed to be telling him it was going to be all right, that they would make it through, even if it was a little rough for a while, but that she'd stick by him no matter what. She certainly *wasn't* supposed to be standing there on the other side of the butcher block, her eyes dry and avoiding his face, with her suitcase half-packed on the bed upstairs. It had to be some kind of dreadfully realistic nightmare. He'd wake up soon enough and find himself in his bed, slick with sweat, heavy with relief, and roll over and put his arm around Steph as she slept on obliviously next to him, still there, still his.

But he didn't wake up, because it *wasn't* a dream. By that night, she was gone. Shane had lain awake on his side of the bed for hours, feeling the yawning emptiness next to him, her pillow untouched, her alarm clock not set. She wouldn't be getting up early to put on her sports bra and go to Pilates class. She'd not roll over when the alarm clock went off, wearing her ADDICTED TO ENDORPHINS! tee shirt, and sleepily whisper, "What do you say, Shaney, should I get my work-out here this morning instead?" Apparently, those days were over. When she'd been standing across from Shane in the kitchen with the butcher block between them, he had been completely unable to believe it was actually happening, that she was really and truly leaving him. But that night, lying alone in their bed and staring up at the ceiling, he'd found it all too believable. She was gone. Maybe she'd come back, but then again, maybe not. It was suddenly a real possibility, even a likelihood, that his marriage was truly over. The realization of it had hung over him like an anvil, threatening to fall on him at any moment, threatening to crush him.

It was true that she wasn't having an affair, but it wasn't true that there wasn't someone else. As the weeks drug on, Shane had learned about the other man, a guy named Todd. He was "a friend", someone Stephanie had met at the YMCA.

At first, they had merely chatted in the weight room, between the machines. Eventually, it had led to sharing coffee at the corner café down from the Y. He'd just been a listening ear, and Stephanie insisted that that's all he still was. Nothing had "happened" between them, but he cared for her, and she cared for him. And the horrible thing was that Shane knew it was true. Stephanie might be a lot of things, but she was not a liar, and she was as straight as an arrow. She'd not disrespect Shane with a betrayal. And that somehow made it worse. He wanted to believe that he was the wronged husband, deserving of the respect of her devotion and commitment, worthy of the work of making their marriage work. But what he felt like was a child getting in the way of Mommy's love life. Her very propriety had reduced him to a mere nuisance. He almost wished she'd just screwed the detestable Todd, realized it was a terrible mistake, and then discreetly forgotten the whole thing. Of course, that might have been worse after all—maybe the human mind just liked to weigh the relative horrors of every possible betrayal—but it didn't make Shane feel any better either way. Sometimes he was angry, other times he was devastated, but it never mattered. Once Stephanie had made up her mind, only Stephanie could change it again.

The divorce had become final in early June. Todd had been long gone by then, although Shane never heard the full story of what had happened. Part of him suspected that Stephanie had gotten tired of him, too, that Todd had merely been a convenient tool, a shoe horn to smooth her transition out of their marriage. Another part of him—the mean-spirited, hurt part—hoped that Todd had gotten bored with Stephanie and had broken things off with her. Maybe she'd learn what it felt like.

In the meantime, they had split up the household. She'd kept the apartment, and Shane had gotten the vacation cottage in Missouri. This had surprised Shane, since buying the cottage had been Steph's idea in the first place. She'd grown up in St. Louis, and had always loved the area. When she'd first suggested a small vacation cabin there, she had been so excited and eager about the idea that Shane had been completely unable to turn her down. They had found the cottage during a house-hunting vacation in the Ozarks. It had been rather outside of their budget, but not so much that they couldn't swing it if they'd really wanted to. And they'd decided they *did* want to. They signed on the property that very week. Their first night in the cottage had been the last night of that vacation, and they'd spent it in sleeping bags, zipped together and laid out on the bare floor in front of the fireplace. The next morning they'd eaten granola out of a plastic baggy on the flagstone patio overlooking the river, feeling the sun shine down, warming them, and Shane decided it had been a good purchase. The cottage was small and a little musty, but it would clean up well, and it was certainly idyllic. They had both come to love it.

When Stephanie suggested that Shane take the cottage, he'd been surprised, but not shocked. Apparently, she was making a break from everything, not just him. This made him feel a very tiny bit better. He decided he'd move into the cottage, just for a while, just until he figured out what he wanted to do with the rest of his life. It wasn't meant to be permanent. But that was before his last phone call from Steph, the one that had changed everything, the one that had turned the world onto its head all over again. Shane had thought it was all over. The divorce hadn't been nice—it had been extremely awful, in fact—but at least the book of their marriage had finally been closed. He could move on. That's what he'd thought, until that one, final phone call. Now, of course, he'd never know.

It occurred to him as he rode his bike through the flickering shadows, pedaling hard, as if to outrun something, that maybe life just doesn't work that way. Maybe the idea of a neat ending is just a myth. Maybe in real life no story is ever really over, everything is unfinished business, and the best you can hope for is just to accept that. It may be frustrating, but fighting it just makes you crazy. Shane knew all about that. Fighting life's unfinished business was a no-win game, no matter how you looked at it. Some things you just had to give up on, even if giving up was the last thing you wanted to do; even if giving up was the absolute hardest thing of all.

He was thinking about these things when he rounded the long curve that bordered the old manor house. As the trees cleared, he glanced aside, looking out across the big weedy yard that fronted the property, and was so surprised by what he saw that he instantly squeezed the brake levers and leaned on the handlebars. The bike scrunched to a halt where the trail intersected the house's ancient driveway, and Shane put down a foot to steady himself. The driveway was made of brick, embedded into the yard and framed with lengths of chipped granite. Normally, the bulk of the house overshadowed the circle drive, especially as the afternoon sun lowered, but now the yard was awash with sunlight, glinting copper on the bricks and sparkling on the cab of the big yellow bulldozer parked on the lawn. The bulldozer explained everything, really. Its tracks were stitched all over the yard, dark and muddy. There was a crane as well, with a wrecking ball hanging from it like a giant iron teardrop. It was parked in back, in the shadow of the tree line with the river sparkling gaily behind it. Shane shouldn't have been able to see it; the house should've been in the way, but of course that wasn't an issue anymore.

The manor house was gone, reduced to a massive pile of rubble that choked the hole that had once been the cellar.

During his previous vacations in the cottage, Shane had ridden past the manor house dozens of times but had never really paid any attention to it. It had been a singularly ugly and dilapidated building, despite how it might once have looked. Slip-shod renovations had hacked the place apart over the years, most recently converting into a duplex apartment, occupied on one side by a permanent resident and on the other by a series of itinerant fisherman and boaters who usually left their trucks and trailers parked on the grass by the front steps. By comparison, Shane's cottage seemed perfectly regal and pristine, and he was glad that the properties had long since been split up. Now that the house had finally been demolished, however, he found himself strangely curious; even, somehow, a little sympathetic. He climbed off his bike, lowered the kickstand, and began to walk up the uneven driveway, examining the wreckage.

It had probably been the most recent flood that had tipped the balance. Maybe the ground had shifted over the decades, or maybe the water had simply risen higher than usual. Maybe it was just that the house had finally outlived the cost of its upkeep. Probably it was all of those things, but the inevitable conclusion was that this last flood had sealed the house's fate. Time and entropy, the hungry step-sisters of Mother Nature, had finally completed their work, transforming the house from what was once probably a glorious architectural jewel into the inevitable pile of rotting wood and broken glass.

As Shane got closer he saw that dust still hung in the air around the wreckage. The air smelled like mold and plaster. The foundation of the entryway was still there, with three stone steps leading up to a broad portico, now littered with bits of wooden siding and shingles. The torso of a not-quite-life-sized marble statue lay on what had once been the doorstep, looking like a fairy-tale crime scene. The front door was half buried in the rubble, split neatly in two right down the middle.

Shane looked out over the wreckage. The footprint of the cellar seemed remarkably small. Of course, the house itself had been larger than the cellar, having been added onto over the decades, but the original house must have been rather cozy, even with its high ceilings and tall, imposing windows. Shane liked classic architecture, with its painstaking craftsmanship and minute details, and he could imagine the house as it might have originally looked, tall and sprightly, its windows thrown open to admit the river breeze, its solid doors creaking on their hinges like contented sighs, huge oriental rugs on gleaming hardwood floors, the clank of pots in the kitchen, the snip of shears in the rose garden.

He could barely remember what the house had looked like when it still stood, in its final configuration, but the image of it in his mind, as it might have looked on the summer it was first built, was strangely, almost eerily perfect. In it, he saw pillars on the portico, two on each side, supporting a high colonial porch roof. He could almost feel them, the cool weight of their shadow. Was it possible he was right? He didn't remember noticing any pillars or high, overhanging porches on the manor house during his summer bike rides. Besides, even if such things had existed in the past, surely they had long since been stripped away, probably resold to some architectural salvage yard somewhere. Shane glanced down, at the front right corner of the portico floor, and then walked over to it, kicking aside a few chunks of rotted wood. Sure enough, there were two large circular scars on the old stone, faded but clearly visible in the bright sunlight. Obviously, he had seen these marks as he'd approached, at least on a subliminal level, otherwise how could he have known that the original house had had pillars framing the portico? Still, the picture in his head was strangely vivid, almost persistent. It nagged at his thoughts, like an itch in the center of his brain, an itch he couldn't quite reach.

Or could he?

An idea struck him, and as soon as he thought it, he knew he had to try it. He walked quickly over to the opposite side of the portico, where the debris lay in a thick pile. There, sticking out of the top of the pile was the perfect thing: a length of wood, broken into a sharp point. Shane wrapped his hand around it, careful to avoid splinters (an artist's hands, after all, were his life) and pulled tentatively. The stick came free easily, about two feet long and heavy, like some kind of hardwood. With the stick in hand, Shane backed carefully down the portico steps, looking up at where the house used to be, letting the mental picture of it solidify, placing it in space. It was so clear he could almost see it. In his mind, the pillars were white, somehow both smooth and rough, like a stone from the riverbed. They tapered inwards as they rose, supporting the squat triangle of the porch roof, and there was a decorative window in the center of that triangle. It was round and intricately patterned, made of leaded glass and wrought iron.

Shane stopped in the center of the circle formed by the driveway. The ground here was packed dirt, with very little grass, and he remembered that this is where the renters had often parked their trucks and boat trailers. It was perfect. He hunkered down on one knee, closed his eyes for a moment, and then opened them again, staring down at the blank ground before him. Using the sharp stick as a stylus, he began to sketch rough lines on the dirt. It was quick work, and utterly temporary, but as he scratched the lines, forming simple shapes, he could feel the sublime sigh of scratching that weird mental itch. The picture in his head had wanted out, that was all. In all of his years as an artist, he'd not felt anything quite like it, or at least not for a very, very long time. Not since he'd been a kid. He frowned studiously down at the lines as he made them, and then adjusted his grip, choking up on the stick to get more leverage with it. Weightier lines now, framing the initial sketch; eight deep vertical scratches to define the pillars, three more for the overhanging porch roof. Finally, leaning close to the dirt and using both hands on the stick now, steadying it, he drew a rough circle right in the center of the triangular porch shape: the leaded glass window.

Shane looked down at his work. A moment later he stood up, listening to the pop of his knees as they straightened, and tossed the stick aside. The sketch looked right. More important, it *felt* right. It felt the way the insistent image in his mind had felt. A long time ago, when the house was new, this was what it had probably looked like. Shane glanced up at the wreckage, and then down again at the drawing in the dirt. If his sketch was right, it had indeed been a rather inviting house at one time. He sighed and dusted his hands off on his shorts.

As he walked back to his bicycle, Shane realized he felt good. Damn good, in fact; better than he had in months, maybe even since the day he'd won the bad luck lottery and lost both his job and his wife in the same three hour period. He tried to remember the last time he had created art for himself, and couldn't. When he'd been a kid, he'd drawn for fun all the time, but not as an adult. Now, art was just work.

He straddled his bike and looked back at the decimated ruin of the old house, smiling with bemusement. Was it possible that the foreman in his head had had nothing to do with the spontaneous house sketch? Was it possible, in fact, that that sketch had come directly from the fabled artist's muse, whose inspirations Shane had spurned all these many years? Had she been the one responsible for that sudden persistent urge, like an itch in the center of his brain, an itch only satisfied by bringing the picture in his head to life? It had been a long, long time since she'd deigned to visit him. He'd forgotten how good it felt. The muse might be a capricious and fickle lover, but when she was good, she was very good. Shane could imagine how easy it'd be to become her slave, like the starving artists he'd seen so often back at Tristan and Crane. That wouldn't happen to him, of course. He knew how to go to the well of creativity all by himself, using his rope and bucket to dip out what he needed, whenever he needed it. But it was nice to know that the muse didn't hold that against him. It was nice to know that she could still show up from time to time, even if it only meant a rough sketch in the dirt, drawn with a sharp stick.

Unlike making art according to the foreman in his mind, making art dictated by the muse had a sort of euphoric buzz associated with it. It created its own sort of endorphins, no less potent than those celebrated by Steph's old tee shirt. And now that he'd gotten reacquainted with the muse, maybe—just maybe—she'd come back. As he pedaled on again, pushing into the heat of the autumn afternoon, feeling that strange, contented euphoria of creation, he thought that might not be such a bad thing at all.

In fact, maybe that was exactly what he needed.

Chapter Two

That night, Shane fell asleep in front of the television, lying on the couch in the cottage's little sunroom. The sunroom was a relatively recent addition, attached to the back of the cottage next to the patio with its ancient brick barbecue. Windows on three sides provided a stunning view of the river bluff during the day, but became blank black faces when darkness fell, hiding the cottage's surroundings. Shane always pulled the blinds at night so he didn't feel like he was in a fishbowl. He'd been watching an old movie on AMC, something with Cary Grant in it. He liked old movies, but they tended to lull him to sleep. There was just something about the black and white images, and the ponderous stroll of the dialogue, at least compared to modern movies. He had been particularly susceptible tonight, however, being weary from his bike ride. After the strange dirt sketch at the site of the old manor house, Shane had seemed to be nearly bursting with energy, and had not only ridden all the way to the floodwall gates of Bastion Falls, but had walked his bike up the grassy slope of the floodwall, onto the gravel maintenance path that ran around the top, and continued on, circling the entire town. When he'd finally gotten back home his legs had felt rubbery and he was so hungry that his hands had been shaking when he'd unlocked the front door. It was a good feeling, overall. It had been awhile since he'd been physically exhausted and ravenously hungry. He'd made himself a hamburger, frying it up in an iron skillet on the stovetop and sticking it between two pieces of toasted bread, slathered with mustard, just like his grandmother used to do for him when he was growing up. He had eaten it sitting on the patio, on one of the old teak deck chairs, looking down at the river and its marching, flotsam-filled current. Just as Shane was finishing his dinner, Tom had come padding around the corner of the house, tail sticking straight up, his nose twitching. He'd purred and twined around Shane's feet, and Shane had tossed him the last bit of hamburger. Tom darted to where it landed, sniffed it to make sure it was, indeed, the source of that intriguing greasy aroma, and bolted it down in one bite. When Shane went back inside, he'd held the door open for a moment. "You wanna come in tonight?" he'd asked the big gray cat. "It's just you and me from now on, Tom ol' boy. Just us guys. Whaddaya say?" Tom had glanced at the open door, then up at Shane, and then dismissed them both. He'd sat down on the corner of the patio and began to lick his flank, washing himself. "Fine, be that way," Shane had said, entering and letting the screen door clap shut behind him.

He awoke on the couch during a late night commercial. Some guy in a denim shirt and a beard that looked like it had been drawn on with a Sharpie pen was yelling about his amazing new cleaning product. He had a bowl of water and was apparently washing something by hand in it, grinning up at the camera and blathering at the top of his lungs. Shane fumbled for the remote and thumbed the power button, making the guy disappear. *His mama never taught him how to use his indoor voice,* he thought sourly. He hated falling asleep on the couch. Whenever he woke up, he always felt surreal and half-drunk, and it was always hard to get back to sleep again once he made it to his bed. He swung upright on the couch and dropped his feet to the floor, groaning, and then froze, suddenly alert, as something clanked in the kitchen.

He listened, waiting, staring through the sunroom door. There were no lights on in the rest of the cottage since he'd retired to the sunroom for the evening while it was still twilight outside. Now, the other rooms had descended into near total darkness. The sunroom lamp cast a bar of light across the wooden floor of the adjoining room, a tiny room that Steph had always called the library, since it held a book shelf, two chairs and not much else. As Shane's eyes adjusted, he could see a very dim greenish glow emanating from the nearby kitchen, cast by the digital clock on the microwave. Nothing moved.

Could it have been Tom? Could he have gotten in? It hadn't been a loud noise, but it definitely hadn't been his imagination. It had been a sort of clank or knock, like a cup being put down on the counter, or a plate in the sink being disturbed by a curious, scavenging mouse. Certainly that's all it had been. The cottage was old, after all, and rife with mice and spiders, bats in the attic and even the occasional snake under the basement stairs.

And yet, for some reason, Shane didn't want to walk through the kitchen. It was irrational, and he knew it, but that didn't make the feeling go away. In the wake of the television's constant noise, the silence felt huge and thick. It didn't feel like the silence of emptiness. It felt like the silence of something being very, very quiet.

Shane was beginning to freak himself out. This was his cottage, damn it. He'd slept here dozens of times. There was nothing here that he hadn't put here, and there was nobody here but him, period. And that was probably the real source of his discomfort, now that he thought about it; apart from last night, every other time he'd stayed here he had been with Stephanie. *And that's the first thing you thought when you heard that little knock in the kitchen, wasn't it?* a little voice in Shane's head said. It sounded a bit like Dr. Taylor. *You thought it was Steph, come out to make herself a cup of tea because she couldn't sleep. And then you remembered: Steph isn't here anymore, and she'll never be here again. Steph is gone. Your marriage is dead. Dead as the manor house a quarter mile down the trail.*

Shane sighed and got up. Maybe that's all it was. Surprisingly, what he felt was relief. The idea of his marriage being dead was a downer, for sure, but it was better than the *second* thing he'd thought when he'd heard that strange noise in the kitchen, when he'd remembered that he was, in fact, entirely alone in the house. That thought had been a lot worse, even if it had been entirely irrational.

Shane reached to click off the floor lamp next to the couch. It snapped off and darkness flooded the room, pouring in from the rest of the house. And something—some *thing* that had apparently been standing in the darkness right outside the sunroom door, invisible in the shadows—*hissed.* The sound came from right outside the entry; long, diminishing, and strangely human, like a deep sigh, or a final exhale, expelled in one weak, sustained gust, rattling as the weight of the chest lowered, collapsing for the last time. Shane's hair immediately stood on end and in the darkness his eyes shot wide open, straining. A dozen thoughts clambered into his head, all shouting possible explanations—Tom the cat, a leaking pipe, a gust of wind through a cracked window—but none of them worked, none of them fit, because there was no mistaking that sound. It was a human sound, but not a healthy sound. It sounded sick, deathly, pathetic, and that made it all the worse. Shane's fingers were still on the switch of the lamp, but they were suddenly shaking so much that he couldn't grip the tiny burled knob. He grasped and fumbled at it, his breath stuck in his chest, going stale. Shane had a vivid artist's imagination, and he could all too clearly imagine the source of that awful, poison breath. He envisioned it moving—no, *floating*—across the floor of the sunroom, invisible in the darkness, reaching toward him with horrible long arms and fingers hooked into talons. He imagined the sort of mouth that could make such a sound; huge and gaping, dry, stricken into a grimace that could almost look like a grin of rapture, bearing down on him. And then, finally, Shane's fingers grasped the floor lamp's switch and he spun it. He turned it too hard, and the lamp clicked on and off instantly, like a bolt of lightning. He turned it again, barking a little yelp of fear, and light flooded the room.

There was nothing there.

Shane gasped a breath and looked around, eyes wide and heart pounding. He caught a glimpse of his own reflection, on the glass of the one uncovered window, the one that overlooked the patio. He looked pale and slightly insane, hunched in a sort of alert crouch, his right hand still buried under the shade of the floor lamp. The room was empty. He peered out, through the doorway that led into the library. It was dim there, but not completely dark. He could see the shapes of the room; the bookcase and one of the chairs, the little round table with the cordless phone on it, its power light glowing green. There was nothing there. There was no one in the house but him. That's how it had been all night, of course, because he lived alone now.

But *what* had made that awful sound?

Shane drew a breath, and then, horrified that he was even giving voice to such a thing, he called out, tremulously, "Smithy? Is that you?"

There was no answer, of course. In truth, Shane was quite certain that, whatever it had been, it hadn't been Smithy. Probably there was no such thing as Smithy. It was just the personality that Shane and Steph had assigned to the house's erratic idiosyncrasies. Probably. Smithy might be mischievous, but he'd never been scary. But there was something else. Whatever had made that horrible, ghastly sound had not been... what? What was the thing? Shane couldn't quite put his finger on it.

His heartbeat was returning slowly to normal. The house no longer felt watchful. It just felt empty. He left the light on in the sunroom and approached the doorway leading into the library. Nothing happened. Slowly, hating himself for being so squeamish, Shane reached around the doorway, found the wall switch for the overhead light, and clicked it on. Brightness flooded the room, chasing every shadow into the corners. The light not only made Shane's previous fright seem a little silly, it made everything in the room feel strangely dull and lifeless, from the bookshelf to the oval rug in the middle of the floor. There were no lurking, gasping ghosts there, that was for sure. Whatever had made that noise, it was gone now.

Was it possible that maybe it had been Tom the cat after all? Shane knew that cats could make eerily human noises, sometimes when they were in pain, sometimes when they were in heat. Maybe Tom was just outside, getting it on with some lady friend beneath the library window. Was the window cracked enough to let in such a noise? Shane looked, and sure enough it was, propped open with one of the books from the bookshelf, something called "the Diary of Mary Todd". One of Steph's old books, apparently. Shane drew a deep breath and let it out slowly, shakily, feeling some sense of relief. A small part of his mind insisted that that sound had been no cat, no way no how, but the rest of his mind shouted it down, like the lone peace protester at a war rally. Still, as Shane made his way through the kitchen, stripping off his shirt and running a hand through his hair, he left the library light on. He'd turn it off in the morning, but for now there was just something comforting about its harsh, banal glow. Nothing wrong with that. He got to his bedroom, stood at the foot of his bed, bare-chested and disheveled, heart still thumping dully from his strange experience in the sunroom, and realized something odd: he no longer felt sleepy. In fact, he felt a sneaking, unexpected energy. Something nagged at him, like a name he had recently forgotten, or a post-hypnotic suggestion. As he stood there, his shirt dangling from his fist, two things occurred to him simultaneously. The first was what it had been about the sound of that awful sigh, what had convinced him that it couldn't be Smithy, even if Smithy *was* real: something in that horrible breath had been distinctly female. Strange that he should be able to recognize that, even in the midst of his shock, but he had. Smithy was a guy's name, and if there was such an entity as Smithy, he was a male. Shane couldn't know this anymore than he could know that that awful sigh had come from the throat of something female, but he went ahead and knew it anyway. Some things you just didn't question.

And the second thing that occurred to him as he stood there in the dimness of his bedroom, staring down at his bed, was that he wanted to paint. For the first time in decades, he wanted to paint at night; not to put in his shift and get the work done, but just for the sheer, unadulterated hell of it. He'd had a refresher taste of creating at the whim of the muse earlier in the day, in the dirt in front of the destroyed manor house, and he'd liked it. Maybe he could duplicate that experience now, tonight, just until he got sleepy again. He was turning away from his bed, leaving the bedroom even as he thought these things. He trotted up the stairs to the little studio, taking them two at a time. He didn't know what he was going to paint, only that he wasn't going to work on the matte painting that was still sitting unfinished on his easel. That was shift work. Tonight, he was just going to paint for himself, just for the thrill of creating.

And who was he kidding? He knew *exactly* what he was going to paint. He'd already made the sketch. It was in the dirt a quarter mile away, but he could remember it very well.

He could remember it perfectly.

The next morning, Shane awoke at his normal time, just as the sun was coming up. He was a little surprised by this, considering how late he'd been up the night before, and how tired he'd felt when he'd finally fallen into bed. Apparently, the body's long habits overruled temporary breaks in the routine. He threw off the covers and padded to the shower, not even feeling particularly groggy, like he had the morning before. That had been the morning after he'd moved into the cottage, the morning after he had "celebrated" the move with almost an entire six pack of St. Pauli Girl beer, in the dark all by himself on the back patio. Shane had never been a heavy drinker, and when he did drink, he always felt it the next morning. Apparently, however, staying up to paint had the opposite effect. Not only did he feel alert and chipper, he felt positively energetic. Maybe today he'd finally finish the matte painting. The moment he did, he'd take it off the big easel, prop it in the corner to dry—his symbolic gesture of *fini*—and head downstairs to call his new agent, a guy named Morrie Greenfeld who worked in a high rise office in downtown St. Louis. That would feel good. It would prove to both himself and Greenfeld that he was, indeed, a can-do artist, one who met the deadline, and with quality work. Shane had been a little worried about that as of late, and he hated to think that Greenfeld might have shared his worries. The matte painting was the first gig Greenfeld had arranged for Shane, even if it had been Shane's portfolio and pencil sketch that had sealed the deal. Shane knew how these things worked. If he couldn't produce the art and impress the client his first time out, Greenfeld wouldn't take the time to tell him to get his butt in gear. Shane would simply not hear from him again. Sure there were other agents looking for artists—this was St. Louis, after all, not Manhattan—but when word got out that an artist was hard to work with, it was a hard reputation to live down. If Shane didn't get this matte painting done quickly, and if the result didn't amaze the client, his shift would probably become eerily, depressingly easy. Thus, Shane looked very forward to finishing this contract during today's shift. The way he felt as he poured his coffee from the percolator and tramped up the stairs, he thought he just might do it, too. The foreman in his head was raring to go; he was back on track, blueprint in one hand, schedule in the other, and ready to make it happen.

In the studio, Shane raised the blinds on the single window, turned around and stopped for a moment. He saw last night's work, lit in the rays of the morning sun, and realized that if he *did* finish the matte painting today, calling Morrie Greenfeld would *not* be the second thing he'd do after taking the painting off its easel. Rather, the second thing he'd do would be to move last night's new painting from where it currently sat, on the old easel in the corner, to the main easel under the M. C. Escher quote. It wasn't just that the new painting was a little too big for the old easel. As he'd painted last night, Shane had come to suspect that this new creation was more than just a bizarre whim. For one thing, it was very, very good;

Shane had recognized it even as the first rough strokes had begun to color the canvas. It was as if the painting already existed, and he'd glimpsed it, memorized it, and all he had to do now was excavate it from the white of the canvas, carefully, and without screwing it up. And even more important than its quality, the painting seemed to *mean* something, even if Shane couldn't quite grasp what it was. The painting was, in fact, possibly the first real *art* Shane had created in decades, the first painting made for itself, not to sell movie tickets, or fabric softener, or political candidates. It was hard to enter the room and not stop to stare at the new work. Even in its current state, rough and unfinished, it had a certain gravity, a gravity Shane wanted to orbit. He nodded to himself. He would finish the matte painting today, and then he would move the new painting, the painting of the manor house, to his main easel, under the Escher quote, where he did his shift work. There were no other contracts for the next few weeks. Instead of lazing around playing Sudoku, going on bike rides and watching television, Shane would take his time and finish the new painting. And when he was done with it, maybe he'd do something with it that he hadn't done with any of his other paintings: maybe he'd frame it and hang it up. Maybe he'd put it right over the fieldstone fireplace in the living room, where it could be visible from almost anywhere in the house. The last time any of his pictures had been displayed just for their art, they had been stuck to the front of his grandmother's fridge, pinned down by magnets in the shapes of plastic fruit. This new painting was different than anything Shane had painted for Tristan and Crane, or for any of his freelance clients, either before or since. Maybe the painting wasn't really as good as Shane thought it was; maybe he only responded so strongly to it because it was the first thing he'd created with the help of the muse in his entire adult life. Or maybe it was just that it showed some idea of the manor house that had once been the big sister of the cottage he now lived in. Either way, it didn't matter to Shane. He didn't care if anyone else liked the painting. This one was just for him, and that in itself was a new, decidedly pleasant experience.

But Shane didn't finish the matte painting that day. The shift went well, and he got close. He even entertained the idea of pushing past his normal two PM stopping time. After all, even bulldozer drivers had to put in a few hours' overtime every now and then, didn't they? He'd push on, at least until the foreman in his head decided to call it quits for the day. But then, unexpectedly, the phone downstairs had begun to ring. Shane froze, listening, his right hand still raised, the brush tip still touching the canvas. Who would be calling him? Who even knew the number? Once again, his first thought was Steph, and he winced inwardly. Steph wouldn't be calling anymore. Still, he supposed he'd been waiting for her to call again ever since that one last conversation, despite everything. The intellect may live in the realm of the logical, but the heart plays by its own rules. Shane sighed and set his brush on the side table, careful to let its tip stick over the ledge. He wiped his hands on an old towel as he tramped down the stairs, following the incessant ring of the cordless phone.

"Hi, Shane, how's it going?" It was Morrie Greenfeld. Shane should've known.

"Great, Morrie, glad to hear from you. I was just finishing up."

"Finishing up for the day?"

"Well, no, actually. I was planning on putting in another hour or two. I meant I'm almost finished with the matte. I thought I'd wrap it up today."

"Glad to hear it," Greenfeld said. Was there a note of chastisement in his voice? Shane was probably imagining it. "I'd love to see it myself. Any chance you could send me a few pics of it before I send somebody over to pick it up?"

"Yeah, that's fine," Shane replied quickly. "I'm happy with it, myself. I'll snap off a few shots and email them to you this evening. Fair enough?"

"Perfect. You do that. If this comes off as well as I expect it to, I might have some more work for you later next week. You up for a quick turnaround on some postcard landscapes? Florida tourism is looking to go retro on some new promotional materials. 'Wish you were here' kind of stuff."

"Sounds right up my alley," Shane answered. For the moment, he dismissed the painting of the manor house. Work was work, and if he scored another quick job, he could take the time off to finish the manor house painting later. "You want me to come out to the office to discuss it?"

"Nah, don't trouble yourself. I still need to nail down the details. They're sending me some concept art on Monday. After that, maybe I'll come out to you for a little sit-down at your place, take a look at the originals from your portfolio, if you're comfortable with that."

"Sure, sounds great. Just let me know beforehand so I can clean up all the empty tequila bottles and ladies' underthings."

"Yeah, yeah, I know how you artist types are. You talk a big game, but you spend most of your time writing emo poems about your long lost innocence and high school sweethearts."

"Not me," Shane said, falling easily into the banter. "I'm the live fast, die young type."

"That explains the cottage out in the boondocks," Greenfeld answered, and Shane could hear him grinning. Shane had only ever met Greenfeld once in person, at his St. Louis office a month earlier, and had decided then that this was the kind of guy most people would find a little too insightful and lot too obnoxiously blunt. Simply put, Greenfeld was one of those rare people who didn't give a damn about getting others to like them. Shane *had* liked him, however, even if he himself tended to be just the opposite, more of a people-pleaser. Maybe it didn't make for a particularly good artist-agent relationship, but then again, maybe it did. Greenfeld went on, "What if I come over sometime middle of next week? Thursday afternoon, maybe? I can show you the Florida concepts and we can talk about the matte painting. If you liked doing it, there are a lot more out there. Less and less of you guys are doing them nowadays, since so many studios are crossing over to making computer generated virtual sets. The few purists who still like the look of paint on canvas are having a hard time finding professionals who are willing to do it. What do you say?"

"I say I still have a beer or two in the fridge with your name on them. I'll see you on Thursday afternoon, Morrie."

Greenfeld ended the phone call with characteristic brusqueness a few seconds later. He took some getting used to, but Shane was glad not to have to waste time on inane small talk. That's one thing he didn't miss about Tristan and Crane. There, as in any other office environment, small talk was like a sort of contagious disease. It was hard not to get sucked into it, and once it caught you, it was even harder to tear back out of it. Shane had never been the kind of artist who could chat the day away while he painted. Steph had always told him that when his shift was on, it was like he was a hundred fathoms deep, like some old-time deep sea diver in a metal suit and a glass face-plate, clanking around on the ocean floor with hundreds of feet of rubber hose connecting him to the surface. It took him a little while to sink that deep, but it took him a lot longer to climb back to the surface, even just to answer a quick question about what he was doing for lunch or to remember the damned oatmeal cookie sitting there on his art table. The call from Greenfeld had been thankfully short, but it had still been an interruption. Shane wasn't fathoms deep anymore. Now, metaphorically speaking, he was sitting on the deck of the boat with his diving helmet off, blinking in the bright, briny sun, wondering if it was worth the effort to make the trek back into the deep again, or if it was time to just call it quits for the day. He couldn't do that, of course. Greenfeld was expecting photos of the finished matte painting emailed to him by the end of the day. Time to get out the rope and bucket and dip deep into the well of creativity. The foreman in his head would probably be a little cranky about being called back in to work, but occasional overtime was just part of the job, and he'd have to deal with it. For now, it was time to make the art happen. After tonight, it'd be all done and he could do whatever he wished.

When he got back upstairs to the studio, however, Shane stopped in the middle of the room. The new painting struck him all over again, and he stared at it. A moment later, he stepped lightly over to it, passing the matte painting on the main easel, but picking up the still-wet paintbrush from the edge of the work table. He leaned toward the new painting, examining it, frowning slightly. Something wasn't exactly right about it, some basic element. He could fix it, and quickly—it was that simple. He just had to figure out what it was. He deliberately blurred his vision a little, making the paint bleed together before his eyes. There it was. One brush stroke, part of the upright of the far right column, wasn't quite right. It pulled the shape of the column out of the gentle taper, made it appear a little awkward and crooked. Shane dabbed, using whatever color was on the brush. It was red. He painted out the sloppy brush stroke. Later, he'd refine it, and cover the red, but just fixing that bad stroke made an amazing difference. He shivered a little. The muse could be a demanding bitch, but she certainly made it worth your while. He stood back again, taking in the painting as a whole. It was incomplete, but it was right. It was going to be excellent, later, when he finished it. But for now, he had to get back to the matte painting. Time to clock a little overtime. Time to get back to work.

Instead, he dabbed at the new painting again, fleetingly. And then he leaned in, painting in earnest. Eventually, fifteen minutes later, he did cross back over to his main easel, but only for a moment.

Only long enough to grab his stool and his palette.

The next day, Shane discovered the old walking path. It was hidden in the front right corner of the cottage's small yard, and he never would have seen it at all if he hadn't been deliberately mucking around outside, trimming a few bushes, digging up weeds, avoiding going back into the cottage.

He'd come out to mow, once his shift was over. He was tired from having stayed up too late the night before, and the last thing he wanted to do was clump around the yard with the old manual lawnmower, wrestling it over the uneven landscape, man-handling it around the trees on the perimeter, but he was determined to do it nonetheless, even despite the bugs and the bright, hard sun that hit the back of his neck like a hammer the moment he stepped outside. Partly, it was the memory of Steph, from their days together here in the cottage. She'd never said it outright, but Shane knew she believed that, left to his own devices, he'd become so entranced by his work that he'd neglect the day-to-day responsibilities of life, things like paying the bills, doing laundry, and yes, mowing the lawn. Shane had never discussed it with her because, deep down, he thought she was very likely correct. Now that she was gone, however, he found that he wanted to prove to himself that he could manage the dull details of life like any other responsible adult, that he wouldn't turn all reclusive and shaggy, even if it meant a nasty sunburn and a dozen bug bites.

But that was only part of it. The more immediate truth was that Shane was putting off calling Greenfeld. *And be honest with yourself, Tiger,* he thought as he pulled the mower out of the shed next to the cottage, *you're avoiding him calling you, right? You're hoping that he gets those photos you just emailed him first, and that he'll be so happy with how the painting looks that he'll forget you finished it barely a day before the shipping date.* Yes, this was surely true, and Shane wasn't shamed by it. He was an artist, damn it, and a good one. He was usually as reliable as the day is long, unlike the moody, temperamental starving artists T and C had occasionally hired back in the day. He could be forgiven one close call in a decade, couldn't he? Granted, the timing of this particular close call was especially bad, but still. Greenfeld would understand, at least once he downloaded the pics and saw the finished matte painting. That's all that mattered, really. Shane had decided to avoid the phone until he could be reasonably certain that Greenfeld had, in fact, received the email with the photo attachments. Shane hadn't sent it the previous afternoon, like he'd intended. He hadn't finished the matte painting until late this morning, in fact. He'd gotten... distracted. But the important thing was that it was done, and it was good. Good enough, at least. Not as good as the new painting, of course, the one of the old manor house. By comparison, the matte painting was a dull, lifeless trinket, but that was no surprise, was it? After all, the matte painting was just client work. The client didn't want art; they just wanted a product, one that Shane was uniquely qualified to deliver. The new painting, however, was inspired. That sort of thing didn't happen very often, but when it did, it was a different kind of art entirely. Once again, Shane thought about how easy it would be to become addicted to the muse's secret embrace, to become her slave. That wouldn't happen to him, of course, but he understood it now. He had a little more sympathy for the starving artists, even if he, himself, would never become one.

He finished mowing the front yard, drew a few swipes of the mower along the sides of the cottage, and decided that it was enough for the day. The back of the cottage was so rocky and steep, dropping toward the bluff and the river below, that it was almost easier to cut it with the weed trimmer. Better yet, maybe he'd just let the field grass and wildflowers grow in, at least until they obscured the view. He stashed the mower back in the shed, parking it next to his bike, and grabbed the big garden shears from their hook on the wall.

He spent several minutes prowling the perimeter of the yard, lopping the bushes into submission and chopping off the occasional errant branch from the encroaching trees. That was when he discovered the abandoned footpath in the front corner of the property. He'd hacked off a particularly stubborn branch from a very old oak tree, and when it finally broke away, it struck the ground with a sharp clunk, as if it had fallen on something much harder than weedy earth. Shane pulled the branch aside and kicked at a thatch of dead grass. There were flagstones embedded in the ground beneath, almost entirely obscured by a blanket of moss. Had this been part of another patio at one time? It was too narrow to be of much use, and rather too deep, extending into the perimeter of the woods. Shane ducked, following the flagstones, feeling for their hardness beneath the weeds, and found that they formed a path, apparently long forgotten, that arced off between the trees. He followed it carefully, pushing aside the intervening branches and stepping over the bushes that had grown up through the cracks, prying the rocks apart. The footpath meandered and curved, but led generally downhill, following the line of the river. Shane stopped occasionally, using the garden shears to cut away some of the heavier undergrowth and reaching branches. There was a splash of color up ahead, where the trail curved around a gully, and as Shane worked toward it, he was surprised to see that it was a drift of hydrangeas, red, yellow and pink, lush in an errant sunbeam. The large flowers bobbed on their stalks, overwhelming the footpath and flowing down into the gully. Bees roamed from flower to flower, humming in the hot, sleepy air. Shane had never seen hydrangeas growing in the wild. Granted, flowers had been Steph's specialty, not his, but he was fairly certain that these were a domestic breed, not a native wildflower. He waded carefully through the waving blooms, trying to stay on the path, and struck something hard with his shin, almost pitching forward into the colorful mass. He swore, and his flailing hands grasped something buried in the flowers, preventing him from falling headfirst into the gaily colored blooms. Whatever it was, it was made of metal, hot in the woodsy sunlight and rough with peeling paint. He pushed the flowers aside and saw wrought iron scrollwork, painted black wherever it wasn't orange with rust. It was a seat of some kind. He brushed more of the thick hydrangea stalks aside, breaking some of them, and found that the vines had grown up through the metal shape, twining into it and completely burying it. It was, in fact, a bench. It leaned precariously backwards, but it had apparently, at one time, been positioned to provide the occupant a view of the low gully and the river beyond, just visible through the intervening trees. Shane was intrigued, even as his shin smarted from its collision with the buried bench.

He pushed on, feeling his way carefully through the drift of hydrangeas and coming out the other side. The flagstone footpath was a little clearer here, where it ambled around the lip of the gully. Moss filled the cracks between the stones, and vines and roots snaked over it, threatening to hook the foot of the unwary traveler, but Shane continued on, stepping carefully, his curiosity piqued. After a few hundred feet, the flagstones gave way to broad stairs, cut from some dark, sharp stone. Shane had seen such stone recently, but couldn't quite remember where. The stone steps were crooked and leaning but still very solid underfoot. They followed the curve of a hill, descending into a density of thick, thorny trees. At the bottom of the steps, where the flagstone path began again, Shane was shocked to discover something else buried in a mass of vines and flowers. He could tell by the height of it that it wasn't another bench. He leaned close to it, examining it, and was completely unprepared for the face that leered calmly out of it. Shane wasn't particularly squeamish; he recognized immediately that the face didn't belong to anything living. It was a statue, almost entirely overcome with flowering vines and dead leaves. Even so, his heart skipped a beat and he gasped a breath when he saw that blank expression, those dead gray eyes suddenly staring down at him from the shushing mass. He reached up and carefully hooked his fingers into the vines, pulling them away. They came only reluctantly, having twined into the cracks of the stone, but as they ripped away, Shane began to recognize the shape buried beneath. It was an angel carved out of white marble, almost life sized, standing atop a pedestal. The wings were partially unfurled from its back, and one hand was raised, palm up, in a vaguely welcoming gesture. An abandoned bird's nest was nestled into the vines that entwined the hand. Shane stood back again, taking in the entire figure. It was somehow both marvelous and a little eerie; beautifully made, but completely forgotten here in the thickness of the deep woods. He realized he was looking at something that had probably not been seen by human eyes for… how long? Decades, maybe?

He looked back the way he had come, up the curve of the hill with its embedded stone steps. It occurred to him that he could clean up the trail, perhaps clear off the bench and the statue, make the footpath usable again. It would be a lot of work, but what else did he have to do with himself when he wasn't putting in his shift? Depending on where the path ended up, walking it could be a pleasant enough alternative to going on a bike ride. He drew a deep breath, considering it, and tramped on, leaving the statue behind. The trees opened and Shane crossed a clearing so covered in dense weeds that he could no longer feel the flagstones beneath his feet. A narrow stream ran through the clearing like a snake, cutting a path toward the river. Large, flat rocks formed perfect stepping stones across the stream. Were they a little too regular to be random? Shane thought they were. Whoever had built this trail had placed them there. Shane might have expected a bridge instead, but on second thought he decided that a bridge probably wouldn't have fit the original designer's intention. He had a strange sense that the footpath hadn't been built as an attempt to subdue and conquer nature, but rather to work with it, following its curves and moods. A bridge would have seemed a bit too bold, somehow. Too... what was the word? Condescending? Maybe. On the other hand, the stepping stones were like a compromise, a sort of truce between the path's designer and the woods it passed through. It was the sort of choice that seemed to say *it's still up to you, nature; if you don't want us passing through, just raise the water, cover the stones, and we'll stay out. We may rule the cities, but out here, you're still in charge. Out here, you make the rules.* For now, the water was low, the stepping stones dry, so Shane pushed on, finding the path again on the other side of the clearing. It switched back and forth descending another hill, leading toward another bright clearing that was just visible through the thick canopy of the trees. This one was much larger and brighter, and Shane was not particularly surprised when he pushed through the weeds and found himself stumbling into the mundane lot of the now-defunct manor house. He looked around, blinking in the sun, and saw that he'd come out of the tree line at approximately the same place where the crane had been parked on the day the house had been demolished. Now, both the crane and the bulldozer were gone. The house's cellar had been cleared out, the debris hauled away and disposed of. In its place, the cellar had been filled with dirt, leaving only a vague outline and a few broken lines of stone, rising out of the landscape like relics from some ancient civilization.

Shane walked idly over to the site of the old house, looking over his shoulder at the wood from which he'd come. It made sense that this was where the footpath had led. After all, both the house and the cottage had once been part of the same property. It was only logical that there would have been some common means of getting back and forth between them. The original owner, Shane recalled, had been an artist, like him. That explained the statue and the bench with its drift of hydrangeas. It explained the stepping stones as well, as opposed to a bridge. Obviously, the original occupant had been a different kind of artist than Shane, but that was all right. What had his name been? The real estate agent had told him and Steph all about it when they'd signed on the cottage. Whitaker? Whitman? Something like that. Maybe Shane would look him up. He'd apparently been rather well known at the time, having made a name for himself painting portraits of politicians and world leaders. Wikipedia would probably have an article about him, at the very least, even if it wasn't perfectly accurate.

Shane was interested to see that the house's portico had been left intact, the only recognizable remnant of the original structure. It had been swept of debris but he could still make out the round marks of the original pillars, two on each side, big as truck tires. The stone floor now overlooked nothing but the grassy lot and the scar of dirt that had once been the house's cellar. The portico looked less like itself and more like a sort of stage, with two shallow steps rising along the front length. Shane climbed the steps and turned on the spot, looking out over the yard and the brick driveway where it curved off into the trees. Lengths of cut stone framed the driveway, and Shane remembered the stone steps along the path, remembered thinking the dark stone had looked familiar. He now knew that this was where he had seen it before, that same cut stone forming the perimeter of the brick driveway. The original owner had apparently liked his stonework. It couldn't have been cheap, even then, especially since it had to have been quarried elsewhere and trucked in, or maybe even brought in on barges. The ground around the river delta was almost exclusively red clay and limestone, not bedrock granite, like that used on the driveway and the footpath. There was probably some story associated with that, but Shane could only guess what it was.

He glanced down, toward the small island of earth in the middle of the circle driveway. Amazingly, his sketch was still there, despite a criss-crossing of tire tracks. It looked a little different, but that was only because he was looking at it upside down. A gust of wind blew, skirling tendrils of dust across the sketch and hissing in the tall grass. Far off, almost inaudible under the groan of the breeze in the trees, thunder grumbled.

Shane decided to head back.

By the time he got back to the cottage the sky was turning decidedly dark and foreboding. Clouds were pushing in swiftly over the river, turning it leaden and threatening an early evening thunderstorm. The air felt thick and metallic, dense with humidity. Wind gusted like the tail of a pensive cat.

The cottage didn't have central air conditioning, and Shane had turned off the big window unit in the bedroom before heading outside. Now, as he walked through the stuffy rooms, he pushed up the windows, letting the hot breeze blow in and billow the curtains. It was only five o'clock, but the lowering sky filled the cottage with drab shadows, and Shane found himself switching on lamps as he went. Passing the entry to the library, he saw that the answering machine light was blinking slowly. Apparently Greenfeld had indeed called while he'd been out. Shane had known he would. Still, he didn't cross the small room and push the "Play" button on the machine. He decided he'd do it later, after he changed out of his sweaty clothes and took a quick shower.

He didn't go straight to the bedroom, however. Instead, he clumped upstairs to the studio. It was especially hot and dark in the small room. He flicked the light switch by the stairs, but the overhead bulb didn't come on. He glanced up at it, frowning a little, and then decided he didn't really need it. He crossed the room and crouched down in front of the matte painting, where it leaned in the corner under the canted attic roof. Carefully, he dabbed the pad of his finger on the upper corner. The paint was tacky, but not wet. If he put a fan in front of it and let it run all night, the surface would probably be dry enough for shipment. The humidity certainly wasn't helping anything, but there wasn't much he could do about that.

He stood up and turned to head back downstairs. As he went, however, he glanced aside at the new painting. It sat on the big easel now, under the Escher quote, and in the dull storm light it seemed to glow faintly, full of unusually bright colors and blocky shapes. Shane paused. He moved a step closer to the painting, studying it. He didn't consider himself a painter with any particular style; he could mimic almost any artistic genre, from realistic to cubist, depending on the requirement of the contract. He'd expected to paint the manor house in a more photorealistic style, since that was his default technique, but as he'd begun it, he'd found himself using much more liberal brush strokes and generalized shapes, blocking out the essential bones of the house in big colorful patches. Instead of carefully blending the shadows, he'd layered them in with purples and blues, creating a sort of conceptual mosaic that most closely resembled expressionism. And yet, it wasn't abstract. It was representational and realistic, even hyper-realistic, like a crayon drawing overlaying a black and white photo. Shane had never painted anything like it before, and he had no idea where this had come from. All he knew was that it was incredible, almost hypnotic. He'd painted it from a slightly different angle than that represented in his original sketch, the one that was still slightly visible in the dirt in front of the old portico. That had shown the house from the front, dead on. In the painting, however, the house was turned slightly, showing the left side in perspective as it receded toward the river. A chimney climbed that side of the house, stately and towering, casting its deep purple shadow onto the white siding. In front of the house, sitting on the stone steps of the portico, Shane had begun the shape of a figure. It was merely a white blob at this point, but eventually it would be a woman in a pale dress, leaning back on one hand, the other raised to her brow, shading her eyes from the sun. He didn't know who the woman was, he just knew that the painting wanted some human focal point, even if it was small and immaterial. A house by itself was just architecture. The woman on the steps would make it a home; she would give the house its story.

Shane felt the tug of the painting. The muse trailed her finger up his back; she wanted him to paint some more, wanted him to continue telling the story of the house. Shane almost gave in, even reached for one of his brushes, but then he stopped. He was hungry, for one thing. And he was sticky with sweat from his work in the yard and his trek along the mysterious footpath. Surely, the muse could wait for an hour or so while he showered and ate. He was just about to turn and leave when something in the painting caught his eye. He frowned a little, leaning in. This time, it wasn't something wrong, exactly; it was something unexpected. Last night, he had begun filling in the house's surroundings, blocking in the tree line, the grassy hill sweeping down toward the river, and the brown curve of the river itself. He'd added a few details here and there; the edge of a rose garden protruding from the rear of the house, speckled with red buds, a wrought-iron W bolted to the bricks of the chimney, and a few decorative details at the furthest edge of the tree line, almost hidden beyond the crown of the hill. It was these details that had caught Shane's eye. He leaned closer, scrutinizing them, the frown lines on his forehead deepening. He'd only noticed it as he'd begun to turn away, catching the shapes with the corner of his eye. In the gloomy light, it was hard to resolve the shapes into anything other than blobs of paint, and yet even now they teased his eye, looking strangely familiar. There was a splash of red and pink, a few strokes of light gray, all of it nearly hidden in the deep green of the distant trees and bushes. He was almost ready to give it up, convinced he was simply imagining things, when the shapes finally resolved and clicked into place. Once that happened, he couldn't *not* see them. His eyes widened and for a long moment he forgot to breathe.

There, in the far corner of the painted yard, he had dabbed in the shape of a statue. It was comprised of no more than four or five quick brush strokes, but they were very economical strokes, like visual poetry. The statue seemed to have one arm raised, palm up, as if welcoming the viewer, as if beckoning them into some secret. Of course, Shane knew what that secret was, for he had seen that statue's sister, covered in vines, leaning and nearly hidden in the woods. Below the painted statue, a drift of red and pink flowers bloomed; hydrangeas, of course. Somehow, Shane had painted the entry to the footpath that connected the manor house to the cottage. He had painted it last night, without even knowing it, believing those lines were just squiggles of color, meaningless details.

He shuddered, and out over the river the thunder grumbled again. A moment later, Shane startled violently and let out a little bark of surprise; the ceiling light over his head had popped on with a tiny electrical snap. Its light suddenly filled the room, bone white and brilliant after the stormy twilight.

And downstairs, for the first time since Shane had returned to the cottage, the toilet flushed all by itself.

Chapter Three

The next day was Saturday, and the phone was ringing when Shane woke up, bleary-eyed and disoriented. He squinted at the sunshine that speared through the curtains, reached for the clock on the bedside table, and groaned when he looked at it. A few seconds later, he rolled out from under the covers and clumped out of the bedroom, following the incessant ring of the phone.

"Hullo,"

"Morning, Shane. Don't tell me I woke you up?" It was Greenfeld again. Damn but he was persistent. Shane wasn't very surprised.

"As a matter of fact, you did. Not your fault, though. I was up late last night."

"Burning the midnight oil? Or living fast and dying young?"

"Maybe a little of both. What about you? Don't tell me you're in the office on a Saturday morning?"

"Maybe I am, maybe I am," Greenfeld replied easily. "I have this artist who likes to finish things on the Friday before a Monday deadline. Means I have to show up bright and early Saturday to arrange shipping and manage the fine print."

"Look, I'm sorry about that, Morrie. Really. It's not like me at all."

"Yeah, you know, in your case I actually believe that. I get a sense of people, and you, you're not a bullshitter, at least about your work. But don't sweat it. This is what I get paid my exorbitant commissions for."

"So you saw the photos I sent?"

"Yes I did. Got 'em late last night, when I got home, otherwise I'd have called right away. Looks good to me, but the ball's always in the air until the client takes shipment and gives us their final okey dokey. You know how it is. I sent the pics off to my contact at the studio, and I haven't heard anything since. Considering how anxious they were about getting this matte just right, I'd say that's a good sign."

Shane felt a knot of tension loosen from his shoulders. He knew the average client well enough to know that Greenfeld was right; these weren't the kind of people who sent handwritten thank you notes full of high praise. The only time the artist ever heard from the client was when there was something wrong with the product. "That's good news," Shane answered. "So are you arranging the shippers?"

"Already set. That's why I called. I'm sending over an intern to get the painting and pack it up, just to be safe."

Shane nodded. Greenfeld was very thorough. "When will they get here?"

"I scheduled the pickup for here at the office at one. Chris is already en route to your place. Should be there by ten. You going to be there?"

"I don't have my interview with Access Hollywood until noon, so I think I'll still be around."

"Sounds good. We still on for Thursday?"

"Sure. You need directions?"

"Nah. I know the general area. I'll call you if I can't find the house number on your cave."

Shane told Greenfeld he looked forward to it and hung up, relieved.

While Shane waited for the intern from Greenfeld's office, he sat at the little computer desk by the living room window, sipping coffee and staring hard at the screen of his laptop. Outside, the previous evening's storms had left the sky bright and hazy. The air was cooler than yesterday, and Shane had left the windows open rather than cranking up the window air conditioner. The curtains next to the desk hung limp, still damp from last night's rain. He had sat down at the computer to check the weather, then to browse the headlines. Eventually, however, he had remembered his trip out to the site of the manor house yesterday, and his plan to look up the original owner. The footpath had piqued his interest, but it was the painting upstairs that was really driving his curiosity. Ever since he'd begun it, he'd developed a rather detailed picture of the original owner—how he'd looked, his personality and history. This was not especially unusual. Shane remembered watching a documentary about a well known comic book artist a few years earlier, remembered the artist saying that when he drew monsters and beasts, he'd sit at his art table roaring and growling, baring his teeth. If he was drawing battle sequences, he'd mimic the sounds of sword clashes, or gunfire, or fists on chins. Shane had grinned as he'd watched, because he completely understood that tendency. It was part of going fathoms deep into the art, becoming one with it, examining it from all the angles so as to best understand it. It was a simple, elementary idea, one that any little kid with a box of crayons understood instinctively: being an artist meant creating in your head before you ever created on the canvas, and the more you gave life to the version between your ears, the more vibrant the final work on the canvas would be.

Thus, as Shane had painted the manor house, constructing it in his head and looking at it from every angle, he had begun to also create its occupants. It had started with the owner, the man who had designed the house and overseen its construction, the famous artist whose name was Whitaker or Whitman—something that started with a W at least, to match the big wrought iron letter bolted to the chimney. He envisioned a tall, thin man, closely shaven, but with thick black hair that he combed across his brow like a raven's wing, Hitler style. He wore white button-down shirts, like Shane when he was working his shift, and gray flannel pants. He had large hands and deep set, heavy-lidded eyes. He was handsome, in a narrow, angular kind of way, and he was particular, almost fussy, about the design of the house, the landscaping, the placement of the garden and the decorative statuary. But he didn't care about the interior of the house. That was the domain of the woman, the one visible on the steps of the house in Shane's painting. He didn't know why he'd decided to paint her instead of the man himself; the painting had just seemed to ask for her. She was young and very pretty, but quiet. Probably, she was the artist's wife. While he, the artist, had hovered around the exterior, primping and overseeing the overall façade of the house, she had worked on the inside, arranging the furniture, hanging the art, populating the bookshelves and hutches. Shane imagined her going on long shopping vacations, returning with shipments of antiques, rugs from junk shops in China, wall tapestries from castles in Scotland. They had both loved the house, but from entirely different directions. They complemented each other in that way, and yet, in Shane's mind, as he painted, he didn't sense happiness. He sensed a sort of wounded sadness, an existence of constant, low-grade anguish, at least for the woman. The shopping trips were a thin mask, overlaying that deep, sharp misery like a mortician's sheet. Shane found himself more and more intrigued by her. More than anything, the story of the manor house seemed to be her story, rather than that of the artist himself. Maybe that was because, while he had designed and built the house, she had lived in it and given it its soul. She had defined it as a home. In a rather poetic sense, the artist might have fathered the house, but the woman had been its mother, nurturing it and raising it, offering it her heart.

These, at least, were the things Shane thought as he worked on the painting, even as he'd painted late into the previous night, filling in, adding detail, while the storm flickered and roared obliviously outside the cottage. It was pure invention, of course; stream of consciousness prose designed to breathe life into the image in his head. But it *felt* like more than that. As he painted, it was almost like traveling in time and space. He was barely aware of the brush in his hand, or of sitting on the stool in his studio. He'd gone into his paintings before, sinking fathoms deep, but never quite like this. He'd never come up out of the painting hours later, disoriented and stiff, his right arm aching deep in the shoulder from working so hard and fast, unable even to recall how long he'd been at it. It made him wonder.

And then, of course, there was the statue and the hydrangeas—the footpath entrance that he had painted into the background of the house before he'd even known there *was* a footpath. That made him wonder, too.

It had been easy enough to locate information about the artist on the internet. Shane had merely performed a Google search for "Famous Missouri Painter Portrait President", which had pretty much summed up everything he knew about the man. He knew he'd recognize the name when he saw it. Within two minutes he had settled on a long article linked from a website about Missouri tourism. Shane cradled his coffee in his hands and leaned back to read:

"Gustav Ferdinand Wilhelm was born on March 12th, 1898, in Cologne, Germany. His parents, Oscar, a shoemaker, and Henrietta, a seamstress, immigrated to the United States when Gustav was four years old. There, they lived in a small apartment in New York City, sharing the space with a Flemish couple that they had met during their crossing. Poor and struggling through their first hard winter, conditions were worsened by a lingering illness (probably scurvy, or 'Barlow's disease', as it was known then) that Gustav had contracted aboard the ship. Nursed by his mother while his father and older brother sought work, Gustav spent that winter in a bed in the corner of the apartment's kitchen, near the stove. Having always expressed an interest in drawing, young Gustav spent this time creating pictures on a small slate that had been given him by his father. The Flemish man who lived with them was a journeyman artist, specializing in miniature keyhole portraits. He recognized young Gustav's talents, and spent many evenings teaching the boy portraiture and the basic artistic elements of balance, perspective and symmetry. Gustav fondly remembered these times, and looked back on this man, whom he only knew by his first name, Letard, as some of the happiest moments of his childhood, despite his illness.

"At age fifteen, Gustav, or Gus as he had come to be known, went to work for the same studio that Letard had worked at. The studio head put Gus to work painting backgrounds for landscapes and architectural scenes. Gus quickly chafed at these assignments, which he found boring and simplistic, and begged to be given a commission for a full portrait. The studio head, a painter named Sylvester Bertoni, allowed Gus his first paid portrait; that of Bertoni's pet bullmastiff. Gus, who even then was known for his quick temper, felt insulted. He refused the commission, and was subsequently banned from the studio. After two days, Gus had second thoughts about the commission, and about the prospect of being unemployed in turn-of-the-century New York, and returned to Bertoni to request a second chance at the portrait. Bertoni refused him, insisting that while the young painter had talent, his ego had already rendered him untrainable, and therefore useless to the studio. This criticism affected Gus deeply. Secretly, he followed Bertoni home and spied on him as his former employer interacted with his beloved bullmastiff. For five days, Gus returned, sketching the dog in charcoal on butcher's paper. Finally, content that he could represent the bullmastiff as Bertoni saw it, he returned to his family's apartment and painted a small portrait. Years later, Gus would insist that it was this experience that taught him how to see his subjects, not as mannequins posed before him, but as living individuals, each with their own unique history and personality. This sensitivity, and Gus's uncanny ability to transmute those stories into his portraits, became the hallmark of his work in later life, and led to his commissions from some of the most influential and important leaders of the day. Upon completion of the bullmastiff portrait, Gus presented it to Bertoni as a gift, asking only to have his position at the studio restored. Bertoni agreed, on the condition that he personally serve as Gus' teacher. Gus progressed under Bertoni's tutelage, and within two years became the most requested portrait artist in the studio's employ.

"In July of 1916, Gus resigned from Bertoni's studio with the intention of traveling to Washington D.C. to pursue a particularly unique opportunity. He explained to his parents that he had read about the recent death of the official presidential portrait artist, Herbert Woosterhouse, and intended to apply for the honor of painting the portrait of the next president. In fact, in the wake of Woosterhouse's death, the White House had announced a search for a new presidential portrait artist, and an article detailing that search had made its way into the New York Times. Gus had determined immediately to move to Washington to apply for the job, despite the fact that the article declared that only artists with at least ten years' experience and the references to prove it need apply. Bertoni himself warned Gus not to throw away his position and his growing reputation in the New York art world on such a foolish lark. Years later, Gus remarked in his memoirs that, despite the warnings of Bertoni and his family, there was never any question in his mind about the move to Washington. In his own words: 'They insisted that by leaving New York, I was risking my future as an artist. What they did not understand was that, by staying in New York, I would have been risking my future as a legend.'

"Gus took what little money he had and moved to the nation's capital. There, he shared a rented room with several other artists and performers, sleeping in a bunk barely twelve inches from the ceiling. Over two hundred artists applied for the position of official government portrait artist. All but twenty were sent home after a portfolio review by then Secretary of the Interior, Franklin

Lane. Despite Gus' lack of experience, he was not among those sent home on the first day. He and the remaining twenty artists were allowed the opportunity to paint a sample portrait of the sitting president, Woodrow Wilson. In his memoirs, Gus described the experience:

"'We were led into the oval office at half past two, just as the man was returning from his rather late lunch. We had to carry our easels, paint pots and supplies, and were instructed to stay well back from the desk, as the president was engaged throughout the day in meetings and various affairs of state. I was positioned in a corner, no less than twelve paces away. Wilson preferred the afternoon curtains to be tied back, with the windows open, and the declining sun dazzled my eyes directly, obscuring the president even further. I was in no way allowed to change my position once the session began, and the president himself was exceedingly recalcitrant to any suggestions of pose. Indeed, after my third request, I was told summarily to be still or be put out. Between the heat of the office, the constant motion of the subject, and the lack of even the barest refreshments, it was by far the least pleasant experience of my professional career. Indeed, I began to wonder if I truly desired the post after all.'

"Despite his doubts, Gus completed his painting of Wilson within the week, injecting it with his usual sense of the personality of the subject. All of the completed portraits were presented to Secretary Lane for his inspection. A week later, Gus' portrait was returned to him at his rented room. A note was pinned to it, penned in Lane's own hand. It read, 'The office of the presidency is a position of honor, not leisure. This work is more suited to the bathhouse than the white house.' The post of official White House portrait artist was later awarded to a veteran painter from Virginia named George W. Hallsley. Crushed and disillusioned, Gus took a job in a kitchen at a nearby hotel, but despite this very bruising setback, his career in Washington was far from over."

Shane stopped reading and leaned back, frowning slightly. He had often thought that he was a different sort of artist than the starving artists he had so often seen lurking in the halls at Tristan and Crane, but he had always thought that with a certain amount of smug disdain. The starving artists may have been more hip than Shane, and some of them may indeed have been equally as talented, but he'd never envied them. They were slaves to the muse, arrogant and temperamental. Gustav Ferdinand Wilhelm, however, had apparently been an entirely different breed of artist, neither like the starving artists back at T and C, nor like Shane himself. Shane felt a certain amount of discomfort in reading his exploits. Here was a man who had been nearly the exact polar opposite of he, himself; an artist who neither submitted to the muse nor rejected her, but who managed to command her affections as his own, and apparently without even trying. Here was a risk taker, a man of ambition and recklessness, of passion and megalomania. And yet, he seemed likeable enough, if a little intense. Shane, on the other hand, was careful, timid, deliberate, and quiet. He tended to downplay his work, believing that if he pointed out its flaws first, no one else would be able to. He never made grand claims about his skills, or expected greatness. Truly, Wilhelm, the man in whose cottage Shane now lived, was a different kind of artist than him. And was Shane a little jealous? Maybe he was. He hadn't yet finished the article about Wilhelm's life, but he knew that things certainly hadn't ended with him working in a hotel kitchen. Things had gotten much better for him. He had indeed eventually painted for presidents, and even for kings and queens. Shane had never even considered such grandiose aspirations. He believed, even now, that he didn't really even wish for such things. And yet...

Just then, Shane heard the crunch of tires on gravel. A dart of sunlight flashed through the curtains next to him as a vehicle turned onto the pull-off in front of the cottage, parking next to his geriatric Chevy pickup truck. Shane glanced at his watch: it was twelve minutes after ten. Chris, the intern from Greenfeld's office, was right on time. Shane had known interns in the past; three or four of them had made their way through the offices of Tristan and Crane during his time there. They were usually college students who spent most of their time hanging around the office kitchen talking about whatever they'd watched on television the night before or how drunk they'd gotten the previous weekend. He'd never been particularly clear what it was interns were supposed to do, mainly because he'd never been interested enough to ask. He didn't know what to expect from the aforementioned Chris. He assumed he would be in his twenties, wearing an expensive, ill-fitting shirt and tie over a pair of jeans. He'd probably be friendly and gregarious in a forced, *I'm-talking-to-a-grown-up* kind of way, and he'd express polite, insincere interest in Shane's work for as long as it took to pack the painting in a crate and lug it out to the waiting van. Shane stood up, coffee in hand, and crossed the living room to the front door. He pulled it open and stood there, blinking in the hazy sunlight, as the driver's door of the gray van swung open.

"Morning," he called to the figure that climbed out, unseen on the other side of the van. Beneath the van, Shane could see a pair of small feet; bare ankles and taupe low-heeled shoes of a decidedly female stripe. He had time to raise his eyebrows in some small surprise—apparently Chris was a Christine, not a Christopher—before she came around the back of the van and all the rest of his expectations were knocked aside as well.

"You Bellamy?" the woman asked, glancing up at him as she pulled the rear doors of the van open.

"No, I'm his butler, Jeeves," Shane said, trying to mask his surprise with humor, "but I'll inform his lordship of your arrival, miss…?"

"Uh-huh," the woman said, pulling a long white box out of the van's dark interior. "I'm Christiana, but you can call me Chris. Everyone else does." Shane studied her while she was turned away from him. She wore tan slacks that stopped halfway between her knees and ankles; were those called capris? He thought they were. Over that, she wore a lilac blouse with short, almost nonexistent sleeves. She had hair so black that it reflected the sun with nearly purple highlights; it was pulled back in a neat ponytail that swung as she turned, hefting the box out into the sunlight.

"Here, let me help you with that," Shane said, remembering himself. He set his coffee on the porch railing and trotted out into the sunlight. Christiana allowed him to take the box, which was nearly as tall as she was. It was very light, but ungainly. Shane felt a little ridiculous, as he almost always did when he was one-on-one with an attractive woman he didn't yet know. She looked at him with an unreadable expression that could have been disdain, could have been professional aloofness, could even have been plain and simple boredom. Her skin was very tan and Shane couldn't help noticing that she had large eyes, almost as black as her hair. She wasn't beautiful, exactly, but she was unique in a way that Shane found immediately attractive. It was hard not to stare at her.

"Christiana Corsica," she said, sticking out her thin little hand, her expression unchanging.

"Oh, ah," Shane replied, dropping the box so that it leaned against him, tall as his chest. He shook her hand; it was warm and dry, her grip firm. "Shane Bellamy. Nice to meet you. Er, coffee?" He gestured toward his own cup where it sat on the porch railing.

"Still have half a cup sitting in the cup holder," Christiana replied, nodding toward the van. "I need to get back to the office quick like a bunny or Morrie will be sending out a posse. He uses up all his slack on his artists. The rest of us have to jump when he says frog or things get ugly. Where's it at?"

It took Shane a moment to realize that she meant the matte painting. "Oh. Inside, upstairs, in the studio. Come on, I'll help you pack it up."

As they moved through the cottage, Shane in the lead, carrying the box and trying to keep it from bonking its big, unwieldy corners on the walls, he talked about the painting, warned her that it might still be tacky in some places, that it had taken him longer than he'd expected, merely spending words, almost nervously filling the quiet morning air. She followed, nodding, glancing around idly.

In the stuffy heat of the studio, Shane unplugged the fan and pushed it aside. Thankfully, the matte painting was mostly dry now, barely tacky even where the paint was thickest. Christiana took one cursory look at it, pressed her lips together and nodded. She held the box while Shane fished out the foam corner grips and began to fit them onto the corners of the painting.

"This where you do all your work?" Christiana asked, turning to look around the room.

"Yes. I like it. It's small, but it's all I need."

"Sure is a big change from the corporate studio in New York, isn't it?"

"I always preferred my own space, even then. I sort of defined it and made it my own. The art table came from there, and so did my Escher quote, the one hanging over the easel..." Shane turned to indicate the hand-painted quote and saw Christiana frowning at the easel, her hand cupping her chin. "Oh, that," he said, a little uncomfortably. Christiana didn't look up; she continued to study the painting of the manor house, the look on her face dark and inscrutable. Shane finished packing the matte painting into the box and sealed it. "Well, that's that. I'll help you get it down to the van."

Christiana spoke without looking up, "You painted this?"

"Yeah. I'm... still working on it."

"Who's it for?"

Shane shuffled his feet a little. For some reason he didn't like the way Christiana was looking at the painting. "I, uh... it's not for anyone. It's just mine."

Christiana finally looked up at him, raising her eyebrows. "Oh," she said. "Well that's cool."

"You... you like it?"

She frowned again and looked back at the painting. She nodded slightly. "I guess. It's well done, at least. I can tell that. There's a lot of realism in it, and yet it's not realistic at all, not in the colors and the overlying shapes. It kind of messes with my eyes. It's just... it's not what anyone would call 'nice'. I hope you don't mind me saying that."

"No. Art is very subjective. And it's still a work in progress. It's just an idea that kind of got stuck in my head." Shane looked at the painting himself, trying to see it the way she did. It was certainly very different than anything he'd ever painted before. Christiana was right that it wavered between realism and abstraction, and yet where she saw conflict, he saw a dance.

"I see what you mean about it sticking in your head," she said, shaking her head and finally turning away. "It's hard to avoid looking at it. I guess that means it's a success, at least by somebody's definition. I just wouldn't want it hanging in my living room. Are we ready to load?"

Shane helped her carry the box back down the steps and around the corner to the front door. The heat was rising as the day turned humid, and by the time the box had been lifted into the van and strapped to the inside wall with bungee cords, Shane's forehead was beaded with sweat. He wiped it away with the back of his hand and noticed that Christiana still looked as cool and fresh as when she'd arrived. She shook his hand again, apparently anxious to leave.

"Good to meet you Mr. Bellamy. I'm sure I'll see you again."

Shane nodded. "I hope so. I have to admit, you aren't what I expected."

"I take it that's a compliment?"

"Well, mainly it's just that I expected some college guy long on attitude and short on attention span. We used to have interns like that back at T and C."

"I'm no one's idea of an intern, apparently," Christiana said, fishing the van's keys out of the pocket of her capris. "And that includes Morrie. I think he keeps me around for the scenery as much as for the work. I don't really mind. Still."

"So why do you do it?" Shane said, following her around to the driver's side door. "I mean, if you don't mind my asking."

Christiana opened the door and looked back at him. She lifted her left shoulder in a quick shrug. "I like art. I can't make it, but I like working with it. I used to be a legal assistant, and was studying for the bar. I woke up one day and realized something important. I realized I hated law. Worse, I hated lawyers. I was only studying to be one because that's what my parents were, and that's what they always expected me to be, too. And I thought, I don't even *like* my parents. They're some of the unhappiest people I know. Why would I want to do what they do? So I quit university, moved out of the apartment my parents had rented for me, and decided to get into art representation. Everyone's got to start somewhere, right?"

Shane nodded somberly. "Impressive."

"You think so?"

"I think it takes a lot of willpower to break out of the orbit of other people's expectations," he answered, and then added quickly, "Not that I've learned that from experience or anything."

"Ah," Christiana nodded, climbing into the driver's seat. "Well, if you say so. See you around, Mr. Bellamy."

Shane backed away as she started the van. "Call me Shane," he said over the sound of the engine. "Everybody else does."

She nodded through the open window, tipped a salute, and began to back up. She performed a neat three-point turn and gunned the van's engine, propelling it down the broken driveway. Sunlight glinted off its rear windows and then it was gone, hidden behind the encroaching trees.

Christiana, Shane thought, bemused. *What a nice name.* He headed back into the house, and had to return a minute later, once he remembered that his coffee was still sitting on the porch railing. It was still warm enough to drink.

The computer was still humming softly to itself, although the screen saver had popped on; the Microsoft logo appeared and disappeared on the screen, changing position each time like some kind of a corporate Whack-a-mole. Shane approached the desk and shook the mouse back and forth on its pad, waking the computer. The Microsoft logo vanished and a field of type appeared; the biography of Gustav Ferdinand Wilhelm. Shane considered finishing the article, and then decided to save it for later. He had plans for today. On a whim, however, he scrolled down to the bottom of the page. There were thumbnail samples of the artist's work there, mostly portraits. Shane recognized some of them. There was Theodore Roosevelt with his dog, seated on a long, sunlit veranda. Below that was an absurdly young Queen Mary, standing behind her husband, King George the fifth, who was seated, smiling cryptically. The paintings were indeed quite good, and very unlike any other portraits Shane had ever seen, especially from that era. They seemed light, whimsical, and even somewhat irreverent, but always in a way that implied the permission of the subjects, as if they were allowing the artist to show a more private and human side of them, a side that was most often hidden by the pomp and circumstance of their offices.

Looking at them, Shane felt a strange sense of relief. He wondered about it for a moment, and then realized where it came from. Part of him had expected Wilhelm's works to appear hauntingly familiar; to be bold and daring with color, somehow both representational and abstract at the same time. In short, he'd half expected Wilhelm's works to look like the painting upstairs, the unusual portrait of Wilhelm's dead manor house, as if Shane was somehow channeling his artistic spirit. It was crazy, of course; so crazy that Shane had not even allowed himself to consider it in the daylight. Only now, as he looked down at Wilhelm's artwork, was he aware of how much that strange suspicion had taken root in his mind. He felt like a man being told by his Doctor that the tests had come back negative, that he was perfectly healthy, only then accepting what had been, up to that point, the very real possibility that the black spot on his chest X-rays had been cancer. He smiled to himself. His imagination had gotten the better of him, that was all. Imagination was a great thing, a profitable thing even, *if* you could keep it on its leash. Let it run wild, and it could turn cannibal. It had happened to much better artists than him. Shane sighed deeply. The painting upstairs was *just* a painting; curious and slightly disturbing, perhaps, but no more so than any number of works he'd seen created by the starving artists, the ones who were the slaves of the muse. And compared to some of those, the painting upstairs wasn't very strange at all; it was even downright quaint.

That afternoon, after lunch, Shane changed into cargo shorts and an old Long Island University tee-shirt, sprayed himself liberally with Deep Woods Off, and went outside. He collected a spade, the garden shears, and the Black and Decker weed-whacker from the shed, piling them all into the old wheelbarrow that sat in the tall grass in back. Whistling happily, he pushed the wheelbarrow to the front right corner of the yard, to the entrance of the mysterious path he had discovered yesterday. Maybe he wouldn't clear away the whole thing, but it was something to do, even if he only made a tiny bit of progress each day. And it seemed like a worthwhile job, even if it took him all autumn.

He had a vague idea that Gus would approve.

He made more progress than he expected that day. It was, in fact, relatively quick work, simply lopping off the branches that barred the path, digging up the occasional bush, and then using the weed-whacker to mow down the undergrowth, revealing the flagstone footpath. Most of the stones were covered with a thick carpet of moss, but that was all right. The moss softened the path and gave it a sense of whimsy, like something elves might skip down in the moonlight, on their way to the cobblers to put in a night's charitable work. Shane made it all the way to the curve around the gully, where the bench was buried in the drift of hydrangeas. The sun had begun to lower, and he guessed it was approaching five o'clock. Had he really been at this for almost four hours? He was hungry and tired, and his back was sore from the digging, and yet none of those things felt especially unpleasant. He'd lived a very sedentary life for the past decade, and the day of hard manual work, much like his unusually long bike ride a few days earlier, was a welcome break. It was good to know that his body was still capable of such exertion. And surely it was good for him, both mentally and physically. He had a sneaky feeling that he'd allowed this most recent painting to get hold of him a little too deeply. That wasn't a bad thing, exactly, as long as he kept it in perspective. The imagination was a great tool, as he'd thought that morning, but give it too much slack and it could turn on you and devour you. The idea of the cracked artist was well known, virtually a stereotype. From

Van Gogh to Jimmy Hendrix, history was littered with the corpses of creative people who had succumbed to the cannibal impulses of an out-of-control imagination. Shane had given it a lot of thought. It was almost as if creativity was too big a current for the human mind to handle very well. It required an awful lot of insulation and careful handling. The volts of the imagination, he'd decided, were careless and indiscriminate; they would either power the artistic machine or fry you in your boots, depending on how far you opened the circuit, how carelessly you loosed the creative current. Shane recognized this tendency even in himself, the tendency to fall into the art with reckless abandon, to let it into his mind like some sort of impish demon. Thus, he'd set up firewalls in his mind; borders and boundaries, hand-painted mental signs that read, "This far, and no further". Getting dressed for his shift each day was one of the firewalls, the simple act of taking his time to button up his white shirt and carefully roll up the sleeves, never arriving in his pajamas, even if that was the way the starving artists did their work. It was one of the ways that he kept the art in check, showed it every day that he was in charge of it, and not the other way around. Another firewall was simply his shift, his discipline of putting in the hours according to an outside schedule, starting promptly at eight and ending right when his internal whistle blew, usually at two in the afternoon. Where other artists had the muse, whose affections were fickle and whose demands were high, Shane had the foreman in his mind. Other artists worked for the muse, obeyed her every whim and wish and begged her to be faithful to them, but Shane bypassed her. The foreman in his mind worked for him, and he was a very good employee, never late for work and almost always right on schedule for the deadline. That had only lapsed lately, probably due to the many dramatic changes in Shane's life, but that was to be expected.

Of course, Shane *was* working with the muse as of late, perhaps for the first time in his adult life. But he wasn't her slave. He'd ignored her siren call the entire day, in fact, spending it out on the forgotten footpath, clearing it and exhausting himself so that he probably wouldn't even paint tonight. He grinned to himself as he finished, tossing the spade into the wheelbarrow behind him and arming sweat from his brow.

"That'll show her whose boss," he muttered to himself, looking back at his work. "Shane Bellamy, that's who. The man who tamed the muse."

He tromped along the path, past what he had cleared, and moved into the sunlit area that curved around the gully. The hydrangeas were very thick, but he kicked through them, clearing his way, and found the hump of the buried bench. Using both hands, secure in garden gloves, he stripped the vines away from the bench, snapping the stems and ripping out the roots wherever he could. He didn't intend to completely clear the bench; he just wanted a place to sit down for a moment. The wrought iron of the bench was contrived to look like curling vines and leaves. Despite the decades of rust, it seemed solid. Shane finally turned and plopped onto it, sighing. It leaned backwards, but held him easily.

Even in its state of overgrowth and rusty dereliction, it was extremely pleasant. Shane immediately understood why Wilhelm had placed the bench here. Its position provided a high, clear view of the boulder-strewn gully as it dropped away toward the river, a hundred yards beyond. Trees clustered along the furthest edge of the gully, but they looked relatively young compared to the woods on either side. It seemed possible, even likely, that the view of the river beyond the gully had originally been completely uninterrupted. He imagined Wilhelm sitting here, perhaps with his wife at his side, watching the huge steamships paddle up the river, splashing and chugging, leaving trails of black smoke in the sapphire sky. Maybe they'd drunk tea from hand-corked bottles, carried in a whicker picnic basket. It was certainly a nice image, and yet Shane didn't think it was exactly accurate. Maybe that kind of thing had happened early in their marriage, before they'd come to Missouri, but by the time they'd built the house, Shane had a strange suspicion that those halcyon days were over. He was probably wrong, of course. These were simply more of those idle narratives, the kind that his mind concocted when he was working on the painting of the manor house, mere creative daydreams, no more accurate than uninformed guesses. He rested there, his arms spread out on the back of the bench on either side, smelling the wild, woodsy smell of the hydrangeas and cut weeds and deepening autumn. The wind blew high in the trees, making them shush and whisper, sending down a snowfall of turning leaves.

As Shane moved to get up, he saw something glint in the thick growth near his feet. He leaned over, and then squatted in front of the bench, pushing the vines and leaves aside. There didn't appear to be anything unusual there. He was about to climb to his feet again, weary and hungry, when he saw it again; a shimmer of sunlight on dull metal. He reached for it, felt around in the thick undergrowth, and finally touched something hard and smooth. He gripped it and began to pull it out. It made a noise, a sort of loose clatter, and for one bright second Shane's mind provided am image of a rattlesnake; it was coiled in the shade of the bench, waiting for him to leave, and he had just grabbed its tail. It wasn't a rattlesnake, of course. Were they even native to Missouri? He hadn't lived there long enough to know, but he doubted it. Shane held the small object up, squinting at it curiously. It was small, barely longer than the palm of his hand, and shaped sort of like a fat tongue-depressor. One half—the handle?—appeared to be made of ivory. The other half was tarnished silver, molded into the shape of a placidly smiling cherub's face, surrounded by curls of hair and blooming flowers. There were three jingle bells attached to the silver end by tiny metal loops. The bells tinkled merrily as Shane shook the object. He had no idea what it was, but it was certainly an interesting find. Obviously, someone had dropped it during their walk along this path, perhaps as they sat on this very bench, resting. It had lain there ever since, lost in the vines and undergrowth, waiting for Shane to come along and find it. He wondered if whoever had lost it had missed it. Had they come back to look for it? Were they still alive out there somewhere? He doubted it. Not quite sure what to do with it, he stood up and stuffed the tiny object into the pocket of his cargo shorts.

The hazy brightness of the day was finally beginning to dim as the sun lowered beyond the trees. Shane decided it was time to head back.

By the time he pushed the wheelbarrow out of the cleared section of the footpath and back into the front corner of the yard, he was sweating again and the sky had grown low and moody. The sun painted long, purple shadows over the yard and up the front of the cottage. Shane lowered the wheelbarrow and wiped his brow again, looking up at the cottage. Because this section of yard was relatively remote and unused, his view of the cottage was somewhat unusual. From here, it crowned the bluff, standing stark against the sky beyond, framed on either side by the marching wood. It looked a little like a lone sentry defending the high ground from some Tolkien-esque advancing army. This was how Wilhelm and his wife would have seen the cottage every time they'd approached it, coming from the footpath that connected it to the main house. That realization gave him a unique perspective on the small stone and wood structure. He tried to look at it as they would have seen it. It certainly did look different from this angle. In fact...

Shane frowned. He blinked and walked around to the front of the wheelbarrow, moving out from under the trees at the edge of the yard. From this angle he could see two sides of the cottage: the front, with its small porch and leaning, mossy roof, and the east side, the side that was most rarely seen, since it faced the nearby woods and the river. The grass portion of the yard on that side was narrow, dominated by the little shed that jutted from the side of the house. A horny old magnolia tree grew up behind the shed, spreading over its roof and obscuring the view of the east face's upper half. Just visible through the lattice of branches and leaves, however, was the shape of a small round window. It reflected the descending sun with a bright pin-prick of light, impossible to miss from this angle.

"What the hell?" Shane muttered to himself, taking a few steps closer, looking up through the branches of the magnolia. The upstairs portion of the cottage was divided into two rooms, the attic and the studio, and Shane had been certain that there was only one window between them, the one that stood over the stairs, facing across the river. That window was not round, like this one. The attic, on the other hand, was merely a dark closet-like area connected to the back of the studio, accessible only by a narrow door in the corner. As far as Shane knew, there wasn't even anything stored there. It was possible, he supposed, that the attic branched off behind one of the side walls of the studio, forming a narrow walkway, but why would there be a window there? And wouldn't he have seen it, at least once, on one of his few trips into the attic? Perhaps, strange as it seemed, it was in a section of the attic that had been walled off. After all, the cottage had gone through numerous renovations throughout its long history. Every owner had placed their stamp on it, adding this, subtracting that, maybe even changing the configuration of the floor plan in such a way as to create some odd forgotten space. It was unsettling, though, that Shane could have owned the cottage for almost seven years and never known that it had a second upstairs window. Maybe later he'd peek into the attic and see if he could ascertain where that unexpected window might be. For now, he returned to the wheelbarrow and hefted it, pushing it toward the shed.

As he approached the cottage, that glint of sunlight played across the tiny round upstairs window again. For a moment, it didn't quite look like sunlight reflecting off the old glass panes; it looked instead like a small interior light source, glowing just inside, like a candle on the windowsill. That was especially impossible, of course.

"Keep the imagination on its leash," he said to himself, shaking his head as he began to unload the tools into the shed. "Don't let it turn cannibal on you, now. Keep the muse in her place and you'll be just fine." He sighed, and for no reason, he thought of the horrible rattling sigh that he'd heard the night after he'd arrived in the cottage. His own sigh turned into a shudder, and he glanced aside, toward the tiny, filthy basement window near his feet. The basement light was off this time.

"Keep the imagination on its leash, Shaney boy," he muttered to himself again. "Keep the muse in her place and you'll be fine. You'll be just as right as rain."

Shane didn't feel as tired that night as he'd expected to. He sat in the sunroom after dinner, thumbing his way through the satellite channels, not finding anything interesting enough to watch. It was funny, he thought (and not for the first time), that the number of good television programs seemed to be inversely related to the amount of available channels. When he'd been growing up, an only child living in a small apartment in suburban New Jersey, his parents had only had one television, an old Zenith console model, and it only clearly displayed three channels, four on stormy nights. He remembered begging to be allowed to stay up one more hour to watch whatever was coming on next; the A-Team, or the Dukes of Hazzard, or Knight Rider, with the irrepressible David Hasselhoff. Sometimes he would be allowed. Sometimes—these were the best of times—his dad would even make popcorn, or scoop bowls of ice cream for himself and Shane, and they'd drape on the couch, watching TV and snacking like kings, cheering whenever Mr. T blew something up or whenever the Duke boys gunned the General Lee and rocketed it over some defenseless creek along the back roads of Hazzard County. Shane's mother was a nurse, and back then she worked the third shift at a large nursing home in Hoboken. She was usually leaving for work, wearing her funny nurse's hat and white crepe-soled shoes, around the time Shane was supposed to be brushing his teeth and heading to bed. She'd appear at the bathroom door just as he was finishing up, and she'd adjust the bobby pins that anchored her odd little white hat in place and glance down at Shane and say, "Don't let your father let you stay up too late, now. Big boys need their sleep. And don't go eating ice cream after you've brushed your teeth." Shane would nod obediently, knowing he'd do both, and with wild abandon, if his dad was in the mood to allow it that night. His mother knew it, too. She'd sigh in a businesslike manner and squat down, still primping her black hair and nurse's cap, and deftly touch the corner of her mouth with a finger, summoning a goodnight kiss. Shane complied easily enough. Back then, he was still young enough to be unselfconscious about kissing his mother. After she'd leave, driving off in the big gold Chevelle, Shane would usually go to bed. But sometimes he'd stand by the entry to the narrow hallway and ask, and his dad would pat the couch cushion next to him, and Shane would run across the living room and hurl himself up onto the couch next to his dad, into the glorious blue glow of primetime television. It didn't happen as often as he wished, but it happened more than his mother knew. That was all right. Mothers knew all about how many vegetables boys needed every day, and how much vitamin D they needed in their milk, but fathers knew other things. Fathers knew about a boy's recommended daily allowance of explosions and car chases.

Shane sighed, still flipping through the channels. Maybe television had just been better when he was a kid. More likely, his tastes had just been simpler. Of course, a big part of the fun had been staying up late, snuggled up next to his dad, who was huge, with giant, meaty mitts for hands and a belly like a medicine ball, round but tough. Both of Shane's parents were dead now; his dad had died of a heart attack when Shane was seventeen, and his mother had succumbed to cancer the winter before Shane's marriage had fallen apart. At least she hadn't lived to see that. June Bellamy had always loved Steph, had always called her the daughter she'd never had. She'd still had black hair then, up until the chemo finally made it disappear. It had probably not been her real color anymore, but she had always been very fussy and careful about her hair, having it done by the same stylist for almost two decades straight, right up until her death. "Only her hairdresser knows for sure," Shane's father used to say, quoting the old commercial. "For all I know, her real color's been gray since the day I married her. She's there every second Tuesday, sure as death and taxes. For what it costs me, I can only hope they're hiding gold bars in those curls."

Shane finally turned off the television. He was surprised at how awake he felt. He realized now that part of the reason he'd worked so hard on the footpath, clearing and trimming it, was because he was hoping to be exhausted and ready for bed early. It wasn't any fun staying up late to watch television anymore, not without his dad and a big bowl of over-buttered popcorn. There was no novelty in it anymore. But more importantly, for the last few days he'd been staying up too late for other reasons, working on the painting of the manor house. He'd put more energy into it by far than he had the matte painting that he'd just finished. It was disrupting his schedule, interfering with his shift. It wasn't so much that he was too tired in the mornings; it was that the painting obsessed him, distracted him from his regular work, even after he'd stayed up late the night before, working away at it. Tonight, he'd hoped to be so tired that he'd forget the painting and just fall into his bed.

Maybe he *was* tired, and just wasn't feeling it yet. Maybe once he got into bed, he'd fall right to sleep. He'd read for a little while from one of the paperback books on the bookshelf. Better yet, he'd take the laptop with him and finish the online article about Gustav Ferdinand Wilhelm. That would surely do the trick.

He sighed and didn't get up. He tossed the remote onto the oversized ottoman in front of the couch and turned his head toward the one uncovered window, the one that overlooked the patio. It was quite dark outside, but the yellow bug light next to the sliding back doors was on, illuminating the flagstones and the big brick barbecue with its weird buttery glow. Moths flitted around the light, lit like tiny constellations. Sitting on the ledge of the barbecue, merely a sleek shape against the black of the night, was Tom. He sat perfectly still, his bullet head raised, peering toward the river.

There was something in the pocket of Shane's sweat pants. He felt the unforgiving shape of it pressing against his hip. He took it out, and it jingled. It was the object he'd found under the bench along the footpath. He held the ivory handle and looked at the smiling cherub's face. The jingle bells were nearly black with tarnish, but they tinkled easily as he turned the object in his hand. And suddenly he thought he knew what it was. He held it up and smiled a little, and beyond it, in the darkness of the library, something moved.

Shane froze, his fingers tightening on the strange silver shape. His eyes slowly went wide and his breath stalled in his chest.

Whatever it was, it was a very pale gray, almost pearlescent, like a shape made of incense smoke. It glowed very faintly against the darkness as it drifted across the library, moving silently toward the kitchen. Bits of it shifted in and out of focus, implying a solid shape, but never quite maintaining it. Shane wasn't exactly frightened of it, but every fiber of his being had come alert, as if he'd never been as awake as he was at that moment. The gray, smoky shape stopped moving toward the kitchen. It wavered and drifted, as if affected by some massive, slow current that Shane could not feel, and then it seemed to turn, to look at him. Shane felt its gaze settle on him, and with it came a sense of simmering rage, indignant and confused. The thing began to approach, moving toward the doorway that separated the library and the sunroom.

"Wai..." Shane said, and his voice came out as a breathy squeak, feeble and weak. He inhaled and pressed back into the couch. "Wait. Wait. No, it wasn't me."

He didn't know what he was saying, and yet the words piled up behind his lips entirely of their own accord. The figure advanced slowly, fighting that strange, otherworldly current. It became more solid as it came, as if the effort was focusing it. Shane could make out the suggestion of arms and legs, clad in something like a streaming robe or dress. Long streaks of hair wafted out behind the head, as if the figure were underwater, pushing upstream. Shane clambered backwards, up onto the back of the couch, gasping for breath.

"It wasn't me," he heard himself say again, his voice high and wavering. "Others came to tear it down. I saw it afterwards, when it was all done, but I didn't make it happen. It was old and falling apart... dangerous..."

The figure suddenly pulsed and grew, and rage beat off it like heat from a furnace. It reached the entry to the sunroom, but couldn't seem to push through. The silent current tore at it. For a fleeting moment, Shane thought he could see a face surfacing out of the misty shape of the head. The features were those of a woman, white and smooth like a statue except for the eyes; the eyes were dead black, as if the eyelids opened onto emptiness. The face pushed through the doorway, fighting that streaming current, and it grimaced in a mixture of effort and fury, baring its teeth.

Terror fell on Shane like a wave, more at the wounded rage of the thing than even its ghostly appearance. He raised his hands to ward it off, just as the shape reared to lunge, trying to force its way into the sunroom. And suddenly, seamlessly, that pulse of broken rage *changed*. It dulled and deepened, sinking back through anger and hate, turning inward, transforming, to Shane's dismay, into a sort of miserable sadness, so huge and seamless that it was like an ocean. Shane had squeezed his eyes shut, but he slowly opened them again. His hands were still raised in front of him, his left opened, splayed, palm out. The right hand, however, still clutched the object he'd found under the bench. The silvery cherub's head and jingle bells protruded from his fist like a cross warding off a vampire. The ghostly figure looked at it, as if entranced by it, and that sense of horrible sadness came off it like cloyingly sweet perfume. The otherworldly current still pushed at it, but the shape hung motionless against it, the hair still streaming back into the library.

"This is yours," Shane whispered. He lowered his left hand, but held the right hand higher, as if offering the tarnished silver object to the ghostly shape. "Isn't it?"

He hadn't expected a response, but the figure looked up at him. Its black eyes looked fathoms deep, filled with sadness. It shook its head very slowly.

"I found it," Shane said, and he realized his teeth were chattering. It was suddenly very cold in the sunroom. "On the footpath. I didn't know what it was at first. But you know what it is, don't you?"

The figure nodded now, slowly, looking back at the silver shape in Shane's hand.

"Do you know whose it was?"

The figure nodded again, even more slowly.

"I didn't knock your house down," Shane said, shivering so that his voice shook. "It seemed like a nice house. I... I'm painting a picture of it."

The ghost glanced up at him again, and the mask of miserable sadness seemed to lighten a little. The shape was fading, drifting backwards now. Shane found he was no longer frightened of it. If anything, he felt a deep sorrow for the pathetic, broken figure. As it drifted backwards, fading, becoming insubstantial again, it maintained eye contact with him. And then, just as it evaporated into nothing, the mouth opened, as if attempting to speak. It made that awful, rattling sigh again, the same one it had made a few nights earlier, only this time the sigh formed a word. It lingered and elongated, falling away to nothing as the shape vanished, leaving only the echo of it in Shane's mind, like a memory of a dream.

"*Riverhouse...*" it had whispered, as if it were a sort of plea. Shane didn't know what it meant, at least not yet, but the sound of it played over and over in his mind, plugging into his imagination, firing it up with hundreds of fizzing, frantic images and ideas.

Shane allowed himself to slide off the back of the couch, plopping down onto the seat cushions. He exhaled harshly. Adrenaline was still throbbing through his body, making his heart trip-hammer and widening his eyes. Whatever that had been, it hadn't been Tom the cat, or a leaky window, or the idiosyncrasies of an old cottage. It hadn't been Smithy. The thing in the library had been a ghost. And Shane had a pretty good idea of whose ghost it was. It was the woman in the painting; the one reclining on the front steps with one arm raised to shade her eyes from the sun. She was the one that the painting—no, the *muse*—had asked for, and Shane had obliged. She was the dead wife of Gustav Ferdinand Wilhelm, and she had suddenly found herself homeless. Somehow, some part of his mind had recognized her almost immediately. Had she actively haunted the main house? Shane had heard stories from the realtor, but nothing very serious, and nothing all that scary. He had a weird sense that the ghost had been mostly dormant in the main house, that she had been awakened only as it had come crashing down around her, shockingly and suddenly. Had she even been aware of what the house had become in the intervening decades, how it had been parsed and pillaged, robbed of its nobility? Probably not. To her, the house had probably remained exactly as she'd left it. When it was taken from her, she'd gone to the only other place that she knew. She'd gone to the cottage, only to find it occupied by a stranger, a stranger she couldn't help blaming for the destruction of her beloved home: the Riverhouse.

Shane shook his head, as if he was trying to order his thoughts. How could he know all this? He knew that the core of any artist's mind was inventiveness, the ability to cobble a story together out of random bits and pieces, but this was something else entirely. It was as if some part of his mind had connected directly with that of the ghost, like the socket had already been there, waiting to be plugged in. He'd felt her emotions; first the confused rage, and then the bottomless sorrow. Somehow, he'd understood her.

It's because you've already met her, one of the voices of his mind said pragmatically. This time, it was the voice of his mother, no-nonsense and imperturbable. *You met her in your painting, in that weird dreamscape between waking and sleeping, fathoms deep, where you go when you're dipping out of the well of creativity. Only this time, someone met you at the well and filled the bucket up for you. The muse? The ghost herself? Maybe, Shaney, they are one and the same. Maybe you should think about that.*

Maybe he should. But not now. His brain was overloaded. Shane had grown up reading ghost stories and watching scary movies. In a manner of speaking, he'd always been a believer—in the general idea of the afterlife, sure, but also in any number of other inexplicable and deliciously morbid ideas; spontaneous human combustion, poltergeists, aliens, zombies in deepest Africa, Big Foot in the untrodden wilderness of the Midwest. He wasn't one of the devout, exactly, like the people who read *Weekly World News* or go to those alien conventions in Roswell, New Mexico. His belief was more of the agnostic variety—everything's plausible, but probably unknowable. It was, he figured, just part of being the sort of person who plied the trade of imagination, who pumped the well of invention on a daily basis. Still, it was one thing to find the idea of ghosts plausible, in a sort of nighttime-around-the-campfire kind of way, and another thing entirely to have confronted one in the mundane reality of one's sunroom. In the movies, ghosts always appeared either to unusually attractive teenagers or well-dressed adults with English accents. Rarely were they seen baring their ghostly teeth at middle-aged men in sweat pants and Dodgers tee shirts. If such a thing was possible, then what about spontaneous human combustion? Or crop circles?

And yet, interestingly, Shane didn't feel especially frightened, even in the aftermath of his confrontation. He lived in a cottage with a ghost, yes, but it was a ghost he thought he understood. He knew who she'd been, and what she wanted, or so he thought. And suddenly he understood something else. She hadn't been able to enter the sunroom—had been forced back from it by that strange, silent current—and it made perfect sense that that should be so. The sunroom was relatively new. It had not been there during the ghost's lifetime. To her, it didn't really exist. No wonder she'd been so confused. The destruction of the main house had forced her awake, forced her to begin to see the world as it is now.

Shane shivered. The room still felt cold, although it was less so than it had been a few minutes earlier. Shakily, he climbed to his feet, preparing to go to the bedroom, and something fell off his lap. It jingled to the floor with a small thump. Shane looked down at it, and then bent down to get it. This was what had really gotten the ghost's attention, not his words. She had recognized it, and known who it belonged to. Shane didn't know whose it had been, but he thought he now knew what it was. It had occurred to him a moment before the ghost had appeared. It was a baby rattle. He shook it in his hand and it jingled merrily. The cherub's tarnished face smiled up at him.

The muse was calling, but Shane resisted. Not tonight. He needed to sleep, and despite everything, despite the strange shock of finding a ghost in his home, he thought he might actually be able to. As the adrenaline wore away, he felt exhaustion finally fall on him like a barrel full of bricks. He stumped out of the sunroom, not even bothering to turn on any lights, and found his way to the bedroom. He fell headlong onto the bed.

Less than two minutes later he was sound asleep, and dreaming.

He dreamed of the Riverhouse, of course. It hadn't been destroyed at all. He had bought it, and paid to have it restored. Somehow, he had sought out all the missing pieces, right down to the pillars on the front portico, and returned them to their rightful places. It was exactly as it had once been, and he moved through it proudly, feeling a great sense of accomplishment and peace. He was alone in the house, and yet he didn't feel lonely. He was attended, somehow. Perhaps it was the ghost, the woman who had originally lived there, breathed life into it, and given it her heart. If so, he didn't see her, but the presence was in every room, sighing from the walls, billowing in the sheer curtains of the open windows, creaking with satisfaction in the tall doors as they rocked in the breeze. Sunlight filled the rooms, illuminating their contents: bright tapestries and oriental rugs, antique chairs and desks with carven legs as delicate as fawns. All of these Shane had replaced as well, finding each and every piece exactly as it once was. He'd known just what to look for. He'd been told. He was content as he moved through the rooms, silently and slowly, assuring himself that everything was, indeed, exactly as it should be. The Riverhouse was his, and it was perfect. As he passed in front of the long, gilt-framed mirror that hung in the downstairs hall, he realized he had no reflection. He was the ghost now, insubstantial as smoke and silent as a memory. That was all right, too. He had done what he needed to do.

Slowly, however, he became aware of a sound, and as he did he realized that it had been going on for some time, nearly hidden beneath the sigh of the creaking doors and the whispering breeze. It was a soft sound, but nagging, distressing in this eternal, sunlit afternoon. It was the sound of someone crying. Shane tried to tune it out, but it followed him from room to room, always sounding like it was just down the hall, or up the stairs, or right outside the window. Sometimes it sounded like a woman, but then, a minute later, it sounded like a young child, whimpering and sniffing, moaning and sobbing. Shane didn't seek it out. Instinctively, he knew he didn't want to see who was making that sound. There was a baby rattle in his pocket. He could feel it there, pressing against his hip as he moved, and it annoyed him that ghosts should even have pockets, much less pointless odds and ends stuffed into them. The rattle made a muffled jingle as he moved. The sound of it became a nuisance, even worse than the sound of the mysterious weeping. Shane decided to get rid of it. He didn't need it anymore.

He left the house, venturing through the huge double doors in back. They were thrown wide open, providing a panoramic view of the river and the surrounding woods. The factories on the other side of the river were gone, replaced with a patchwork of fields and hills, dotted with brown cows. It looked like something from an Andrew Wyeth painting, and yet the noise of that jingling rattle soured it. It should've been a happy sound, but it wasn't. It was becoming nearly maddening. He moved through the intricate pathways of the rose garden, stepping over the gardening shears and the weed whacker. His wheelbarrow lay on its side, abandoned on the lawn. Finally, at the edge of the yard, where it fell away to rocks and then the brown, forgetful face of the river, Shane stopped. He pulled the old rattle from his pocket, held it up, and stopped. The silver cherub's face had changed. Instead, a nappy brown bear's head protruded from his fist, smiling its black stitched smile. It wore a yellow rain hat, and Shane recognized it; this was Paddington Bear. The rattle was embedded in the yellow plastic handle in his fist; it clattered as he held it up. He'd seen this rattle before, had held it in his hand. It all came back to him and landed on him with horrible, suffocating weight.

"No," he said, and sobbed, lowering his arm, unable to throw the rattle away. He'd meant to heave it into the river, where it could be forgotten. The river was good at forgetting; that was nearly its job. But he couldn't do it. He couldn't forget. And an idea occurred to him. Had it been his own weeping he'd heard as he moved through the house? Was that why he'd never been able to escape it? Why it had always followed him from room to room, nagging at him, echoing, always just out of sight?

It was a good theory, but it was wrong. Shane turned around, back toward the house, and she was standing right behind him. Tears streaked her cheeks; her eyes were red and swollen, but bright, panicked. She was wearing the light blue tee shirt, now faded and threadbare, the black letters across her chest barely legible: ADDICTED TO ADRENALINE.

"I lost it, Shane!" she cried, stumbling toward him and raising her hands. They were very white, wherever they weren't splattered with bright, wet red. "I lost it! I've been looking, but I can't find it anymore! It was the only thing I had to do, but I couldn't do it! Help me Shane! *Help me look!*" Her voice was ragged, splintering into madness. She fell on Shane, pushed him backwards, and her tears fell onto his cheek, her blood streaked his clothes. He fell backwards, over the rocks, toward the river below. Stephanie clung to him, still shrieking and sobbing. The Paddington Bear rattle was still clutched in his hand, so tightly that his knuckles whitened and his fingernails dug into his palm, as if it were a lifeline. But it wasn't a lifeline. If anything, it was just the opposite.

Together, they fell and fell, waiting for the darkness to swallow them up, waiting for the forgetful bliss of death. It didn't come, and Shane didn't wake. He shifted in his sleep, moaning and sweating, trying unsuccessfully to thrash himself to consciousness.

And in the darkness over his bed, silent and patient, something watched.

Chapter Four

By the time Wednesday morning came, the day before his visit from Greenfeld, Shane had made his way through most of the groceries in the cottage fridge. He put on a flannel shirt and an old pair of jeans, dressing for the seasonal mildness of the morning, and went out to his brown Chevy pickup truck. It started easily enough, despite its age, and he silently thanked the old Missouri farmer who had surely been its original owner. The truck bounded gamely down the rutted dirt path to the valley road, and Shane cranked the steering wheel hard left, angling toward Bastion Falls.

He turned the truck's old AM radio on, scanned the stations, and then turned it back off again. It was a short drive; he could stand a few minutes of amiable silence. He rolled down the window and listened instead to the thrum of the road and the rush of the cool autumn air. A few minutes later, he slowed and passed under the shadow of the huge floodwall gate, entering the town proper. Bastion Falls was really not much more than a collection of old factories and sprawling industrial complexes, randomly peppered with bars, auto body shops, and carry-outs. A warren of crammed residential streets clustered around the outskirts, mostly populated by the employees of the local industries, their driveways full of shiny pickup trucks, ATVs and boats on trailers. In the center of the town, where the factories finally gave way, was a short main street with slant parking on one side and six sets of railroad tracks on the other. At the end of the street was a small square park, sporting some of the town's few trees and an old world war two Sherman tank on a concrete platform. The IGA grocery store was situated on the far side of the park. Shane steered his truck up into the small parking lot, content to find a space near the chain link fence in back.

He shopped slowly, almost indulgently, listening to the in-store muzak and even humming along a little. He was in an unusually good mood. Last night, he had finished his latest painting. The portrait of the Riverhouse was finally complete. Years ago, one of Shane's college art instructors had taught him the immortal axiom of finishing art: "the artist never finishes his work," he'd said gravely, almost warningly, "he just abandons it. Never make the mistake of trying to finish it. The best you can hope for is to quit the work before you kill it." Shane had long since learned that lesson, and yet the Riverhouse painting had been different. He'd disciplined himself to work on it in the evenings, only after he'd finished his regular shift (he was working on some Oriental Tibetan mountain scenes for a tea company contract, emailed to him by Greenfeld on a take-it-or-leave-it basis) and after he'd gotten some exercise and had his dinner. The arrangement seemed to work for the muse, albeit grudgingly. She had taken to leaving him alone until around five-thirty or six, and then she would jump on his back like an impatient monkey, demanding and hungry. Sometimes Shane would still wait an hour or so, watching television or sitting on the back patio, watching the river, stroking Tom when he'd jump up on his lap, purring like a motorboat. He did this just to prove to himself that he was still in charge, that the muse was not his master. If Gustav Wilhelm had been able to train her and make her his own, maybe little old Shane Bellamy could, too. Maybe some of the old man's indomitable spirit had even settled on Shane, since he was living in the last remnant of his once grand artist's compound.

When he did paint, however, he did so with a sort of speed and fury that was a little scary. And he was less and less aware of the passage of time as he was doing it. It was, he thought, eerily like abandoning his body to some outside force, allowing it to come in and puppet him, letting it create through him. He supposed all artists felt like that sometimes. Otherwise, why would they have invented the myth of the muse, the external imp of inspiration, whose fickle passions were really just the embodiment of the artist's own quirky moods? Still, Shane had never experienced the power of creation like he had when he'd been working on the Riverhouse painting. As his arm swept over the canvas, his mind sank away into the scene, living inside of it, moving all around the house and steeping in its story. More importantly, there was the woman on the portico. As he'd painted her, he'd watched her, studied her, been her voyeur. She was pretty, but not beautiful, sad but not broken, strong but not domineering, quiet but not shy. Shane respected her, even loved her a little, and in his wandering thoughts, he watched her move through the house, growing old inside it as it developed around her. There were others there as well—servants, friends, art dealers, associates and fellow painters—but they moved through the scenes like blurs, silent and unimportant. The woman was all that mattered, because she was the woman in the painting, the heart of the house. She was the ghost, of course. In his semi-dreaming mind, he wondered if the painting had summoned her ghost, or if her ghost had somehow influenced the painting. Surely there was some kind of connection.

He had felt her presence in the evenings sometimes, but had only seen her once more. The previous night, she had stood at the top of the stairs of the studio, almost invisible in the shadows, watching as he'd painted. He'd sensed her there, sensed her eyes on him, and hadn't even been alarmed by it. He'd glanced aside, stopping in mid stroke, coming up out of the painting only long enough to verify what he suspected. Her black eyes were unblinking. He thought she'd been looking at him—it was hard to tell, with those featureless, colorless eyes—but she was actually looking at the painting. Shane had gone back to work, amazed that one could so quickly grow accustomed to the supernatural. He lived with a ghost. She left him alone, mostly, and he returned the favor. It had probably happened to lots of other people, but they just never talked about it. How could you? Everyone knew ghosts didn't exist. Everyone taught their kids that from an early age, preaching it like it was one of the infallible doctrines of life. If Shane had had a child, he'd have taught her the same thing, even now. Life, he thought, was full of constructive lies like that; they were the asphalt that paved the way for civilization smoothing the edges, making existence seem manageable and predictable. Most people knew it was all a sham, but that was all right. It was a useful sham. Deep down, though, the truth was undeniable. The truth was a rattling sigh that came out of the darkness, lost and confused. The truth was the coldness Shane felt on his back as he painted, as someone watched over his shoulder, someone who wasn't really there.

And despite what his art teacher had said, the Riverhouse painting *had* gotten finished. He'd been plowing along, laying on the paint, stroke after stroke, sometimes smearing it with a pallet knife or even his thumb, lost in the fathoms of the house's story, when the muse had suddenly just vanished. He'd stopped, blinking, and lowered his arm. The painting had been finished. One more stroke would have been too much; one less, too little. It was as simple as that. He'd never been surer of anything in his entire artistic career. With the muse departed, Shane realized just how exhausted and beaten he felt. It wasn't a bad feeling, however; it was the feeling of hard work that had been worth doing. He'd stood up, stretched his spine, and backed away from the painting. In the hard glare of the overhead light, it dominated the room. It almost seemed to suck the color out of its environment, drawing it into itself, transforming it into something magical. And was it all good magic? Shane knew it was not. Christiana had been right; there *was* something about the painting that messed with the viewer's eyes. It was in the way it almost seemed to be two paintings overlaying each other, sometimes competing for attention, sometimes complementing each other. Shane liked the effect. It turned the painting into something that was very nearly alive.

He'd looked back toward the top of the stairs, almost hoping that the ghost was still there. He was proud of the painting, and wanted to share it with someone. The stairs were completely empty, however. Maybe the ghost had never really been there at all; maybe that had just been another invention of his daydreaming, fathoms-deep mind.

Shane finished his shopping, filling his cart with the sorts of things that all men who live on their own are wont to stock their kitchens with: mostly lunch meat, condiments, and frozen microwave meals. He'd also gotten another six pack of St. Pauli Girl. Greenfeld was coming over tomorrow at one, but Shane had known enough people in the art world to know that midday wasn't too early to offer one of them a beer, or even a martini. The rest of the people in the small store seemed to be women in their forties, mostly unhappy-looking, drifting through the aisles as if in slow motion. The checkout area had three lanes, but only one of them was open, manned by a young, skinny guy in a black tee shirt and a stained green apron. Across the top of his tee shirt, printed in faded, silvery letters, were the words *Avenged Sevenfold,* hovering over what appeared to be a skull with bat wings. Shane could only guess it was the name of a band. For better or worse, he had stopped paying attention to the world of music around the time Kurt Cobain had decided success was a burden too heavy to bear. He sighed and looked around. The front wall of the IGA was comprised of glass windows plastered with hand-lettered sale signs. The glare of the morning sun on the white signs turned the checkout area into a sort of human terrarium. It was not unpleasant, despite the drab, eighties-era cash registers and conveyer belts and the shocked, frozen faces of the people on the covers of the tabloids. The guy working the scanner was humming to himself, and despite his shirt, Shane thought the song he was humming was *Bad Moon Rising* by Creedance Clearwater Revival. He even whistled part of the chorus as the woman in front of him studiously wrote out her check.

"Morning, paper or plastic?" the guy said, glancing up at Shane as the woman ahead of him pushed her cart disconsolately toward the front doors.

"Surprise me," Shane replied, unloading his cart.

"You got it," the guy answered, swiping the six pack of beer over the scanner. "And hey, just so you know, we had to send back a whole pallet of that Macarena salsa. It was all rancid. Had a bunch of people bringing it back. I'm not supposed to say anything about it, but the boss is down at Nick's getting coffee, so screw him, right?"

Shane blinked and looked down at the salsa in his hand. "Thanks. Maybe I'll skip this one, then." He set it aside, on the metal plate at the end of the conveyor.

The guy in the green apron scanned the groceries with practiced speed. "It's just that you look like a man who knows his salsa, and I'd hate for you to have to drive all the way back into town to return a bad jar."

"I appreciate it," Shane said, glancing at the nametag on the guy's apron. "Er, Alex."

"S'not really my name," the guy said, grinning up at Shane. "I lost my name tag. Probably under the front seat of my Honda. I borrowed this one from a locker in the back room. Alex is actually a girl. She's hot, too. Works in the deli. I'm Brian."

Shane smiled, bemused. "Nice to meet you, Brian. By the way, how'd you know I was from outside of town?"

"You're kidding, right?" Brian said, now stuffing the groceries into plastic bags. "I see the same faces in here all week long. Most of them I've known all my life. That lady behind you used to babysit me even, back when I was a snot-nosed brat. Isn't that right, Mrs. Baker?"

Shane glanced behind him, to a large black woman in her fifties. She stirred and said, "What, you mean you aren't still a snot-nosed brat?"

"Good times, Mrs. Baker," Brian answered unperturbed, and then glanced up at Shane again. "Besides, you live out in the river cottage, right?"

Shane raised his eyebrows. "Er, yeah. I do. Just moved in about a week ago."

Brian nodded. "Don't worry, it's not like we've all been spying on you or anything. My Grandpa used to be caretaker out there, and he still keeps tabs on it. He took me there sometimes when I was a kid. I've been in your place a few times, back before it *was* your place. Grandpa worked at the house, too, way back in the day, when he was my age. Started when the Wilhelms still owned the place. Shame they finally tore it down, after all these years. I guess time marches on, eh?"

"It sure does," Shane said, frowning a little. "You say your grandfather worked there when the Wilhelms were still there? He must be getting up there himself. They built the place in, what, the thirties?"

"He'll be ninety-five this Christmas," Brian replied, as if he was personally responsible for his grandfather's longevity. "Still drives his own car. Washes it, too, once a month, rain or shine. I try to get him to wash mine too, but he's a stubborn old coot. That'll be seventy-nine, twenty-nine."

Shane fished out his wallet and handed Brian his credit card. "I'm Shane Bellamy, by the way," he said. "You'll be seeing me around more often, so I might as well become one of your regulars."

"Good to meet you Mr. Bellamy," Brian said, swiping Shane's card. "You should go talk to my Grandpa sometime. He could tell you stories about that old place. You wouldn't believe some of the stuff that's happened out there. You know they used to have other artists come out there and spend the summers? One of them lived in a teepee in the woods for two months straight, wearing Indian war-paint and smoking peyote. Artists, eh?"

Shane smiled and nodded. "Speaking as one of them, you don't know the half of it."

"Oh, you'd be surprised," Brian said, handing Shane back his card and a pen. "I've heard plenty of stories. You paint too?"

"I do."

"I used to draw, but I gave it up. I'm in college now, over in Webster. History major."

"Good luck with that," Shane said, signing his name to the little slip Brian pushed toward him. "And I would be interested in talking to your grandfather sometime, actually. Does he live here in town?"

"Just around the block, at Denny Acres. He's always around, except for Friday nights. That's when he goes over to the Eagles to meet with his war buddies and play pinochle. His name's Earl, last name Kirchenbauer, just like me. He'd be glad to talk to you, I bet, especially now that the big house has been torn down."

Shane hefted his plastic bags, preparing to leave. "I imagine he was pretty sad to see it go," he said. "Seeing as he used to work there and knew the place."

"Not at all," Brian shook his head, laughing a little. "Grandpa hated that place. He would've burned it down himself, if he'd been able to. He about danced a jig when the paper announced the city was demolishing it."

Shane frowned, confused, and Brian shrugged. "He hated the old place," he said again. "Not the cottage, where you live, but the house, even though he spent all those years keeping it up. Must have trimmed one too many hedges or something back in the day, I guess. Wilhelm was a tough guy to work for."

"I can sort of imagine that," Shane replied thoughtfully.

"Look grandpa up," Brian said, beginning to swipe the next load of groceries over the scanner. "Number fifty one. He'd love to talk to you about it, believe me. What'll it be today, Mrs. Baker, paper or plastic?"

Shane stood in the sunlight, holding his groceries in their white plastic bags. After a moment, he turned and stepped on the black ribbed matt in front of the automatic doors. They hissed open, letting in a gust of still-cool morning air, and Shane walked out into the parking lot, wondering what in the hell "Denny Acres" was.

One block east of Main Street, Shane pulled his truck into the narrow lot next to a white sign that read "Valley Acres Retirement Community". It didn't appear to be much of a community, really. There was only one building, made of white brick, single story but sprawling, dotted with identical, mostly curtained windows. There was a circle drive in front, curving under a teasingly grand façade, complete with statuary and a long burgundy canopy. Shane avoided the curved drive, parking instead on the side of the building, in a slant space between an EMS van and an immaculate Chevrolet Caprice with a fake Shih-Tzu dog glued to the dashboard. As he got out, he saw that the retirement home shared a parking lot on this side with an old but well-maintained Denny's restaurant. That pretty much explained the nickname, at least.

There were doors between some of the windows, but none of them had numbers on them. Even if they were doors to interior hallways, they'd surely all be locked. He walked around the corner to the front of the building, entering the shadow of the canopy. The entrance was a set of double glass doors, flanked by a pair of somewhat unhealthy-looking decorative trees. As the doors shuttled open, Shane read the small white letters just below the name of the facility: *No Smoking – Oxygen in Use.*

Shane's mother had worked in a nursing home. She'd never liked it, even though she'd met her best friends there, friends she'd kept for years after retiring from the big assisted living facility in Hoboken, friends who'd stayed with her right up until her death. Most of them had been at the funeral, and Shane thought that they'd looked even sadder than he had. Probably it was just that women in their sixties were much more comfortable with expressing their emotions than were thirty-something-year-old men, even if the man in question was an artist. Years after she'd retired, Shane's mother had told him stories about her night shifts at the nursing home. Some of them were funny, like the time old demented Mrs. Kubrick had raved for days about how she'd won the lottery and was going to buy the home and fire all the nurses, and everyone had merely rolled their eyes at her, until one of his mother's friends, a first shift nurse named Norma Rigby, had actually found the winning ticket stuck in Mrs. Kubrick's latest Jacky Collins paperback as a bookmark. As it happened, she'd only won a hundred and fifty thousand dollars, which wasn't enough to buy the nursing home. It *was* enough, however, to get her a room in a much more cushy retirement community in Aspen, Colorado. "Take that, you skinny bitches!" old Mrs. Kubrick had cackled as they'd wheeled her out for the last time, under the big hand-painted banner that read CONGRATS AND GOODBYE LOIS KUBRICK. "Take that! I told you, didn't I?

That'll teach you to change the channel in the middle of Jeopardy! I told you I'd see you put out on the streets!" She laughed and laughed, and most of the nurses laughed with her, waving and shaking their heads.

Some of the stories that Shane's mother told, though, weren't funny at all. Some of them were sad, and some of them were just plain creepy. The one Shane remembered most was the one about the home's oldest resident, a hundred-plus year old woman named Mrs. Jerzyck. She lived in a room in the back corner of the top floor, an area the nurses secretly referred to as "the Waiting Room," since it was the place residents were moved to when they were deemed terminally ill, or when their dementia or Alzheimer's had progressed to the point that they no longer recognized their family, or even themselves when shown a mirror. In the nurse's lounge, one nurse might ask another about a suddenly empty bed in the home's main residence, and her friend would answer, "Oh, Mr. Herbert was moved to the Waiting Room this morning. Took his number from Dr. Gordon. The cancer's spread to his lungs." Shane had learned that places like nursing homes were full of that sort of black humor. It was a basic defense mechanism against the ever-present reality of human decay. Once residents got moved to the Waiting Room—once they "took their number"—it was only a matter of time, usually measured in weeks rather than months, before they "graduated". That was another black humor term they used around the nurse's lounge. Nobody ever died in the Waiting Room; they merely graduated, as if all of life thus far had just been a tedious school term meant as preparation for whatever happened next. Mrs. Jerzyck, however, hadn't graduated, even by the time Shane's mother herself had retired. She'd lived in her little nook in the Waiting Room for sixteen years, floating in and out of lucidity like a waterlogged tree stump bobbing occasionally to the surface of a river. When she was awake and alert, Shane's mother had said, Mrs. Jerzyck was very sweet. She was chatty and pleasant, if a little dotty, sometimes believing it was 1951 and she was living in Poughkeepsie, other times knowing what year it really was and asking to read the newspaper to see how her beloved Ronald Reagan was faring. Late at night, however, regardless of whether Mrs. Jerzyck had been lucid or not during that day, she'd talk to herself in her room.

"I always hated doing my rounds down at that end of the top floor," Shane's mother had told him. "It was dark down there, because it was in the oldest part of the building and none of the lights had been updated. Her door would be closed, and you'd only hear her just a little, only when you walked right by, but she talked *all* the *time* at night. She must have been doing it in her sleep, but it was still an eerie sound. And then, one night, my curiosity got the better of me. It was around three in the morning, and I was passing by her door. I heard her, and I leaned in close to listen. She wasn't just talking to herself; she was having a *conversation*. And the worst part was, she was speaking in different voices. She was herself, as a child, and then she was her mother, and then, worst of all, she was her father. When she spoke in his voice, her old lady's voice turned rough and deep, and I could have sworn there was someone else in the room with her, carrying on his end of the conversation. The voices were arguing, fighting over something, and then Mrs. Jerzyck let out a scream. She did it in her little girl's voice, as if she'd been slapped. My instincts kicked in and I pushed the door open, running in to see what had happened. Mrs. Jerzyck was sitting up in bed in the dark, and I saw her head turn toward me. I asked her if she was all right, and she just looked at me, her eyes confused and bleary in the light from the hall. And then, in her little girl's voice, she said, 'who's that lady, Mama?' And then the father's voice came out of her mouth, making it big and sort of liver-lipped. 'Make her go away. Get rid of her or I'll do it myself,' it said, and Mrs. Jerzyck's mouth grinned at me. It almost *leered*. I couldn't help it. God forgive me, but I ran. I just backed out of the door, turned on my heel and ran all the way back to the elevator. I never listened close to that door again, I'll tell you that. I took as wide a berth around it as I could from that night on."

Shane had been a teenager at the time, morbidly interested in his mother's creepy tale. He'd asked her if she thought Mrs. Jerzyck was crazy, and she had shaken her head. "There's more out there in the world than we understand, Shaney," she'd answered. "More than I care to know, and that's the truth. I don't think Mrs. Jerzyck is crazy. She's demented, yes, but I think maybe she *is* being visited in the night. Not by the ghosts of her parents, mind you, but by *things*. Things that take pleasure in tormenting people when they're at their weakest."

"Demons?" Shane had asked, borrowing a term from the Baptist church he and his mother attended sometimes.

"Maybe," she'd answered dismissively, flapping her hand as if the technical terminology was unimportant. "Maybe not. Maybe they *are* ghosts, but not human ghosts. Humans don't need to stick around here in this world once they're time is over, unless maybe something keeps them here, some serious unfinished business. And even then, I suspect they'd have better things to do than have ninety-year-old arguments with their still-living relatives. I think the things that torment poor old Mrs. Jerzyck are just mean-spirited imps, preying on the living when they're at their weakest, when they're too feeble or too out of it to fight them off. Just a bunch of invisible bullies, if you ask me. In the end, how much you want to bet that God kicks all their scrawny, invisible rear ends straight to Hell's front door?" And she'd grinned at Shane, a crooked *I-wouldn't-say-that-to-anyone-else* grin, and Shane had smiled himself, and then laughed.

As Shane entered Valley Acres Retirement Community, he found himself approaching a large, round desk, busily manned by nurses in gaily colored scrubs, not at all like the old white jumper and cap his mother had worn during her third shifts. All around the nurse's station, clustered like barnacles, were wheelchairs populated by residents. Most leaned in various stages of morning doze, mouths open or chins on chests, but a few looked up at Shane, their eyes bright and avid. One woman waved a skinny, liver-spotted hand at Shane, beckoning him over, her mouth turned up in a hopeful, toothless smile. He smiled back, meeting her eyes, and angled towards her.

"Be a dear and fetch me a cigarette," she said, reaching up and taking his hand. Her fingers were cold, brittle-feeling, but strong. "There's a machine in the restaurant if you don't have any with you. I have money."

"I don't think you're allowed to smoke, ma'am," Shane replied, leaning over so she could hear him. She was still gripping his hand. "The sign on the door says—"

"Never mind that. Just bring me my goddam cigarettes. I've asked you at least a dozen times, now. The money's in my purse, hanging by the back door."

"I'm sorry, ma'am," Shane said. He pulled his hand gently away and she let go very reluctantly, seeming to sink into herself as she did, still mumbling. He glanced up at the nurse's station, to see if anyone had observed his interaction with the unfortunate old woman, but no one was paying any attention. One of the nurses, a young man with greasy black hair, was apparently listening to an iPod.

"Excuse me," Shane said, approaching the desk. "I'm looking for a resident."

The man with the iPod headphones plugged into his ears ignored him, but a fat woman with very thick glasses spoke up. "Name?"

"Oh," Shane said, surprised. He hadn't even noticed her sitting there; the counter had hidden her until he was right next to it. She stared at him, unsmiling. He cleared his throat. "I'm looking for Earl. Earl, uh…" Suddenly, he couldn't remember the last name that the kid in the IGA had told him. "Er, he's in room number fifty one."

"You a relative?" the woman asked, typing quickly on a keyboard.

"No, but I was sent by one. Guy named Brian. He works at the grocery store one block over. Kirchenbauer," he said, blurting the last name the moment it came to him. He hoped he'd remembered it correctly. The fat woman didn't respond. She stared at the screen, chewing a piece of gum. Finally, she said, "You a solicitor? Insurance or funeral planning or anything like that?"

"No," Shane answered, feeling strangely guilty. All he wanted to do was ask the old guy about the history of the cottage, but suddenly he felt shifty, like he should lie about his name or produce a phony badge or something. "No, I just want to talk to him. I'm sort of a friend of a friend, I guess."

"No solicitors allowed," the woman said, not really listening. "He's in room fifty one. Go down the hall on your right, take a right at the cafeteria, and then a left at the first corridor. Better hurry, though. Lunch is in a half hour."

"I'll be sure to beat the rush," Shane said, turning away.

The retirement home seemed to be divided into two sections; assisted living in the east wing, and independent living in the west. Apparently Mr. Kichenbauer, despite his age, resided in the independent living wing. There were less wheelchair-bound sleepers here, and the few doors that were propped open showed small, tidy apartments, most with the televisions turned on, displaying soap operas or The Price is Right. Bulletin boards adorned the walls between the doorways, all of them colorfully decorated for the holidays. He passed one framed in scalloped brown construction paper with cutouts of pilgrim's hats and pumpkins stapled to it. In the middle, a sign-up sheet proclaimed the upcoming "THANKSGIVING DAY DANCE", complete with "LIVE MUSIC" and an exhortation to "GOBBLE UP THE FREE CIDER AND COOKIES!" To Shane, the bulletin boards looked disconcertingly like they belonged in a grade school hallway rather than a retirement home. As he reached the cafeteria, he passed a woman with a walker, grimly making her way into the unmistakable odor of boiled green beans and macaroni and cheese. He glanced up at the numbers on the plain metal doors, counting up. After a left turn into a narrower corridor, he finally found number fifty-one. It was cracked open, propped with a rolled up issue of TV Guide. Shane knocked lightly.

"Mr. Kirchenbauer?" he called softly. He could hear the sound of the television. It was loud enough that he could tell what was on. The eleven AM news was just starting on channel five. Shane pushed the door open a little and peeked inside. "Mr. Kirchenbauer?"

There was a very old orange Laz-E-Boy recliner in the corner by the little kitchen, but no one was sitting in it. A coffee cup and a crossword magazine lay on the side table, which reflected the glow of the wall-mounted television. Shane pushed the door open further. On the nappy carpet in front of the chair, looking like a Rorschach ink blot, was a splatter of dark liquid. An alarm bell began to go off in Shane's mind. Had something happened to the old guy? Should he go and alert the nursing staff? He could imagine how that would go. Crack team that they were, they'd surely rush to the rescue by sometime that afternoon, at least once lunch was over and they'd all finished their smoke breaks. Instead, he decided to check on Mr. Kirchenbauer himself. He entered the small living room, allowing the door to ease shut behind him, closing on the rolled up magazine. There was a door in the back of the living area, across from the kitchen. It was mostly shut, showing only a bar of shadowy dark: probably the bedroom. Shane inched toward it, afraid of what he might find when he opened the door. He reached out for the handle, and when his fingers touched the cheap metal it was very cold. And then, shocking him so that his knees nearly unhinged, a toilet flushed almost directly behind him. It was so loud and so sudden that it sounded like an F-18 launching from an aircraft carrier. Shane spun on the spot just in time to see movement in a second doorway, kitty-corner from the bedroom. A small, antiseptic bathroom lay beyond, complete with bright fluorescent lights and a thick, stainless-steel handbar next to the toilet. A small man was crossing the living room floor, hitching up his pants and ignoring

Shane completely. Shane struggled to settle his heartbeat, and grinned at his foolishness. The small man eased himself into the orange chair, sinking into it so that his knobby knees poked up like dock pilings. He eyed Shane with no surprise, his eyes magnified behind a pair of horn-rimmed glasses.

"Well, get on with it, why don'cha?" he declared, flapping a large, knuckly hand. "What're you waiting for? A written invitation?"

"I'm sorry?" Shane said, taken aback. "Were you expecting me?"

"What do you think I'm spending all my sociable security on, if it isn't for you lackeys to clean up a spot of spilled coffee? I called down an hour ago already, told you I'd leave the door propped open so I wouldn't have to get up again. It's probably sunk right into the padding by now, and it serves you right. Where's your cart, anyway? What you gonna do, *suck* it outta the carpet?"

Shane couldn't help grinning. "Sorry to say it, Mr. Kirchenbauer, but I don't work for the facility. I just came over to talk to you. Your grandson told me about you."

"My grandson," the man said, still eyeing Shane severely. "Shaun or Brian?"

"Er," Shane replied, searching his memory again. "Brian. He works over at the IGA. That's where I met him, and where he told me about you."

"Oh, well why didn't you say so? Sit down then. That Brian, he's a good enough boy, if you don't count the fact that he's about as soft in the head as a November cabbage. Not like that uppity cousin of his, though; lives up in Chicago and thinks he's ten different kinds of high and mighty. Works for some government office there, undersecretary of some stuffed shirt or other. I'll take dull over uppity anyday. You know my Shaun, do you?"

"No," Shane said, seating himself on an old sofa near the chair. The television blatted away over his head. "No, I just met Brian this morning. He told me about you. Said you might be an interesting person to talk to."

"That Brian, now," the man said, pushing his glasses up onto his bald brow with a horny thumb. "He's all right enough. How long did you say you known him? It don't matter anyway. Any friend of his is a friend of mine, long as they don't interrupt my Royals games. You follow the Royals, er, what'd you say your name was?"

"My name's Shane, Mr. Kirchenbauer. Shane Bellamy."

"Bellamy, huh?" the man said, his eyes bright. "Sounds familiar. You from around here?"

"No, sir. I grew up in New Jersey. I spent the last ten years or so living in New York City."

"Is that so!" the old man replied, impressed. "Well doesn't that beat all! New York City. Had you a couple of decent ball teams, then, didn't you? I went to a ball game there once, had to be sixty-four or five. I was there with my wife, but she didn't come to the game. She never was one to go to ball games. She didn't like the drinkin' and the yellin', always told me I should've gone in for a gentleman's game, like golf. Golf! Can you believe that? I told her the day I start chasing a little white ball all over God's earth is the day they may as well put me in a box. You golf, er…"

"Shane. No, sir. I used to, when I was a kid, but I never really got a taste for it."

"Better off," the old man said, waving a hand as if to disperse a nasty smell. "Buncha uppity son's o' bitches waltzin' around like lords of the earth, chasin' a white ball like it was the most important thing they ever saw. My Shaun goes out golfin' with all his Chicago politico buddies. I always told him there was nothing for it once you started buying into that west county bull. Give me a ballgame, a beer and a frankfurter any day of the week. Brian took me down to see the Royals last year. He tell you that? They lost, but I got down close enough to the field to smell the grass and hear the chatter in the bullpen, just like when I was a kid. Some things never change and that's the truth." He finished and drew a huge sigh.

"Mr. Kirchenbauer," Shane began, but the old man interrupted him.

"Name's Earl. I never stood on formality. Only person that ever called me Mr. Kirchenbauer was my banker down at First Federal, and he's been dead for twenty years now. You hungry? It's almost lunch time."

Shane stood as the small man gripped a cane and hoisted himself to his feet. As he followed the old man toward the door, he shook his head, amused. "Earl, then. Are you at all wondering why I came to see you?"

The man stopped in the middle of the doorway. He turned back and looked up at Shane, frowning slightly. "I only just now remembered you didn't come to clean up the stain on my carpet. What do you expect from me? I'll be ninety-five this winter. Be glad I remembered to put on my trousers this morning. You got some pressing matter for me to attend to, then you best make it quick, in case I keel over on the way to the cafeteria. Even if I live that long, the food there'll probably finish me off. You got the floor, Mr. Shane from New York City."

Shane followed the tiny man as he limped down the corridor, leaning heavily on his cane. In spite of his dire predictions, however, he moved down the hall quickly, almost as if he thought he was being chased.

"The truth is, Earl," Shane said, walking alongside the small, wizened man. "Brian mentioned you when I told him where I was living. My wife and I bought the property a few years ago, but I just moved in full time now, since we got divorced. Around here, I guess they call it the river cottage. It used to be part of the Wilhelm estate."

Earl didn't break his limping stride, but he glanced up at Shane for a moment, his eyes sharp. "Is that so, then? *That's* why your name rung a bell."

Shane nodded. "Brian said you used to work out there, way back when it belonged to the Wilhelms. He said you knew Gus Wilhelm himself."

Earl shuffled around the corner, joining a sort of slow throng in the main hallway, heading toward the cafeteria. He didn't respond for a long moment. Finally, he said, "You say you're divorced?"

Shane looked aside at the old man. He nodded. "Yeah. It wasn't my choice."

"Never is, is it?" Earl said, and cackled suddenly, loudly. "Shame about that. It really is. That place needs a woman's touch. You ever think about trying to work things out with the little lady?"

"Frankly," Shane said, frowning a little, "That's pretty much out of my hands. I did everything I could."

"Then what in hell made you want to move into that goddam cottage full time?" Earl said, finally glancing aside at Shane, almost furtively. "Does that really seem like such a good idea?"

Shane stopped walking. "I don't know what you mean, Mr. Kirchenbauer."

"Again with the 'Mister'," the old man said, turning aside and gripping Shane's elbow, as if for support. His grip, like the old woman's out front, was surprisingly strong. "I told you to call me Earl. Don't be getting all uppity on me now. I'm just asking a simple question, that's all, same as you."

"I don't think I've asked any questions at all, yet," Shane replied.

"Yeah, but you were planning to, and I know just what kinds of questions you want to ask. I'll save you the bother. You don't really want to know any of the answers, Mr. Shane Bellamy. That house went and got torn down, and that's that. Your cottage is all that's left. Why you'd want to go living there, especially all by yourself, I can't imagine, but you can suit yourself, just like the rest of the world."

Shane looked down at the old man, suddenly feeling as if he'd wasted his time. Earl was obviously a few exits past rational, even if he did wash his own car once a month, like Brian had said. He nodded his head. "Sorry to bother you, Earl. Thanks for your time, anyway."

But the man didn't let go of Shane's elbow. He stared up at Shane piercingly. "Just out of curiosity, Mr. Bellamy," he said, his voice low now, without a trace of the previous cackle. "What do you do for a living?"

Shane considered asking Earl why in hell it should matter, but knew that would just be petulance. Earl had piqued him about being divorced, and he was still smarting from it. Instead, he answered truthfully. "I'm a commercial artist. I work at home."

"Is that so, then," Earl replied, nodding, not seeming particularly surprised. "Imagine that. You're a painter. Quite the coincidence, wouldn't you say?"

"That had occurred to me, yes."

"Brian's right, dull as he is," Earl said, his face sagging a little, resigned. "I used to work out there. Knew the Wilhelms both, s'far as anyone from around here could. They kept their distance. All I can say to you is good luck with the place. It's better for you the main house was torn down. You'll be fine out there. Or, at least, that's the hope."

Shane shook his head in consternation. "Look, all I was planning to do was ask what the place had been like back when it was first built, but I'm getting the feeling that that's no small answer. Is there something I should know about the property? What can you tell me?"

"Not much, not much," Earl said, looking away, toward the cafeteria. "I stopped working for the Wilhelms in forty-seven, a year after Gus Wilhelm took off and left the place to the Missus."

Shane blinked. "Brian said you were the caretaker when he was a little kid. He said you took him out there sometimes."

"True enough," Earl nodded, still not meeting Shane's eyes. "But that was later, after the official caretaker gave it up. I was the only one left in town who'd originally worked out at the property. They called me to take up the job. I didn't want to, but it was good money, paid right out of the old Wilhelm estate. Of course, the house was different by then. The Missus was dead, and the place had been converted into a sort of museum, staffed by volunteers. Hardly anyone ever came out to tour the place, though. Too far off the beaten path, for one thing. Not that many people even remember Wilhelm anymore, either. The man was most famous for his portraits, for Chrissake. It isn't like folks today are clamoring to hang up prints of some old archduke or goddam secretary of state. They closed the museum down in the late seventies. I stayed on as caretaker until eighty-eight, when they sold off the cottage. The Wilhelm estate finally ran out of money for keeping the old house up, and the bank took it over. It's city property now, since the last owner defaulted on their loan and the bank handed it off for a song. I wasn't there during the time the Missus ran the place, though, if that's what you're curious about. That was Stambaugh's tenure. He'd tell you everything you want to know about that strange time, if he could."

Shane was indeed curious, and even more so for the tiny bits of information he was gleaning from Earl's cryptic statements. "Stambaugh's long dead, I assume?"

Earl nodded slowly, finally glancing up at Shane. "In a manner of speaking, yes. That's close enough for government work, you might say."

"What do you mean?"

Earl smiled a little crookedly and nodded toward the cafeteria doors. With his hand still on Shane's elbow, they moved toward the open doorway.

"See that skinny old cuss over there by the kitchen doors?" Earl said, gesturing. Shane saw him. A very old man was bent almost double in his wheelchair, his hands hanging loosely over the armrests, fingers thin and bony. To Shane, they looked like the legs of giant albino spiders. A male nurse sat next to him, spooning something white and dribbling into his slack mouth, wiping his lips with a napkin after each spoonful. "That there's Stambaugh," Earl went on. "He hasn't said a meaningful word in ten years. Before he floated away, though, we used to talk about the old place. Oh yes. *He* had some stories. He was the last person to know the Missus, of course. He watched what she did to the house during those last years. Hell, he even helped her with some of it, when she asked him to. It was the job, and like I said, it paid well, at least by our standards."

Shane felt uncomfortable watching the old man being fed. It was like catching someone in the middle of some embarrassing but necessary act, something that should be done in private, not in front of a crowded cafeteria. No one else seemed to notice, though. Maybe his presence was even vaguely comforting to the rest of the residents. After all, compared to Stambaugh, Earl himself looked spry enough to break into a jig.

"I'm keeping you from your lunch," Shane said, extracting his elbow from the old man's grip. "Thanks for your time."

"Look," Earl said a little gruffly. "I don't mean to be stand-offish, all right? It's not your fault. There's still a little bad blood between the folks around here and that old property. The less you know about it, the better. Either way, it's in the past now, specially now that the house's been torn down. The cottage is all right, though. It was part of the property back in the day, but hardly anybody even remembers that."

"What *was* the cottage?" Shane asked, hoping to leave with at least one question answered. "Was it a guest house or something?"

Earl blinked at Shane, a little incredulous. "You really don't know?"

"Earl, before a few days ago, that cottage was just the place my wife and I spent a week or two every summer for the last seven years. I didn't even remember the name of the original owners until I looked it up online a few days ago. I came to talk to you just because I was a little curious, that's all. So no, I don't know what the cottage was originally used for. I was just wondering."

Earl grinned, showing a set of big, yellow dentures. "Why, it was Mr. Wilhelm's studio," he said, as if it was the most obvious thing in the world. "That's where he did all his painting, and what you might call his... *entertaining*. He and his models worked right there, in the upstairs, in the space between the windows, where the light was best. Nobody else was allowed in there. Not even Mrs. Wilhelm. That's what I mean about the place needing a woman's touch. Every home needs that, don't you think, Mr. Bellamy? But some need it more than others. Oh *yes*."

Shane stared at Earl, speechless, but Earl just cackled again, a little softer this time, and turned to limp into the cafeteria, dismissing him.

Chapter Five

Greenfeld was driving a slate gray Audi when he arrived, the next day. He steered the car with almost prissy deliberation, babying it along the rutted path and into the gravel turn-off. Shane sat on the porch, watching, a book of Sudoku puzzles on his lap. Greenfeld parked, killed the ignition, and climbed out into the sunlight. He peered over the roof of the car toward the cottage, spied Shane, and called, "You aren't out here seeing how long you can grow your fingernails and collecting jars of your own urine, are you?"

"I can't afford to be that eccentric," Shane called back, smiling. "The best I can hope for is unique. Come on up. It's mostly safe."

"Keep your pants on, I gotta get my shit together," Greenfeld replied, thumbing a button on his key fob. The trunk of the Audi popped open. Shane got up and ambled out to the car, joining Greenfeld as he produced a large manila portfolio from the depths of the trunk. Greenfeld was short, built like a jockey, with a wiry handshake and immaculate style. Today, he wore a white button-down shirt under a navy blazer, tieless. His short black hair was combed forward from his temples, and Shane thought he looked a little like a diminutive modern-day Caesar. Greenfeld pushed the portfolio toward Shane and reached for his attaché. Shane saw his own reflection in the mirrored shades clipped to Greenfeld's glasses.

"Let's get inside and have a look, whaddaya say?" Greenfeld said, grinning. "I've got to say, Shane, your name on my client list has opened up an interesting new branch of work for me. Let's just hope you can keep that savvy New York artist aura going out here in the sticks."

Shane shrugged as they entered the cottage. "I don't think I ever really had that savvy New York artist thing down, even when I *was* one."

"Well, perception counts for a lot," Greenfeld replied, crossing to the sofa. "At least we have that working for us. Here. Just got that portfolio from the agency down in Tampa. I've looked at it already and given them a tentative thumbs-up. Frankly, based on your previous work, I think you can do this in your sleep, but go ahead and take a look."

Shane sat down, opened the flap of the portfolio and pulled out a thick sheaf of paper. Some of the sheets were poster-sized, printed on heavy matte paper, showing enlargements of classic postcard art: grinning, bikini-clad women on the beach, a woody station wagon with a surfboard on top, a giddily colorful Florida sunset over the ocean with waving palm trees in the foreground. The original artwork was grainy, resplendent with day-glo colors, printed with poorly aligned processing so that the red of the woman's lips didn't quite match the black outline of her smile. The rest of the prints, however, showed updated versions of the classic style, created for other state boards of tourism. One version showed a starburst of happy family travelers enjoying the Grand Canyon, complete with an image of a grinning, pipe-smoking dad planning the family's vacation on his laptop. It was fairly typical stuff, kitschy and edgy, marrying the halcyon sense of the classic with modern ideals of convenience and hipness. Shane had, indeed, done stuff like it many times before. He said as much to Greenfeld.

"That's exactly what I thought," Greenfeld nodded. "The question isn't whether you can do it. The question is whether you can do it in *time*. The muckety-mucks at the agency handling this account want to see final shipment by the middle of November. They're planning on rolling out this campaign by late January, in time for the spring vacation push."

Shane put down the last of the posters and leaned back on the couch. "How many do they want?"

"Six versions, one for each market. Keys, coast, family, diving, historic and water sports. Each one will include five to seven scenes and the word 'Florida' in those big, three-dimensional block letters. You don't do any computer generated stuff, do you? Photoshop, that kind of thing?"

Shane shook his head. "Sorry, I'm pretty old school. We had a whole department for that kind of thing at T and C. None of those guys could paint, and I couldn't draw with a mouse. Call it job security. Why?"

"No point in painting the Florida hero word six times, that's all," Greenfeld replied, taking off his glasses and sticking them in the inner pocket of his blazer. "Paint it once, we can get a scan of it and place it in the other scenes, maybe alter the color digitally to keep them all distinct. Don't worry about it. I have a guy that can manage that angle on the cheap. It'll save you some monkey work, painting the same thing over and over. You can just leave a space in the middle. Make sense?"

Shane nodded. It would indeed save him a lot of time. "What about reference material for the scenes? Do they know what they want to show? Or is that up to me?"

Greenfeld swept an arm over the scattered images. "Keep it market specific, but other than that, anything you see here you can use in the final. If you get any bright ideas, feel free to block them in. We can start with basic mock-ups, small scale, and get them approved. After that, no client contact until final proof. So what do you say?"

"I can do it," Shane said carefully. "But what's the budget?"

"This is a government contract," Greenfeld replied. "It's coming to us through an agency in Tampa called Bullseye. I've worked with them before, but never on anything like this. They bid the job for fifty thousand. After all the pie gets cut up, that means five thousand a shot for you. I know that's not New York walking around money, but it's a start. You nail this one, there'll be more to come."

Shane was actually very pleased with the amount. His living expenses had dropped to almost nil, now that he'd off-loaded the Saab and moved into the cottage. If he was careful, he could even live off the income from the Florida gig for a couple of months. He'd almost forgotten what it was like in the feast-and-famine world of contract work, but he thought he could pick it up again, if he was disciplined about it. He told Greenfeld he could do it.

"That's what I like to hear," Greenfeld announced. "You know, I wasn't kidding about you being a bit of a curious commodity around here. People are watching to see how this pans out. You'll never get the kind of big-money contracts you used to get at Tristan and Crane, but the economy is different here, as I'm sure you've noticed. If we dance the dance, you can do all right."

"I'll let you dance," Shane said, standing. "I can't even do the funky chicken. Last time I tried, I almost knocked myself out. Come on, you want a beer?"

"Twist my arm, why don't you. Don't forget you were going to show me your studio, too."

Shane produced two bottles of St. Pauli Girl and tossed the caps in the kitchen trash. A minute later, he led Greenfeld up to the studio. The window over the stairs had been pushed open, letting in the cool autumn air, freshening and brightening the small space. Along the canted right wall, Shane's collection of works leaned in the sunlight. Most of his artworks were sold in their original form, usually leaving him with nothing more than printed copies, but he did retain almost all of his mockups, sketches and several final works that had been done on spec. One of them, the first one in the line, was a large painting of a girl running through a golden wheat field, her blonde hair streaming, one hand flung out behind her in the rapture of the moment, white in the sunlight. It had been painted for a book cover, but the publisher had eventually gone with something edgier, with a slightly older, sexier woman in a white dress. Greenfeld hunkered in front of it, nodding.

"Nice," he said. "It's a different thing to see the original, that's for sure. Still, even up close, I can barely see the brush strokes. Good, tight work here."

"Thanks, sensei," Shane said, looking around the room. He was somewhat anxious to get back to work. Not on the Florida mockups, though. That could wait a day or two. He had another idea in mind. It had occurred to him the night before, when he'd gotten back from his bike ride. He glanced aside, to the blank canvas on the big easel.

"This the original sketch for the matte painting?" Greenfeld asked, gesturing at a large drawing taped to a piece of white cardboard.

"Yeah. You want it?"

"You bet," Greenfeld nodded. "This kind of stuff is great for hanging in the office. I've got too many calligraphy verses and greeting card scenes as it is. You don't mind?"

"Not in the least. Take it."

Shane wandered over to the stool in front of the easel and sat down, suddenly feeling impatient. He wanted to paint. Coming up to the studio had apparently awakened the muse, and she didn't care that Greenfeld was there. She just wanted to create.

"Good stuff," Greenfeld said, straightening up. "But where's *your* work?"

Shane furrowed his brow. "What do you mean? This is all my work."

"No, no, I mean *your* work. Chris told me that you do your own painting, too; said you showed it to her when she came to pick up the matte painting. Real artsy stuff. She said I should be sure to get a look at it."

"Oh," Shane said, frowning. "That. Yeah."

"What? Don't tell me you're suddenly all secretive and shy about your own work. I mean, I understand completely if it's the kind of thing you pull out to impress the pretty girls, but come on. It's me."

Shane smiled at Greenfeld's wounded expression. He shook his head and stood up. "It's no problem. I just wasn't finished with it, then. I wasn't *showing* it to her, exactly. It just happened to be out. It's right over here now."

The house portrait was sitting on the smaller easel, where Shane had initially begun to paint it. Now that it was completely dry, he had covered it with a piece of muslin. He carefully lifted the fabric away and tossed it onto the nearby stool. Greenfeld joined him in front of the painting, and then leaned in, squinting a little, his hands on his knees. There was a very long moment of pregnant silence, and Shane felt himself growing uncomfortable. Finally, Greenfeld straightened again. He backed up, not taking his eyes from the painting. Shane backed away as well, moving toward the stairs. When he got there, he turned back, and saw Greenfeld looking at him over his shoulder. He gestured at the painting with one manicured hand.

"The hell is this?" he said, almost as if he was offended.

"What do you mean?"

Greenfeld dropped his hand and looked back at the painting, shaking his head. "You have any more paintings like this?"

"No. Frankly, I've never painted anything like it before."

"You're serious." It wasn't a question, so Shane didn't respond. Greenfeld went on, "I know this is the sort of thing you creative types really hate, but I have to ask, Shane: where'd this come from?"

Shane didn't really hate the question. He'd heard variations of it before, and it had usually been pretty easy to answer. Then again, his artworks were usually inspired by nothing more than a creative director's sketch, or a block from a storyboard, or a collage of images printed from the Internet. He realized it was a harder question to answer when the picture had been dictated by the muse. He shrugged and frowned. "It just came into my head. I was on a bike ride."

Greenfeld glanced aside at Shane again, one eyebrow cocked. "You know what this is?"

Shane half nodded, half shrugged again. Greenfeld answered for him, returning his gaze to the painting once more. "This is art, Shane. The real deal. I'm not prepared to call it *great* art, you understand. True art isn't really my bread and butter. I'm just a working stiff, helping push the product out the door. That's one of the things I like about you. You understand that philosophy. But this is different... this is the real thing. I may not deal in it, but I know it when I see it."

"Don't tell me you want to hang *that* in your office," Shane said, smiling as if it were a joke. To his surprise, Greenfeld looked up at him again, his face serious.

"Would you let me?" He stopped himself and shook his head. "No, no. Never mind. That's not the venue for it. You're right. It'd scare the shawls off the ladies from Homespun Greetings. Hell, it'd probably put a shiver down the spine of the guy from Swank Pictures. Not the biggest clients, but long term folks, from back when I was getting started. No, no, not the office..." Greenfeld covered his mouth with his hand, thinking hard. He shifted his eyes to Shane again and spoke through his fingers. "Did you know Chris and I are putting on a gallery show at the art museum downtown?"

Shane shook his head, not liking where Greenfeld was going. Greenfeld didn't notice. "It's really Chris' show. She's trying to break into the world of art herself. She wants to run a gallery, help undiscovered talent get their big break, that kind of thing. *Real* art. Problem is, she doesn't have the capital or the reputation to get started yet. I'm helping her get the second half of that equation. I pulled some strings to help get her into the main floor of the art museum. Even called in a favor with some people from the *Post Dispatch*. They're sending over one of their Lifestyle writers to review the show. Even if it sucks, it's good press. Whaddaya say?"

"What do I say about what?"

"Whaddaya say about displaying this piece of yours in the show?"

Shane furrowed his brow. "Seriously? I mean, I've never had anything shown in a gallery before. I'm just... you know, not *that* kind of artist."

"And that's supposed to be a deterrent?" Greenfeld asked, finally abandoning the painting and joining Shane at the stairs. "Who wants to look at any more self-righteous emo crap produced by all those guys convinced that they're the next Jackson Pollack? Guys who paint with pigeon guano and rivet doorknobs to overcoats and hang them from actual human skeletons and give their works names like 'Pathos Princess Number Sixteen'? Believe it or not, the art world is getting a little sick of those guys. At least the art world around St. Louis. I can't speak for New York. The fact that you don't think your crazy haunted house picture belongs in a gallery showing is exactly why people will be curious about it. It's not intentional. It isn't so deliberate that it's a caricature of itself. Like I said, Shane, it's the real deal."

Shane blinked as he led Greenfeld down the stairs. It was the term "haunted house" that had struck him. He'd never thought of it that way. Was that how it looked to others? He decided not to press Greenfeld about it. Instead, he shook his head and said, "'Pathos Princess Number Sixteen'? How long did it take you to come up with that one?"

"I only wish I had. I didn't make any of that up. The doorknob overcoat on the skeleton was in Chris' first gallery show, late last year, before she knew how to separate avant-garde from basic silliness. She's learned a lot since then, but she'll probably never live that one down."

"You think she'd want my painting in her show?" Shane asked, taking Greenfeld's empty beer bottle and following him to the door.

"Sure. She'd probably have asked you herself if she'd known you'd be done with it by now. She needs something a little crooked and dark like that. She's being a little too careful this time, afraid of producing another freak show. Still, nobody will take her seriously if there isn't something a little bit... I don't know. Unsettling? No offense."

"None taken, I guess," Shane said, shaking his head, bemused. "You really are serious about this, aren't you?"

Greenfeld nodded. "Nobody is going to be turning that little number of yours into a Thank You card, but that doesn't mean it doesn't have its own odd attraction. My first thought, looking at it, was that I wanted to burn it. That's how strong it was, I'm dead serious. Art that strikes someone like that, though, that's nothing to sneeze at. Loads of artists aim for that sort of visceral reaction, and all they achieve is a sort of bland offensiveness. That's easy. Anyone can be offensive. Hell, give *me* a paint set and a canvas and *I* can offend someone. That piece upstairs, though… it's a little like a Salvador Dali painting mixed with a Pablo Neruda book. That probably doesn't make any sense, but that's what I think." Greenfeld stood in the light of the front screen door and shook his head wonderingly, meeting Shane's eyes, and Shane realized something that shocked him: Greenfeld was truly excited. He was nearly panting, as if he'd just discovered a Rembrandt at a garage sale. Shane felt increasingly worried by Greenfeld's response.

"All right," he said slowly, "if it's OK with Christiana, I'll agree to show the painting. On one condition."

Greenfeld narrowed his eyes a little. "Name it."

"It's not for sale," Shane said flatly. "Not as an original, at least. The original is mine."

"That kind of defeats the purpose, Shane," Greenfeld said pedantically. "Seriously?"

Shane nodded. "Yeah, sorry. I'm… not done with it yet."

"I thought you said you finished it?"

Shane shrugged and didn't say anymore. Greenfeld sighed and spread his hands. "I'd never have expected it from you, Shane Bellamy, but you get artsier every time I talk to you. That's not a bad thing, as long as you don't go all native on me. I'm not done squeezing you dry yet."

"I'll call your office if I decide to go crazy and cut off my own ear."

"I appreciate it," Greenfeld said, nodding gravely. He opened the screen door and stepped out into the sunny afternoon. "The showing is this Saturday. It's late notice, I know, but I suspect you can squeeze it into your busy schedule if you really try. You know where the museum is? Downtown, Forest Park?"

"Er, yeah," Shane blinked. "Why?"

Greenfeld turned back to Shane as he reached his car. "So you can bring the piece. You do know you'll need to be there yourself, don't you?" He grinned and shook his head. "You really are a newbie at this. That's excellent. The *Post Dispatch* people are going to love you. You're the *artist,* Shane. People will want to talk to you about that wacky painting of yours, *especially* if you aren't selling it. The show starts at six, but if you can get there by five, latest, that will give us time to get set up. Can you make it?"

Shane nodded slowly. "Sure. I guess. I just didn't realize. Yeah, that's fine."

Greenfeld clapped Shane briskly on the shoulder and turned to get in his car. "I wouldn't have guessed it," he said, dropping into the low seat and draping his hand over the steering wheel. "You've really never painted anything like that before?"

Shane stepped back from the car as Greenfeld started the engine. "Not even close. It surprised me as much as anyone."

"It was the woman on the front step that did it," Greenfeld said, peering up at Shane, his smile gone. "My first thought was that I wanted to burn it, like I said, but then I saw her."

"Yeah?" Shane said. "And then what did you think?"

Greenfeld's eyes grew unfocussed and he squinted. "I thought: 'It's all just a stage. The first act is about to begin, and she's going to be the main character. I wonder what happens next.'" His eyes sharpened again and he studied Shane's face. "That's the point, right? Why's she sitting there, watching, waiting? Who's coming up the path, and what happens when they get there? That's what I was thinking, at least. At first, I hated it. Then I saw her, and I still hated it, but I was too curious to look away." He shook his head again, quickly. "I don't know how you did it, Shane, but it's quite a trick. Keeping that balance must be like walking a tightrope." He smiled crookedly at Shane and tapped his temple twice with his left index finger.

Shane smiled and nodded, not quite knowing what the gesture meant. Greenfeld shifted into reverse and backed gingerly out of the turn-off. A minute later, Shane was alone again. He walked back to the cottage a little dazedly. For some reason, he didn't really want to put his new painting into the gallery showing, and yet he hadn't been able to say no to Greenfeld. Probably because he had no good reason to refuse. It was just a strange, gut feeling. Somehow, the painting wasn't meant for the rest of the world. It was for him, alone. But that wasn't entirely accurate, either, and he had to be honest with himself about it. The painting was for him, and it was for the ghost.

And suddenly Shane thought he understood what Greenfeld's head-tapping gesture had meant. He'd said that painting something like the house portrait—the "haunted house", he had called it—was like a balance, like walking a tightrope. The head tap showed that Greenfeld understood where that tightrope existed. It was a tightrope of the mind. The balance was between realism and abstraction, between ugliness and beauty. Shane had felt that balance, that strange tension, from the very beginning, from the first night he had begun to paint the house, responding to the insistent prodding of the muse. But now another question occurred to him: what happened if he fell off the tightrope?

In the warm afternoon sunlight, Shane shivered.

The second painting started differently than the one of the main house. With that one, Shane had known what it was going to be from the start, and had begun with the basic shape. He'd blocked in the house in one quick sitting, and then spent the following days filling in the details. Now, with the second painting, it seemed to be happening in reverse.

Shane had sat in the mid-afternoon light of the studio for half an hour, merely staring at the blank canvas, trying to see where the first brush strokes were supposed to go, but nothing had come. The muse still had her fingernails dug into him, but she wasn't offering any specific help for the moment. Now, she merely provided the hunger to make, but not the details. Shane had stared at the canvas, his brow furrowed, his lips pressed together, until he'd gotten frustrated. In a gesture of annoyance, he'd reached forward with his brush and slashed at the canvas, making a quick, tapered black stroke. And then he'd stared at it. Maybe it had just been the cathartic gesture he'd needed to break free from some unexpected artist's block, but the stroke seemed like more than a random slash of paint. It looked like a shape, like the suggestion of something much more complex, buried in the white. Shane had studied it, trying to divine its meaning. Then he abandoned that logic; that was the sort of thinking that had left him stymied for the past half an hour. Instead, he leaned forward once again, raised his right arm, and added a second line, an arcing sweep that curved under the first line. Suddenly it wasn't just two lines. It was the beginning of a face. Realizing that, the picture suddenly clicked into place. The next half a dozen strokes had come a little more easily, with less thought. After that, he was hardly even aware of the brush in his hand. After that, he fell into the canvas.

This painting was like a puzzle, or piece of complicated origami, unfolding as it went. It had begun with a face, and Shane had been dimly aware of whose it was, even as he'd drifted deep into the canvas, sinking fathom after fathom into the story. It was neither of the Wilhelms; he knew that immediately. There was no life in the face, no vibrance or story. And then he realized why this should be so. He was not painting a face, technically; he was painting a *painting* of a face, duplicating one of Wilhelm's portraits. It expanded out of those initial brush strokes, filling the middle quarter of the new canvas, quite small, but rich with color and detail. It was the portrait of Woodrow Wilson, the one Gus Wilhelm had painted in an effort to win the post of official White House portrait artist. As Shane painted it, he turned it over and over in his mind, wondering, inventing. Gus Wilhelm had not received the post he had painted the portrait for. Shane knew that much from the article he'd read on the Internet. The post had instead been awarded to another artist, a veteran portrait painter named Hallsley. Wilhelm's portrait of Wilson had been returned to him with a note pinned to it: "This work is more suited to the bathhouse than the white house." Wilhelm surely would have kept that portrait, and the note as well, perhaps even leaving it pinned to the work, a constant reminder of his first major setback. Based on what he knew of Wilhelm, Shane imagined he'd looked at the portrait as a motivational tool. *I'll show them,* he'd have thought to himself, firming his jaw, balling his hands into big fists. *Reject me, will they? I'll see them seeking* me *out someday, pleading with me to return and paint their damned portraits. And will I do it? Yes, I will, and I won't even tell them how they once rejected me. That will be my little secret. That will be the jaunty feather in my cap, the one that only has special meaning to me, and me alone.*

Shane imagined Wilhelm hanging the portrait in the Riverhouse, years after he had achieved fame and wealth, long after he'd met the challenge of that snide little note. And yet the painting remained, and always enjoyed a place of high honor. Why? Because despite his braggadocio, that note had wounded him. He'd remembered it with great, vivid clarity, remembered the shocked numbness of that rejection. It lived in his mind, even after the writer of the note had been replaced, even after Wilhelm had indeed gone back and painted succeeding presidents. Because none of those latter portraits had bested that first one, the one that had begun in the hot confines of the Oval Office, surrounded by other artists while the sun dazzled just over the President's right shoulder. Secretly, Wilhelm had believed it was among his best works, and he'd hated the fact that it had failed. He often recalled the day of that rejection, remembered examining the returned portrait, confused and crushed. He had painted the president exactly as he had witnessed him; his glasses pushed up on his forehead, leaning over his desk with his chin resting on his cupped right hand. Wilson's face was shaded, but a line of brilliant orange sunlight followed the angle of his cheek, his left ear, and his severely combed hair, glowing in the drab office like a halo. Wilhelm had been confused because he'd felt that the portrait had perfectly captured the intensity of the man in his work. The line of backlit sunlight was like a streak of molten gold, starkly accenting the president's features, implying the Olympus-like grandeur of the highest office in the land. Later, however, Wilhelm had seen the winning entry, and had understood. The winner of the post had painted Wilson in a completely invented pose; standing, fully lit, chin raised and hand on hip. Behind him the artist had even injected a pastoral scene of rolling fields and idyllic forest. Wilhelm had then realized that the winning painting, with its invented nobility and stiff formality, was the very antonym of his own portrait, which delved into the ethos of the man himself. Apparently, presidential portraits were not meant to be portraits at all; they were only architectural renderings, displaying the mere meat of the man's body and some contrived sense of what people expected of their leaders. Wilhelm told himself that, if such was the case, he had been granted a divine blessing in being passed over for the post. Perhaps he could even find it in his heart to pity the man who had bested him, George Hallsley. Then again, perhaps not. Hallsley was perfectly content with creating mere painted waxworks. And he had been condescending to Wilhelm, looking down his long, skinny nose and peering through a fussy little pair of Pince Nez glasses, as if Wilhelm had been someone's dirty-faced child with a slate and a chunk of colored chalk. Deep down, Wilhelm had hated Hallsley, and hated the rejection he represented. Gustav Wilhelm had spent the next decade furiously working to live down that failure. He'd succeeded everywhere except in his own mind.

Hardly aware of what he was doing, lost in the fathoms of the story, Shane painted. The portrait of Wilson hung in the middle of the canvas, complete right down to the old, yellowed note pinned to the top right corner and the ornate gilt frame that surrounded it. And then, slowly, more shapes began to evolve around it, sketched in with quick strokes, expanding outward; a room. As the picture took shape, the story in Shane's head changed. It stopped being about Gustav Wilhelm. After all, while this was still a painting of the Riverhouse, the perspective had switched; it had moved inside. The exterior of the house was Gustav Wilhelm's domain, but the interior belonged to his wife, the woman that Earl Kirchenbauer had referred to simply as "the Missus". For the moment, the room in the painting was empty, but Shane instinctively knew that that would not continue to be the case. Everything thus far was merely background. This was going to be a portrait, a portrait of the woman of the house. He didn't know what she'd looked like, and yet he had seen her, in a manner of speaking. Her ghost now haunted his cottage, at least occasionally, when the sun went down. Besides, Shane hadn't known what the Riverhouse had originally looked like, either, and he had painted that accurately enough, right down to the mysterious footpath entrance. He didn't know how he'd gotten it right, but he didn't doubt that he had.

When it came time to paint the woman of the house, he knew that he'd get that right, too. He didn't know how, but for the moment, he decided that the less he thought about that, the better.

Shane didn't paint on Friday morning, however. Instead, he put on his garden gloves and cargo shorts and worked on clearing more of the footpath. He made it to the top of the granite stairs, sweating and smarting from nettle stings on his legs, but happy with his progress. It really was going to be a very nice walk; not a long one, exactly, but pleasant and thoughtful, winding and humping over the bluff, dipping toward the site of the old house. The granite stairs were fairly solid, carpeted with grass and moss, and Shane decided to leave them as they were, almost hidden, embraced here and there by old tree roots. He liked the mysterious secrecy of the stairway, liked how it curved around the bowl of a steep hollow, descending into the shadows of the wood. He followed them carefully, enjoying the cool of the shade and the still air. The angel statue stood at the bottom, waiting, buried in flowering vines. As he neared it, he wondered if he should simply leave the rest of the path wild, mostly concealed in the tall grass beyond the angel statue. After all, if anyone discovered this end of the path, it would lead them to his cottage. Shane wasn't a hermit, but he did value his privacy. The last thing he wanted was to encounter a bunch of granola types hiking curiously across his front yard. He glanced up at the vine-encrusted statue as he moved under its shadow. The upraised arm looked like a benediction. The face peered out of the vines, its blank gray eyes looking vaguely out over Shane's head, seeking the horizon beyond the trees.

"What do you say?" Shane asked the statue, pausing and putting his hands on his hips. "Should we leave you covered as well? We wouldn't want anyone ripping you up and carting you off in the back of a pickup, would we? All in favor, raise your right hands."

A puff of breeze moved through the valley and whispered the vines of the statue. Shane nodded.

"Motion passed," he said, and walked on.

The grassy plain beyond the statue was turning pale yellow as autumn fell. Shane walked briskly, listening to the pleasant sound of the grass as his feet combed through it, flattening his hands to let the tips of the stalks tickle his palms. He could see the stream that cut across the valley, and as he approached, he could hear the happy trickle of the water. He stopped at its edge and looked for the stepping stones. He couldn't see them, even though the water was crystal clear, revealing the pebbly bed under its cold surface. He walked along the edge of the stream, heading away from the river, looking for the large, carefully placed stepping stones. After a minute, he stopped and squinted in the hazy sunlight, putting his hands on his hips again. The rocks were nowhere in sight. He turned around, looking along the length of the creek in the opposite direction. Obviously the stepping stones were closer to the river than he'd thought. He squinted into the distance, looking. A set of old dock pilings poked out of the river near the mouth of the stream, rotted and warped, but the stepping stones were nowhere in sight. He considered walking back in that direction, maybe examining the ancient dock, and then decided against it. Even if he did find the stepping stones, there was no real reason to continue on to the site of the manor house. In truth, the big empty lot was a little depressing, with its vestigial driveway and cellar packed with dirt. It was probably almost two o'clock, anyway. His shift was over. He turned and began to head back.

With some amusement, he realized that he had, in fact, put in the same hours working on the path as he normally did on his art. A shift was a shift, apparently, regardless of how he spent it. Besides, clearing the footpath wasn't that much different than his normal shift work, was it? Whether he was working on a blank canvas or carefully grooming the path, his task was essentially the same. Either way, it was a matter of revealing that which was buried. By Monday morning, he'd be back to his normal shift work, pushing out the product, as Greenfeld called it, but for now it was nice to mix it up a little. He was proud of the path, almost as if he had designed and created it himself. As he walked back, he took his time. For some reason, he found himself whistling something from an old movie, something he had seen a snippet of on Turner Classics while channel surfing the previous night. By the time he got back to the cottage, he realized what song it was, and sang part of it out loud.

"See the sugar bowl do the Tootsie Roll," he called cheerfully, wondering how in the world he'd remembered such inane lyrics. "With the big bad devil's food cake. If you eat too much, oh-oh, you'll awake with a tummy ache."

He was still humming the old song even after he finished his lunch and prepared for a short bike ride.

Chapter Six

She is holding a piece of paper, staring down at it in her hands, and the expression on her face is pale and dead, as if all the life has drained out of it. Shane watches her, still and breathless, ghostlike. She cannot see him. For all intents and purposes, he isn't really there. *After all,* he tells himself, *this is just a dream.* Still, it is an amazingly, painstakingly detailed dream. He can smell the varnish of the hardwood floor mingled with the musty scent of an old tapestry on the wall to his right. He knows that the tapestry is one of the house's most recent additions, and that it came by ship from Scotland, rolled between two huge sheets of muslin and wrapped in brown paper, tied with twine. He even knows that the twine from that shipment is still in the house, carefully balled up and stored in a bottom drawer in the kitchen. The woman that the workers like to call "the Missus" tends to save things like that, just in case they might prove useful at some later date. Living out here, it is a good idea to save things. One never knows when the river, their nearest neighbor, will rear up and hem them in, blocking the roads, turning the house into an island. It's a good idea to have things on hand, just in case. It's a good idea to be prepared.

Sounds come from the kitchen, along with the smells of cooking dinner, and Shane knows that the woman and her husband are planning on eating fish stew for dinner, prepared by the young black cook. Her first name is Clara. Shane could probably produce her last name if he really tried, but he is too distracted. All of his attention is focused on the woman in front of him. She stands there holding the piece of paper, staring at it silently, frozen in shock and disbelief. Shane tries to read the paper, but it is turned away from him, with only the top third folded down on itself, showing the first line, the heading: *Dear M,* It is a letter, and yet Shane is certain that it does not contain good news. The contents of the letter have changed this woman's life forever, knocked it neatly aside like a child kicking over a house of blocks. There will be no fish stew tonight, despite the smells wafting from the kitchen and the amiable clank of pot lids. Not now. Those days are over. Slowly, almost imperceptibly, the woman's eyes grow thick with tears. Shane watches as one of the tears trembles on her black lashes and spills over, tracing down her cheek. In her shock, pale and vulnerable, she is beautiful. She has forgotten to breath. Suddenly, she inhales, almost gasps, and raises her eyes. She is looking right at him, seeing him, and Shane is afraid. He is afraid because *she* is afraid— terrified, in fact. She backs up a step, retreating from him, her eyes wide, magnified with tears, and yet she doesn't lower the letter. It rattles in her hands as she shivers. Shane looks down at it and sees that her hands, like those of Steph in his previous dream, are covered in blood. The letter is stained with wet, red fingerprints.

And then the dream changes. The room vanishes into mist, leaving Shane cold and shuddering, looking around. He is in the woods, on the path, and something is in the woods with him. It is not following him on the path. It is in the wood all around, watching and waiting, like the woman on the front steps in his painting. The thing is not human. It is not even truly alive, and yet it is hungry. It breathes in the whisper of the leaves, moves in the massive creak of the ancient trees, sighs in the gurgle of the brown river, unseen beyond the mist. All of these sounds together seem to say a word, over and over, repeating on itself like an echo, sometimes forwards, sometimes backwards, like waves lapping at a rocky shore. Shane can almost hear the word. It is the same word the ghost said to him, on the single occasion that she has spoken. *Riverhouse... Riverhouse... Riverhouse...*

And then, rising over the treetops, much larger than it could possibly be, Shane sees it, and it sees him. For the first time since childhood, Shane feels his bladder loosen of its own accord. He wants to run, but there is no point. His knees unhinge and he falls down, tumbling backwards onto the hard stones of the path, his eyes still nailed to that horrible, massive shape as it looms over him, pushing the trees aside like grass, groaning and creaking a deafening chorus.

And Shane takes the only escape he knows of.

He awoke.

He was sitting up in bed, panting, his forehead beaded with sweat. His lungs physically hurt, as if he had just run a marathon. But it had just been a dream—a nightmare, really. Even now, it was breaking apart around him, tattering like a vampire in the sunlight. He looked down at his hands and saw that they were covered in blood. A strangled bark of horror erupted from his throat and he scrambled backwards, pushing up against the headboard of the bed, as if to escape the sight of his own red-stained fingers. *Caught red-handed,* a voice in his head sang gleefully. Was it Stevie Burkett, the kid who'd lived down the street from his parents' apartment in New Jersey, the kid he'd shot hoops with on lazy summer afternoons? Stevie always did have a very strange, mean sense of humor. *Caught red-handed, Shane-brain! What'd you do now? Boy, are* you *gonna get it!*

Shane squeezed his eyes shut, still panting from the nightmare, his heart pounding in his chest. A moment later, he reopened his eyes and focused on the bedroom window. Dim, pink light lay beyond; a cloudy pre-dawn, cool and pearly. Shane raised his hands again and looked at them. They were still stained with red, but it wasn't blood. Blood turned brown as it dried, but this was still bright and vivid, like clown make-up. He pressed the fingers of both hands together and pulled them apart again, feeling the tacky stickiness. It wasn't blood, it was paint. Somehow, that realization didn't make him feel much better.

He got out of bed and went out to the hall without turning on the light. The dawn glow permeated the cottage, making everything strangely flat and shadowless. He turned and climbed the stairs to the studio. On the left of the stairway, just above the banister, three streaks of drying paint were smeared, as if left by a careless, dripping hand. They were red. Shane stopped at the top of the stairs. He didn't need to go any further to verify his suspicion. He could see the painting from here, lit in the first rays of the morning light as it angled through the window over the stairs.

It was much further along than he had left it the night before. The woman in the painting was almost entirely finished. She stood exactly as he had seen her in his dream, dominating the foreground, partly obscuring the carefully painted portrait of Woodrow Wilson over the fireplace. Her face was pale and expressionless, staring down at the piece of paper that she held in both of her small hands. The top third of the letter was folded back, revealing the first line, the salutation: *Dear M,*

For a moment, Shane was sure that he had painted her hands splattered with blood, as he had seen her in the dream just before it had evaporated, but that was just a trick of the dawn light. Her hands were white, spotless. The red had come from the fireplace in the background. He had painted it as embers, a pile of glowing coals in the grate, spilling their bloody light across the floor behind the woman. The colors, like that of the portrait of the Riverhouse, were shockingly bright, almost garish, laid on so thick that each stroke created its own miniature topography of dried paint. The red paint tube was still open, sitting on the side table, nearly empty.

The strength drained out of Shane's body and he leaned back against the wall next to the window. He remembered riding home on his bike the previous evening, just as dusk was setting, remembered walking the bike around to the shed on the east side of the cottage and then looking up, looking for the round window hidden in the branches of the magnolia tree. That glimmer of light had been there again, reflecting sunlight from the dying day. But that hadn't made sense, because it was cloudy. The sky was a huge blot of gray from horizon to horizon, masking the sun. The glimmer of light in the window was a candle, lit just inside, sitting on the windowsill. Impossible, of course. Shane had decided to go in and check it out that very evening. He would let himself into the attic via the door in the back of the studio, look for the strange, hidden space, and figure out what was making that weird light.

But he hadn't. Why hadn't he? Once he'd gotten inside, he had just... forgotten. Was that all? Shane leaned against the wall, staring at the painting of the woman with the letter, and knew that wasn't it. He hadn't forgotten. He had been distracted. The muse had landed on him the moment he'd gotten inside. She wanted him to paint, and to paint at that very moment. The canvas was waiting on the easel; the background was finished. Now it was time to put in the main character, the woman. Shane hadn't known what she was going to look like, or what she'd be doing, but the muse would take care of that, if he'd let her.

But he'd resisted. He was stubborn about it. She didn't control him, damn it. He wanted to shower and eat. He was tired. The painting could wait. Maybe he'd paint Saturday morning instead of work on the footpath. All that evening, the painting called to him, but he refused it. He was not the slave of the muse. He controlled the art, not the other way around. As he'd fallen asleep, he'd felt the muse loosen her grip on him, and he'd thought, *I've won. I've shown her. I'm still the boss.* But she *hadn't* been letting him go. She'd just decided to take a different approach. She'd waited until he'd gone to sleep, and then she'd jumped on him all over again, animating him in his sleep, walking him like a zombie. She'd taken him to the well of creativity and used him to draw up bucket after bucket, bringing her vision to life. It was horrible to realize that the muse could be that powerful and persuasive. Is this how it always was for the starving artists? If so, Shane could begin to understand the hollow-eyed pathos that was so often apparent on their faces.

He shivered and looked down at his hands again, at the red paint packed under his fingernails and layered darkly in the folds of his skin. He had painted the fireplace with his fingers. He knew it instinctively, just like he knew that the Wilhelm's cook had been named Clara. He had completely foregone the brush and smeared the paint on with his bare hands. He had done it in his sleep, while he'd dreamed, and then he had stumbled back to his bed, leaving a smear of paint over the banister as he'd gone, and probably staining the sheets with bloody red handprints.

Outside, the wind blew, moaning in the drainpipes and thrashing the trees along the bluff. The sound of it was horrible, almost like a voice, repeating the same word over and over, not quite clear enough to understand, but just clear enough to tease. The sound filled Shane with dread. He turned his back on the painting, tramping back downstairs and heading for the shower.

Late that morning, Shane found the cordless phone on the counter in the kitchen. He used it to call Greenfeld's office. The line rang half a dozen times, and then clicked over to Greenfeld's voice mail. Shane wasn't surprised. The recording offered to let Shane leave a message, and Shane was prepared to do so, but then the voice also offered Greenfeld's cell phone number, "for urgent matters". Shane considered it, and then hooked a pad of paper toward him on the counter. He jotted the number down and broke the connection. Immediately, he dialed Greenfeld's cell number.

Most likely, Greenfeld and Christiana were already at the museum getting things ready for that night's show. He didn't want to risk the message being missed until Monday. By then, it would be too late. Greenfeld answered on the third ring, sounding impatient.

"Yeah?"

"Hey Morrie, Shane Bellamy."

"I had a weird feeling I'd be hearing from you today. Tell me you aren't calling to cancel on me, old buddy."

"Nope. In fact, I think you'll call this good news. I've decided to go ahead and offer the house painting for sale, if anyone wants it."

"Well," Greenfeld said, sounding genuinely surprised. "That *is* good news. He wants to sell his painting after all," this, Shane could tell, was for someone else's benefit. Christiana was probably with him. Shane imagined her looking at Greenfeld, her eyebrows raised. Greenfeld went on, "If you don't mind me asking, what changed your formidable mind?"

"I decided you were right, I guess. I was just being a little too artsy for my own good. There's no real reason for me to hang onto it. I'm already working on another one."

"More good news," Greenfeld replied. "Glad to hear it. Do you have an asking price in mind?"

Shane shook his head in the empty kitchen. "Beats me. Ask Christiana. She'll know better than me. But make it cheap. If I'm going to sell it, I want it *sold*. Understand?"

"Clear as a bell," Greenfeld said quickly. "Oh yeah, and what should we call it? We got title cards printed for all the other works already, but Chris has fabulous handwriting. She's making yours herself. You have a name for that thing?"

Shane thought about it, but only for a second. "Riverhouse," he said. "That's its name."

"Riverhouse. Straightforward and to the point. See you tonight with the work in hand. You sure you don't want me to send Chris over to pick you up?"

"I can handle it. Don't worry. I'm not going to bug out on you. I'll see you at five. Tell Christiana I said good luck."

"Will do, Shane. See you then."

Shane thumbed the red button on the cordless and saw that the battery was getting low. He carried the phone to the library and plugged it into the charger. Being single and having virtually no friends or family, he was not much in the habit of checking his telephone messages. He saw the red number one blinking on the top of the answering machine and was mildly surprised to realize that he had forgotten to play the message from several days earlier. When he had first seen the message light blinking, he had assumed it was Greenfeld calling to tell him he had received the photos of the matte painting. Now, though, he knew it couldn't have been him. Greenfeld had said that he hadn't gotten Shane's email until very late on the night Shane had sent it—so late that he hadn't even tried to call Shane until the next morning. If it wasn't Greenfeld, then who could it be? He reached to press the "play" button, and then stopped. Did he really want to know who it was? After all, who else even knew he was living here? Probably, it was just a wrong number, or a telemarketer. They had a no-call list here in Missouri, but Shane had never taken the time to sign up for it. The cottage's phone number was unlisted, so sales calls were a rarity, but not entirely unheard of. He didn't want to hear it if it was just some annoying monotone voice asking him to call back for information regarding an amazing deal on aluminum siding or special subscription rates for many popular magazines. But there was more to his hesitation than potential annoyance, and he knew it. Shane was actually afraid to push the button. It was probably just some residual nervousness from his unsettling discovery that morning—the discovery of the painting he had worked on entirely in his sleep—but that didn't make it any less worrisome.

He told himself he was just being silly. It was only a phone message, after all, and probably just some annoying telemarketer. Maybe it was Greenfeld after all. Hell, maybe it was the city calling to tell him that his property tax was due, or to remind him that his work-from-home business license had expired. It was better to know for sure than to give in to some nameless, irrational fear. Before he could change his mind, Shane pushed the big gray button marked "play".

An electronic female voice said, "One… unheard message." There was a pause, and then a voice took a breath, loudly. "Hi, Mr. Bellamy, this is Janice Hayes from Price, Hayes and Whitaker. We've taken the liberty of sending all the remaining paperwork regarding your recent case to your current address. I just wanted to ensure that our records are all up to date. Feel free to give us a call if you don't receive the package in the next week or so, or if you have any questions at all. Thanks much."

There was a clatter as the phone hung up and Shane sighed, reaching to push the "erase" button. His finger was almost touching it when the electronic voice came back on. "One... unheard message," it said again, and Shane paused, frowning. There was a moment's silence, a click, and then a thin, whistling sound, as if someone had called from a car with the windows rolled down. The sound wavered and grew louder, and there was something buried under it, a tinkling sound, like music on some distant radio frequency. Suddenly, it rose in volume, growing much louder than the tiny speaker of the answering machine should have allowed, and Shane jumped backwards, his hair standing up.

"On the good ship... Lollipop!" the voice of Shirley Temple trilled giddily, threaded with static. "It's a sweet trip to the candy shop! Where bon-bons play... on the sunny beach of Peppermint Bay!"

Shane lunged forward, stabbing at the "erase" button, but his finger missed and the voice sang on, grinning, crackling through the tiny speaker, "See the sugar bowl do the tootsie roll with the big bad devil's food cake!" Shane finally managed to hit the button, but the voice didn't stop. It sang on, hurting his ears, making his eyes water with shocked dismay. "If you eat too much, oh-oh, you'll awake with a tummy ache!" He stabbed the button again and again, to no avail. Finally, he dropped to his knees and scrabbled at the cords beneath the table, finding the power cord for the answering machine. He followed it to where it was plugged into the wall, next to the bookcase, and yanked it as hard as he could. It popped out of the wall, and for a horrible second, the singing still didn't stop. It blared on, and Shane flailed forward, grabbing the machine with his hands, prepared to smash it on the floor, prepared to do anything to silence that inane, grinning voice. Before he could, however, the voice changed. The singing shut off, suddenly and completely, and then another voice spoke, sounding perfectly natural and normal, like any other voice on any other answering machine. It only said one word, but it was enough to freeze Shane in place, still clutching the answering machine, his eyes wide and wild.

"Shane?" the voice said, and then fell silent. The lights on the machine blinked off. It lay there, dead in his hands, and Shane stared at it, his eyes bulging, his heart trip-hammering. He exhaled shakily, dropped the machine, and fell back into the corner next to the bookcase, shivering, feeling like he was going to be sick.

It wasn't that the voice had said his name.

It was that the voice had been Stephanie's

Part II: Dear M

Chapter Seven

The art museum was a huge stone building perched atop a grand, treeless hill in the middle of Forest Park. Shane remembered reading that St. Louis' Forest Park was second in size only to New York's Central Park. He was very familiar with Central Park, of course, having spent many a summer afternoon there, riding his bike or just walking with Steph, watching the joggers and the beggars and the dog walkers. Even at night, Central Park was usually busy, full of activity. By comparison, Forest Park seemed like acres of rolling farmland, with vast tracts of mostly empty hills and manicured woods. The roads through the park meandered and looped back onto themselves, making navigation difficult. As he drove, glancing down at the map on the empty passenger's seat and occasionally swearing to himself, he recalled that Forest Park had been developed to be the site of the 1904 World's Fair. This was another detail that their real estate agent had impressed upon him and Steph during their swift tour of the St. Louis downtown. Over twenty million people had crowded the park during the international event, eager to view the sites, including a passable representation of Venice Italy, "human zoos", displaying sallow-faced native Americans in their "traditional clothing and habitats", and the world's largest Ferris wheel, with individual cars the size of San Francisco trolleys. Shane had heard a strange legend about the Ferris wheel, related by an old woman at a junk shop in nearby St. Charles. The legend stated that the Ferris wheel, despite its incredible size and notoriety, had virtually disappeared after the World's Fair, never to be seen again. Apparently, no one had claimed the gigantic amusement machine, since it was simply too big for most venues, and too expensive to transport, in any case. Thus, while the rest of the buildings were being disassembled and carted off piece by piece, leaving gaping holes in the landscape of the park, the workers had chosen the most obvious solution. They'd merely dumped the components of the massive Ferris wheel into those holes before they were refilled with earth, burying it anonymously throughout the rolling hills. Perhaps the cars themselves, large as they were, had been auctioned off one by one, converted into diners or storage units. Then again, perhaps they had all been buried in the bed of the ersatz Venice canal, which was now the floor of one of the park's many lakes. According to the old lady in the junk shop, on one hot summer night in 2004, on the one hundred year anniversary of the World's Fair, several dozen people claimed to see the Ferris wheel standing in the middle of one of Forest Park's largest lakes, its lights glowing, reflecting in the water, turning with ghostly silence. It was a nicely creepy story, but one that didn't amuse Shane at all as he finally followed the curving road up to the art museum, realizing he'd been looking at it up on its hill for twenty minutes while he circled, trying to decipher the signage. As he walked up the steps to the front doors, carrying his painting under his arm, he looked back at the monstrous statue of St. Louis that overlooked the park, one of the original remnants from the World's Fair, left exactly where it had stood a century earlier. *If he could talk,* Shane thought sourly, looking up at the huge statue on its stony steed, *he could tell where that Ferris wheel was buried. And if Forest Park is anything like Central Park, he could tell where a few* other *things are buried, too. Things that would be a lot less pleasant to dig up.*

The gallery showing was held in a small hall to the left of the main lobby. The room had high ceilings and marble floors, making Shane's footsteps echo as he entered. The normal displays had been cleared out, and in their place had been hung a wild assortment of photography and paintings, each representing a different style. There was a cluster of people standing around a table in the back right corner of the hall, and Shane immediately recognized them as belonging to the worldwide clan of the starving artist. They dressed a little differently here than they did in New York—here, there was a greater emphasis on beads, beards and colors, implying a stronger hippie influence—but the posture and overall expression was immediately recognizable. The starving artists didn't smile much, and even when they did, it didn't affect their eyes. The eyes almost always looked the same; sad and empty, like burnt-out light bulbs. Several people turned to Shane as he approached, but none of them greeted him or smiled. A few of them were holding tiny white plates or flutes of champagne, but most seemed to have foregone the refreshments. They talked among themselves, quietly and morosely.

"Mr. Bellamy," a woman's voice said from behind him. Shane turned to see Christiana approaching, her high heels clicking on the floor, echoing. She wore a simple black dress that stopped just above her knees. It swished distractingly as she sped toward him, unsmiling, her hands held out. For a moment, Shane thought wildly that she was going to hug him, and then he realized that she was reaching for the painting under his arm. "Yours is the last installment. You're just in time. Have you met everyone?"

Shane allowed her to take the painting from him. "I suppose I have," he said, glancing back at the small group around the white table. "Er, what am I supposed to do?"

"Well, you can follow me to make sure you approve of the display. We'll be putting your work on an easel instead of hanging it on the wall. Right over here, at the entrance to the next hall. It'll function as a barrier as well as a focal point. Sorry, the rest of the wall space was used up by the time your piece became available."

"I suppose I should be the one to apologize," Shane said. "I didn't want to cause any trouble by coming in so late. Morrie was sort of insistent. I never would have even known about the showing if it wasn't for him."

"Yeah, I know how Morrie can be," Christiana said, hefting the painting. The two of them positioned it carefully on the easel. "When he gets an idea in his head, he's a bit like a bulldog. Small but stubborn."

"Well, stubborn is a quality I generally respect," Shane said diplomatically.

"Yeah, me too. But it's like anything else, isn't it? Location, location, location."

"What do you mean?"

Christiana shook her head, as if she'd only been talking to herself. "Never mind. There's your title card. Everything spelled right?"

Shane peered at the small white card attached to one of the legs of the easel. In neat printed letters, it read

"River House"
By Shane Bellamy
Oil on Canvas

"Yeah," Shane said slowly.

"What?" Christiana said, looking down at the card. "I spell your name wrong?"

Shane caught a whiff of perfume and shampoo as she leaned in next to him. "No," he said, a little sheepishly. "It's nothing. Really."

"What, what?" she said, sounding almost frantic.

Shane realized that she was extremely nervous. He laughed. "It really is nothing. It doesn't even matter, really. A quirk. In my mind, the title is all one word. Riverhouse. That's all. I should have been more specific if it really mattered, which it doesn't. I just... didn't recognize it at first."

"You want me to change it? I can make another one. Still have the marker in my purse."

"What I *want*," Shane said, touching her lightly on the elbow, "is for you to try to relax. You're making *me* nervous already."

Christiana looked up at him for a moment, her eyes tense, and then she sighed and slumped. "I can't help it. I am a little nervous. Does it show that much?"

"It shows," Shane said, shrugging. "But only because the show hasn't officially started yet. By the time people start arriving, you'll be fine. That's how it always is, right? You're only nervous until the curtain goes up. After that, instinct just takes over."

"Is that right?" Christiana said, glancing up at Shane again. "I wouldn't know. I've always been the one in the audience, never the one behind the curtain. I'm a pretty tough critic, too."

"I can tell," Shane replied, nodding. "Go grab a champagne. You'll feel a little better."

"I can't drink before the show. My stomach's too rumbly. Afterwards, it'll be a different story. Talk to me then."

Shane nodded. "You'll be fine. If the people around the table are any indication, this is going to be a true art show. Don't worry."

"I hope you're right," Christiana said, laughing a little. "I've juried this thing as well as I know how to. I turned away more people than I wanted to this time, just to make sure. Frankly, I'm still trying to figure out how this whole business works. Morrie's been a little help, but..." She gestured vaguely at the hall, at the crowd of artists gathered around the table, as if to say *how much help could any one person be*?

Greenfeld appeared at the lobby entrance of the hall, carrying a large white sign and an easel awkwardly under his arm. Christiana saw him and hurried over. A moment later, once the sign was erected, Shane drifted over to read it.

Introspection and Abstraction: Microscopic Views of a Telescopic World
Various Artists and Media, presented by Christiana V. Corsica and Greenfeld Media Management, LLC

A woman meandered into the hall, looking from face to face, and then brightened as she saw Greenfeld. She approached, smiling and holding out her hand. Greenfeld took it and bowed theatrically, despite the fact that the woman was already at least two inches taller than him. She looked slightly older than Shane; pretty, but painfully skinny, with dramatic tortoise-shell glasses, short blond hair and a long, narrow nose. Christiana watched Greenfeld's handshake and bow with a strained, plastic smile, and Shane guessed that the newcomer was the arts columnist from the *Post Dispatch*. The blond woman shook Christiana's hand next and then looked around, still smiling a brilliant white smile. Shane couldn't help thinking that that smile looked a little predatory, but decided he was just responding to stereotype. The woman was probably perfectly pleasant, even if her grin did look like something from an old Vincent Price movie. He dismissed the scene by the entrance and wandered over to the table, looking for some champagne, looking to give his hands something to do. After all, he was a little nervous as well.

Eventually, people began to drift into the hall, usually in twos and threes, chatting in low voices. Christiana and Greenfeld met all of them near the sign, smiling, pointing out the refreshments, laughing lightly. To Shane, the whole thing looked a little forced, but that was probably because he knew how nervous Christiana was, knew how important this show apparently was to her. He couldn't guess what Greenfeld's stake in it was. The two of them made a fairly attractive couple, standing there together by the lobby entrance. Most of the people who came in probably thought their hosts were a couple, and yet Shane felt fairly confident that Christiana, at least, didn't see Greenfeld as a romantic possibility. Greenfeld, for his part, seemed to play it up. He curled his arm lightly around her waist, leading her toward the door as another group arrived. What had Christiana said when he'd first met her? That Greenfeld kept her around "mostly for the scenery"? Shane guessed that Greenfeld had made his attraction to Christiana fairly obvious, and that she, in the interest of keeping her position and getting his professional help, had politely pretended not to notice. Or was that just wishful thinking on Shane's part? He turned away again, realizing with some dismay that he was watching the two of them a little too closely, with something akin to jealousy. Feeling a little ridiculous and foolish, he turned his attention to the crowd milling nearby. One of the artists, a gangly man with comically thick glasses and a shock of Andy Warhol-like white hair, was looking openly at Shane, his expression severe. Shane looked back at him, surprised, and then shrugged and waved. The man didn't reciprocate, but he did shift his gaze away, suddenly, as if he'd been caught doing something naughty.

"Is this yours?" a nearby female voice asked. Shane glanced aside and saw an older woman in a black sweater and pearls looking at him out of the corner of her eyes. Her face was turned toward his painting.

"Yes, it is," Shane replied quickly. "I'm Shane Bellamy."

"Apparently," she said, dismissively. "It's hideous."

Shane didn't know how to respond. He looked at the painting, then back at the woman. She took a breath.

"How much?"

"Excuse me?"

"How much? What's the selling price?"

"Oh," Shane said, taken aback. "I'm not entirely sure. Miss Corsica is sort of in charge of—"

"Are you the artist or not?" the older woman snapped. "How much are you asking for it? I'd like to buy it."

Shane smiled, unsure if he should be offended or amused. "I thought you said it was hideous?"

"You heard me correctly. You agreed, or else you'd have argued with me. Therefore, you'll be happy to unload it. How much?"

"I... can we talk afterwards? I really just don't know. This is my first showing."

The woman studied Shane severely, her eyes squinting in nets of fine wrinkles. "Mr. Bellamy, I don't plan to stay for the entire show. I am happy to write you a check right now."

"How much?" another voice asked, startling Shane. He turned. It was the other artist, the one with the white Andy Warhol hair. He peered at the older woman, and then shifted his gaze to Shane, his eyes huge behind his glasses.

"He hasn't yet said," the woman answered.

Shane laughed and shook his head. "Look, I'm not trying to be difficult. I'm a commercial artist in real life. I have agencies that usually price my work for me. I have no idea how to do it myself. After the show—"

"You're a *commercial* artist?" the white-haired man interrupted. "And you painted this? Who'd you paint it for?"

"No one. This one was just for me."

"What was your motivation, if you don't mind my asking?" This came from a third voice. Shane looked and saw the skinny woman with the dramatic tortoiseshell glasses, the newspaper columnist. She looked at him with an expectant smile, even more shark-like than her earlier grin. Shane felt his cheeks redden.

"I... you know. It just..." he stammered, looking back at the painting. The sight of it calmed him a little. He took a breath and ordered his thoughts. "It came to me when I was on a bike ride. That's all. It... sort of followed me home."

"Look Mom," the columnist said, amused, "It followed me home. Can I paint it? Please?"

"Is it a real house?" The white-haired artist asked, his face stony.

The old woman clucked her tongue. "This is an art show. Is *anything* real?"

Shane smiled. "It's based on a house that used to be near my home. It's been torn down now."

The old woman looked at him sharply. "Where do you live?"

"In the river valley, south of the city. Between Bastion Falls and Kirkwood."

The woman nodded to herself. "It's the Wilhelm house. I knew it looked familiar."

"The Gustav Wilhelm residence?" the columnist asked, glancing between Shane and the old woman.

"Not really," Shane said quickly. "It was torn down. This is just… how it might have looked. A long time ago."

"'Might have looked' nothing," the old woman said, raising a pair of glasses on a fine chain around her neck, peering at the painting through them. "It's like a photograph. Granted, a photograph somebody drug through an abattoir. All those awful colors and overlying shapes. I'd never have recognized it under all of that, but now that I know…"

Shane was simultaneously intrigued and hesitant. "You knew the house?"

She glanced up at him. "I was there once or twice, when I was a girl. My mother was an artist, a friend of Mrs. Wilhelm, who painted as well. The house was not a nice place. It was beautiful, of course, but creepy, especially by that time. In a way, it was just the opposite of your painting, here. Your painting is creepy on top, but underneath the hideous part, it's beautiful, too. Like a sunrise reflected in a dead man's eyes. You see that, don't you?"

"I may quote you on that, Mrs. Grand," the columnist said, producing a small pad of paper from her bag. "You must spend all day thinking up things like that."

"It's called inspiration, dear," the old woman said indulgently. "Look it up."

The artist with the Andy Warhol hair drifted away, called back to his own work as a small crowd gathered there. The columnist stepped forward in his place, reaching to shake Shane's hand.

"Penn Oliver, Mr. Bellamy" she announced. "I write for the *Post Dispatch.* You've caught Mrs. Grand's eye, which is no small feat. Frankly, I just follow her around and look at whatever she looks at. Saves me a lot of time and effort."

"You give yourself too little credit," Mrs. Grand said, obviously meaning just the opposite. She turned to Shane again. "Mr. Bellamy, may I assume that Ms. Corsica is your representative?"

"I guess you may," Shane replied, glancing across the hall to where Christiana stood by the entry, nodding, deep in conversation. "After all, this is her show."

The woman nodded curtly and drifted on.

"That's quite an accomplishment," the blond woman, Penn, said, watching the older woman walk away. "Is this really your first showing?"

Shane sighed. "It is. I've been painting for years. Just not quite like this."

"Well, Dolores Grand likes your work, which means something. Congratulations."

"She said it was hideous."

Penn looked at Shane closely. "And that disappoints you?"

"Well, it wasn't what I was intending, exactly."

"What *were* you intending?"

Shane shrugged and shook his head, smiling sheepishly. "Are these typical art column questions?"

Penn smiled as well and stuffed her notepad back into her bag. "Sorry. Yes, I guess they are. You shouldn't be disappointed. Art is meant to illicit a reaction. On the canvas, good or bad is entirely subjective. Yours at least gets the conversation going. That's the point, right?"

"You're the writer. I'll take your word for it," Shane said. "I just painted it the way it came into my mind."

Penn studied the painting again for a moment, frowning. Shane noticed that most people seemed to frown when they looked at Riverhouse, even if they were just passing, letting their eyes roam randomly over the collected works. Without looking up, Penn asked, "Who's the woman in the foreground?"

"I don't really know," Shane lied. "Just a focal point. Human interest."

"Who's she looking at?"

Shane furrowed his brow and peered down at the painting. "It's funny you should ask. Morrie asked the same question."

"So why's it funny?" Penn prodded, smiling a little crookedly.

"Well, because I didn't mean to paint her looking at anyone. She was just supposed to be resting, sitting in the sun. But people seem to see her as watching, looking for someone. I don't have any guesses about who it might be."

Penn nodded. "Some paintings just seem to have a life of their own, don't they? Are the rest of your works like this?"

Shane shook his head. "Not really. That was sort of a one-time thing, I think. I *am* painting another work for myself, but it's... different."

"Then can I assume you'll be appearing in more of Ms. Corsica's shows?"

"Maybe," Shane said, hedging. "I don't know."

"I hope so," Penn announced, nodding to herself and turning back to Shane. "Anyway, it was good to meet you, Mr. Bellamy. It's nice to meet an artist who doesn't know why he makes what he makes."

Shane blinked, but Penn laughed and touched his arm lightly. "That's high praise, if you ask me. Most artists try too hard, that's all. You, though, you've tapped into something. You're letting the picture tell its own story. I'm willing to bet that's what Dolores Grand noticed about your work. Like she said, her mother was a painter, and pretty well known amongst the local scene, at least back in the day. She taught at the Sam Fox School of Design at Washington University. I saw her speak once, a few years before she died. She said that the best artist was the one who offered the least interference. Does that make sense to you?"

Shane thought about it and nodded. "Yeah. I guess it does."

"Most of the rest of these people don't get that. Frankly, I don't get it either. But I can see the difference in the works of those who do. You're a bit of a curiosity, Mr. Bellamy."

"Oh?" Shane said, raising his eyebrows. "Just because I painted a somewhat strange picture of a house?"

"Yes," Penn nodded, smiling enigmatically. "But not just because of that. Here." She reached into her bag and produced a small white card. "Call me if you plan to be in any more shows. If you want, I'll email you a preview of the column. It'll probably run next Wednesday."

"Thanks," Shane said, taking the card. He glanced at it. It was very plain, containing only her name, the name of the newspaper, and her telephone number and email address. Apparently, her given name was Penelope. Shane produced his wallet and slipped the card into one of the inner pockets. When he looked up again, Penn had moved on already, following the trail of Mrs. Grand.

"Well, you did say to sell it," Christiana said, swirling her wine, watching it in its glass.

Shane shook his head in wonder. "I guess I did. I just didn't expect it to happen so fast, or for so much. How'd you know how to price it?"

Christiana sat her wine glass on the bar and shrugged languidly. To Shane, she looked like a cat preening on a windowsill. All around, the little bar droned and murmured, dark and crowded. He touched his own wine where it sat near his elbow but didn't pick it up.

"Do you remember a year or so ago," Christiana said, as if she was changing the subject. "When the market started to go all to hell and everyone was scrambling around trying to figure out where all their money went?"

"For a little while I was one of them," Shane nodded. "Although, I admit, it ended up being the least of my concerns. Most people got hit a lot harder than me."

"Hmm. Well, fortunately, *I* was fine," she said. "For once, it was a good thing *not* to have socked away for the future. My parents got whacked pretty hard, though. They're still reeling, although like most people they're right back at the grind again, plodding on."

"You think that's a mistake?"

She shrugged again, as if it didn't really matter what she thought. "The point is, my parents' accountant tried to explain what happened to them in the beginning. My father told me what he said. He said that the money they thought they had was never really there at all. All their stocks and stuff, it was always just *potential* money, waiting to happen. He said that everyone had been trading on that potential money for so long that they'd forgotten that it wasn't real money at all. When the potential dropped out, everyone thought they'd lost actual dollars. Understanding the difference between *real* money and *potential* money was the key to getting back on their feet, the accountant said."

Shane nodded slowly. Talking about money usually made his eyes glaze over, but Christiana managed to keep his interest. "Makes sense, I guess."

"Yeah," she said, looking at him. "I suspect it would, because you work in the world of potential money every day. That's the point. I understood what that accountant told my father, because art is one of the best examples of potential money. It's right up there with Beanie Babies and… and, you know, anything people collect not so much for the love of the thing, but because there's this group of other people who are collecting the same thing, and it's like a big competition. A 'he who dies with the most toys' contest. Sorry, the wine went straight to my head already. I need something to eat." She rummaged in her bag for a moment and produced a half-eaten energy bar still in its wrapper. Shane watched her take a bite. She looked up at him again. "Does that make sense?"

"Sure," Shane replied, glancing over her shape where she sat on the barstool next to him. "You're slight. Alcohol doesn't have very far to go."

"No, silly," she said, smiling suddenly. Her dark eyes twinkled. "I mean about the idea of art as potential money. Like a Beanie Baby, or... oh, what were those things everyone collected when we were kids?"

"I don't think we were kids at quite the same time," Shane replied, meeting her smile.

"Pogs," she said. "I'm older than you think. You remember pogs?"

"Sure, I guess. I never caught that particular rage, myself. I was more into the world of baseball cards. That's still a thriving industry, in fact."

Christiana nodded enthusiastically. "Sure. That's the best example of all. I mean, why is any particular baseball card worth what it is? It's not because of the two cents that went into its raw materials. It isn't even because it has a picture of some special player on it. It's because more than one person out there wants it, and is willing to pay a buck more than the other guy just to make sure *he* doesn't get it. That's what potential money is all about. It's about wanting something more than the other guy. Without the other guy, the potential drops to nothing. Without the other guy, the baseball card is only worth the cardboard it's printed on."

"So that's how you knew how much to ask for my baseball card?" Shane asked, finally taking a sip of his own wine. "You just guessed at how many 'other guys' there were?"

"No," Christiana admitted, shaking her head. "I wish I was that good. When I priced your work, I just priced it to sell, like you said. Someday I'll be good enough to know how people are going to respond to any given work. I hope so, at least. For now, I just go on my own instinct. Every now and then, fortunately, that instinct is right on. I had no idea that that weird painting of yours would be received the way it was."

"Eighteen hundred dollars," Shane said for the third time since they'd arrived. "That's some serious potential money."

"It's not potential anymore," Christiana said, patting her bag on the bar next to her. "Assuming the check clears. If it does, *that's* the difference between potential money and the real thing. Now, its potential money for the *new* owner. For you, it's the real deal."

Shane furrowed his brow. Nearly everything about tonight had surprised him. "Do you know her very well?"

"Penn Oliver?" Christiana said, chewing another bite of the energy bar. "No, not really. She and Morrie used to date, although it doesn't sound like it ever really got past the flirty-email phase. I've read her columns, of course. She's usually pretty fair, I guess. There are other people who take a perverse delight in the power of their words to destroy. She's usually not like that. Still, having her there scared the living bejeezus out of me."

"I have a feeling things are going to turn out all right," Shane said. "She seemed happy enough."

"She obviously liked *your* work," Christiana replied, smiling crookedly. "One star per show is about all anyone can hope for. Who'd have guessed it would be the newbie latecomer?"

Shane shook his head, embarrassed. "I think that was a perfect example of the power of the one other person. Penn Oliver only wanted the painting because she saw how that other lady, Dolores Grand, responded to it. I'm not sure she'd even have noticed it, otherwise."

"There you go," Christiana said, gesturing toward Shane with one hand. "That's the way the market works. Hooray for capitalism. If we can get Dolores Grand to come to every show and announce her intentions to buy something, we'll be golden. Too bad we can't pay her off."

"I get the feeling she's not the kind to be bought, at any rate."

Christiana blew out a breath. "At least not for any price we could afford."

There was a silence between them, and Shane allowed it to spin out. He was pleased to be here with her, surprised that things had turned out as they had. It was one thing to have sold his painting, and for what seemed to him to be a rather shocking price, but it was another thing entirely to have ended up here, sitting close to this young (not as young as she looked, perhaps?) woman at the dim little bar, watching her sip her wine and look around, studying the way her black hair captured the light and tossed it around as she moved. Part of him insisted it was foolishness to inspect her so unabashedly, but she didn't seem to notice, or to mind if she did. He decided, for the moment, not to worry about it.

"So," he finally said, raising his wine again. "Whatever became of Morrie?"

Christiana pressed her lips together slightly and then said, "Oh, don't worry about him. He's got bigger fish to fry than meeting us here. He's got shoulders to rub, contacts to make, people to impress. Somebody's got to do it, and he's just so damn good at it."

"You don't like Morrie?"

She made a vague flapping gesture with her hand. "Morrie's all right. He's a bulldozer, that's all. Like I said, some people have to be. I just don't think they should enjoy it so much."

"I wouldn't be here tonight if he hadn't bulldozed me a little," Shane said, frowning slightly. "I have to say, I'm glad he did."

"I am, too. If the showing gets as good a write up as I hope, it'll be due mainly to your Riverhouse. I mean, she did buy the painting, after all. That's got to be a good sign. But don't think that Morrie asked you to show your piece because he was trying to help you or me out. At least, not for those reasons alone."

"What do you mean?"

She sighed and stared at her wine again. "Nothing. I shouldn't. Like I said, Morrie's all right. Let's just say he doesn't miss a golden opportunity when it comes his way. He knows how to play all his cards. It's a gift, really."

"So, you two aren't...?"

Christiana glanced at Shane, her brow furrowed, and then laughed. "What? Dating? No, not at all. Heavens, no."

Shane bobbed his head noncommittally, trying not to look too pleased.

Christiana went on, "He's been a great help, honestly, even if his reasons for helping are a little mixed. It's a hard business to break into without someone on the inside. He's happy to be that someone for me, and I'm happy to let him. He flirts, sure. Some guys just can't help themselves. Guys like him are about as subtle as dogs yapping from behind a fence. It doesn't really mean anything, though. Morrie's a businessman at heart. By helping me, he gets to show off his own artists in a 'legitimate art environment', which is good for his business cred. And I get access to the venues and attendees that I could never hope to get on my own. It works for everybody, for the most part."

"So is that why he asked me to be in the show?" Shane asked. "To help his 'business cred'?"

"Are you surprised? At least yours was real art. It'll get written up in the paper and he'll clip it out and frame it. More importantly, he'll use it as the basis for a press release and send it out to all of his clients, telling them about how this artist he represents is making a 'big splash in the underground art scene', or something like that. Like I said, he's a businessman at heart. He knows how to play all of his cards."

Shane shrugged. "I suppose I should be offended, but I'm not."

She nodded. "I see that. I envy you. Seems to me, lately, that I've been offended more often than not. It's getting harder and harder to be patient."

"Patient with Morrie?"

She laughed and lowered her eyes. "No. Well, yes, I suppose. But with everything else, too. Work. Life..." She drew a quick sigh. "You know. Everything. This isn't where I expected to be by my age. When I was growing up, age thirty was sort of the high-water mark. It was the deadline for getting serious about life, you know? I knew I'd have my life and career all arranged by then. I'd probably be married, I'd certainly be an attorney, just like Mother and Father, and I'd be living like the lawyers on TV, the ones who hustle and bustle through every day, tackling the big important legal cases, putting away the bad guys, and then spending their evenings in trendy nightclubs working out the kinks of their intensely interesting personal lives."

"Damn those lying people on TV," Shane said, smiling crookedly. "Damn those lying courtroom drama shows."

Christiana smiled back, sheepishly. "I *so* wanted to be Ally McBeal. Give me the coed bathroom and the dancing baby hallucination any day. I wanted her problems. I almost dyed my hair to be like her."

Shane shook his head. "You're better off brunette. Leave the dirty blonde to Ally."

"I left the whole thing to Ally," Christiana replied. "Life doesn't look like it does on TV. I guess real life just can't fit on a TV screen. So here I am, contrary to all my plans and expectations, thirty-two and still trying to figure out what life is going to look like."

"What are you hoping for now?"

She glanced at Shane, and then looked back out over the bar. "A gallery of my own, I guess. That's what I really want. But I won't show just anyone. I want to promote artists who paint what's really there. Not just the ugliness in their own heads or the made-up feel good stuff that most people seem to want to look at. Nothing pretentious and nothing plastic. I suppose that makes me pretentious in my own way. That's all right with me—for now, at least. Life is just a lot more complicated and interesting than most art would have us believe. It isn't just emo abstract ugliness and it isn't just clown's faces on black velvet. I mean, it *is* those things too, but those are just the boundaries… just the hard edges. Most of life happens in the middle, *between* those two extremes. That's where most of us live and work and move every day. That's what I want to see in art. That's the kind of gallery I'll open someday, if I can."

"It's a gallery I'd go to," Shane said seriously.

Christiana looked at him again. "You keep painting and maybe you'll have a good reason to."

"You'd display my work?"

"Maybe. I may not love your stuff myself, but it fits the description. It's not beautiful, but it's not ugly either. There's nothing forced about it. And what the hell, it apparently sells."

Shane laughed. "So Morrie's not the only one with business in his soul."

"I'm the daughter of two lawyers," she replied, straightening on her barstool and affecting a stern demeanor. "Some things are just bred in the grain."

"Well, at least one part of your teenage dream has come true," Shane said, lifting his wine glass. "You're sitting in a trendy nightclub discussing the weighty intricacies of life."

"Hmm," she said, raising her own wineglass and clinking it to his. "But I'm not being fought over by the district attorney and a young, hot-shot lawyer under the guise of an argument about today's grisly murder trial."

"Well, there's Morrie and me," Shane said, feeling a little bold. "Which one of us is the D.A. and which one is the young hotshot lawyer?"

She shook her head, smiling a little and sipping her wine again. After a moment, she said, "So what about you, Mr. Shane

Bellamy? What about the mysterious New York artist who suddenly relocated to the buggy backwoods of the Midwest. What's your story?"

Shane exhaled wearily. He raised his hands, palms up. "It's a long, unhappy tale."

"Thus the painting," Christiana said, nodding. "Who was it that said that art grows best in the fertilizer of life's crap?"

Shane grinned. "I never heard that one. Maybe it was you."

"Maybe it was. Go on."

Shane shrugged again and looked away, scanning the people gathered around the bar. "I'm like you in some ways. I grew up knowing exactly what I wanted out of life. The difference was, I *got* it. I had that life for several years. And then, suddenly, it all went away. I guess that's what it all boils down to."

Christiana took another, smaller sip of her wine. "Morrie says you used to be married."

"Well, you know how it is," Shane replied. "Nobody keeps secrets from their agent."

"So what happened?"

Shane looked back at Christiana, saw her studying him carefully, her dark eyes serious. He sighed. "She just got bored with me, I guess. It's the same story as everybody else. She says I got lost in my work, stopped paying attention to her."

Christiana didn't blink. "So was it true?"

Shane frowned and looked along the length of the bar. "I don't know. Maybe..." He shook his head. "How can you argue with somebody else's perception?"

Cristiana laughed a little hollowly. "Some people do it all the time."

"Well, there was no point in arguing with Steph once she'd made up her mind. But no, I didn't think it was true. I've thought about it a lot since the day she told me she wanted out. At the time, I was too stunned to think back on it, but since then... that's about all I've done. I was no model husband, but I wasn't a slouch. I did make efforts. I loved her. A lot. And you know what's weird? She loved me, too. You can just tell when someone says it and they mean it, can't you? I mean, people are pretty insecure, generally. It's natural to doubt someone when they say something really important and personal like 'I love you'. But if they say that to you and you never have the slightest question in your mind about whether they mean it or not... if you never once doubt it... that's got to mean something, right? I used to look at my friends, at their marriages, and think to myself, 'I'm very lucky. Steph and I have it good.' We weren't perfect, but..." Shane stopped, sighed, and shook his head again, slowly. He looked back at Christiana. "She laughed at my jokes. I guess that sounds pretty stupid, but that was the first thing I thought the day she told me she wanted a divorce. I thought, 'but you laugh at my jokes. You have any idea how rare that is, after eight years of marriage? How many couples still enjoy each other's company enough to laugh at their jokes? And you're willing to just throw that away?'"

Christiana frowned. "But you didn't say that to her."

"No, I didn't. It seemed like a dumb thing to mention at the time. I just knew there was some magic bullet, some perfect thing that I'd be able to say to change everything back to normal, to remind her of what we had. I was just waiting for it to come into my mind. It never came, though. Soon enough, she was gone, and I just kept thinking that same stupid thing over and over, like a broken record: you laughed at my jokes. How can you just throw that away? You get me. You understand me better than anyone. And *I* understand *you*. Who will understand you if you leave me? Who will get you? And who will laugh at my jokes?"

Christiana nodded and didn't say anything for a moment. Finally, she said, "What do you think it really was?"

"What what really was?"

"Why she decided to leave you."

"I don't know. We only talked about it a few times, but she never really said anything more than she did on that first day. Basically, I just wasn't there for her. I was too busy. She felt alone."

"That's baloney and you know it. You said you understood her."

"I did."

"So why did she really leave you?"

Shane blinked at Christiana, but she didn't look away. She stared at him expectantly. Finally, he drew a deep breath and let it out slowly. "Maybe... probably, it had something to do with having a baby."

Christiana nodded again, knowingly. "She wanted one, and you didn't?"

"At first, yeah, sort of. I was less excited about it than she was. She could tell, but I was willing to go along with it for her. I'd never been the kind of guy who loved kids, but I figured I would learn to love my own baby, once we had one. Problem was, we couldn't. We tried for over a year before we went to see a doctor. Nothing worked. We never got to the point of finding out exactly why. Maybe we didn't really *want* to know. But I think it affected her a lot more than it did me. I think... maybe she blamed me. Maybe she thought it was my fault."

"Because she knew you weren't as excited about it as she was?"

Shane nodded, barely listening. "But the thing was, I *was* excited about it. Not at first, like I said, but the more I thought about it... the longer we tried..."

"You caught the bug?"

Shane thought for a moment, smiling to himself. "I was walking out of the grocery store one night, carrying my bag and shaking out my keys, and I was following this guy pushing a cart with a little kid in it, up front in the baby seat. I'd begun noticing kids everywhere I went. That's how it is, isn't it? You buy a red car, you start seeing them all over the place. So I was watching the kid. He was a boy, not even two years old. He pointed up toward the sky, his little chin raised. His dad saw him and followed his pointing finger, looking up over his own shoulder. Then he says to the kid, 'that's the moon'."

Shane stopped. He blinked and swallowed. "'That's the moon,' the dad said, like it was the most normal thing in the world, having to explain something so obvious and mundane. The kid just sat in the cart, looking up at the sky, his face somber and amazed, awestruck. He was awestruck by the moon. I looked at that little boy and his dad and for the first time I thought, 'I want that. I can do that. I want to explain to a little person what the moon is. I want Steph and me to have a baby so I can do that someday.'"

Christiana was looking at Shane, her expression serious but otherwise unreadable. Shane shook himself. "Maybe that's a silly reason to decide to have a baby, but that's what pushed me over the edge. Problem was, we just couldn't. At first, it was sort of a fun challenge. And then, after a few months, it became a steady, nagging worry. Finally, after a year, it was an out-and-out fear. I think it took its toll on Steph, and I think it contributed to the end of our marriage. But it took its toll on me, too. If I did withdraw, it was because of that. I was... I don't know."

"Stressed?" Christiana suggested. "Worried?"

"I was ashamed," Shane said, looking her in the eye. "That's all. I wanted to give her what she wanted. I didn't know if it was my fault we couldn't—not yet, at least—but deep down I suspected it was. I think she did, too. I hated not being able to give her what she most wanted. So I buried myself. I did what I could do for her instead. I worked, and I provided income. That, at least, I could control. If she was alone in the end, that was why."

Christiana shook her head ruefully. "That doesn't give her an excuse. What she did...it's still an awful thing to do to somebody."

"Yeah, I guess."

She changed her expression, lowered her voice a little. "You think there's any chance you'd ever be able to work things out with her again?"

Shane laughed. It was a hard, humorless sound. "No, I'd say that's pretty much out of the question."

"Why?"

Shane looked at Christiana, tried to smile, and then let it fall away. He sighed instead. There was no pretty way to say it. "She's dead."

Christiana nodded soberly. "I wondered. You kept referring to her in the past tense. What happened?"

Shane shook his head minutely. He shrugged.

"I'm sorry," Christiana said suddenly. "Never mind. I've got no reason to ask. I'm too curious and too blunt, most of the time. It's another thing that's just bred in the grain."

"It was a car accident," Shane said, smiling a little. "She was hit by a drunk driver. And I don't mind. It's kind of refreshing." He reached across the bar and touched her hand, covering it with his own. She looked up at him, studying his face.

"I'm seeing someone," she said.

Shane blinked. "Hmm?"

She sighed quickly. "I'm seeing someone. It's not Morrie, but it's someone. We've been dating for a little over a year now. He's a law student."

Shane withdrew his hand slowly. "OK. I didn't..."

"I know you didn't," she said, interrupting. "But I have a habit of... of leaving out certain important details. It's also bred in the grain, right alongside being curious and blunt. I'm telling you now because if I don't..." She lifted her shoulders and raised her hands, palms up. "I may not tell you at all. And I think that might be a mistake. A mean mistake, even if it's unintentional. All right?"

Shane nodded, feeling suddenly very foolish. "Yeah. I get it."

There was a long silence between them as they looked around the bar, watched the laughing, talking faces of those around them. It was a less comfortable silence this time. Finally, Christiana picked up her nearly empty wineglass and held it by the stem. She looked at Shane over it.

"Money's not the only thing that gets traded on its potential, is it?" She said, smiling a small, crooked smile.

Shane tilted his head and raised his eyebrows.

"Here's to life," she said, nodding toward her glass. "Here's to figuring out the difference between potential life and the real thing."

Shane lifted his own glass and nodded agreement. "The best toast I've heard in years."

Their glasses clinked and they drank. A little while later, Shane walked Christiana to the parking lot at the end of the block. He wanted to link arms with her, even if just as a sign of camaraderie, but he didn't. They said goodnight at her car, a little awkwardly, and Shane turned toward his truck as she pulled out onto the busy street. He drove home thinking about her toast, thinking about the difference between potential life and the real thing. It was a lot to consider. It really had been one of the best toasts he'd ever heard.

Chapter Eight

Over the next week, Shane worked his normal shift from nine until two, plugging away at the Florida tourism paintings. It started slow, but by the middle of the week, he had hit his old stride. The foreman in his mind called out the brush strokes like a quarterback calling out plays in a huddle. Shane's hand obeyed diligently, and the paintings sprang quickly to life. The corkboard under the Escher quote had been cleared of the reference material from the matte painting and refilled with printouts of surfers and scuba divers, water skiers and sunlit beaches. By Thursday, Shane had nearly finished the first painting in the series, ending with a large representation of a woman in a white bikini leaning against a surfboard stuck upright in the sand. He'd printed the reference photo for this picture from an image he'd found on the Internet. In the reference photo, the woman was wearing jean shorts and a yellow tube top, and she was leaning against a Coke machine instead of a surfboard. She was laughing, holding a cigarette in her right hand. Shane had found the image on a photo sharing website called Flickr, and even though all the minor details were wrong, the woman in the photo had the perfect pose and expression. For Shane, getting the poses right was the hardest part. Once he'd sketched the woman's essential shape, the act of redressing her in a bikini—as well as removing the cigarette and giving her a voluminous blond hair-do instead of the mousy brown locks in the photo—was easy work, nearly effortless.

It was fun painting the young woman in the photo, because painting was a strangely intimate thing. In his mind, as he painted her shape, he chatted her up, asking her where the photo had been taken, who she'd been with. The young woman modeled for him in his mind, and told him she'd been on a road trip with her girlfriends, skipping a Friday of classes at Georgia State University to drive down to the coast and blow off some steam. She was dating this guy, a poly-sci major, who hadn't approved of the road trip, had been jealous of her and her girlfriends. He'd called her on her cell phone to complain and ask why she wasn't spending her time with him instead, and she'd told him to go have a good cry and get over it. This had offended him immensely, but had reduced the young women in the car to gales of caffeine-induced laughter so raucous that they'd had to pull the car over at a gas station to recover. There, to commemorate the event, they had taken pictures of each other, posing and snapping them off with one of the other girls' cell phone cameras. It had been a fun day, a day of irresponsible delights perfectly suited to the lifestyle of a young college girl on her way to a disappointingly conventional suburban future.

The timestamp in the bottom right of the printed photo said 05.07.03, and as the young woman in Shane's mind modeled for him, he saw that those days of free-wheeling carelessness were now long over. In his mind she had married the poly-sci major (who hadn't had a good cry since he'd been seven years old) and had born him two kids. In Shane's mind, the woman never went on road trips anymore, never shirked a Friday's responsibilities to blow off steam. She missed those days, missed them sorely, although she never admitted it to anyone. She loved her kids desperately, loved her husband a little more prosaically, and spent her evenings scanning old pictures and posting them on Flickr and on her Facebook page. By doing that, she relived the old memories. She revisited the laughter. As she'd scanned the photo of herself leaning against the Coke machine, she'd smiled ruefully and thought, *'go have a good cry'. Damn that was funny. We laughed so hard.*

Shane finished painting the refurbished adaptation of the woman in the photo and said goodbye to the version of her in his head. She wasn't real, of course. She was just a daydreaming concoction of his subconscious mind, bringing the woman in the photo to life for the time it took to transfer her onto the canvas. In his mind, her name was Renee, but the title of the image on Flickr had been "Lisa and me at Cape Canaveral". Maybe Shane had changed the name on purpose, just to be safe. He'd felt a little strange while he'd painted her, even though he knew the version of her in his mind was entirely made up. As he finished for the day, he realized what it was. The other painting, the one of the woman with the letter in her hands, standing in front of the blood-red fireplace, was on the smaller easel across the room, facing him. He'd had the weird sense that she'd looked up from the letter while he'd been painting the other woman; that she'd watched him, trying to decide if she should be jealous or not.

"She's just a model," he said, scrubbing his hands with an old handkerchief, cleaning up after his shift. "You've got nothing to worry about. You're still my main squeeze, M, whatever your full name is."

He smiled to himself. Of course the painting hadn't been looking at him. That sense of being watched was common enough during his shift, especially lately.

And besides, he *did* know her full name, despite what he'd told Penn Oliver at the gallery showing. He simply wasn't particularly comfortable with admitting it. Her name had been in his head ever since the morning he'd woken up with red paint drying on his fingers. It had come to him repeatedly during the previous evening, flitting in his thoughts like a bat at twilight, as he'd finished painting in the fine features of her nose and lips, adding the highlight of a tear in the corner of her left eye. Her name was Marlena.

"Marlena," he said idly, approaching the painting and studying it. It was nearly finished, but not quite. Maybe he'd finish it later that night. He had fallen into a routine with the muse, painting at night, when her influence was strongest. It also happened to be the time when the presence of the woman's ghost was most apparent, when he saw her sometimes flitting through the library, attending to her own otherworldly agenda. Often, she'd look at him as she went, just a passing glance, her face calm, her eyes black and bottomless. Shane had almost gotten used to it. Sometimes he'd close the sunroom doors while he was watching television in the evenings, not wishing to be surprised by her wafting, misty shape as he watched the Mets on satellite. Other times—most of the time—he left the doors open. In a bizarre but undeniable way, he rather liked sharing the place with a woman again, even if she was a little creepy and somber. Earl Kirchenbauer had been right: the cottage did need a woman's touch. The ghost wasn't much, but her presence was pervasive, especially at night. Morning might be the domain of the mysterious and mischievous Smithy, who still flushed the toilet sometimes and turned on and off the basement light, but the night belonged to Marlena. She left the basement lights alone. After all, she had the candle in the secret window.

Shane shook himself. In the painting, Marlena studied the letter, her face pale and oddly expressionless except for that subtle glimmer of a tear in her left eye. The painting was nearly done. When it was finished, he'd put it away. Hell, maybe he'd put it in the attic. She'd probably be happy there.

Not for the first time, Shane felt a secret relief that the Riverhouse painting was gone. Somehow, keeping both the Marlena painting and the Riverhouse painting in the cottage at the same time seemed like a bad idea. That's why he'd decided to sell it, after all. It had been a good decision, too. Now that it was gone, he felt a little bit saner, a little more in control. He hadn't painted anymore in his sleep, for one thing. And his shift had come back, along with the foreman in his mind. Everything was jake. Selling the painting had been a very smart move.

Even if he did sort of miss it.

Recovery, Dr. Taylor had said, is a slippery slope.

Shane remembered when he'd first heard the man say it. They'd been in his office just over the river in New Jersey, a month after Stephanie's last phone call, and it had been raining outside. "You don't get over something like this," Norm Taylor had said, taking off his glasses and putting them in his shirt pocket. He was skinny, and the glasses made a heavy lump on his shirt. Shane had stared at it, willing his eyes not to tear up for the umpteenth time. Taylor had sighed and gone on. "You get over a cold. A shock like the one you've experienced is more like pneumonia. In today's medical world, most people don't die of pneumonia, but it isn't unheard of. It can still be fatal. You don't just 'get over' pneumonia. You recover from it. You endure, you take your meds, and you eventually survive it. And just like any other recovery, it's often a slippery slope. Just when you think you're finally past it, it'll come back and hit you in the back of the head. Your experience is like that, Shane. Just like any recovery, it'll take time. Don't expect it to go away easily or quickly. Just when you think you're over it, something will happen, and *bam*. You'll be right back in the middle of it again."

Shane had raised his eyes at that point, and they were indeed shiny with tears. He'd hated the tears, hated how easy they were in those days. "Sounds pretty damn bleak," he'd croaked.

Norm Taylor had smiled. It was a sardonic smile, but sympathetic. "Welcome to the buffet of life," he'd said quietly. "Sometimes the kitchen's all out of Kobe steak. Sometimes all they have to offer up is ten courses of tough shit. What're you going to do, Shane? You still have to eat, right? We all do. We have to eat whatever life dishes out."

Shane hadn't thought those were the kinds of things psychologists were supposed to say, but then again, Norm Taylor didn't often seem like a typical psychologist. The first time they'd met, they'd talked about the Mets for the entire hour. Shane had been reluctant to discuss the real reason he'd called Taylor's office, even though he'd known he needed to. He'd sat ramrod straight on one end of the big couch, mentally convincing himself that he was actually fine, that he was entirely capable of managing things on his own, and knowing it was a lie. Dr. Taylor had begun their session by commenting about the previous night's baseball game, and Shane had blinked. He hadn't watched it, of course. He'd been at his wife's funeral. Taylor hadn't even paused. "Shame you missed it. It was a corker. Martinez drilled seventy-seven pitches against the Braves. At least that's what the Times says. I wasn't counting, but you can bet I was watching. Says he's thinking about retiring next year. You think that's a good idea?"

Shane hadn't. He liked Martinez. He'd said so, and within ten minutes he and Dr. Taylor were deep in conversation about the Mets playoffs chances, about Martinez and his hamstring injury and his Cy Young awards, and whether or not his glory days were behind him, and Shane had eventually forgotten why he'd originally called Taylor's office. By the end of their hour, Shane was leaning back on the leather sofa, his arms thrown back on either side, his foot cocked on the corner of the ottoman, even smiling a little. Taylor's glasses were in his shirt pocket, making that hard, heavy lump on his skinny chest. "What do you say, Shane?" he'd asked at the end. "You want to do this again next Tuesday?"

"What," Shane had answered, shaking his head, still smiling. "Talk about the Mets?"

Taylor had shrugged. "We can talk about the Mets. Or the Giants preseason. Or how far the stock market's fallen down the crapper. Or, of course, we can talk about your wife. If you want. You think you'll want to?"

Shane had drawn a huge sigh. He didn't answer. He did, however, meet Dr. Taylor again the next Tuesday, and for nine Tuesdays after that. They talked about Stephanie, as well as a few other things. Shane remembered a lot of what Dr. Taylor had said. Often, he recalled his comments about how the buffet of life sometimes ran out of Kobe steaks, but that you had to eat no matter what, even if the only thing on the menu was ten courses of tough shit. Mostly, though, he reminded himself of the thing Taylor had said most often: recovery is a slippery slope. Just when you think you've made it to the top of the mountain, something will come out of the blue, and *bam:* you're right back in the middle of it again.

On Friday, the day after finishing the painting of Marlena, Shane got two packages. One came in the morning, and the other came in the afternoon, after his phone call from Christiana. Much later, looking back, Shane would think that that was when things had really begun to slip out of his control. Two harmless deliveries, both completely unconnected (or so it seemed) and both utterly innocuous, at least on the surface.

Bam.

The first one was a manila envelope, thick and heavy, neatly sealed and stamped on the back with red: PRIVATE DOCUMENTS – TO BE OPENED BY ADDRESSEE ONLY. The return address was also stamped, and Shane groaned inwardly when he saw it. It was from Price, Hayes and Whitaker, the law firm that had handled first his and Stephanie's divorce, and then the disbursement of her assets after her death. Janice Hayes, the woman who'd left the message on Shane's answering machine several days earlier, had been Stephanie's lawyer. He'd completely forgotten about the phone message, as well as the package the message had mentioned. He stood in the early morning sunlight at the end of his long gravel driveway, looking down at the envelope in his hands, and it occurred to him that his posture was eerily similar to the pose of Marlena in the painting back in the upstairs studio. He lowered the manila envelope, folded it over the rest of the mail, and stuffed the whole thing into the pocket of his jeans. He closed the mouth of the big black mailbox and turned to hike back toward the house. The coffee percolator was probably boiling by now. He'd have a cup on the back patio and watch the river for awhile before starting his shift.

The leaves were in full color now, after all, and there was a pleasant crispness to the morning air.

He'd ignore the big manila envelope. There was nothing in there that he needed to see, nothing that demanded his immediate attention. How could there be? For one brief, black moment, he imagined opening the envelope and finding one sheet of paper on top of the legal records, blank except for six type-written words: YES, YOUR WIFE IS STILL DEAD. He grinned at the absurdity of it, and then laughed harshly, and the laugh was partly a sob. He choked it back and looked up at the trees. *Recovery is a slippery slope*, he thought. *Just when you think you've made it to the top of the mountain...*

He wouldn't open the envelope. He didn't need to. He knew what was in it, had seen all of it before. One of the things in the envelope was a photocopy of a highway patrol report, complete with a grainy black and white printout of a photo showing Stephanie's silver Honda. In the picture, it was hard to tell what kind of car it was. Frankly, it was a little hard to tell that it was a car at all. The first time Shane had seen it, he'd thought it looked more like mechanical hamburger. The only recognizable part had been the passenger's door, which jutted up out of the mess like the wing of a dead bird.

"I need to tell you something," Steph had said during her last phone call. "I don't want to tell you on the phone. Can we meet somewhere?"

Shane had still been in the apartment then, and he remembered standing there by the refrigerator, clutching the phone to his ear, unsure what he should say. Some small, petty part of him said he should refuse her. If she had something to say, she could damn well say it on the phone, or she could come back to their old apartment and tell him there, maybe right there in the kitchen with the butcher block between them. But he didn't say that, of course. For the most part, Shane wasn't a petty person. And besides, he still loved her. He knew her. He understood her well enough to recognize the tone of her voice. Something had changed. She hadn't sounded like this ever since that awful day two months earlier, the day he'd lost both his job and his wife in a single hour. The divorce had gone remarkable quickly from that point—Janice Hayes was exceedingly efficient—and Shane had signed the papers only a week earlier. So why was Stephanie calling him now? What had happened to bring about that change in her voice?

"Can we meet at the Spring Garden?" she'd asked, and Shane suddenly thought he knew. After all, the Spring Garden was more than just an outdoor bar on the corner of fifty-seventh and Park. It was where he had proposed to her, seven years earlier. He realized that the tone of her voice didn't so much signify a change of heart. It signified weariness and resolve, as if she'd finally dropped a charade that had been very difficult to maintain. What he heard in her voice was sincerity and relief. She was doing something she'd wanted to do for awhile, but had chosen, for any number of complicated, convoluted reasons, to resist. She was coming clean. Somehow, Shane had always expected this. After all, she laughed at his jokes. He understood her. You didn't just throw something like that away. The divorce might be final, but they weren't. How could they be? Fate wouldn't allow it.

He agreed to meet her at Spring Garden for lunch that day. He kept his own voice casual, as if there was nothing particularly special about her choice of meeting place. It was almost as if he didn't want to jinx it.

She'd never arrived, of course. Shane had sat at one of the tall tables that lined the wrought iron railing, nursing a Rolling Rock beer and watching the crowd mill past. Stephanie had been living in a small apartment in the Meadowlands at the time, less than ten minutes away on ninety-five. She had her own particular brand of punctuality; she was almost always ten minutes late, but never more than fifteen. Shane imagined that she'd barely even left her apartment until the time she was supposed to be meeting him, and that she'd come breezing along the sidewalk at a quarter after one, breathing heavily and fanning herself with one hand, apologizing distractedly. Shane had seen it a hundred times, and it was, if anything, somewhat comforting. It had been one of the familiar small dramas of their marriage. He'd waited and sipped his beer and watched the people on the sidewalk, gazed over the cabs that crawled beetle-like in the hard afternoon sunlight. By twenty after she still hadn't come. After half an hour, Shane had begun to wonder about her.

By one-fifty, he'd known something was very wrong.

It had happened less than a mile before her exit. The pickup truck that hit her Honda had been traveling at over a hundred miles an hour, driven by a young man named James Herk. He'd been very drunk, and as was so often the case, he had managed to survive the crash. Shane had never spoken to him, but Janice Hayes had assured him that Herk was very sorry for what he'd done, that he had no memory of the event whatsoever, and that he'd promised, tearfully, to join Alcoholics Anonymous as soon as he was released from the hospital. Shane doubted it, but he didn't really care. James Herk didn't matter. Shane had expected to be angry at the guy, but he wasn't. He couldn't muster the strength for it. All that mattered was that Stephanie was dead. She'd never make it to Spring Garden again, never tell him whatever it was she'd meant to say. He'd meant to give her back her tee shirt, the light blue one that said ADDICTED TO ENDORPHINS. He still had it in his backpack, freshly laundered and folded. When he'd gotten home that night, he'd taken it back out again and just looked at it. Folded, it read ICTED TO END. He read it over and over, not really seeing it, his mind reeling numbly.

"This isn't an official part of the proceedings," Janice Hayes had said on the day Stephanie's assets were disbursed. "All of your wife's belongings will be turned over to her mother, her closest surviving relative. This, however, was retrieved from the car after the accident. I understand she was on her way to meet you. I thought you might like to..." For once, Janice Hayes had seemed to be at a loss for words. She'd shrugged and set the object on the table of the conference room. It was Stephanie's purse. "I'm just going to go get some coffee. Would you like some coffee?"

Shane had said that he would. Janice Hayes had nodded and left, closing the conference door softly behind her.

The purse was scuffed. The strap had been broken off, leaving a ragged hole on one side. For nearly a minute Shane had simply stared at it. Finally, he'd pulled it toward him. He'd felt strangely guilty opening it, almost as if he was snooping. After all, at the time of her death, she had no longer been his wife. Nevertheless, he had loved her, and this had belonged to her. It had been with her when she died, had probably been propped on the passenger's seat next to her. Sitting on the conference table, scuffed and torn, it had still smelled like her, the mingled scent of her perfume and the hand lotion she used. Inside had been a mostly empty package of Raspberrymint Orbit gum, a tube of Blistex, her lipstick, a travel pack of Kleenex. He'd placed the objects reverentially onto the table next to the purse, lining them up as if they were museum exhibits, or crime scene evidence. Her tortoiseshell compact had been cracked; brittle bits of the mirror sifted onto his hand when he moved it. Her cell phone, broken, the battery dead. Her wallet. A granola bar. A travel-size bottle of Anacin.

And then Shane had stopped. Everything he had taken out so far he had expected. Seeing her things laid out on the table was strangely cathartic. Seeing the gum she would never chew, the lipstick she would never wear, the phone she would never again forget to charge, all of these things were heartbreaking, and yet they made the reality of her death seem somehow manageable, like something he could begin to grope around the edges of. These were her things, things she would never again touch or see, things he himself had seen a thousand times during their marriage, things that represented her, even symbolized her.

Except for the last thing. It had settled to the bottom, buried beneath her sunglasses and a paperback copy of Zagat's restaurant guide. Slowly, Shane had reached in and felt the object, gripped it, drawn it out into the light. It was small, mostly yellow. It made a happy little clattering sound as he lifted it. It was a baby rattle. The handle was plastic, but the top was soft plush, fashioned to resemble Paddington Bear. His little stitched mouth was black and demure, smiling slightly, as if he knew a secret. Shane was still holding the little rattle, staring down at it in his hands when Janice Hayes came back. She settled two coffees onto the conference table, near the collection of Stephanie's things, and sat down in the chair at the end. After a moment, Shane drew a breath. His voice came out very calmly, so much so that it surprised him.

"Did you know?"

She looked down at the two coffees steaming on the table, and then up at Shane, meeting his eyes. She pressed her lips together slightly. She didn't say anything at all.

Shane figured that was answer enough.

Stephanie had been pregnant when she died. Shane knew it, knew that's what she'd meant to tell him. He imagined it over and over in his mind, dreamed it relentlessly, as if he could change reality just by willing it hard enough. In his dream it was always the same. In the dream, she met him at Spring Garden, took a sip of his Rolling Rock beer while she waited for her own drink, an iced tea with lemon. In the dream, Shane commented on her choice of beverage, and she nodded cryptically, unsmiling. In answer, she reached into her purse and drew something out. She took Shane's hand and placed the object in it, watching his face, watching to see his reaction. The little Paddington Bear rattle sat in the palm of his hand and he stared at it dumbly, speechless, his mind racing. Finally, he met her eyes, saw the scrutiny in her face as she watched him, hoping he'd understand.

"Does this mean...?" his dreaming self asked her.

The dream Stephanie's expression didn't change. Her eyes remained on his, unguarded. Her eyes were two different colors; one green and one blue. Not many people noticed that. Slowly, almost imperceptibly, she nodded, and Shane realized that the reason her eyes looked so bright was that there were tears in them, trembling, not yet spilling over her lashes.

"I found out after I left," the dream Stephanie said, keeping her voice low, almost a whisper. "I swear it, Shane. I didn't know it that day in the kitchen. I'd stopped hoping. But later, after things had gotten going with the divorce, I missed my period. I told myself it was just stress, but... well... after two months, there was no denying it. I didn't want to tell you until I was absolutely sure. Oh, Shane..."

In the dream, Shane touched her hand and held it, and his own eyes thickened with tears. He'd shed a lot of tears in the last few months, but never like this. Never out of happiness. The two of them looked at each other, blinking back tears, and laughing a little helplessly, and the Paddington Bear rattle clattered merrily between them, held between their clasped hands.

But that hadn't happened, of course. Instead, Stephanie had been hammered to death by a drunk kid in his dad's GMC pickup truck. She'd died with the baby still inside her, died probably before she even knew if the baby was a boy or a girl, before seeing it born and healthy, before discovering if it had two different colored eyes. There'd been no funeral for the unborn baby, of course. If it hadn't been for Janice Hayes and her uncharacteristically gracious choice to allow Shane to find the Paddington Bear rattle, he never would have known at all. Sometimes he wondered if the baby wasn't even his, but never for very long. Of course it was. Steph wouldn't have told him to meet her at Spring Garden to tell him she was pregnant with someone else's child. Nor would Janice Hayes have led him to the discovery that his dead wife had been pregnant if the baby hadn't been his. She was a lawyer, but she was also a woman. Shane didn't know her very well, but he knew that Steph had considered her a friend. Janice Hayes had known, and she had decided Shane deserved to know as well, regardless of what was legally required. Maybe even in spite of it.

Shane thought about all of this as he painted that morning. The scenes played over and over in his head, full of heartbreaking clarity and forgotten details. He remembered the sound of Stephanie's voice when she laughed, and the way she looked in the morning before she got dressed, the annoyed sound she always made when her hair got in her face. If she had only divorced him, it would have been much easier. He could tell himself that she was still out there, probably with another man, that her rejection of him had been final and complete. It would have been awful, but he could have moved on. Instead, he was left to wonder. Had she wanted to get back together? Would the baby have been healthy? Would the three of them have been happy together? Maybe, but then again, maybe not. It was easy to create elaborate idyllic fantasies about it, to gnaw on the infinite possibilities of a failed what-if. And yet he couldn't let it go. Her last phone call hung over him, vibrating in the air like an unresolved chord, constantly nagging, teasing, speculating about an answer that could never come.

Shane painted quickly, almost feverishly. By two o'clock, he was nearly done with the third of the Florida paintings. The Marlena portrait sat on the smaller easel in the corner. It was finished, and Shane was glad. Whatever bizarre passion had gripped him and pressed him to create those two strange images, the Riverhouse and Marlena, it had fallen away now, at least for the moment. Maybe he would put the portrait in the attic after all. Or maybe he'd merely leave it there on the little easel. On its own, it was a rather captivating picture. It told a story. The woman in the painting was beautiful, if only because of the stunned vulnerability on her face as she looked down at the letter. Her white hands were perfectly crafted, lovingly shaped and shaded as they gripped the paper. Where the Riverhouse painting had been disturbing, the Marlena painting was strangely heartbreaking. The viewer didn't need to know what the letter said to know that it had devastated her. One couldn't help wanting to reach out to the woman, to comfort her and soothe her, if that were possible. In its own way, the Marlena portrait was no more pleasant to look at than the Riverhouse painting, and yet her misery was undeniably enthralling to the outside viewer. It was very nearly indulgent. Shane found himself staring at the portrait once his shift was over. His arm ached and he was ravenously hungry, and yet he didn't feel like moving. He sat on his stool, his head turned to the side, and studied Marlena. He thought of Stephanie, but no more tears came to his eyes. He seemed to have used up all of his tears over the past few months. He no longer felt that exquisite sadness at her loss. That was old hat now. Now, he just felt empty. Empty and alone.

He stared at Marlena, because he thought she knew that feeling. He thought she knew that feeling very well.

Downstairs, the phone began to ring.

"Hello?"

Nothing. There was a clatter, a sound like a car with the windows rolled down. A shiver coursed down Shane's spine, but then a voice spoke.

"Shane?" It was Christiana.

"That's me. Chris? What's going on?"

"Hi. Sorry, I probably shouldn't have called. I... believe it or not, I don't have a lot of friends at the moment. Not since I dropped out of school and started working for Morrie. I... where are you at?"

Shane blinked. "I'm at home, standing here in my library. What's wrong?"

"Of course," Christiana said, as if talking to herself. "You don't have a cell phone. I knew that. I forgot. God, I'm sorry. I shouldn't have called." She sounded strangely hectic, distracted.

"Chris, just tell me what's wrong. Where are you?"

"I'm driving. I'm downtown. I'm... I guess I'm heading back to work. I was supposed to have the afternoon off, but..."

Shane was becoming alarmed. "Chris, I can tell something's wrong. What is it? You obviously called for a reason."

"It's nothing," she said, and laughed. It sounded high and forced. "I just wanted to chat with someone. Sometimes you just want to hear someone's voice and say hi, talk about whatever. You know? Maybe that only happens to girls. Do you mind?"

"Not at all," Shane said, clutching the phone to his ear. "You want me to meet you somewhere? We could get a drink or something, like the other night. That was nice. What do you say?"

She replied immediately. "No, no, that's fine. I don't want to interrupt you. I'm sure you're in the middle of work. That Florida series must be keeping you plenty busy. Morrie would probably kill me if I kept you from your work."

Shane frowned as an idea surfaced in his thoughts. It was an awful idea, but it was strangely compelling. "Chris, are you all right? Is someone with you?"

"I'm fine, I told you. I'm alone. Why do you ask?"

"You sound... I don't really know. You sound like you're afraid."

She laughed again, that high, forced laugh that sounded so unnatural coming from her. "You're imagining things. I'm a little stressed out, that's all. Things have been crazy since the show. Everything's fine. Look, like I said, this was stupid. I was just feeling like chatting, taking a little sanity break, you know? Maybe we will get together for a drink again soon. I think I'd like that. Not tonight, though. Gotta take a rain-check. All right?"

Shane nodded to himself, slowly. "All right. You can call me anytime you want, Chris. I mean that. I like hearing from you. Do you believe me?"

There was another long pause. Shane could hear the wind blowing through the car, whistling and roaring. Christiana blew out a breath. "Yeah, I do," she said, sounding a bit more like herself. "And there's something I need you to believe, too, all right?"

"What's that?"

"I'm fine. Believe me when I say that. I'm a little shaken, yes, but that's no big deal. Life's a little crazy right now. Look at how pathetic I am. I've spoken to you, what, twice? Three times counting this phone call?"

Shane was perplexed. "Why's that pathetic?"

She laughed a third time, but there was no humor in it. "It's a long story. Maybe I'll tell you later. Not on the phone. I should get off now anyway. I'm about to get on the highway."

Shane shuddered again, but forced himself to keep his voice even. "Look, you can come over. I'd love it. I don't have any wine, but beer's in the fridge. I can grill us up something. Strictly business. Well, business and bratwurst. What do you say?"

"I gotta go, Shane," she said, distracted now. "I'll take you up on that soon. I promise. See ya."

"Wait—!" Shane said, almost barking into the phone, but she was gone. The whine of the wind through her car clicked off. He lowered the phone and stared at it, his eyes a little wild. He considered calling her back, was already reaching to press star sixty-nine for the automatic trace-back, but stopped himself. It wouldn't do any good. In her own way, Christiana was a lot like Steph. Once she'd made up her mind, there was no changing it. Slowly, as if in a daze, Shane placed the phone back onto its charger.

Outside the window, something moved. Shane glanced toward it, jumping in surprise. It was huge and brown, lumbering, pulling a plume of dust behind it: a UPS truck. Shane walked toward the window and leaned to peer out. The truck leaned and bounced as it descended the driveway. Shane could hear the sound of the radio coming out of the truck's open side door. The driver was listening to Rush Limbaugh.

Puzzled, feeling a disconnected sense of growing dread, he approached the front door. The morning's cool had burned away in the autumn sunlight, leaving the front porch stuffy and still as Shane stepped out onto it. Tom the cat lay in the far corner of the porch, dozing in the sunlight, his eyes slitted sleepily. He looked up at Shane and flicked his tail. There was a large, flat box leaning against the side of the cottage, half in the shade of the porch roof. Shane approached it slowly, that sense of dread creeping up his back, sinking deep, chilling him in spite of the afternoon heat. The front of the carton was split into two huge flaps, affixed with a long, neat strip of packing tape. Shane used a pen to split the tape. Gingerly at first, and then with mounting impatience, he pulled the flaps open, ripping the tape apart, tearing the flaps at the bottom. Sunlight poured into the carton, glaring on its contents. Shane stepped back weakly, dropping the pen onto the gravel drive.

It was the Riverhouse. The painting stood in the carton, neatly packed, with foam buffers affixed onto its corners. There was a note pinned carefully to the top right corner. Handwritten in neat blue ink, it read:

> *This painting is better suited to your River House than my house. I had the sense that you were reluctant to part with it, so consider this my gift. Cheers!*
> *Penn Oliver*
> *P.S. I want to see more of your work! Call me.*

Shane stared at the painting, and at the little note pinned discreetly to its corner. After a few minutes, he sighed deeply and carried the painting into the house. He left the carton on the porch, but didn't remove the note attached to the corner of the painting. Somehow, it just seemed appropriate to leave it there.

Unseen in the upper window on the east side of the cottage, almost hidden behind the lush leaves of the magnolia tree, a candle flame burned and flickered, flickered and burned.

Chapter Nine

The next morning, Shane stood in the front room with his coffee in hand, wearing only his boxers and a faded gray tee shirt. Mist rose beyond the windows, bright in the early sun. There was a distant thump and hum as the furnace in the basement switched on.

For a moment, he wondered if Penn Oliver was playing some kind of elaborate practical joke on him. He stared at the painting where it stood on the small mantel over the fireplace, his hand cupped to his jaw and his brow mildly furrowed. It was his painting, the Riverhouse, and yet it was different somehow. For several minutes he couldn't put his finger on what it was. It was like the afternoon when he'd discovered the abandoned footpath in the corner of his yard and then returned to realize that he'd drawn the footpath entrance into the painting the previous night. When he finally saw it, it was like an optical illusion clicking into place, like seeing the two black silhouetted faces instead of the white candlestick. Once he saw it, he couldn't *not* see it anymore. In the Riverhouse painting, the woman on the front portico wasn't alone; there was someone on the path approaching the house, someone coming to meet her. The second individual was not physically visible on the path—they were just outside the range of the painting—but their shadow was there, in the lower right corner, spilling across the foreground and forming an irregular shape on the arc of the brick driveway. Shane had no recollection of painting that shadow.

He stepped toward the painting and touched the bottom right of the canvas, brushed it lightly with his fingers. The ridges of dried paint were as hard as stone, as distinct as the whorls of a fingerprint.

He recognized the strokes of his medium sized sable brush. The shadow had obviously been placed there by his own hand. How could he have missed it before? The shadow changed the picture in a subtle but important way. When Shane had first painted the house, he'd added the woman on the portico simply for human interest—after all, a house without an occupant is just architecture. He hadn't known her name at the time, had simply meant to show her leaning in the sun, content with her work, a pair of gardening shears and a stack of neatly cut roses lying nearby. He'd painted her with one arm raised, her forearm crossed over her brow to shield her eyes from the sun. It had been meant to be a languid pose, but the shadow in the foreground transformed the pose entirely. Marlena was not just resting in the sun. She was looking up as someone approached, shading her eyes to see who it was. Suddenly, Shane remembered something Greenfeld had said when he'd first looked at the painting. "It's all just a stage," he'd said, sitting in his car and looking up at Shane. "The first act is about to begin, and she's going to be the main character. That's the point, right? Why's she sitting there, watching, waiting? Who's coming up the path, and what happens when they get there?" Greenfeld had apparently seen it immediately. Maybe everyone had. The unsettling thing was that Shane felt rather sure that, when he'd first painted the woman on the portico, he'd painted her with her head turned slightly, looking out of the left of the picture. Now, however, he saw that she was looking toward the right of the picture, peering into the foreground, toward something just out of sight. The setting sun cast a bar of impenetrable shadow under her raised arm, hiding her eyes, and yet she was unmistakably looking up, peering toward the source of the shadow, her expression mild, unreadable. It was a very slight difference, but it was unsettling. Had the painting always looked that way? For a fleeting moment, Shane wondered if he had sleepwalked again, unconsciously gathering his brushes and painting the shadow and the subtle shift in Marlena's pose. He hadn't awoken with paint on his fingers, however. And the paint on the canvas was bone dry. Obviously, this is how the painting had always appeared, and he had just never quite seen it. It was funny how one missed detail could change the story.

In the front room, Shane shook his head slowly. He'd known the muse could be tricky. He hadn't known that she could be secretive.

Later that morning, Shane painted. His shift came and went and he made some decent headway on the fourth of the Florida paintings. He was two-thirds of the way done with the series, and was very pleased with himself. At this rate, he'd be done well before the deadline. Greenfeld would probably have kittens, he'd be so delighted. More importantly, however, the Florida paintings were *good*. They were simultaneously campy and edgy, colorful but cohesive. The foreman in Shane's head was back on the job, calling out direction with his mental megaphone, telling Shane's right hand where to go, and what to do when it got there. It had taken a little while for the foreman to hit his stride again, but things had finally clicked. Everything was jake. At two-thirteen, Shane stopped, cleaned up, and went downstairs for some lunch.

A little while later, he went for a bike ride.

He thought very little as he pedaled. The air was cool and bright, with beams of stark sunlight cutting through the trees, lighting the foliage like fireworks. The path was carpeted with fallen leaves. Red, yellow and green crunched gaily under his wheels as he sped on, leaning into the turns, watching the river where it lay like a giant brown ribbon in the valley. He made it to the grassy floodwall of Bastion Falls and turned around immediately, right where the path crossed the road in front of the open floodgates.

He stood on the pedals and pumped, gaining speed, pushing himself forward and leaning hard on the turns. His thighs sang with the effort. Vaguely, Shane realized that when he rode like this, he was usually trying to outrun something. Today, what he was outrunning was Christiana. Her last phone call replayed over and over in his head, mingling unsettlingly with his recent thoughts about Stephanie, James Herk, the Spring Garden, and the Paddington Bear rattle. Other than the fact that they were both women and somewhat stubborn, Stephanie and Christiana had almost nothing in common. Stephanie had been fair and blond, so skinny that she was almost bird-like, single-minded and possessed of a sort of innate confidence that struck most people as arrogance. Christiana, on the other hand, was dark, athletic, and random, filled with equal parts self-doubt and unshakable determination. Still, the two women were uncomfortably linked in his thoughts, emerging repeatedly like jokers in a trick deck of cards. *Maybe I'll tell you later, not on the phone,* Christiana had said, sounding eerily like Steph during her final phone call. *I should get off now anyway. I'm about to get on the highway.*

Shane shut off his thoughts again. He was getting somewhat good at that. He rounded another curve and the river swung into view, bright and brown, lying low in its banks. Dragonflies darted out over it, chasing their reflections, glittering greenly, as if they were made of recycled beer bottles.

Near the end of his ride, Shane passed the lot where the Riverhouse had once stood. He slowed and coasted, squinting in the lowering sun. The city had converted the lot into a sort of storage facility for the Parks and Recreation crews. Huge concrete blocks had been erected on the weedy lawn, forming low walls and dividers. The dividers enclosed mounds of mulch, gravel and peat. Parked in the middle of the old brick driveway was a yellow front-loader, its bucket raised. Shane stopped his bike on the path and leaned on one foot. He was interested to see that the foundation of the house itself had been left undisturbed. The yard was stitched with the tracks of the front-loader where it had navigated around the storage bunkers, but the cellar of the Riverhouse, now packed with dirt, looked completely untouched. Curiously, no weeds had even begun to grow on it. The remaining portico floor caught the sun and threw it back blindingly. From his position on the bike path, Shane could just make out the circular scars where the pillars had once stood.

For a moment, the sunlight illuminated something in the air over the portico. It glinted, almost as if it were shining on some tall, invisible shape. Shane blinked and frowned. His mind was playing tricks on him. For a moment, he seemed to see sunlight reflecting off of tall windows and drawing pencil-thin highlights down the necks of pillars. High up, taller than the trees themselves, something glimmered, forming a small round shape, like a decorative window, almost like the secret window on the east side of his cottage. Shane armed sweat off his forehead and swiped at his eyes; they were dazzled in the sun, that was all. When he looked again, there were no phantom shapes in the air over the old foundation.

A crow launched from one of the trees that bordered the right side of the driveway. Shane watched it flap up and out over the yard, heading toward the river beyond. Interestingly, it seemed to bank suddenly, to wheel around in a long arc. For a moment, Shane thought it looked as if the crow was avoiding the airspace over the dirt-filled cellar. He smiled to himself and shook his head. That was crazy, of course.

He stepped on the pedals and pushed on, entering the shadow of the trees, leaving the Riverhouse, and his chasing thoughts, behind him.

There was a car in the turn-off next to the cottage, parked crookedly next to Shane's pickup. Shane saw it sitting in the sun as he navigated his bike up the gravel drive. It was a Pontiac Bonneville, huge and old, with brown fleck paint and a cream hardtop. Its fat chrome bumper tossed the sun back and forth like a mobster flipping a quarter. Shane furrowed his brow, scanning the yard, but no one seemed to be there. He coasted, slowed, and then hopped off the bike and pushed it the rest of the way toward the cottage.

"Mr. Bellamy!" a voice called. It came from the shadow of the porch. Shane shaded his eyes with his hand and saw a thin figure standing there, peering out at him. "Hey Mr. Bellamy! It's me, Brian. We came out to see how you're getting along," he turned and glanced aside, toward someone Shane couldn't see. "Here he comes. He was on his bike, that's all."

There was a mumbled response and another figure moved in the shadow of the porch. Shane smiled, recognizing Earl Kirchenbauer, the old man from the rest home in Bastion Falls. He had been sitting on the porch's single piece of furniture, a very old metal lawn chair with flaking red paint. It creaked as he pushed himself to his feet, leaning on his cane. He glared out at Shane, his expression unreadable in the shadows.

"Hi Brian," Shane called, waving a hand. "And hi to you, too, Earl. What a nice surprise."

The old man didn't respond. Brian glanced back at his grandfather, and then returned his gaze to Shane. "Sorry, Mr. Bellamy. I hope we didn't freak you out or anything. It was Grandpa's idea. I think he wanted to make sure you were keeping all the cracks spackled up nice or something,"

"Shut up, boy," the old man said mildly, then to Shane, "Hope you don't mind us dropping by. Just wanted to see how you're faring out here is all. Looks like you've been keeping the place up all right, for the most part."

Shane shrugged and armed sweat from his brow again. He popped the bike's kickstand and approached the porch. "There's not a whole lot to do, frankly. The place is small enough that it sort of takes care of itself."

"That so?" Earl said, unsmiling.

"You two want something to drink? I've got beers and water and a few cans of Coke."

"Beer's good for me," Brian said, nodding and smiling.

"Beer will probably do us all good," Earl agreed. "But not inside. Let's sit out back, assuming you've kept the patio cleared off. I recall it used to get pretty chock full of leaves and twigs this time of year."

Shane caught the man's eye, saw that he was studying him critically. "Just swept it off yesterday, as a matter of fact. Come on through. There're only two chairs back there, but I can sit on the wall."

As they cut through the narrow alcove into the kitchen, Shane sensed Earl looking around sharply, his bushy eyebrows low and furrowed.

"Looks nice," Brian said. "Small, but comfy. A lot better than the last time we were here, right Grandpa?"

Earl didn't reply. Brian didn't seem perturbed. "You decorate the place yourself, Mr. Bellamy?"

"My wife did," Shane answered, popping the tops off his last three bottles of St. Pauli Girl. "Sorry, guys, looks like first call is also going to be last call here at Bellamy's bar and grill. I don't often entertain, so I'm a little short on suds."

"If I'd have known I'd have brought some with me from the store," Brian answered magnanimously, taking the proffered bottle. "In fact, if you want me just to drop off your groceries sometime, I'd be happy to. It's only a few minutes—"

"Man can carry his own groceries, Brian," Earl interrupted, heading toward the sliding glass doors. "Leave him be. Come on and quit prattling. There'll be enough of that outside."

Shane followed Earl out into the sun again. Despite his previous efforts, a thin carpet of leaves had already collected on the stone floor of the patio. They formed a small drift in the corner of the low wall, next to the barbecue. Earl tilted a look up at Shane but didn't say anything. The three sat down, Earl and Brian on the deck chairs, Shane on the low stone wall. The stone was very cool in the lowering sunlight.

"Place looks good," Earl said, gesturing with his beer bottle. "Nice to see it being used and all."

"I'm glad you think so," Shane replied. "Seeing as you used to maintain it."

Earl nodded slowly, not meeting Shane's eyes. "You found the old trail, I see."

Shane blinked. "Oh. Yes. The path that used to connect the properties. I did. I've been clearing it out again."

Earl finally looked at Shane, his eyes bright and his brow lowered. "You have, have you?"

Shane nodded. "Sure. It's nice for walking. Not very long, but scenic. Of course, you know that. I'm sure you've walked it a hundred times."

The man grinned, showing a lot of yellow dentures. "You'd think so, yes. Truth is, I've never set foot on that trail. Nobody did. We weren't allowed."

Shane frowned. "Weren't allowed?"

"That trail was the domain of Mr. and Mrs. Wilhelm and invited guests, period. It was mostly him that used it. Us grunts had to take the long way around every time. He said he didn't ever want to pass us on the trail, uglying it up and turning it into a thoroughfare."

"That's pretty selfish," Shane said. "The path probably cuts fifteen minutes off the trip. That would have been especially important back in the day, before you guys had access to golf carts, like you see all the maintenance guys using nowadays."

"Oh, we had us a truck for the trip," Earl sighed. "Wilhelm bought it and kept it in a barn to the right of the drive. It was an old model A, with only one working gear and no reverse, and it used to get hotter than hell in the cab, especially after it'd run for more than a few minutes, but we used it, sure enough. Point is, we didn't want to be seen on that trail. We kept as far away from it as possible." He eyed Shane.

Brian chuckled. "Didn't want to be running into the boss, I guess. I know how that is."

Shane didn't think that was quite what Earl had meant, but the old man didn't contradict him. He was still looking at Shane, unsmiling, his eyes bright. Shane smiled crookedly back at him. "See something green?"

Earl's face remained impassive. "Nope. I was just thinking."

"What were you thinking about?"

"About what it was you were wanting to ask me that day when you came to see me."

Shane frowned and looked out over the river. "I was just curious about the old place, that's all. I did a little research online, but couldn't find much. I mean, I found plenty of information about Wilhelm, about his career and his art, but nothing about the house or the cottage. Then Brian here told me you used to work out here, back when it was all first built. I came to see you, but... well, you made it seem like my questions were best left unanswered." Shane looked back at Earl. "Since then, I've pretty much put it out of my mind."

Earl cracked a grin and then laughed. He slapped his knee with the hand that wasn't holding his beer. After a moment Brian grinned and joined in, laughing alongside his grandfather. Shane smiled but didn't laugh.

"Put it out of your head, did you?" the old man wheezed. "I just bet you did. Good for you."

"Well," Shane replied, still smiling but feeling a little piqued. "I was just taking your advice if you recall."

"Oh, I recall what I said. I'm just not used to other people listening. Not at my age." Earl drew a deep sigh and let it out, still grinning. He took a swig of his beer, emptying a third of it.

"Truth is," Shane went on, "I'm a little surprised to see you out here. I had the impression you'd be happy never to see the place again."

Earl shrugged one shoulder. "Oh, I never minded the cottage. It was the house I hated. Now that that's gone, I expect the rest doesn't matter. I thought about it after you left. Decided I'd been a little too testy with you, maybe. Truth is, I changed my mind. I decided a little knowledge might actually do you some good. Forewarned is fore-armed. That's what we used to say during the war."

Shane nodded slowly. "Fair enough, I guess. I don't want to shake any skeletons out of any old closets or anything, if that's what you were worried about. This is my home now. I was just interested in learning about its past."

Brian swirled his beer and laughed ruefully. "You mean besides the insanity stairs and the bottomless pit?"

"Hush, boy," Earl said quickly. "Can't you see he don't know about all that stuff? Let the man enjoy his bliss awhile. We'll come to that, if he wants. Leave it up to him."

Shane glanced between the two of them. "Bottomless pit?"

Earl closed his eyes and shook his head, not dismissively, but impatiently. "Fool's talk, that's all. The poor Missus had her... let's call them her fetishes. When she got older, some of the furniture in her mind started coming loose and sliding around. Like I said, we'll get to that if you want, though I'll warn you, I don't know any of it first-hand. You'd have to talk to Stambaugh to get any real dirt on those years, and if you remember him, you'll know his days of giving interviews are long over."

Shane did remember Stambaugh, remembered him slouched almost double in a wheelchair, being fed tapioca in dribbling spoonfuls. It was an unpleasant memory. "Tell me what you do know, then," he said. "Whatever you want. I'll just listen."

"Heh," Earl chuckled humorlessly. "Problem's not what I *want* to tell you, but what it's *safe* to tell you. But like I said, I'm probably just being old and foolish. Wouldn't be the first time. The house's gone now, chopped down to a hole in the ground. Good riddance..." His voice trailed off and his eyes roamed out over the river. "Good riddance to bad rubbish. That's another thing we used to say during the war. I wasn't in the war, of course. Bad back and crummy eyesight. Most of my friends went, though. A few of them even came back. That was later, though. When the war started and everyone left, that's when I first came out here. It was the spring of forty and I'd just turned twenty four. The Great Depression was ten years old by then and work was still hard to come by. That's what brought me out here that day. Word around town was that Wilhelm had lost some of his groundskeepers to the draft. I came out here and lied about why I wasn't going to the war myself. I was afraid if he knew about my back and my eyes, he'd never hire me. I told him I'd been granted a special circumstance because I was the last boy in my family and my mother was on her sickbed. Truth was, I had four kid brothers and my mother worked ten hours a day at the textile mill downriver, but Wilhelm didn't check out any of my story. He was barely listening. He just pointed to a group of men working on a stone wall around the back of the house and told me to go help them. He said to me, 'If you're still upright at the end of the day, and those men say you're worth my dollar, I'll start paying you tomorrow. Today, you prove yourself.'

"I worked like a mule until sunset, and my back was singing the Spanish aria by the time I was done, but I never let on. The next day, I came back and started it all over again. I was never officially hired, but no one ever told me to go home. At the end of the week, Wilhelm gave me twelve dollars fifty, and that was my pay for the next two years, until he went ahead and promoted me to chief groundskeeper. I think he suspected I had troubles with my back, although I never once complained. As chief of the grounds, I had a lot less to carry with my back, but a lot more to carry with my mind. I was up to it, though, and that's when I really started learning how things worked in the house. That was when I first formally met the Missus, and started understanding the gears that that marriage turned on. They weren't happy gears, let me tell you. Maybe that's true for most families, when you get right down to the nitty-gritty, but it's still an ugly thing to see up close. I learned a lot more than I wanted to, but back then, secrets were a thing we kept. Back then, what a man did in his house, even a man as famous as Gus Wilhelm, well, that was his business. We saw it all, but we didn't really see any of it, if you know what I mean. Loose lips sink ships. Heh. I bet even Brian here remembers that one."

Shane watched the old man as he spoke. Earl seemed to sink into the words as he said them, as if he was reconstructing the memory around him, settling deep into it. Shane's artist's mind could easily imagine Earl Kirchenbauer as that young man of twenty-four, thin and tan, his glasses stuffed into his back pocket so no one would see them. Mentally, Shane erased the wrinkles, thickened the white hair and turned it glossy black, straightened the back and neck. Earl went on, and even his voice sounded younger, less raspy, void of that old man's gruffness. Even Brian seemed entranced.

The sun slowly lowered into the trees. The river turned first golden, and then deep copper. And on the patio, rapt and intrigued, Shane listened.

Chapter Ten

"The Wilhelms first came to the valley in the summer of thirty-three. I remember it was in the paper. Famous artist and his wife were coming to live among us, and they were bringing their artsy friends and all their money with them. We all had mixed feelings about it, but not *too* mixed. Like I said, those were the days of the Depression, and anything that looked like work was welcome. Those were the days when men rode the rails from town to town, looking for anything they could do for a buck. Paint fences, hoe gardens, lay bricks, anything. My own father took that road, and we never saw him again. He left on a Monday morning when I was seventeen, walked down to the train yard with his friend Clete, each one carrying a lunch pail and a change of clothes wrapped in a bindle. They said they'd find some work and send home what they could. We never did see any money come in the mail, and we never saw my father again, neither. My brothers were just kids at the time, but they were wise to the ways of the world. They thought father had just run off, but they didn't know him like I did. I didn't think he'd just run off. I thought something bad had happened to him, out there in the hobo camps and Hoovervilles. People say things are bad nowadays, what with people shootin' one another over a pair of hundred dollar shoes, but things were a different kind of bad back then. Back then, people'd kill each other for a pair of leather boots, not because they wanted to, but because they were desperate. That was the real ugliness of it. Half the time, you couldn't even hate the people who'd done the crime. Half the time, you were only one step away from being them yourself.

"When Wilhelm and his caravan came into town, we didn't throw any parties, but we didn't throw any stones either. We just watched. He'd picked himself out that lot down by the river, already had it cleared so he could set about building his house. He hired mostly local fellows to do the construction, but the foreman and the crew leaders were all New Hampshire men that had come with him from up north. He'd hired them to come down and stay while the place was built. The first thing they built was this very cottage, and they used it as a dormitory while they finished the main building. Wilhelm had planned it all out. In the beginning, the cottage was the anchor, holding everything together while they built the house, and in the end, the cottage was still the anchor, so far as he was concerned. It was his studio, where he did all his work, where he even slept two, three times a week. For Wilhelm, this was the real heart of the place. This cottage was his real home. The manor house was his showpiece, the thing he presented to the world to prove he was one high and mighty lord of the earth, but this cottage was his true castle. This was where he holed up, where he fortified himself. When he was working, no one else was allowed inside, except for his models, when he wanted them. Even when he wasn't here, he had a general rule that no one was allowed inside without his specific instruction. That went for the Missus as well, and she abided by that rule, oh yes. That was the tragedy of the place, if you ask me. But I'm getting a little ahead of myself. Let me back up.

"Wilhelm met the Missus back when they were still in Washington. She was one of his models, when he was still struggling to get a name for himself, before he got famous and rich and arrogant. Well, truth was, he was always arrogant, according to the stories. Arrogance is free, after all. Back then, I suppose that's about all he could afford. He was doing portraits for some senators and local politicos. Sometimes he painted the families, but more often than not, it was usually just the women, the wives and mothers. Wilhelm was doing them for next to nothing, just to get his work out there. I think the men who hired him did it as much to shut their wives up as they did it for the paintings themselves. Wilhelm had a way with the ladies. He could get them excited about him and his work, and they'd go to their husbands, talking him all up, begging to get family portraits made. Problem was, the men that hired him knew Wilhelm was a charmer. They didn't want their wives sitting with the fellow for hours and days at a time while he painted them. Wilhelm promised he'd only need one quick session with the ladies, though. He'd sketch them in their homes and paint them later in his studio. There, he'd more often than not hire girls to come in and pose for the portraits, painting their bodies with the other ladies' faces on them. Sometimes he'd hire prostitutes for the job, other times local teenagers eager for any sort of work that didn't require them to get on their knees, either for scrubbing floors or... well, you get the picture. Marlena Havelock was one of those girls. According to the old ladies that used to run the museum at the house, she fell in love with Wilhelm immediately, but I have my doubts about that. I watched them together over the years I worked here, and I'll tell you what I saw.

"Wilhelm was a man who was used to being adored and admired. He very nearly commanded it from people. And the funny thing was, most people *wanted* to give it to him. There was just something about him that made you want to get on his best side, made you feel that if he liked you, approved of you, that some of him would rub off on you. Even the workers here at the property, they used to cuss him up one side and down the other when he wasn't around, but whenever they were in his presence, it was another thing entirely. It was like he was made out of something other than plain old flesh and bone, like his blood had something magic in it, something from the old stories about the Greek gods and goddesses. You wanted to get some of that for yourself, or at least be near it. That was the effect Wilhelm had on people. Like they always say: women wanted to be with him, and men wanted to be like him. But Marlena was different. I don't think she loved him right away. I couldn't tell you how I knew that, since I wasn't there when they met and courted and got married, but I saw them later. I saw the way she looked at him, and the way he *didn't* look at her. Marlena was a proud woman, tall and pretty and severe, but when he was around, she went soft. He'd beaten her. Not with his fists, mind you. I never once saw him raise a hand against her, or anyone else, for that matter. Wilhelm didn't beat people with his fists. Sometimes I think it'd have been better if that was all he'd done.

"I think when she first met him, he disgusted her. I bet you a million dollars that she thought he was one uppity son of a bitch the first day she saw him, there in his rented room in the city. I bet she did the job all right. I mean, how hard could it have been? All she'd had to have done was sit still for a few hours. He wasn't even painting her face, so she coulda looked out the window the whole time, or closed her eyes and daydreamed, anything she wanted. But

I'd bet my right eye that when it was all over, she took his dollar and left without hardly a word. And I'll raise that bet with another: I'll bet that that annoyed the ever-loving hell out of Wilhelm. Because like I said, he was used to being adored. He thrived on it. He didn't paint all those portraits for the money, after all. The money was just a fringe benefit. Wilhelm painted so that people would love him and tell him how almighty great he was. It was like a drug to him. I think Marlena wasn't impressed by him, and it made old Wilhelm crazy. I think, for a fellow like Gus Wilhelm, if the praise isn't unanimous, it doesn't count. If the rest of the world cheers and one person boos, the boo is all he'd hear. I think he pursued her from that day on. Maybe it was love. Maybe it was as close to love as a guy like Wilhelm could ever get. Even so, deep down, I think his love for her was never really anything more than misdirected love for himself.

"So he chased her. He chased her all the way to New Hampshire when her family moved her out there. Up and left his Washington art career in the same way that he'd left his New York art career a few years earlier. Of course, by then, he was finally beginning to get the renown he'd always dreamed of, and his reputation started following him around. In New Hampshire, he vowed to Marlena that he'd win her love with a major contract. He made her promise him that she'd marry him if he could take care of her in the way that she deserved. She agreed, and I think by then she really was falling in love with him. Women will do that, you know. They'll fall in love with the worst bastard in the world sometimes, if he's around long enough, and persistent long enough. Hell, sometimes I think being a bastard is the best way to get women to flock to you. If I'd have known that when I was a young man, I might have fared differently myself. Heh. Maybe not, but it's the truth no matter how you slice it. Worst thing about most women is the men they choose to hitch themselves to.

"So Wilhelm went out and got himself that contract. Like I said, his reputation had followed him. The New Hampshire art world was a lot easier to break into than it was in Washington, and Wilhelm got himself in good graces with enough of the right people that he got an appointment with the governor. The governor took one look at Wilhelm's work, especially a portrait he'd done of President Wilson, and hired him to do a whopping huge portrait of the whole family for the state capital. Wilhelm insisted on painting them outdoors, the governor and his wife and their three young kids.

There used to be a big print of it in the main house, in the days when it was a museum. Wilhelm had even included the family's dog in the picture, a pissant little ratty thing with eyeballs that looked like marbles jammed into the sides of its head. When he finished it, the portrait was twelve feet tall, and so far as I know, it still hangs in the New Hampshire capitol building to this day. That cemented Wilhelm's career, not only in New Hampshire, but all over the country, at least among certain people.

"Soon enough, he went back to Marlena, this time with a ring. She was as good as her word, and they were married in the summer of twenty-nine, when she was only nineteen years old. Wilhelm was nearly thirty by then, but nobody cared about such things back in those days. Back then, that was pretty much the norm. He was older and established. He could take care of her. Her family was happy to approve of the marriage. Wilhelm and Marlena moved into a big house in the country, all built out of solid New Hampshire granite, and the old ladies in the museum said that the two were happy there, at least for awhile. And who knows? Maybe they really were. I doubt it, though. By that time, Wilhelm had beaten Marlena. Not with his fists, like I said, but that didn't make it any better. She'd finally loved him. He'd beaten her by making her fall for him, making her finally give him her heart and her adoration. By then it was too late for her to realize that that was all he'd ever really wanted from her. Not to *accept* her love, but just to be offered it, just like everyone else always did. He never really wanted her affection. He just needed her to want to give it. Once she'd done that, he was done with her. She was beaten.

"Trouble was, love was a one-way street for her. She was like that blasted old model A truck Wilhelm bought for the grounds crew. She didn't have any reverse. Once she'd fallen in love with him, she was stuck there. It didn't matter what he did with her love. Most of the time, what he did with it was nothing. But she just kept offering it. She was helpless not to. It was a sad thing to watch. It was almost a perversity. I've seen plenty of women in my time willing to offer up their bodies to men who didn't care, and that was bad enough. To watch a woman, especially a woman as strong and beautiful as Marlena Wilhelm, offer up her *heart* to a man who just didn't care... who didn't even invest enough time in her to scorn her, who just ignored her straight up... well, that was almost like a blasphemy.

"She stayed in New Hampshire while Wilhelm came out here to build the new house. He called it the River House and he'd designed most of it himself. It had been his idea to move out here from the beginning. He said he wanted to build 'a community of the arts'. A place where artists of all kinds could come and stay and create. What he really wanted, I expect, was to be adored by an all new group of people. He'd won over the art buyers, the important men in high places, and now he wanted to win over his fellow artists as well. He came to Missouri because it was right in the middle of the country, easy to get to by anyone from anywhere. I suppose he picked the river valley because it was pretty. Not that he thought so himself, mind you, but because he thought everyone else would. Land was cheap enough then, and he bought up this whole plot south of the river, from here right up to the city limits. Once he finished the cottage and the house, Marlena finally came down to join him. She moved in and started to set up housekeeping. Wilhelm was fussy about the outside of the place, about the grounds and the trail, the gardens and the main barn, and especially about this cottage, but he left the inside of the main house to her. She was an artist herself. Not many people remember that, but it's true. She painted sometimes, even did a little sculpture, but once she moved into the house, it became her canvas. She decorated it all herself. She'd go on long shopping vacations, picking up bargains and treasures all over God's green earth. She'd be gone for months at a time, and when she'd get back, she'd be accompanied by whole truckloads of things, especially at the beginning. She was smart, though, and never paid more than she had to. Hell, half the time she barely paid anything at all. The trick back then wasn't finding the bargains, it was getting to them, and having the wherewithal to carry them back with you. She was good at that, and shrewd as the devil. Never really stopped working on the house, from the day she moved in. She hired workers to come in and make little changes and additions, to put in doorways here, close them off there. And she always watched them work, watched them like a hawk. Most of the men I worked with assumed she watched just to assure herself she wasn't getting ripped off, but I thought different. I thought she watched because she wanted to know how the work was done, almost as if she wanted to learn how to do it herself. She was that shrewd and careful with the money. If she could do any of the labor herself, she wasn't above getting in there and doing it, even if it meant getting dirty and looking unladylike. Of course, in the end, that was a big part of the problem. That didn't come until much later, though. We'll get to that in good time, if you decide you really want to hear it.

"I was working out here by then, of course, but even before I got to being here full time, I'd heard the rumors. They flew all over town. The Wilhelms were the richest and most famous thing to happen to Bastion Falls in forever, and they were always the juiciest gossip, even if we all knew most of it was only half true, at best. Plenty of crazy things did go on out here, especially in the summers, when Wilhelm opened the house and property up to his gaggle of artist friends. 'The Wanderers', they all called themselves. They'd come out and stay for weeks and months on end, living in the house, or in rented canvas tents when the weather allowed it. They'd drink and smoke and whoop it up all night long, and sleep until noon more often than not. Not Wilhelm himself, of course. That man probably did sleep sometimes, but I never knew right when he did it. He had a bed upstairs in his studio, and I expect he took naps sometimes, when he wasn't using the bed for other shenanigans. He painted all through the night, though, often enough. He was one hell of a night owl, that man. Once I became the chief groundskeeper, I was expected to stay late on some nights, especially when the parties were in full swing. Wilhelm thought of me as something like his right hand man on those nights. It was my job to keep the barrels filled with ice and beer, to manage the cook and make sure none of those dandy ladies and gentlemen guests of his wandered off drunk and dunked themselves into the river, or capsized Wilhelm's prissy little rowboat, or got lost in the woods. Most of the time I had my hands plenty full, just keeping tabs on everyone, keeping the bonfire going, carrying loads of dishes and tureens from the kitchen to the patio and back. Wilhelm had brought his own cook with him from New Hampshire, an old colored woman named Clara, and she cooked from sun-up to dark those days just trying to keep up.

"They were wearisome times, but they were also kind of exciting, truth be told. Somehow, we all knew that we were seeing something not many people saw, watching a lifestyle most other people could only dream of. Those artists were some of the most self-centered, strange, empty-headed people one would ever expect to meet, and at the same time, they were some of the smartest, saddest, most generous folks I'd ever known as well. One time, a fellow by the name of Clearwater took me aside and told me he needed to be sick. He said it as if he was telling me it would soon be half past two in the afternoon, as calm and debonair as you please. He'd been smoking something and drinking heavy and could barely keep his feet under him, and yet he talked like he was giving a speech in front of Jesus and the saints. I led him to the downstairs bathroom and Clearwater bent at the waist as if he was going to bow. He was sick in the commode, wiped his mouth, and turned to me with tears in his eyes. Next thing I know, he falls into my arms and starts a-bawlin' on my shoulder, just as free and shameless as a baby. He just keeps saying the same name over and over. I remember it to this day. 'Wendy' he says, again and again, just sobbing and crying, his nose running and mixing with his tears. I was a little disgusted, but mostly I was just sad for him. I didn't know what it was about, not then and not now, but when he was done, he straightened, blew his nose and sat down on the commode, shivering a little. 'Do you have a daughter,' he asks me then. I didn't, but I had a boy, Sammie, Brian's uncle. 'Do me a favor someday, will you?' Clearwater says to me. And he reaches into the pocket of his jacket and hands me a gold watch on a chain. 'Give this to him,' he says to me. 'Don't tell him where it came from. Tell him you found it somewhere. Tell him you got it for him special. Tell him to keep it forever. Will you do that for me, Earl?' I could tell he meant it, and that it really wasn't a gift he was giving to me, or to little Sammie. That watch was probably worth more than I made in six months, and yet I knew by the way he asked me that he wasn't just being nice to me. It was me doing *him* the favor. I could see it in his eyes, red and swollen as they were. I didn't balk. I took that gold watch and put it in my pocket and I promised Clearwater, as truthful and honest as I knew how, that I would do exactly as he asked. He nodded and shuddered and a minute later he shook my hand with both of his. Next thing I knew, he was outside again with his friends, laughing and whooping it up with the best of them.

"Fourteen years later, on Sammie's graduation day, I did give him that watch. I told him it was a gift from me and a family friend. That's all he needed to know. Brian here knows the truth now, but I trust him to keep it a secret. After all, since Sammie never had himself any kids of his own, that watch might go to you someday, boy. Fact of the matter is that it'll probably mean more knowing where it really came from. But if you tell your uncle, I'll whup you good. Don't think I can't still do it, either.

"Lot of rumors flew around town during those summers. Some of them were true, a lot of them weren't. A few, even I didn't

The Riverhouse

know for sure. Some people said that Wilhelm himself was a dandy, that he'd married Marlena to keep it a secret, but that he and his male models had themselves a little hanky-panky up in the studio sometimes. If that was true, all I know is that Wilhelm was the original equal opportunity employer. He had his share of ladies up there, too. Most of them were models. He hired them just like he did back when he first met Marlena, only by then he was doing it to create his own art, not portraits. None of the stuff he did for himself was ever as good, or as famous, as his portraits, but by the time I was working out here, that was most of what he was doing. He painted those women and men in the nude more often than not, usually draped on the furniture in his studio with a bunch of cloth pinned up behind them and the sun falling all over them from the open window over the stairs. Sometimes he had several models up there at once, and posed them altogether. Disgusting, a lot of the men I worked with said, and I suppose it was, but I never said so myself. He was the boss, and as his groundskeeper and occasional right hand man, it behooved me to keep some semblance of loyalty out in the open. After all, once the men started seeing me bad-mouth the boss, it was only a matter of time before they'd start bad-mouthing me as well. When that happens, everything else goes pretty much straight to hell.

Marlena knew about Wilhelm and his affairs. He wasn't particularly secretive about it, really. She hated it, but what was she going to do? Once, for her birthday, Wilhelm had the gall to give Lena—that's what he always called her; Lena, never by her full name—he had the gall to give her a little painting of one of the girls he'd been diddling with. I can't even begin to imagine what he was thinking. Honestly, I don't think it even occurred to him that she might be offended by it. Maybe he was arrogant enough to think she didn't even know. The end result was that she hurled that picture right out the front door on the day he gave it to her. I found it myself in the middle of the driveway, the frame broken and the glass all shattered. I tried to give it back to Wilhelm, but he told me to throw it away. I didn't. I kept it myself, and sold it a few years later, to an art dealer in downtown St. Louis. I suspect that if Wilhelm had ever found out I'd done it, he'd have fired me for sure, but he had his own distractions by then, and I had a good idea that my time there was nearly done anyway.

"The thing that finally brought everything to a head was the baby. Wilhelm wanted a son from the beginning, but Marlena hadn't been able to give him one. She'd gotten pregnant once, early on, while they were still in New Hampshire, but it hadn't taken. She'd miscarried the baby in the first few months, according to the old ladies who ran the museum. By the time they lived here, they'd begun to argue about it. I used to hear them sometimes, we all did, upstairs in the house. Wilhelm claimed that that was the only reason he was messing around with those other women. 'I'm just looking for someone to give me my son, Lena, someone to carry on after me,' I heard him say one of those times. 'If you can't do it, someone has to.' He said that if she was any kind of wife, she'd help him look for the proper substitute, like Sarah had done for Abraham in the Bible. Marlena begged him to keep trying with her. He said he would, but insisted it was no use, and he was getting too old to wait much longer.

"And that's when the ugliness really started. Word got around town that Wilhelm was looking to have a baby with whoever could give him one. Like I said, even though the depression was a decade old by then, those were still desperate times. For a lot of the girls in town, and even some of their families, the prospect of getting attached to Gus Wilhelm was close to what winning the lottery might be today. Women started showing up at the house, ostensibly looking for work as maids and cooks, but obviously trying to catch the eye of the man of the house, trying to hook his attention. Problem was, Marlena was in charge of interviewing the house help. She found herself in the very position she'd most detested. She might have been questioning a girl about her ironing skills and her ability to darn socks, but she also knew, on some level, that she might very likely be choosing the mother of her husband's child. She turned most of the girls away out of hand. After all, the house wasn't that big. There were only so many cook's assistants and maids the place really needed. But they did hire one local girl. Her name was Madeleine Cross, and I remember her very well because she grew up on the street behind my house. She was young and pretty, plump by today's standards, but that was considered the style back then. She was quiet, though. Quiet and serious, with black hair and dark skin—so much so that some of us thought she might have had a colored father, although none of us ever knew for sure, since he was long gone by then; run off, as far as any of us knew. Madeleine was hired as a maid, and she worked in the house exclusively. Marlena saw to that. Not that it did any good, though. Wilhelm liked the girl straight off. We all saw it. He wasn't especially subtle about it.

"I honestly don't know if Madeleine came out to the house intent on becoming Wilhelm's mistress. She was too quiet to ever let on one way or another. I've thought about it a lot over the years, and even now, I can't say for sure. I think maybe she just got carried along, like a log on the river when it's in full flood. Either way, once Wilhelm had set his sights on her, there wasn't much question that things would turn out any different than they did. Wilhelm was used to getting the things he wanted. Madeleine became one of those things. From that day on, nothing was ever really the same in the Riverhouse again. When Wilhelm started his affair with Madeleine, that was when the place started to die. We all felt it, and knew that the days of midnight parties and tent dormitories were almost over. Once Wilhelm started up with Madeleine, he didn't have a mind for much of anything else.

"In August of nineteen forty-four, Hector Wilhelm was born. It happened over the weekend, right there in the house. None of us ground crew were there that day. Clara was there, of course, since she pretty much lived there, and Madeleine was there, too. The first any of us knew of the baby was when we were coming to work on the following Monday. When I saw him, he was being held on the front stoop, crying his fool head off, that little squall that all babies have when they're still brand new. He had a bunch of black hair, even then, and a little red face and tiny fists the size of walnuts. And he was being held by Marlena. She was smiling. That was the thing that struck me most about the scene, even more than the baby himself. That smile on her face as she looked down at that baby, and then up at us who were coming in to work that day, and then down at the baby again. I didn't see Madeleine at all that day, and we all just assumed she was still getting herself together after the birth. After all, that's how it was all supposed to have worked out, why she'd come out to the house in the first place, regardless of whatever job she'd interviewed for. But that's where things start getting really hairy in this story. Because none of us knew for certain that Madeleine *had* been pregnant. Sure she'd put on a little more weight in recent months, maybe even enough to start some rumors, but you could hide an awful lot under those horrible maid uniforms and aprons. Fact was, none of us ever really could tell for sure. And to further complicate matters, both Wilhelm and Marlena claimed that that baby was their very own.

"I had to think back on it. The fact of the matter was that Marlena had been travelling an awful lot over the past months. None of us had hardly seen a wink of her. When she'd gotten back, only three weeks earlier, it had been late at night, and she had apparently been ill. She'd been in her bed most of the time since then, and none of us could even remember seeing her once during that time. Crazy as it sounded, it began to seem entirely possible that Marlena *had* been pregnant, at exactly the same time that the scuttlebutt had been going around about *Madeleine* being pregnant. For her part, Madeleine never said anything. Only person who ever had the gall to ask her about it was one of the gardeners, a young pup named Pickering. I wasn't there when it happened, but apparently Madeleine slapped him, almighty hard, right on the cheek, but standing there just as calm as a frozen pond. She told him she'd never been pregnant at all, and either way, she said, it was none of his cotton-picking business.

"I thought about asking Clara the cook, but I never did. If anyone in the house knew the truth, it was her. Hell, she'd probably mid-wifed that baby into the world with her own two hands. I had a feeling that she wouldn't admit to anything, either way. She was as loyal to the Wilhelms as paint is to a wall, and truth be known, she gave me the heebie-jeebies just a little bit. I know that sounds crazy, but there's no sense denying it. I never did ask her, and she never did tell.

"Hector got big fast. He was a strong baby, crawling by the end of his first year, babbling like a brook most of the time, shaking his rattles and tootin' his toy horns. Wilhelm loved that boy like he'd never loved anyone else in his life. He used to play records for the boy on the old Victrola in the den, cranking it up so loud that the whole house could hear. Wilhelm would dance around the living room and make that baby just cackle. It was sweet to see, in spite of everything, and for a little while, I'd begun to wonder if maybe everything was going to be all right after all. Marlena seemed happy enough, raising Hector, feeding him and reading to him, even though Madeleine had been appointed to be his nanny. Wilhelm had even begun sleeping in the house most nights, instead of staying out to all hours up at the cottage, painting and carousing. My boys and I had just finished putting in the new rose garden out back, and were getting ready to start shutting the house up for the fall, putting up the storm windows and getting the woodpile chopped and cut to length. There was even talk of inviting the Wanderers out for the summer again the next year, something that hadn't happened for two years in a row. They had scattered like dandelion seeds in the years since, like they always did whenever they weren't camping out in the front yard or in the woods between the house and the cottage, but I had no doubts they'd come back next spring if Wilhelm sent out the invitation.

That never happened, though. And the fall of forty-seven was my last year there at the Riverhouse. That was the year of the big spring flood, and the year that everything finally fell apart at the place. It took a long, long time for that damned house to finally die, but that was when the fatal blow fell, believe you me. And it happened right here, right in this cottage.

"Wilhelm had asked Madeleine to be Hector's nanny, like I said. It was a strange arrangement, we all thought, and yet Marlena herself seemed pretty much all right with it. The truth is, I think she thought she'd won after all. Whether or not that baby was really hers, she thought that the baby had brought Wilhelm back to her, that she'd finally captured his love. She believed that Madeleine was no longer a threat. Either Madeleine had failed to produce the baby Wilhelm had wanted, and Marlena had, or Madeleine had performed the service she had really been hired for, giving them the baby and allowing them to present it as their own. In either case, I think Marlena believed Wilhelm was done with that younger girl. Keeping her there was Marlena's way of proving, both to herself and everyone else, that she really had come out on top of the whole thing. She had helped Wilhelm get the son he'd so desperately pined for, and in so doing, she had captured his heart once and for all.

Unfortunately, none of that was true. Wilhelm *was* still seeing Madeleine. Only this time, he was doing it much more secretly. The bastard could be as cunning as the devil himself when he really wanted to be. It turned out he'd made up a system. Most days, he never saw Madeleine at all. He'd be outside, overseeing me and the grounds crew most mornings, then he'd be up here at the cottage by mid-afternoon. There was no telephone between the house and cottage, not then, and there was no way to communicate between the two. But that didn't stop him, of course, not when he was in the mind for dickens. That's when he came up with his little system. You see, the cottage here is on the highest point of the bluff, and when Wilhelm looked out the little round window on the east of the studio, the one that looked down toward the Riverhouse, he could see the peak of the main roof coming up just over the trees. It was at an angle to him, and there was another window, almost exactly the same size and shape as his own, built into the top of the Riverhouse, right over the porch. He could see that window from his own window up there in the studio. And someone standing inside that *other* window, down at the Riverhouse, if they leaned to the side and looked just right, they could see *his* window up atop the bluff. Wilhelm's system was very simple. He'd told Madeleine to check that window every night, before she left. The window was in the attic of the Riverhouse, but there was no problem getting up there. The attic was probably the biggest room in the whole house, full of trunks and crates and endless bits and pieces that the Missus had bought on her trips and never yet found a place for. You got up to it by an angled stair at the back of the house, over the kitchen. Madeleine checked every day, peering out that window in the attic just like Wilhelm had told her to. And when he was in the mood for some shenanigans, he had a very simple sign he'd give her. He'd light a plain white candle and set it in the window on his side. If Madeleine saw it, instead of walking back home to town that night, she'd go up the other way. She'd steal up the trail to the cottage and meet him.

"If Wilhelm had been content with that, things might have ended differently. He might have kept his little secret until he got bored with it, until he sent Madeleine away and found somebody else to amuse him, but he was getting older and flighty by then. No one knows for sure what he was really thinking when he decided to run away with Madeleine. Maybe it was true that she really was the mother of his son, Hector. Maybe what Marlena had thought was true for her—that giving Wilhelm the son he'd wanted had secured his love for her—maybe that was true in reverse. Maybe Madeleine really had been the boy's mother, and that had made Wilhelm fall in love with her. Maybe it broke his heart to see her acting as the nanny to the boy that really was her own flesh and blood. Then again, maybe Wilhelm had other reasons entirely. Maybe he'd finally gotten tired of the charade, of the fame and success. Some people—*most* people probably—just aren't wired to know how to handle that kind of thing. It spoils them from the inside out, takes all the flavor out of life. Hardly anyone believes that, of course, but I've seen it up close and personal. I remember it all. The parties and the drinking, all covering over the sadness and desperation. I remember Clearwater bawling on my shoulder like a baby, handing me a gold watch, begging me to take it, like it was a terrible burden, or some kind of mummy's curse. I've seen what success and fame does to people. Maybe Wilhelm was smarter than any of us gave him credit for. Maybe he wanted a chance to taste life for real, outside of the gilded cage he'd built for himself. Wouldn't surprise me one little bit. Either way, it happened on May eighth of that year, the day before the first major flood came to the Riverhouse, lapping right up over the patio steps and filling the cellar four feet deep. Took me and my men two weeks to clean it up afterwards, but we didn't say a word about it. Wilhelm was gone by then, and we figured we would be, too, soon enough. We were glad for whatever work the job still had to offer, slick and muddy and disgusting as it was. It was hard to feel sorry for ourselves, not when we were in the same house as poor Marlena.

"He'd left her a note. I only know that because the housekeeper, a woman we all called Mrs. Wren, told us about it. She'd seen the Missus reading it on the night Wilhelm left. She'd been standing there in the parlor, still as a stone and white as a sheet, reading that note, and Mrs. Wren said you could almost hear the poor woman's heart breaking. The note revealed everything: Wilhelm's continuing affair with Madeleine, the white candles in the window, and his plan to leave her forever, to leave her there, along with the Riverhouse and the cottage and everything in them. He was leaving her everything.

"But Wilhelm did take one thing with him. Besides Madeleine, he took the one thing that mattered most to him in the whole world. He took Hector, his son.

"Mrs. Wren told me that Marlena stood and stared at that note for two minutes straight, right there in front of the fireplace with the rain pouring down outside the tall windows. And then, all of a sudden, she let out something like a low scream—a sort of deep, gut-wrenching yowl, and she started toward the house's front door. She still had the letter in her hand, and by the time she got to the door, she was nearly running. She yanked that door open so hard it hit the wall and left a mark in the plaster, a deep dent in the shape of the door knob. She ran out into the rain, still picking up speed, her feet splashing in the grass as she rounded the house, heading toward the back. I knew where she was heading even if Mrs. Wren didn't. Marlena was heading for the trail, meaning to run all the way up the trail to the cottage. I don't think she could stop herself. I think she meant to find them if she could. Some part of her just got stuck on that tiny hope—that desperate hope that they had stopped up at the cottage for some reason, and were still there, Wilhelm and Madeleine and Hector. Maybe she thought that if she caught up to them, she could talk some sense into him. Maybe she thought she'd be able to say just the right word to change it all.

"I don't know if she made it all the way there that night, what with the rain and the mud and the rising floodwaters, but some part of me always kind of believed she did. I think she made it all the way up to this cottage, probably panting fit to fall over, wet to the skin, covered with mud and dead leaves. I think she made it inside, all the way up to the studio, her face probably covered with her own tears by then, though nobody'd be able to tell, wet as she was with all that rainwater. I always expected that she found the place empty and dark, except for thing. I knew Wilhelm, after all. I know what kind of man he was. I think she found that white candle still a-burning on the windowsill. He'd probably had it lit for Madeleine, lit it for her to follow as she carried little Hector there to meet him. And after she'd gotten there, he'd just chosen not to put it out. What did he care?

"And as crazy as this sounds—after all, I'd have no way of knowing this, no way at all—I don't think Marlena put that candle out either. I've seen her that way in my dreams sometimes. Truth is, part of me loved that poor woman. Not like she loved Wilhelm, mind you, and not more than I loved my own wife, but I loved her anyway, with a sort of pitiful, sad love. Because she didn't deserve none of what she got dealt. She may have gotten a little unhinged in the years afterward, and a lot of people may have made fun of her about that, but none of them knew her like I did. None of them saw what she'd gone through, and the loss she'd felt.

"In my dreams I used to see her standing there in front of that little round window, her face lit in the glow of that damned white candle. I'd see her looking out, thinking in her addled, fevered brain that maybe, just maybe, that candle was magic. Maybe if she kept it burning, it'd bring them all back to her. She'd of known it was crazy, but that wouldn't have mattered, not one little bit. By then, crazy was about all she had left to hold onto. Maybe that candle would bring them back to her, just like it'd brought Madeleine and Hector to Wilhelm as he'd waited there in his studio for the last time. In my dreams, I used to see Marlena just standing there in the dark, lit only by that little yellow flame, dripping rainwater onto Wilhelm's damned studio floor, still panting a little from her run up the trail, and she'd just be watching. That's all. She'd just be watching and waiting."

Earl finished his uncharacteristically long monologue and drew a deep sigh, as if the story had exhausted him. His voice had grown dry and rough again as he'd progressed, so that by the time he was done it had attained that gravelly rasp that is the strict domain of very old men and lifelong smokers. Shane shuddered as the evening wind cooled. It pushed aimlessly around the patio, rustling the leaves and singing momentarily in the back door screen. Brian had long since finished his beer, but both Shane's and Earl's were still a third full. Earl looked down at the bottle in his hand for a long moment, and then finally raised and emptied it expertly, his Adam's apple clicking up and down on his stubbly neck. In the wake of the story, Shane felt strangely detached, almost ethereal. After all, listening to Earl hadn't been like hearing a story he'd never heard before. A lot of the details had already been familiar to him, if only vaguely. The effect of Earl's story was similar to what someone might feel after watching half of a movie with the focus and sound out of whack, leaving the picture blurry and muffled, only to have the projectionist come back from a long bathroom break and fix the film, bringing everything into crisp, clear focus. Shane had known a lot of the general details already, had picked them up from his paintings and his dreams, from the secret osmosis of living with the ghost of Marlena herself. Very little of Earl's story had surprised him, not even the very end. Shane had found Hector's rattle in the woods, under the bench, probably dropped by the boy himself as the nanny, Madeleine, had carried him along the trail on that fateful night. Maybe Madeleine had heard the rattle drop, but had been in too much of a hurry to stop for it. Or maybe it had been raining even then, drowning out the sound of the little rattle. Maybe Hector himself had been crying, upset at being carried out into the darkening woods and the cold rain. Either way, the rattle had fallen, tumbled into the flowers growing around the bench, and Marlena had probably run right past it on her way up to the cottage, had likely splashed it or even stepped on it during her hectic passage. The rattle had lain there for the intervening decades, glittering hotly throughout dozens of summers, frozen in the dark of endless snowfalls, just waiting for Shane, of all people, to come along and find it in the science fiction year of two thousand nine. The ghost had recognized that rattle. It must have been an incredible shock for her to see it in Shane's fist that night, held up like a tarnished talisman. It must have struck her as deep magic; that familiar silver rattle, suddenly appearing in front of her. Shane wondered how much of her ghostly forbearance of him was due to the cosmic serendipity of that night in the sunroom, the night he'd happened to have that rattle in the pocket of his sweat pants. Maybe quite a lot.

Brian was the first to speak after Earl fell silent. "So how'd old Mrs. Wren know what the letter said?"

Shane expected Earl to snap at his grandson again, but he didn't. He was still staring down at the river below the bluff, watching as it gathered into dusk. "She didn't. Not for sure, at least not then. We all just sort of pieced it together for ourselves. Mrs. Wren knew about the windows and the candles, Wilhelm's damned system. She'd seen Madeleine sneaking upstairs every evening right before she left for home, seen her peeking askance out that window, looking for something. I expect one of those evenings, Mrs. Wren herself stole up there and peeked, too, after Madeleine had gone. She saw that candle probably, and figured it out. Later, Marlena told Mrs. Wren about the letter, of course. Those two women were about the same age, and Mrs. Wren was probably the closest thing the Missus had to a friend, even though she was a townie, like the rest of us. Later, after Wilhelm had been gone long enough to prove he wasn't ever coming back, Marlena told Mrs. Wren everything. She needed to tell someone, I expect, and Mrs. Wren was safe. She herself never told the whole story to anyone else except me, and that wasn't until some years later. And I never told anyone except the two of you. Never had much of a chance to, really. Nobody ever wanted to know about Marlena and Wilhelm in the beginning. Everybody seems to have pretty much forgotten about those early years, before the poor woman started slipping her gears. I think that's a big part of the reason I decided to tell you that old story, Shane Bellamy. When you first showed up at my door, I thought you were just like the rest of the muckrakers, come to dig up more stories about how the old lady went crazy, all shut up in that big house. That's all people care about nowadays. Once you'd left, though, I thought about it, and it dawned on me that you didn't know anything about all that. It occurred to me you really were just curious about the people, not the craziness, about Gus Wilhelm and Marlena herself, when the house was new and none of the ugliness had happened yet. I hope I was right about that, because if I wasn't, I'll feel like a damned fool."

Shane shook his head. "No, you were right, Earl. When we first came out here, my wife and I, the real estate agent told us a few stories about how the place had been rumored to be haunted, and said that there was an interesting story about the house itself, even though it had long since been sold off and converted into duplex apartments. She didn't tell us about any... what did you call them? Insanity stairs?"

Earl grimaced and pushed himself upright in his seat. "Probably not a surprise she left all that out. That stuff's only interesting if you don't live right on top of it. Your agent was probably Darcy Harrold, right? I know her from way back. She probably figured she'd have a harder time selling the place to you if you knew the real story about this property and the Riverhouse. Darcy may be a chatterbox, but she knows when to shut up when a sale is on the line, oh yes. She doesn't have those billboards with her picture on them up on the west side of town for nothing."

Shane stirred on the low stone wall. "You don't have to tell me any more than you want to, Earl. You've told me plenty already, and I'm grateful for it. But I do have two questions if you'll indulge me."

Earl looked up at Shane, his bushy eyebrows low on his brow. He nodded slowly, not really promising anything.

Shane drew a breath. "What ever happened to Wilhelm? Where'd he and Madeleine end up?"

Earl chuckled weakly. "Not here, that's all anybody really knows for sure. Some people say he wound up out west, in California. They say he'd changed his name and become some kind of art teacher out there, at U.C.L.A. or Berkeley or some such. There're stories about how he became a sort of pop culture icon in the sixties, the sage old hippie with his own harem of adoring teenage girls and pothead disciples. Every few years, some yarn goes around the locals that a long lost Gus Wilhelm portrait's showed up, found at some garage sale or flea market out west, painted long after he left our neck of the woods. Sometimes it's a portrait of Madeleine and Hector, all grown up and mysterious, signed by Wilhelm with his real name, like he was blowing a raspberry at history itself. One time, a decade ago—this one was my favorite—they said it was a portrait of Elvis that showed up, found in a storage garage in San Bernardino, complete with a diary and sketches by Wilhelm himself, penned in his own hand. Maybe those stories are even true, who knows? Point is, nobody knows for sure where he and Madeleine and Hector ended up. The stories come and go. People like me, people who were here back in the day, we really just don't care. Good riddance."

Brian nodded somberly. "Good riddance to bad rubbish."

Earl glanced at his grandson and smiled crookedly. "There's hope for you yet, boy." He leaned over and clapped Brian on the knee. For the first time, Shane noticed that Brian was not exactly the young man he had originally thought him to be. Despite his dead end job and talk of college, Brian was probably closer to thirty than twenty. Brian grinned at Earl, and Shane noticed something else: despite the gruff words and age difference, these two loved each other.

"All right, Mr. Shane Bellamy, we've talked your ear off long enough," Earl said, leaning back slowly in the deck chair. "You said you had two questions. Go ahead and ask the last one, if you want."

Shane considered it, and then looked the old man in the eye. "I understand why you might have hated Gus Wilhelm, Earl, after your story. I even get why there might be some bad blood between the town and the estate, considering everything, considering the rumors and scandal. But there's one thing I don't understand."

Earl studied Shane's face. Unsmiling, he said, "What's that?"

"Why did you hate the house so much? Why were you so happy when Riverhouse got torn down?"

"I'd have thought it was obvious," Earl said. His voice had degenerated into a deep rumble, almost a growl. Shane had a feeling that the man hadn't spoken so much in one sitting in decades. "I hated that goddamn place because of what it did to Marlena. It was all she had left after that bastard left her, like I said, and she clung to it like it was a life buoy. She clung to it even though it was poisoning her. It started sinking its fangs into her the moment she got that note, the moment she ran up to the cottage that night and found them gone, all gone. It never stopped killing her from that day on, and it was a slow death, believe you me. It was an outright torture. That house toyed with her and drove her mad, because it was Wilhelm's. You see that, right? It was like he'd left a part of himself there for her, locking her down, imprisoning her, teasing her and making her madder and madder every day. It took almost twenty years for it to finish its work, and by then, there was hardly anything left of her. By then, that house had grown fat on her madness, gotten huge and ugly and sprawling, and it had sucked her dry, sucked her right down to nothing but a used up husk. And then she was dead, and all that was left was that monstrosity of a house. It killed her. I hated that place because it killed her, and I had loved her. You understand that? Maybe I caught a little bit of her craziness, but even so, I don't deny it. Crazy is like that. It can be catching. That was part of what I was warning you about, Shane Bellamy, that day you came out to see me. I was trying to protect you, believe it or not. Because sometimes, crazy is catching. Sometimes crazy is as contagious as the goddamn plague."

Shane could tell that Earl was getting worn out. His original cantankerousness seemed to have rallied and reasserted itself, so that the old man looked even older now than he had when Shane had first seen him on the front porch, leaning on his cane and peering out at him. Brian stood and helped Earl get to his feet.

"I appreciate everything you've told me," Shane said, standing and leaning in through the back door, clicking on the yellow bug light. It chased back the twilight and lit Earl's and Brian's faces with its harsh glow. "I got more than I expected, to tell you the truth."

"That's how life is, ain't it?" Earl said, leaning on Brian's arm. "Ask for an inch, it'll give you a mile."

"I always heard that the other way around," Brian said, frowning a little. "I thought it was something about taking an inch, when people give you a mile, or something like that?"

"Shut up, boy," Earl said mildly, stepping through the sliding back door of the cottage.

Shane led them through the kitchen and breezeway, purposely standing between them and the front room. The dusk was gathering thickly in the cottage, and the only lights that were on were the overhead in the kitchen and the bug light out back, but Shane didn't want to take any chances. The last thing he wanted was for old Earl Kirchenbauer to see the painting of the Riverhouse sitting on the mantel over the fireplace, especially after the old man's comments about craziness being catching. He had a strong suspicion that that painting would be especially hard to explain. Brian and Earl didn't even glance in the direction of the fireplace, however. Shane followed them outside onto the porch, and watched as Brian led his grandfather to the passenger's side of the Bonneville. The door squeaked as Brian pulled it open, and the interior light popped on, lighting the front seat brightly.

"Good luck, Bellamy," Earl said, turning to peer back over his shoulder. "Be good to the place. It'll probably be good to you."

"I will," Shane replied. "Scout's honor."

Brian helped settle his grandfather into the passenger's seat, then shut the door and tossed Earl's cane through the open window of the back seat. "Good seeing you again, Mr. Bellamy," he said, rounding the back of the big car—Earl's, Shane guessed, the one he still washed and waxed himself, as hard as that was to believe—and shaking out a set of keys. "See you around, all right?"

"You bet."

Brian started the car and Earl powered down the passenger's side window.

"She killed herself," he said, struggling to make his voice heard over the rumble of the engine. He said it almost as if he couldn't stop himself, as if he'd been waiting for Shane to ask. "She wasn't in her right mind. Hadn't been for years. She was still young, in her fifties, but she was just done. The house had used her up, like I said. You'll remember that, right? She did it herself, in the end. Jumped out of that window, the round one at the front of the attic, up on the peak of the Riverhouse, the same one Wilhelm used to summon his mistress. I heard Marlena had something in her hand when she did it. It was broken on the driveway next to her when they found her. It was a painting, one of her own, but just a little one. I don't know if it was true or not, but that's what they say. A painting of her missing husband and son, and herself too. The paint was still wet when she jumped, like she'd just finished it. Remember that, will you? I'm tired of doing it myself. It's like that damned gold watch Clearwater gave me. I don't want to carry it anymore. It's too heavy."

Shane nodded slowly. "I'll remember it, Earl."

Brian had waited patiently. When he saw that his grandfather was finished, he shifted the big car into reverse, clicked on the headlights, and began to back up. Shane watched the Bonneville rock and squeak on its springs as Brian did a three point turn, aiming the car down the long, sloping drive. Half a minute later, the spray of its headlights had disappeared into the woods, leaving Shane leaning on the porch railing, listening to the chirr of the autumn crickets, watching the lightning bugs stitch glowing gold patterns amongst the trees. At the perimeter of the yard, barely a gray shape slinking in the darkness, Tom the cat prowled slowly, his tail held high, his head low, stalking something in the weeds. Shane watched, thinking about Marlena, wondering if he'd see her tonight.

Wondering if she'd been listening.

Chapter Eleven

A few days passed before the third artwork revealed itself.

Shane worked on the Florida series, finishing the big splashy representation of the state's name, centering it on its own canvas, ready for Greenfeld's Photoshop artist to cut it out and composite it into the six background images. He decided that, once the paint had dried, he'd call Greenfeld and tell him it was done, ask him how he wanted to take possession of the work to give to the next guy on the assembly line. In the meantime, he rode his bike and worked on the footpath, clearing it as far as the little grassy plain with the stream running through it, dragging wheelbarrows of debris out of the woods and piling them in the back corner of the yard, unwilling to merely toss them to either side of the path lest they clutter up the view, make it seem haphazard and messy. He was very proud of his progress, realizing on some level that he had become somewhat obsessed with it. This didn't bother him. Shane was an observer of people, and he believed that most individuals spent their lives buried in various obsessions. Some were unhealthier than others, and some were more pervasive or dangerous or silly, but the saving grace of almost all of them was that humans, almost by definition, are fickle and easily bored. Obsessions pass, and are replaced by new ones. Shane knew that he was somewhat obsessed with the footpath to the old property, but he also expected that that obsession would pass soon enough, like so many others had. For now, he enjoyed the exertion and the sense of progress, the measurable difference as he cleared the path and groomed it, even going so far as to strip the vines off the old angel statue and scrape off most of the moss, despite his earlier decision to leave it alone. On the Thursday after

Earl's and Brian's visit, Shane found a gallon can of old white paint in the back of the shed, still half full, albeit thick and gloppy with age. He thinned it with a cup of turpentine and slapped a gleaming white coat onto the bench that overlooked the gully. He was absurdly proud of how it looked when he was finished, despite the pasty drips that spattered from beneath, spattering the leaves of the hydrangeas in the bench's shadow.

He had time to think that he'd been unnecessarily worried about having both the Riverhouse and the Marlena paintings in the house at the same time. The muse seemed to have forgotten him again, leaving the foreman in his head plenty of room to do his job everyday from nine until two. The Riverhouse painting still stood on the mantel downstairs, the Marlena painting on the small easel in the corner of the studio. Maybe eventually he'd display them together. They were obviously part of a series, with their garish colors, their mix of bizarre modernism and strict realism, like a scene glimpsed through a semi-transparent kaleidoscope. Maybe both paintings had simply been cathartic exercises, just part of the process of getting over Stephanie and the loss of his previous life. Stranger things had happened. He'd display them in the years to come, and explain that they were sister pieces, the two signature works from his "Shane Bellamy Insanity Stairs" series. The thought made him smile, and yet, for now, he was content to leave the two paintings in their respective places. Not because he was superstitious, not anymore. Just because the time wasn't right yet. The paintings weren't... ripe. It was a weird thing to think, but he was an artist, even if he did wear khakis and white button-down shirts to his shift, even if he did occasionally watch sports on TV. He was an artist, and artists were prone to think weird things sometimes.

But that was before Friday evening, when Shane decided to go down to the basement to check on the furnace.

It had been thumping a bit harder than usual, and taking longer pauses between the thump and the gentle whoosh of the vents. The last thing he wanted was to go into a long Missouri winter with his furnace on the fritz. Not that he knew anything about such things. He knew there was a filter that needed to be changed sometimes, part of a humidifier addition Steph had arranged to have installed the year after they'd purchased the place. Other than that, the furnace was simply a huge black monstrosity in the rear corner of the cellar, festooned with snaking ducts and pipes, like a sort of iron-age octopus. Still, he had some idea that, when he called the repair guys at Trane Heating and Air Conditioning in Bastion Falls, it'd behoove him to at least be able to say he'd gone downstairs and taken a quick look at the thing himself. Thinking that, Shane flicked the light switch at the top of the cellar stairs. It clicked loudly, but the basement remained dark.

"Smithy," Shane scolded automatically, and then laughed to himself. He retraced his steps back to the kitchen and retrieved the old silver Maglight from the junk drawer next to the stove. He clicked it on, saw the satisfying cone of light it made, and turned to tromp down the steep wooden stairs into the basement.

Like always, the basement smelled of dirt and mold. Cobwebs swayed in the spaces between the upstairs floorboards, drifting at his passage like seaweed in an ocean current. Shane shone the flashlight around in a wide arc, looking around the cellar. A pile of old cardboard boxes were stacked in the corner under the stairs, scrawled with words in black marker: *living room, den, kitchen stuff.* Steph had had a rule that if anything stayed packed for more than a year after a move, it was trash. Apparently that rule hadn't applied to the cottage. A thick layer of dust and mouse feces covered most of the boxes. In front of them, an old exercise bike loomed like a skeleton, covered with cobwebs, an old rag dangling from one of its handlebars.

Shane sighed and approached the furnace in the opposite corner. It looked just as incomprehensible and ancient as ever, despite the relatively shiny box of the humidifier attachment. Two Honeywell filters sat neatly on the floor next to the furnace, still in their delivery boxes. Steph's work, of course. She had ordered the replacement filters on the internet, and then placed them there on the basement floor, waiting for the day when they'd be used. Something on top of one of the boxes caught Shane's eye. He blinked slowly and peered closer, adjusting the angle of the flashlight. On the top of one of the boxes, four narrow streaks lay in the dust. More dust had almost filled them in, but not completely. There was no mistaking what they were; they were Steph's fingerprints. She had been down here during their last stay together, and had checked the filters. She had moved this box, probably to get a better look at the current filter inside the humidifier attachment, and she had left those four streaked finger marks in the dust.

Shane drew a deep, shaky breath, and was amazed to feel tears suddenly blurring his vision. Dr. Taylor had had a term for this. He'd called it death lag, and he'd said it was the opposite of grief. Grief was when you walked through life fully aware of the loss of a loved one. It may be painful, but it was functional; grief helped you move on, allowed you to live your own life again, even if it felt a little like cheating. Death lag, on the other hand, was that awful moment between seeing a sign of your loved one and remembering, suddenly and horribly, that they are no more. Norm Taylor had said the instances of death lag would decrease over time, but they'd probably never go away completely, no matter how long Shane lived.

Shane raised his left hand, the one that wasn't holding the flashlight, and held it over the top of the box. The flashlight cast the shadow of his hand onto the box, covering Steph's fingerprints with the shadow of his own fingers. He pretended he could feel her hand. He pretended he could reach through time, back to that moment when she had been here in the basement, probably in the middle of the summer of two thousand six or seven. He pretended that he could touch her, and that she'd felt him, felt his ghostly, magical hand cover hers. Maybe it had startled her a little. Maybe she'd thought it was Smithy, reaching out to squeeze her hand for a moment. Perhaps she'd gasped and drawn her hand back suddenly, making those streaks in the dust. But then she'd probably stopped, and put her hand out again, cautious but curious. That, Shane knew, was exactly what Steph would have done.

Tears spilled from both of Shane's eyes and ran down his cheeks. He dropped his hand and lowered his head. It was all just his imagination, of course. Steph was gone. As gone as the Riverhouse.

Feeling very weak and tired, Shane pushed himself upright. The flashlight dangled from his hand, harshly illuminating a spot on the gray basement floor. Long ago, the floor had probably been dirt, but at some point during the intervening decades, someone had decided to pour it with concrete. Now, the concrete was cracked and chipped, spread with dust and water stains from the leaky basement windows. Shane stared down at the cone of light on the bare floor, feeling hopeless and exhausted and terribly sad. Something lay on the floor next to his foot. It was cylindrical and pale yellow, worn down to almost a nub; a piece of sidewalk chalk. Shane frowned. Vaguely, he recognized the chalk. It was part of a box of colors that he and Steph had bought no less than five years ago, thinking it'd amuse Steph's nieces when they came to visit. The plan had been to let them use it on the patio out back. The nieces had been entirely disinterested in the chalk, however, being old enough for iPods and Hannah Montana and High School Musical by that time. Thus, the chalk had ended up down here in the basement, probably stuffed into one of the boxes under the stairs. How, Shane wondered, had this one gotten out onto the floor?

He raised the flashlight a little. There was another one; green, also worn down to nearly nothing. And there was something else—a shape, drawn in chalk, curling out of the shadow of the dark basement. Shane's frown deepened on his brow. He walked slowly away from the furnace, raising the flashlight so as to broaden its cone of light. More shapes and more worn out chalks. It was a drawing, huge and complicated, but completely indecipherable from so close up. Shane began to feel that familiar chill falling over him, starting in his stomach and spreading out and down, making him shudder. He saw his own footprints in the chalk dust, smearing the image where he'd walked over to the furnace, oblivious of what lay under his feet. His eyes widened as he began to recognize one of the shapes of the drawing. A surge of hopeless frustration welled up in him as he backed away, toward the stairs, and then began to climb them, backwards, holding the flashlight higher and higher, illuminating the entirety of the basement floor with that cold, bony light.

The scene was enormous, filling almost all of the cracked basement floor, scribbled in haphazardly but with a cruel eye for detail. Shane easily recognized it now. It was the Valley Road, the one that the cottage driveway emptied onto, the road that led into Bastion Falls. Gaily bright fall leaves adorned the trees on both sides of the road, and a childishly blue sky made a gigantic V between the trees, pointing down toward the ribbon of asphalt. The perspective was all off, however, so that both ends of the road could be seen. One side, nearest the furnace, diminished toward the floodwalls of Bastion Falls, just visible in the chalky distance. The other, under the front cellar window, led up the hill of the valley toward that awful blue sky. Shane could see his own mailbox drawn into the space next to the stairs, crammed in, destroying all sense of perspective.

But the worst part was the vehicles. On the Bastion Falls side, drawn with scurrying, frantic strokes, implying speed and recklessness, was a big red pickup truck. Acres of silver grill dominated its front, and in the center of that grill were scrawled three letters: GMC. On the other side, drawn with nearly loving care and detail, was Steph's silver Honda Prelude. There was a shape behind the glass of the windshield, and Shane recognized it. He sunk to a seat on the stairs and dropped the flashlight. It clattered to the floor and rolled crookedly, spraying harsh light over the scene, illuminating the silvery Honda and that eerily familiar silhouette. Shane shuddered and covered his face with his hands, but his eyes peered out, bulging between his fingers, still wet with tears, still looking at that shape on the floor. He couldn't help himself

The silhouette behind the wheel of the Honda wasn't Steph. That would have been bad enough.

It was Christiana.

He couldn't paint at all on the morning after finding the chalk drawing on the floor of the basement. It was Saturday, and yet some part of him insisted that he should still try to put in his shift. He needed to paint, needed the mundane normalcy of the foreman in his head. Unfortunately, the foreman hadn't gotten the memo about putting in a little overtime on Saturday. He was apparently off for the day, fishing somewhere, watching Sportscenter, maybe mowing his lawn. In his absence, Shane merely sat on his stool, slumped in front of the canvas. It was the fifth of the six Florida paintings, the one that celebrated the Florida Keys. A fan-boat carrying a gaggle of grinning people dominated the bottom left of the painting, only half finished. Shane stared at it, his right hand dangling across his knees, the brush held loosely in his fingers. It was no use. He could tell that there would be no painting today, no matter how much he might wish for it.

He was worried. Craziness, Earl had said, was catching. Was that what was really happening here? Was he going insane? A few years ago, while waiting in his dentist's office, Shane had read a magazine article about the top ten most stressful events that could occur in a person's life. The top three had been losing a spouse, losing a job, and moving to a different city. Shane had experienced all three of those things during the previous year. It was all too plausible that, in response to those events, his mind had simply swung loose of its bearings a little. Maybe he'd given up seeing Dr. Taylor too soon. Maybe he should find someone else here, someone to talk to about... everything. But could he really do that? It was one thing to walk into a therapist's office and admit that thoughts of suicide had flitted through your mind in the wake of the loss of your job and your wife. It was another thing entirely to admit that you were painting phantom visions from a dead house and entertaining a moody ghost. That was the sort of thing that summoned the men in the white coats, at least according to the stereotypes in Shane's head. He didn't think he was quite ready to lay down on some strangers' couch and start talking about Marlena and the Riverhouse. Maybe he could have done it with Norm Taylor, but Dr. Taylor's office was several states away now. Too far to go to admit maybe you had a few screws loose.

But the funny thing was, Shane didn't really believe it was true. He didn't *feel* crazy, despite the crazy things that seemed to be happening around him. His worst fear, when he'd found the chalk drawing on the basement floor, had been that the sleep-walking had happened again, that he'd been animated by the muse, zombie-like, and marched down to the basement to make that drawing. It was possible, of course, but the more he thought about it, the more he wondered. For one thing, the style of the drawing was different than anything he'd ever created. It was distinct from both his normal work and his two new pieces, the signature works from his "Insanity Stairs" series. The chalk drawing was somehow minimalist and expressionistic at the same time, with details haphazardly crammed in here and there, especially around the vehicles. It wasn't the most compelling evidence that those drawings hadn't come from Shane's hand, but there was something else as well: he'd never awoken with chalk on his fingers. Maybe the muse had gotten smart enough to have him wash his hands when she was through with him, but what would be the point? Why would she hide it?

Of course, if Shane hadn't created that drawing, either asleep or otherwise, that left one big, burning question: who had? And why? Had it been Marlena herself? Was she really capable of such a thing? And if so, had it been a warning of some kind? Or even a threat?

Slumped on his stool in front of the canvas, Shane shook his head. There was no point in thinking about it any further. Nor was there any point in attempting to work on the Florida painting. The foreman was gone for the day, and he wasn't answering his phone. Shane reached and set the paintbrush down on his little side table. He wouldn't do any painting today, but that didn't mean he couldn't work on something else. An idea had been forming in his mind, secretly, as if backstage, waiting for the right moment to present itself. He could work on something different if he wanted, something sort of special. It was probably a little crazy, but it just might make him feel a bit better. Either way, it was harmless. Perfectly harmless.

Shane stood up, stretched, and crossed the studio. He took the stairs two at a time, rounded the corner past the kitchen, and stopped at the top of the basement steps. The door was open, providing a wide view of the cellar floor. Watery mid-day light spilled across it, illuminating the drawing and casting dark shadows next to the nubs of used sidewalk chalk. Almost all of the chalks had been worn down to stumps, but Shane thought there was just enough left to do what he had in mind. He wouldn't need much, really.

Slowly, he descended the basement stairs. At the bottom, he squatted and pinched a piece of yellow chalk between his right thumb and forefinger.

The muse didn't whisper to him this time. This time, the art was entirely his own.

By the time Shane was finished, he'd used up almost all of the remaining chalks. His fingers were sore from pinching the nubs in order to draw with them on the rough concrete floor. He was mostly satisfied with what he'd done, even if it was a little crazy. It fit. He'd always been good at mimicking whatever artistic style a job required. This job, in fact, had been easier than most. The style of the chalk drawing was blissfully simplistic, almost instinctive. Shane stood up and dropped the fragment of blue chalk. He brushed his hands carelessly on his thighs and realized he was hungry. He considered going upstairs and making himself a sandwich, but then thought better of it. It was Saturday. If the foreman in his head had decided to take the day off, maybe Shane should as well.

Besides, he was still out of beer.

He didn't even take the time to change. There were still chalk streaks all over the thighs of his khakis and ground into the knees where he'd crawled around on the basement floor but he didn't care. He rolled down the window of the pickup truck as he steered it down the driveway and pulled out onto the Valley Road. The road made him think of the chalk drawing again, of course, with its two vehicles, each bearing down on the other with nothing but destiny between them. He put it out of his head, reluctantly but firmly.

He stopped at a diner just past the Bastion Falls industrial district. The diner was pushed back from the road, giving it a view of the river on one side and a big gray parking lot on the other side, surrounded on two sides by chain-link fence and filled with more pickup trucks. Shane's truck was older than most of the shiny new examples in the parking lot. *GMC* he thought disconnectedly as he pushed through the diner's side door, into the sound of clattering plates and lunchtime banter. He sat at the bar, next to a trucker wearing a plaid flannel shirt and a NASCAR ball cap, black, with a big white number three on the front. The man was talking politics when Shane entered, and he absorbed Shane into his monologue without even pausing for breath. In terms of politics, Shane tended vaguely toward the conservative, which was, of course, just one more thing that separated him from the ranks of his fellow artists. He'd learned to not even mention it, lest he become the subject of scorn and ridicule among his much more impassioned community of coworkers. Even now, in the presence of the trucker, Shane found himself merely nodding noncommittally and grunting. He didn't mind. In fact, the timber of the trucker's voice, the metronome-like motion of his elbow as he shoveled eggs and hash browns into his mouth between sentences, was strangely comforting. As long as there were guys like this out there in the world, pontificating loudly while they lugged around the world's essential loads of toilet paper, big screen televisions and Keebler cookies, things would probably be all right, no matter who was in the White House. Shane ordered a cheeseburger and fries and enjoyed the buzzing warmth of the sunlight through the diner's plate glass windows while the cook prepared his lunch. On the whole, it was very nice. At least for the moment, it was easy to forget all the craziness—the ghost and the paintings and Earl Kirchenbauer's story. And the chalk drawing, of course.

Shane ate ravenously, and even topped it off with a piece of apple pie from the glass dome at the end of the counter. Then he left a ten on the counter, tucked just under the lip of his plate, and left. The trucker was leaving at the same time. He was driving a big Freightliner, parked crookedly at the edge of the diner's unusually large gravel lot. Its engine was running, throbbing in the cool fall air.

"Gotta make Kansas City by dusk," the trucker said, adjusting his cap and gazing up at the bright blue sky. "Radio says a storm will be blowing in this afternoon, too. Gonna have to haul ass if I want to beat that."

"I have a feeling hauling ass is something you're pretty comfortable with," Shane said, cranking open the door of his own much smaller truck and glancing back.

The trucker grinned at him and put on a pair of mirrored sunglasses. "Haulin' ass is an important life skill," he said, starting across the parking lot. "You never know when it'll come in handy. After all, everything in life is practice for everything else. My dad taught me that. Said if I remembered that I'd do just fine."

Shane nodded. It seemed like good advice. Maybe some of the best advice he'd ever heard.

Brian wasn't working at the IGA checkouts that afternoon. Shane waited in line with his beer and meager basket of groceries. A twenty-something year-old girl was working the only open lane, attractive but unsmiling and bored. As Shane approached, he saw that her nametag read "Alex". It was the girl that Brian had talked about, the one whose nametag he had borrowed on the day Shane had first met him. Hadn't Brian said she normally worked in the deli? No wonder she seemed a little disgruntled. Still, cute as she was, Shane had a feeling that she probably wasn't the nicest person in the world. Brian was probably better off spending his afternoons with his grandfather. Thinking that, Shane considered driving over to Denny Acres himself to see if Earl was around, and then decided against it. Something about Earl's last visit made Shane think it'd be best to give him a few weeks before dropping by again. He couldn't quite put his finger on why, but didn't question the general instinct. Earl had resurrected a lot of old ghosts in order to tell Shane the story of the Riverhouse. Best to give him a little time to bury them again.

When Shane got home, he climbed the stairs up to the studio and checked the Florida title painting. The paint was finally dry to the touch, ready for delivery. He clumped back downstairs, took one of the new beers out of the fridge and found the cordless phone on the kitchen counter. Morrie probably wouldn't be in the office, but Shane figured he could leave a message. Sure enough, the answering service clicked on after the third ring.

"Hey Morrie, I just wanted to let you know I've got most of the Florida series finished," Shane said, popping the cap off his beer. "The title piece is dry enough for you to get, if you want to send it off to your Photoshop guy. I could take some digital pics of it myself, but I figured he'd rather manage that end of things on his own, if he's anything like the digital artists I knew back at T and C. Give me a call back and let me know how you want to manage things from here. Thanks."

He thumbed the power button and carried the phone into the library. Once he'd plugged it into the charger base, he meandered into the sunroom and plopped onto the couch. Outside the big sunroom windows, Shane saw Tom lying on the end of the stone wall that bordered the patio, asleep with his tail curled around him, touching his nose.

"You've got the idea, Tom old boy," Shane said, sighing. He'd planned on whiling away a few hours watching television, but suddenly it occurred to him that, like Tom, what he wanted most was a nap. Sleeping in the afternoon seemed like the sort of thing only old people did, but Shane decided he could give himself a pass this time. After all, it was Saturday. He drained a third of his beer, set the bottle on the end table, and kicked back, crossing his ankles on the arm of the couch. Five minutes later he was asleep.

Twenty minutes after that, he was dreaming.

It was confusing. He knew he was dreaming, because the view outside the sunroom windows was different. Featureless black pressed against the glass panes, and Shane could tell that it wasn't the black of mere darkness; it was the black of emptiness, like the eyes of the ghost of Marlena. It was cold as well, as if the sunroom hadn't felt actual sunlight in ages. He moved to stand up, and realized he already was. It was that kind of dream, bizarre and inexplicable, where things happened in jerks and whirls, with no reference to actual time. He moved toward the door that led into the library, first tentatively, and then frantically. The sunroom was breaking away from the house, silently falling into that abyss of cold blackness beyond the windows. As he passed through the French doors into the library he shuddered, as if he'd pressed through a sort of invisible boundary. The coldness diminished, and Shane glanced back. The sunroom was gone, but not fallen away, as he'd feared. It simply didn't exist. It was as if it had never been there at all, or hadn't yet been built. The doorway looked out onto nothing. In the dream, Shane himself could barely remember what the room had even looked like.

The rest of the cottage was there, but it was different. It was as if every day of the cottage's existence was crammed into a single moment. Nothing moved, and yet everything seemed to be strangely in flux, shimmering, night over day, winter over summer, decades and seasons all pressed together until they blended into a single seamless tone, like a ringing in the ears.

Boundary lands, he thought for no reason. It was like a memory, one he couldn't quite place, spoken in a woman's voice. *We're drawn to the boundary lands of life... rivers and valleys, shores and cliffs... but this one is unusual. Here, the boundary line is a lot deeper... deeper...* The voice was familiar, but Shane couldn't place it. All he knew for sure was that it wasn't Marlena, even though—

He looked up. Marlena was there. She stood in the doorway that led down into the basement, her back to him. Shane tried to speak to her, but no sound came. It was as if there was no air, no medium to conduct the sound waves of his voice. He pushed forward, toward her slight, straight frame. He meant to touch her, for here, unlike in his waking hours, he thought he truly could. He wanted to comfort her, soothe her, draw her into his arms. The cottage swam past him with infuriating sluggishness. It was that kind of dream as well, the kind where space is plastic, elongating in front of you so that you never quite seem to reach your destination, as if some capricious force was constantly pushing you backwards. And yet he did reach her, suddenly, as if time had once again slipped its gears, launching him forward so that he nearly barreled into her where she stood on the top of the stairs, her back to him, her posture rigid and tense. He reached for her, but before he could touch her, she seemed to sense him. She turned, very slowly, and once again, time became sluggish, focusing in on that single action, as if Marlena herself were standing still and the entire world, Shane included, was swiveling around her, forcing him to look into her face.

Her eyes were as blank and black as ever, but they were no longer cold. They were blindingly hot, pulsing like a blast furnace. Shane tried to stop himself from touching her, but the inertia was too great. He pressed against her, and she was as rigid as a statue, suddenly towering over him, looking down at him as if from a great height. She was monstrous, her face calm, but her eyes flaming darkly, as if they could turn him into ash right where he stood. In that moment, he was terrified of her. Not because she meant to hurt him, but because he had disappointed her. He didn't know how, or why he should even care, but he did. The weight of it crushed him, pressed him down, and she seemed to tower even further over him. The cottage itself drifted away around them, shredding like paper, incinerating into dust. And then, for the first time, Marlena spoke.

"See the sugar bowl do the Tootsie Roll," she said, her voice huge and clanging, ringing madly like lead weights in a watery grave. "If you eat too much, uh-oh, you'll awake with a tummy ache."

It should have been funny, but it wasn't. The words were terrible, heartbreaking, lonely, lost. Shane tried to cover his ears to drown out the sound of them, but it was no use. He wasn't hearing them with his ears.

Darkness fell, and all that was left was the echo of those awful, senseless words and the heat of her eyes, baking out of the darkness, consuming everything. And yet, Shane did not wake. He tossed and turned, sweating, shivering, his pupils switching under the hot film of his eyelids, mumbling to himself.

Outside, Tom the cat had woken up. He sat on the stone wall watching the sunlight wane and die, watching purple storm clouds crowd in over the trees. His ears pricked as Shane thrashed and muttered, but he didn't turn his head to look. Only his tail moved, twitching and writhing, as if it had a mind of its own.

Chapter Twelve

Shane awoke to the nagging warble of the cordless phone in the next room. He rolled over, not realizing where he was, and nearly fell off the couch. He threw out an arm and caught the top of the ottoman, saving himself from crashing face first onto the sunroom floor. Feeling stiff and stupid, he groaned and pushed himself upright.

The phone rang. Shane stumbled into the library.

"Shane?"

"Yeah," he answered, rubbing his eyes. "Hey Morrie." The light outside the library windows seemed wrong somehow. Too bright.

"You sick or something, pal? You sound awful, if you don't mind my saying."

"Why would I mind that, you insensitive prick? I'm fine."

"Glad to hear it," Morrie replied cheerfully. "Even gladder to hear about how things are going with the Florida series. You really have the title piece done and ready to roll?"

"I do. It's upstairs now, calling your name. How do you want it?"

"Any way I can get it. I was thinking about sending somebody out there this morning, but no couriers are running today. I'd do it myself, but I got priors. My nephew's available this afternoon around two. I thought it'd be best for me to check in with you first, anyway. You going to be around?"

"Today," Shane repeated, confused. "You mean tonight? Isn't it a little late?"

"What do you mean? A little late for what?"

"For anything. I mean, it's got to be…" Shane trailed off, looking out the window again. He'd been about to say *it's got to be seven P.M.,* but that couldn't be right. It was far too light outside for that. If it was seven, it'd be mostly dark outside, wouldn't it? Instead, the sun shone brightly, sparkling on the wet grass of the side yard.

On the phone, Morrie went on. "I know, it's Sunday, but I'm a control freak, all right? An extra day is an extra day, and my Photoshop guy doesn't have your sparkling penchant for deadlines. Sooner I get that canvas to him, the better. But if it's no good for you, don't sweat it. We'll work something out for Monday."

"No," Shane said distractedly, carrying the phone into the kitchen, peering through the window over the sink. The sun was bright over the trees on the other side of the river. Could he have actually slept through the entire night on the couch in the sunroom? He'd never done such a thing before. It was extremely disquieting. "No, that's fine. Send your guy on over. If I'm not in, I'll leave the painting in the front room and a key under the mat."

"Great," Morrie agreed. "His name's Derek. Tall kid with glasses and a tat on his neck. Looks like a damn skinhead, but don't let him fool you. He's a decent kid. Two or three this afternoon, all right?"

"Sounds fine," Shane replied, still staring out the kitchen window. Suddenly, he blinked and glanced aside. "Wait. What about Christiana?"

"What about her?"

"Er, I was just thinking, she's the one you sent last time. Sorry, I'm probably being nosy. Just curious."

"Well, she *is* a lot easier on the eyes than Derek, I'll give you that, but it's Sunday. I wouldn't call her even if I thought I'd get hold of her. She's been M.I.A. for a few days."

"What?" Shane said, feeling suddenly very cold. "What do you mean? Is she on vacation or something?"

"Nah. She just hasn't shown up at the office. Not since Thursday. Not answering her cell either. She left me a message saying she might have to take some time off, but I figured she meant to arrange something, not just up and vanish on me."

Shane clutched the phone tightly and struggled to keep his voice even. "That seems pretty strange, don't you think?"

"Nah, she's done it before. She has a pretty loose schedule here, works whenever she wants to squeeze it in, unless I need something special. She's never been gone this long before, but she'll turn up, acting like nothing's happened, like everything's perfectly normal. That's just how she is. Besides, I'm sure I'd have heard about it if she was found dead in a ditch somewhere."

Shane couldn't say anything. His lips felt sewn shut. Completely unbidden, snippets of last night's dream sprang up in his mind: *Boundary lands*; Marlena's searing black eyes, the dead clang of her voice, saying *if you eat too much, uh-oh, you'll awake with a tummy ache.*

"You cool, Shane?" Morrie said, his voice sounding tiny and unimportant in the telephone earpiece. "You sound like you're fading out on me there."

"I'm here," Shane said, amazed at how normal his voice sounded. "I'm cool."

"Great. Nice work on the Florida series. Let me know when you get the last pieces done and maybe I'll come collect them myself and we'll hoist a few, all right? See you, Shane."

"Yeah," Shane said, and then dropped the phone on the floor as he reached to turn it off. He heard it clunk onto the kitchen tile and looked down at it dazedly. The dial tone buzzed up at him from the floor; Greenfeld had hung up, thankfully. Feeling strangely numb, Shane squatted to retrieve the phone. His fingers were shaking as he reached for his wallet and opened it. Christiana's card, the one she had given him at the art show, was tucked into a pocket in the back. He pulled it out and stared at it. Two numbers were printed underneath her name, one marked "office" and the other marked "cell". Knowing it was no use, Shane dialed the second set of numbers. He lifted the phone to his ear and listened. The electronic burr of the rings began. He counted them. After nine rings, the phone still hadn't clicked over to her answering service. Shane lowered the phone, not even bothering to hang it up. Dangling at his side, the earpiece continued to burr incessantly. Shane listened, feeling weak and utterly hopeless. Time seemed to have overlapped on him, taken him right back to that day at The Spring Garden, the day he learned that he'd never hear from Steph again because she was dead, struck down by a red truck with GMC printed on its huge chrome grill, just like in the drawing sprawled across his cellar floor. He'd thought he could change it, alter it with a few bits of leftover chalk, but of course that had been silly. You couldn't change destiny. He felt vaguely sick.

Uh oh, a voice in his head chided gaily, *you'll awake with a tummy ache...*

Shane lifted the phone to push the "end" button, and then stopped. There was something odd about the sound of the incessant ringing in the earpiece. It almost seemed to be echoing. Shane stood very still and listened. The phone in his hands burred, and almost immediately afterwards, very faintly, came a sort of electronic chime. Shane frowned, straining to hear. The noise seemed to be coming from outside, near the front of the cottage. Still carrying the phone, listening to the burr of the ring in the earpiece and the subsequent distant chime, Shane walked through the library. Sure enough, the chiming sound grew slightly louder. It was coming from outside. Shane began to walk faster, approaching the door. He pulled it open more forcefully than he'd intended to, clambering out onto the little porch that overlooked the driveway, his eyes widening and his heart suddenly pounding. There was a car parked on the woods side of his pickup, a bottle-green Saturn. Shane had seen it before, but only once. Its rear windows were open slightly, and out of them came the persistent chime of a ringing cell phone.

Shane hunkered down to peer into the side window, cupping his hands to his face to cut the glare of the morning sun. There didn't seem to be anyone inside. And then behind him, shocking him so much that his knees nearly unhinged, a voice spoke.

"Peeing outside is a lot easier for men than women," the voice said, sounding bleary and vaguely annoyed. "I'm too tired to explain much more than that right now."

Shane turned around, a grin of helpless, monumental relief spreading across his face. Christiana was approaching from the direction of the woods, her dark hair mussed and her blouse untucked, flapping over a pair of jeans. She'd obviously slept in her car, right here in his driveway. Shane couldn't begin to guess why, but for the moment, he didn't care.

Christiana stopped ten feet away and squinted at him. "What are you smiling about, anyway? Aren't you wondering why in the hell I'm here?"

Shane shook his head wonderingly. "Just my lucky day, I guess." He drew a deep, shaky breath and nodded toward the cottage, still smiling. "What do you say? You want some coffee this time?"

"I'd like to say that I didn't know what Randy was like. It feels so stupid. To have known, almost from the very beginning, probably from the first time we ever went out, and to still stay with him. I wish I could say he kept up a really good image for a long time, until after we'd been together long enough to make me care about him. Long enough to make it hard to walk away. But that's not true. My parents didn't raise any idiots. I knew he was trouble, right from the very beginning. I didn't know how *much*. There's that, at least. But that's no excuse. I kept telling myself he'd never turn it on me. Later, I told myself it'd never be more than words. He'd never actually raise a hand to me. He wouldn't stoop that low. Then, after that, I told myself the same thing that all women in abusive relationships eventually tell themselves: I told myself it was my fault; that I'd asked for it. When I heard myself say that, that's what finally woke me up. I looked in the mirror, at the bruises on my upper arms where his fingers had dug in, where he'd held me and shook me, and I realized I'd begun to believe it—that I deserved it, that it was my fault for making him so angry. And I stopped and just stared at myself, my mouth dropped open. It would have been funny, at another place and time, that look of comic surprise. And I thought, 'When did I become *that* girl? The weak one? The one who makes excuses for the abuse she takes?'"

Christiana stopped and pressed her lips together. She sat on the patio next to Shane, cupping a large red mug of coffee between both of her hands, staring out at the current below the bluff. She was sitting in the chair that Brian had occupied during his and his grandfather's visit. Shane sat in the other chair, watching Christiana as she watched the river. She was wearing a long-sleeved button-down blouse, tangerine colored, still un-tucked. The sleeves were unbuttoned and rolled up, but not enough to show her upper arms. She'd been virtually silent since Shane had invited her in. She'd merely perched on the edge of the kitchen counter and hugged herself, warming by the stove as Shane made the coffee. He'd been content with the silence, not knowing what her story was, but knowing that when it came, it probably wasn't going to be very nice. Shane had known a few women who'd been in abusive relationships. He knew enough about the dynamics of such relationships to know you could never guess what kind of woman might be involved in

one. In Christiana's case, he was surprised, but not quite shocked.
She drew a long, deep breath and went on.

"I've been with Randy since my second year at law school.
We met in copyright law. I was interested in that class because I was
interested in art, and copyright is an important issue with the arts,
especially in the digital age. He was smart and funny. Decent-
enough looking, even if he did dress a little like a grown-up version
of Alex P. Keaton. You remember him? Michael J. Fox in that
show, 'Family Ties'? Huh. Hardly anybody remembers that
reference anymore. Randy carried a briefcase. I mean, lots of guys
carry briefcases in law school, but with Randy… it was kind of the
whole package. He wore sweater vests and wingtip shoes and slacks
with creases right down the leg, razor sharp, like his butler had
ironed them fresh that morning. But I knew he lived alone, in an
apartment off-campus, a little basement flat with nothing but a
bedroom, a bathroom, and a cook-top. I knew that because he'd
dated one of the other girls in class, a friend of mine named Angel.
They'd gone out once or twice and she'd gotten bored with him. She
said he was nice enough, but too intense. Too serious. He packed
his own lunches and carried them in his briefcase. If it had been two
or three years earlier, I'd have thought he was a hopeless geek, but I
was in college then, and prided myself on my open-mindedness, my
fairness. I could tell that he was interested in me. Randy was quiet,
but he wasn't timid. He had this insufferable, stupid confidence that
drove me a little crazy. He seemed to believe that I'd go out with
him, no matter what. It was like he knew that, anywhere else, he'd
never have a chance with a girl like me, but there, in law school, in
copyright law, he was in his element. There, he was the smart one
with the bright future. There, he was the big fish in the little pond.
Naturally, the girl fishy in that little pond would recognize how great
he was. And the stupid thing is, he was right. That's exactly how it
happened. Back home, I'd never have dated a guy like him. Not just
because he was skinny and arrogant and dressed like Alex P. Keaton,
but because some part of me knew he was trouble, right from the
beginning. Probably, that was even part of what drew me to him.
And don't tell me that it was a stupid thing to do. I already know
that. I knew it then, even. All girls do. I went along with him
because he was trouble, because I was already feeling some
resentment at my parents for pushing me into their world, and I
wanted to revolt. I wasn't ready to quit school yet, like I did a little
while later, but I was ready to rebel against my parents, at least in

some small, secret way. I knew my parents would never approve of Randy. My father would have smelled him from across a crowded room. My parents would have hated him. That was enough reason for me to be with him, in spite of everything. Take *that,* Mom and Dad.

Of course, they never even knew about Randy. Not until after I left school completely and moved out of the place they'd rented for me. By then, they had bigger fish to fry. The more they tried to push me back into their mold, the more I ran back to him. I hate to admit that, but what's the point in hiding it now? For awhile, I even had the gall to blame it all on my parents. I told myself that if they hadn't pushed me so hard, I wouldn't have had to run so far away from them. I wouldn't have had to cling to Randy like I did. But that's all a lie. It's the opposite of the lie I told myself about deserving Randy's abuse. I blamed my parents for my decisions, and blamed myself for Randy's. For a while, it was a vicious cycle. I became exactly the sort of woman I've always hated. That's how it always is, isn't it? It's like the homophobic guy who's really just responding to his own gay tendencies. We all hate the thing we most fear becoming. I'd always hated the weak women who stayed with the men who hurt them. I scorned them, and had no patience for them. I even considered getting into domestic law, just so I could sit across the table from those women, the ones who defend the men who beat them, who make excuses for them and protect them, even after those men have nearly killed them. It wasn't that I wanted to help those women, necessarily. I just wanted to lean across the table and grab them by the collar and shake them, and say 'Why? What in the hell is wrong with you? Why do you protect the one who hates you? Women like you are the reason men like them always get away with it! Women like you are the reason rapists go unpunished! You are as much to blame as they are! What is WRONG with you?'"

Christiana stopped again. Her voice had risen, grown loud and shrill, splintering on the last few words. She was shaking a little, struggling to hold her coffee cup steady. She exhaled and shuddered and reached to set her cup on the stone wall next to her.

"You don't need to tell me all of this," Shane said quietly. "He's not here now. There's no point in upsetting yourself."

She was shaking her head, making her hair flop limply around her face. "That's not true. There's *every* point in getting upset now. I've been numb for months, for over a *year.* I've been fooling myself. I was so adamant that I could never become one of *those* kind of women that I didn't see it when it actually happened. I didn't see it until I was standing there in the mirror, dabbing at the bruises on my arms, and telling myself it was my own fault for getting him so riled up. Those were the words I thought, too. I actually said them in my head. 'I shouldn't have gotten him so riled up'. Like he was a dog I had teased, a dog that didn't know its own strength, or how sharp its teeth were. I was amazed. I wanted to reach through the mirror and grab myself, like I'd always envisioned grabbing those pathetic, abused wives and girlfriends. I wanted to grab myself and demand those same answers. And that's when I realized the truth about it all. Nobody *plans* to get into an abusive relationship. Some of us just don't plan *not* to. And once you start sliding down that slope, it's all too easy to just put on blinders and hope it won't be as bad as it could be. You start making excuses from the very beginning. And let me tell you, once you start making excuses..." —she laughed; a shrill, hopeless bark— "you just never stop. It's like giving the guy Carte Blanche. Do whatever you want, sweetiecakes, because you'll never have to pay for it. I'll forgive you every time. I'll cover for you. Just don't take off my blinders. Keep telling me the lies about how you regret it, about how you'll never do it again, and how it's all because of how much you love me. As long as you keep telling me the lies... as long as you let me wear the blinders..."

Her voice trailed away again. She reached to pick up her coffee cup, and then took a long, deliberate sip.

"So," Shane said, trying very hard to keep his voice even, trying to simply give her what she needed so that she could say whatever needed to be said. "Why did you end up here last night?"

Christiana looked at him full on, perhaps for the first time since beginning her tale. Her face was remarkably composed, her eyes steady, almost grave. "Because," she answered, "He didn't keep his end of the deal. The stupid bastard. He did the one thing he wasn't supposed to do."

Shane asked, although he thought he already knew the answer. "What did he do?"

Christiana drew a sigh and looked away again, out over the bluff. In a businesslike voice, she said, "He took off my blinders."

Shane called Greenfeld while Christiana lay down to sleep for a few hours, borrowing one of his tee shirts to use as a makeshift nightshirt. She hadn't wanted to, but Shane had insisted. She obviously needed the sleep. By the looks of it, she hadn't had a decent night's rest in several days. He stood in the kitchen and looked toward his cracked bedroom door as the telephone line clicked through. After three rings, Greenfeld's answering service droned to life. Shane waited for the beep, then told Greenfeld that if he got the message in time, he could tell his nephew to stay home and play a few more hours of World of Warcraft; he and Christiana would be coming downtown themselves later in the day, and they'd drop off the Florida title painting when they did. He hung up, feeling fairly confident that Greenfeld would get the message, despite his previous engagements—his "priors", as he'd called them. Shane had considered offering some explanation for Christiana's presence at his cottage, had even begun to concoct a rather elaborate lie about showing her some works-in-progress for a future gallery show, but had decided at the last minute not to say anything at all. It wasn't Greenfeld's concern why Christiana was there. She hadn't asked Shane to keep her presence a secret. Besides, they were all adults. If Greenfeld was curious about it, he could ask.

Thinking that, Shane climbed the stairs to the studio. He took the Florida title painting off the big easel and placed a fresh canvas there, setting it on its side, in "landscape" position. He pulled his stool up to it and sat down, resting his chin on his right hand. For several minutes, he simply stared into the white. Like all artists, blank space tended to both calm and mesmerize him. His mind wandered.

Shane had had only one good friend back in New York City, a writer named Desmond. Desmond wrote crime mysteries under a female pseudonym, and while he didn't earn a terribly fine living at it, he was prolific enough to have been able to quit his advertising job of ten years and write full time. He and Shane had only ever talked about the craft of writing once or twice, but on one of those occasions, Shane had asked Desmond what it took to make a really awful villain. Was the worst bad guy a rapist? A murderer? A pedophile? Desmond had shaken his head wisely and peered crookedly at Shane, as if the answer to that question was a sort of trade secret, rather like the answer to how a magician saws a girl in half. Shane hadn't thought his friend was going to reply at all. When he did, his response had both surprised and dismayed Shane. Now, staring at the bottomless white of the canvas before him, Shane thought again about Desmond's answer to the question of what made the worst villain. For the first time, he thought maybe he understood.

Randy had given Christiana a pet rabbit. Christiana had told Shane this with a wry laugh, as if it was the sort of gesture that was typical of Randy—*close but way off*, as Shane's dad used to say. She'd wanted a cat, but Randy apparently hated cats. He was allergic to them, or so he had said. He'd bought the fat brown rabbit as an apology gift, after a particularly vicious argument, the one during which he had gripped her arms hard enough to embed deep bruises in the flesh of her biceps, shaken her violently enough to give her a splitting headache that lasted until the next night. Randy was apparently an expert at that sort of violence—the kind that didn't leave marks in obvious places. He was almost a connoisseur of careful abuse. There were never any black eyes or bloody lips, but there were plenty of headaches and hidden bruises, plenty of sore ribs and dry heaves in the bathroom afterward, listening to him stalk the floor just outside, breathing curses and threats, telling her how it was all her fault, fretting about how she'd asked for it, demanding to know why she made him do such things. Randy was wont to return the next day with dramatic ovations of affection and apology, offering Christiana gifts, flowers, often even heartfelt tears of sorrow. Over and over, Christiana had wanted to end things with him, but had never found a way to do it. When he beat her, she was too scared of him to proclaim her intentions to leave him. When he apologized, he was too sincere and pathetic.

I'll do it sometime when things are normal between us, she'd told herself. *When he won't hurt me, and when I won't crush him. When we can be like normal people, talking, being rational. I'll do it then. Then I'll be free.*

The problem was, things were never normal between them. They were constantly swinging wildly between the polarities of his violent rage and his pathetic, wretched remorse. Further, Christiana had come to fear Randy, even in his 'I've been a bad boy' mode. This was because some part of her knew that his remorse, dramatic and sincere as it seemed, was just a ruse. It was simply the price he had to pay for the privilege of hurting her whenever he wanted to. For most men, apology meant giving away a part of themselves; it meant breaking off a part of the ego and presenting it as a gift. For most men, apologizing cost them something, and that was what made it meaningful. For Randy, apologies didn't seem to cost anything. That was why it was so easy for him, so natural and indulgent. He didn't really ever think he'd done anything wrong. Putting on the 'I've been a bad boy' façade was merely a dull obligation, like leaving money on the hooker's dresser. Christiana was terrified of knowing this, of knowing that Randy's apologies were meaningless. Because if that was true, then the only real emotion Randy ever felt was the rage, and it was probably always there, hidden just under the surface, under the misty eyes and the oh-so-sincere smile of regret. The rage didn't need to stew to a boil before it flashed out at her. It was *always* there, simmering, ready at any moment. This was never more apparent than the day of her birthday, less than a week earlier.

Christiana had named the pet rabbit Percy, even though it was a girl. It lived most of its days in a hutch on the back porch of her apartment, but Christiana took it out for a while most evenings. She'd hold Percy on her lap and stroke her deliciously soft fur. The rabbit was typically timid. It didn't arch its back when she pet it, like a cat would, but it sat perfectly still, as if it were catatonic, merely twitching its nose and breathing in quick, panting puffs. Despite this, there was something pleasant about holding the small animal, about stroking Percy's luxurious brown coat. She'd been holding Percy on her lap, sitting on a lawn chair on the back porch, when Randy had gotten home that evening. He'd announced his intention to take her out for her birthday, acting magnanimous, throwing his arms wide and grinning.

Christiana had been less enthusiastic than him. She'd told him she was tired, and that she'd already started some dinner thawing in the sink. Randy's grin had vanished. He'd nodded, curtly, and announced that he'd already made reservations, so whatever was thawing in the sink would just have to wait for another night. She could wear her new black dress, he'd suggested, the one with the spaghetti straps. He liked that one. He'd bought it for her. He'd even gone to the trouble of laying it out on the bed, along with the shoes he liked for her to wear whenever she dressed up. He'd already done all the work for her, so there was no reason for her to complain. Christiana had known she was treading on thin ice, but she really had been tired. She'd been looking very forward to a quiet evening at home. She'd tried to soothe Randy with her voice, telling him how nice it'd be to just stay in for the night, to snuggle on the couch and watch something she'd recorded on the DVR.

"Besides," she'd said, smiling up at him and cocking her head. "Percy is so content right here on my lap. I'd hate to stick her back in her hutch. She's been in there all day. Maybe she can cuddle with us on the couch. I bet that would make her happy." She looked back down at the rabbit and stroked her fur. "What do you think, Perce? Would you like that?"

Randy seemed to relax a little. He sighed and smiled thoughtfully, hunkering down on one knee in front of Christiana. He was still wearing his sweater vest and tie, although he'd left his briefcase on the kitchen table, like he usually did when he got home from class. He'd reached forward to pet Percy, scratching her between her big, floppy ears. Then, before Christiana had realized what he was doing, he'd wrapped his hand around the rabbit's neck. He reached forward with his other hand, gripped the rabbit's head, completely engulfing it in his fist, and twisted. Percy's neck snapped audibly. The rabbit lurched once, violently, and then went still on Christiana's lap. It felt no different than it had a moment before, except that its quick, metronome-like breathing had stopped.

"There," Randy said, neither grinning nor frowning. "Now Percy doesn't care what the fuck we do tonight. Go put on your dress. Our reservation's at seven."

Three minutes later, Christiana was in her bedroom, standing in front of the cheval mirror, half-dressed and shuddering violently. From the hall, Randy's voice came. "Maybe we can make her into a really little bitty fur stole for you to wear with that dress. Would you like that? Will that help you to remember to listen?" And he'd laughed, delighted with his wit.

Shane stared at the white of the canvas, stewing, thinking of Randy and Percy. Thinking of his friend Desmond, the writer.

"If you really want to make the reader hate someone," Desmond had said, leaning forward and smiling thinly, "Make him kill an animal. Something cute. A kitten. You have your villain do that—easily and with no remorse—and they will *despise* him. They'll want his head on a pike. No death will be too gruesome for that guy."

Back then, Shane had thought that that was some pretty screwed up logic. Why would people feel a greater sense of vengeance for a man who killed an animal than somebody who murdered his fellow human beings? Now, however, it made an eerie kind of sense. Murder is heinous, Shane thought, but it is rarely, except in the most deranged cases, committed lightly. If someone can kill an animal, though, without the slightest compunction, something inside them is truly dead. Whatever invisible thread exists that connects people to the brotherhood of humanity, it does not embrace the person who destroys life lightly. For that individual, the only difference between murdering an animal and murdering another human being is one of personal consequences, not morality. One can get away with killing a rabbit. It is much harder to get away with the casual murder of one's fellow man. This is the only real barrier preventing such a person from becoming a serial killer, and it isn't much. Shane had read enough to know that. Ask any police profiler. Almost without exception, mass murderers began with torturing and killing animals, usually while they were still children. The average person didn't need to be told that, however. People understand a lot of things instinctively, whether they know it or not. People understand that a man who could easily kill a rabbit could just as easily kill his girlfriend, if the mood struck him and he thought he could get away with it. That's what Desmond, the crime fiction writer, had meant when he'd said that the best way to make readers hate a villain is to have him kill an animal.

"But is that enough?" Shane had protested. "Doesn't he have to follow it up with an actual murder of another person?"

Desmond had shrugged, as if the answer didn't really matter. "What are you more afraid of, Shane?" he said in reply. "The poisonous spider that's already bitten you, or the one up in the corner of your bedroom, hanging over your bed, watching you, pondering, deciding whether or not it wants to strike?"

Shane hated spiders. He'd shuddered at the mere thought. Desmond nodded wisely, not needing to elaborate.

Christiana had told Shane the story of her previous few days, not because he'd asked, but because she seemed to need to. Keeping Randy's violence a secret had apparently become a deeply rooted habit. Breaking that habit was an important, if symbolic, act. Shane was secretly gratified that Christiana had chosen to break her silence with him, instead of with Greenfeld or her parents, but he didn't think too much of it.

"After Randy killed Percy, he was in a sort of weird, giddy good mood for the whole rest of the night," Christiana had told him, her voice strangely flat and expressionless. "It was like someone had given him a shot of B-12 or something. He joked with the waitress at the restaurant and ate like he hadn't had a meal in weeks. I wasn't hungry in the least, but I made myself eat, because I knew he'd get angry again if I didn't. When we got back to my apartment, I wanted to throw up. That would have been the worst of all. I sat as still as I could and just willed myself to keep it down. Percy was dead in her hutch out back—Randy had put her body there. He was whistling when we got back, and he just walked through the apartment and out the back door. He didn't change his clothes or anything. He dug a little hole in the back yard and buried Percy back there. I almost expected him to call me out there, to try to have a little funeral, like I was a kid whose goldfish had died. He didn't.

I went to my room and locked the door, glad to finally be out of his presence. I thought he'd try to come in when he was done. I just sat on my bed, staring. I was stunned. I didn't know what I'd do when he came back. I just kept thinking about how it had felt, when he'd been petting Percy one moment, and then snapping her neck in the next, without even blinking. I kept thinking about how she'd died on my lap, as I was stroking her fur. I hadn't been able to protect her. And I thought *who will protect me? Who will stop him from doing the same thing to me if he wants to? Would my neck sound the same as Percy's? Would he bury me in the back yard?*

"He did come back, when he was done burying Percy. I heard him come in and close the back door. He wasn't whistling anymore. After a minute, I heard him come down the hall toward my bedroom. The doorknob rattled, but just a little, like he was just resting his hand on it. He didn't try to come in, and that was good. He wouldn't have liked that I'd locked the door. He just stood there for a minute, and then I heard him let out a big sigh. 'Happy birthday, Chris,' he said. 'I'm willing to put all this ugliness behind us. I know you're tired. Sleep tight. See you tomorrow.' And then I heard him walk away. A minute later, his car started out front, and he was gone.

"I went to work the next day. It was my half day. I had plans for that second half of the day. I was going to come home after lunch, and I was going to break things off with Randy. He'd still be at class until four, so I'd have plenty of time to make arrangements. Some of his stuff was at my place, some clothes, a few books, that kind of thing. I was going to pack them up in a box and drop them off at his apartment, along with a note. I suppose that seems pretty weak, but there it is. I couldn't bring myself to tell him in person. I could hardly bring myself to think about even being in his presence again. It was like..." She shook her head, then looked up at Shane, her coffee cup long forgotten on the stone wall of the patio.

"Did you ever hear that if you try to poison someone by giving them arsenic, if you give them a little too much, the body will sense it and just throw it all up? A small amount, built up bit by bit over time, that'll kill somebody, but if you give them just a tiny bit too much, the body's alarms all go off. After that, you can bet your life that that person won't ever trust you to get them a smoothie again. Right? It was like that. Randy had been spoon-feeding me abuse for almost two years, and I swallowed it all, even as he ramped it up, even as it got worse and worse. But when he killed Percy, that did the trick. It set off all my internal alarms. It took off my blinders. It's stupid, really, that that's what did it, but it did. It was just like with the arsenic story. I wanted to vomit all of it out, every night I'd ever spent with him, every moment, every word and look and touch. Not just the bad stuff, either; *everything*. It was like taking a breath of fresh air for the first time in years. I couldn't bear to think of seeing him again. I thought I really would puke if I did, or I'd lash out at him, or worst of all, lose what resolve I'd mustered and never find it again.

"My plan was just to pack up his stuff, write a short note telling him it was over and that I never wanted to see him again, plop it all on his doorstep, and then go away for a few days until it all blew over. My parents have a little vacation place up in the Ozarks. It isn't much, just a little cabin with no heat or electricity, but it's quiet and peaceful. I have a key, even though I haven't been there for years. None of us have. I was going to pack up a few things and head there, spend a few days alone. I'd be there now, if things had gone a little differently.

"When I got back to my apartment, I went straight to the living room and started pulling Randy's books off the bookshelves. They were all legal stuff, textbooks and law books, things he'd left at my place over the last few years. Nothing good. Nothing readable. I started getting angry as I pulled them off the shelves, intending to stack them all in a box I'd found in the basement, but missing it mostly, just tossing them on the floor, not caring if they got damaged, hoping they would. I got madder and madder, baring my teeth and throwing them over my shoulder, taking my anger out on those stupid damn books. The last one was big. It was some encyclopedia of legal precedents for the state of Missouri. I picked it up with both hands and spun around, heaving it across the living room and letting out a little scream of rage.

"Randy was standing there in the hallway, watching me. His face was blank. Completely dead, like he'd been switched off. He just stared at me, his eyes on mine. I was panting and sweating and suddenly completely terrified. I knew he had a key, but he'd never come in before without my knowing it. At least, that's what I thought. Very slowly, he looked down at the books on the living room floor. I had time to notice there was a big paintbrush in his right hand. The tip was black and wet. He looked back up at me, still real slow, and finally he opened his mouth.

"'Bad day at the office dear?' he asked me, completely deadpan. I was shaking, partly from the rage, partly from the fear. I couldn't bring myself to respond, not even to shake my head or nod. The books all over the floor said everything. He just stared at me, and then, after almost a minute, he smiled. 'I'm guessing you meant to put those in that box. A lot of guys would get mad about seeing their stuff thrown around, but lucky for you, I'm the understanding sort. I don't care about any of those, anyway. That's why I left them here. They've served their purpose. What do you say we box them up and stick them in storage? I'll wait while you pack them up. Fair enough?'

"He came into the living room then, and stood there, right in front of the pile of books, and just smiled at me. The smile was the worst part. No matter what he said, he knew exactly what was going on. He knew why his books were all over the floor. Suddenly, I was aware of how many heavy, blunt things there were in the living room: the lamp on the side table, a little bronze sculpture on top of the bookcase, a pair of pewter candlesticks, a lump of volcanic rock from Hawaii that I used as a bookend. I wasn't thinking of these things because I was worried Randy might use them to hurt me—his abuse was usually very personal, using only his hands. I was thinking of them because of what I wanted to do to *him* with them.

"I was afraid, because in that moment I was still so very, very angry. I wanted to kill him. Not a figure of speech. I wanted him dead on my living room floor. I was afraid, because I knew if I lashed out at him, if I gave voice to that rage, he'd come for me, and if he did, I'd grab whichever one of those big heavy objects was closest and I'd use it on him. He'd never expect that, and I can be fast when I want to be. I wasn't afraid that he might stop me and overpower me. I was afraid that he wouldn't. Once I started hitting him, I didn't think I'd be able to stop. And in my mind, I wouldn't be paying him back for all the times he'd hit me. In my mind, I was thinking only of Percy; poor, defenseless Percy, who had been too timid and scared to even try to jump off my lap when I held her, whose only defense was trust—the hope and belief that the people holding her wouldn't try to hurt her. Randy had taken advantage of that trust, had violated it in the most basic, permanent way. And I knew that if he ever wanted to, he'd do it again. I had a sense that the rabbit's only chance was to bite, and to bite so hard that there was never any going back.

"I was wavering between two options—reaching for the hunk of volcanic rock on the bookshelf or squatting down to stack Randy's books in the box—when I heard a sound. It was a sort of scratching. It was coming from the back door. I looked in that direction, and Randy moved. He was so fast, so… cunning… that I barely knew what he was doing. He grabbed me by my hair, right at the top of my head, and shoved me in the stomach with his other hand, forcing me to bend over, driving me down to my knees. 'Isn't this what you *mean* to be doing right now?' he said through his teeth. He was panting all of a sudden, almost like he was turned on, like this was some kind of twisted foreplay. His voice went low, distracted, and he said, 'In the box, Chris. Put them in the box,' but underneath the actual words, what he really seemed to be saying was, I *dare you not to, Chris. Please, make me* make *you do it. I* want *to make you do it.*

"I think he knew. I think he saw that I was on the edge of fighting back. And you know what's really sick? I think he liked it. I think he thought it gave him the excuse he needed to really let go. Does that make sense? He wanted to push me to it. Later, then, maybe he could say he hadn't meant for things to turn out the way they did, that it had all happened so fast, that I'd pushed him and pushed him, that a man can only take so much. Maybe he'd call it temporary insanity. And the crazy thing was, most people would probably believe it. After all, how could the guy in the Alex P. Keaton sweater vest really be a premeditated murderer?

"And then I heard it again—that scratching, coming from just outside the back door—and it all made sense. I almost laughed out loud. He'd bought me a new rabbit. He had come over while he thought I was at work, put the new rabbit in Percy's old hutch, and was repainting the name over the door. He thought he was doing something sweet. He really and truly did. I wondered for a moment what name he had chosen for the new rabbit. He'd never liked the name 'Percy' anyway. Apparently, he'd decided naming duties were best left to him from now on.

"I started putting his books in the box. He still had his fist wrapped in my hair, forcing my chin down to my chest. I think he was a little disappointed when I actually obeyed. He didn't let go. He hunkered down in front of me and sighed and said, 'I love you, Chris, you stupid bitch. You need me. You can't go anywhere, and you can't get rid of me. What were you thinking? Without me, you're just a silly little bird flying around, not knowing what to do, banging off the windows, just hurting yourself. You need me to keep you grounded and to watch over you. And I need you, too, Chris. Do you realize that? Without you, I just don't know what I'd do. I love you. You make me angry sometimes, but that's just because of how much I care. I hope you know that. If you haven't learned that by now, well, I guess I just need to work a little harder at teaching you. I've been a little soft, maybe. It's my fault. I accept that. Fair enough?' And he nodded down at me. I sensed it, I could feel it in the way he was still holding my hair, forcing me down.

"I was still putting away his books, stacking them in the box. The biggest book, the one I had thrown last, was the only one left on the floor. It was just out of my reach, right by Randy's feet. He saw that I was nearly finished, and he finally let go of my hair. In a different voice, more like his normal Randy voice, he said, 'here, let me help you with this big one,' and he picked it up with both hands. He pushed himself upright, and his knees cracked as he did. I started to get up myself, and that's when the book came down on my head. He hit me with it, right on the top of my head, using both his hands and all his weight. I fell down onto the floor face first, just missing the box with my head, and everything went gray and swimmy for a while. I vaguely remember a thump, like he was dropping the book he'd hit me with, plopping it onto the pile in the box, and then there was the sound of him walking away. It was probably only a minute or so later, but it seemed like hours before I came back to myself. I was still lying on the living room floor, my face pressed into the carpet and the top of my head throbbing. I heard Randy whistling. He was out on the back porch again, probably finishing painting the new sign over the hutch door. I got to my feet, feeling woozy, grabbing onto the chair for support, and started for the front door. I tried to be quiet, but he heard me.

"He called out, 'Going out for a little while, sweetheart?' I could tell by the sound of his voice that he was smiling. He said,

'I'll wait here. Go get some air. When you get home, I've got a little surprise for you. I think you'll like it. I always hug you after I spank you, you know. So don't be too long, hmm?' I was running, stumbling, really, by the time he started whistling again. I nearly fell through the front door. I didn't know where I was going. I made it to my car, sure he would come out from behind the apartment, maybe reach into the open window and pluck the keys out of my hand. He didn't, and I finally got the car started. I just started driving, not really knowing where I was going. Maybe I'd go back to work. Maybe I'd go ahead on up to the cabin. And then..."

Christiana had stopped at that point, staring down at her hands on her lap, shaking her head minutely. "And then, I thought of you. I don't really know why. I waited until I'd calmed down a little. The further I got away from my apartment, the better it got. That's when I decided to call you. I needed to talk to someone... someone sane and normal and... safe. I didn't want to talk about what had happened. I just needed normalcy. But you knew, somehow. You could tell something was wrong. I was worried that you'd guess it all if I stayed on the phone. For some reason, it seemed very important to me that you not know about Randy, about... about how he was with me. I was ashamed. And keeping secrets... it has its own weird kind of inertia. It's hard to stop doing it once you start.

"I started to go back to work. And then I started to drive down to the cabin. Part of the way there, I became paranoid, though. Randy knew about the cabin. He'd never been there, but I'd told him about it, early on in our relationship. We'd planned to go there for a long weekend sometime. He didn't have a key, but he knew where it was. He could find it, and if he did, he could surely get in. I even started thinking maybe he'd made a copy of the key, maybe even copies of *all* the keys on my key-ring. Like I said, he's cunning. I knew it was crazy and paranoid of me, but after finding him there in my apartment, I was feeling a little off-kilter. My head still hurt. I needed to rest. I just wanted to sleep. I ended up stopping at a Super Eight motel. I stayed there for the night, but I could barely sleep. I kept thinking Randy had followed me somehow, tracked me down. Every time I heard footsteps on the sidewalk outside my room, I'd be sure it was him. I stayed there through the whole next day, never even leaving the motel, eating crackers and drinking Pepsi from the machines out front. That next night was the worst one. I barely slept at all. I knew I was letting my fear take over, and that it was irrational. I considered going to my parents, but Randy knew where they lived, too. He would probably never go there, but probably wasn't good enough. My cell phone rang a few times, but I didn't even look at it, didn't even want to see his number on the little display. Finally, yesterday, I decided it had to stop. I didn't know what to do, really, I just knew I had to get out of the motel, get to where I could finally tell someone what was happening. Not my parents. Not Morrie. Not any of my friends from college, the few that are left. I checked out of the motel and thought about it as I drove, thinking of this person or that person, not knowing for sure what to do or where to go, but knowing I needed to go somewhere, and tell someone.

"I went by my apartment first, though. I just sort of ended up there, not really knowing where else to go. It was the hardest thing to do, but I guess I needed to see, needed to force myself to at least look. Randy's car wasn't parked anywhere in sight. I was about to go in, but then, paranoid as I was, I drove around the block, just once, slowly. He drives a white Corolla. I saw one parked along the street behind my apartment. I told myself it wasn't his, that even he wasn't *that* crafty, but when I got closer and drove past it, I could see that it was. There was his university parking sticker on the front windshield, and the dent in the left of the rear bumper. The bastard was there, waiting for me, watching for me, like some kind of damn snake.

"I thought about calling the police, but what would they do? I'd given him a key, after all. Maybe they'd believe me about how things were between us, but then again, maybe they wouldn't. Randy rarely left any obvious marks, and he could be very convincing. I couldn't bring myself to take the chance. And that's when I decided to come here, Shane. I don't know why, really. It just seemed like a good idea. Once it came into my head, it seemed like exactly the place I needed to be. Like somehow, at least for a while, I could just stop and catch my breath. And tell someone. After all, it almost seemed like you already kind of knew. You sensed something when I called a few days earlier. Didn't you? So I came, stopping only long enough to get a fresh change of clothes and some toiletries, picking them all up at a Walmart along the way. I got here last night around seven-thirty. I knocked, but you didn't answer. I figured you were painting, maybe, or gone, even though your truck was still here. I waited for a while, and then knocked again. I pounded on that door, but you never came. Somehow, though, I knew you were here, or that you'd be back. I waited in the car. Later, though, I decided not to bother you. The shame had started to creep back. Besides, weird as it sounds, I felt safer just being here, even sitting in my car, parked next to the pickup. It was like a little cocoon. Randy might try to find me, but I knew he'd never find me here, not up that long, gravel drive, hidden up in the woods on the river bluff. He could look all night, if he wanted, but he'd never think to look here. Somehow, I just knew that. And I slept, a little. Better than I had the previous few nights, even though it isn't any too comfy trying to sleep in the car, with the seat pushed all back. I had a blanket in the trunk that I covered with, though, and it was better than I'd have expected. I woke up a little while before you found me. I had to pee and I was cold. And that's how I came to be here."

Christiana had finally stopped her long story at that point, still not looking directly at Shane. She sighed. "I hope you don't mind. I'll leave if you do. None of this is your problem. I don't want to push it on you, or anyone else. Like I said, I can't really even explain why I came here. I'll go if you want me to. Do you want me to go?"

Shane looked at her. The sun had risen high over the trees by now. It painted her features with striking clarity, shone on her black hair where it hung loose, framing her face. Tom the cat lay beneath her chair, sleeping in its shadow. Christiana waited for his answer, looking down at her hands in her lap. Finally, she looked up at him, her face composed, prepared for the worst.

Shane shook his head. "No," he said simply. "I don't want you to go. I want you to stay."

And she did.

Chapter Thirteen

The afternoon drew out slowly as Christiana slept. Shane sat in the studio and doodled a little, drawing meaningless scribbles and cross-hatches on the pages of a yellow legal pad, filling in the space, watching his right hand like it was a rambunctious kid that didn't know how to sit still. The canvas on the easel was still blank. Shane had an idea of what was supposed to go on it, at least for starters. There was one more painting in his head, one final addition to the Shane Bellamy Insanity Stairs series. Unlike the previous two (he wasn't counting the chalk drawing on the cellar floor, since he wasn't entirely sure he himself had actually drawn it, aside from the little editorial work he'd performed on it a few days earlier) the new painting in his head felt fragile, almost tenuous, like a soap bubble, ready to pop out of existence at the slightest provocation. Where the previous two works had felt more like freight trains, thundering through his head and out onto the canvas, this one was like a feather, tickling so lightly that he could barely feel it. It made him curious. This time it didn't feel like the muse. This image, more than the other two, felt like his very own, like it was being drawn from that same mysterious well, but by his own hand this time, without the heavy influence of the muse to push him, to guide the strokes. And yet, just as when he'd begun the previous two images, the picture in his head was only a fragment. It was like an anchor chain, coming up link by link, pulling something heavy, something that would only show itself once all those rusty links had been laid out on the deck, drying in the sun. It was going to be slow, patient work, but Shane was going to give it his best shot. For now, he simply stared at the canvas again, and saw the first stroke in his mind, even if he hadn't yet painted it. It was a vertical line, pencil thin, curving a little, fading from black to red; the first link in the chain. Shane would paint it soon. Maybe tonight. Not now, though. Not while Christiana was still there, sleeping, recouping. Later.

At one o'clock Shane headed back downstairs to find something to eat. The bottom of the stairs was gloomy, full of shadows now that the sun had officially begun its afternoon descent down the other side of the cottage. Shane was barely looking, stepping lightly on the steps so as not to wake Christiana, when one of the shadows moved.

Shane startled and stumbled a little, catching himself with a hand on the right-side banister. The shadow coiled, turned, and grew solid. It was Marlena. She'd been standing there, at the bottom of the stairs, watching the mostly-closed door of Shane's bedroom. In the silence, Shane could hear Christiana's breathing, long and slow, drifting through the crack of the door. Marlena's face spun toward him and she advanced on him, growing in size, towering up into the hot, still air over the stairs. Her eyes were black holes, widening, deepening, eating into her face, and her mouth drew down into a gruesome leer, gaping, melting like wax. She let out a long, harsh breath, a sighing scream, barely audible, and yet it seemed to shake the walls. Shane fell back onto the stairs and scrambled backwards, no longer worried about being quiet. Marlena looked like she wanted to eat him, or smother him, or rip him limb from limb. Rage and misery beat off her like heat waves, and her hands came up, hooked into white claws, growing huge and bony. Then, just as she seemed ready to fall upon him, she pulled back, as if conflicted, torn between him and the cracked doorway below. Her face collapsed into a sort of silent wail and her hands dropped down. She shrank away once more, drifting backwards, one hand reaching toward the door of the bedroom, toward the sound of Christiana's breathing, and the other reaching toward Shane. The hand reaching toward him was beckoning, palm up, plaintively beseeching. The one pointed toward the door was contorted into a hooked grapple, shaking with malice. Marlena faded again, but as she did, she looked back up the stairs, toward where Shane lay collapsed on the steps. The look on her face was terrible. It was heartbroken, utterly wasted and bereft. Her black eyes implored Shane, begged him. And then she was gone.

Shane let out a shaky breath. He was panting, his heart thundering in his chest. She was gone, but only for now. And she was unhappy. Shane didn't know why, but there didn't seem to be any doubt about it. For some reason, he thought of the drawing on the cellar floor, and of his dream, the one that had begun with Marlena standing atop the cellar stairs, looking down, and had ended with her turning on him, filled with black disappointment. She'd been unhappy about what she'd seen down there. Was it the picture itself that had disturbed her? Or had it been Shane's changes? Shane had a terrible, creeping feeling that it was the latter. When Marlena had first arrived in the house, she had seemed bereft, sad, solemn, but essentially harmless. Now, Shane wasn't so sure. Now, for the first time, he began to seriously worry.

A little while later, Christiana woke up. She came out into the kitchen, bleary-eyed and tousle-haired, still wearing Shane's tee shirt. It swayed around her thighs, making her look much younger than she really was. Shane was sitting at the tiny table in the kitchen, doodling, making nonsensical scribbles and shapes, fingering something in his left hand.

"What's that?" Christiana asked, pulling out the other chair and plopping onto it.

Shane didn't look up, but he closed the pad of paper and set down the pencil. "Just something I found in the woods," he said, closing the object in his fist. It glittered a little, and let out a tiny, jolly jingle, like a memory of Christmas. He smiled up at her wearily. "What do you say, you want to ride into town with me?"

They packed the Florida title painting in the back of Christiana's Saturn, putting the rear seats down and laying it flat on top. Shane closed the trunk and jingled the keys.

She looked up at him crookedly, squinting in the sun. "Are you sure you don't mind?"

He merely shook his head. She nodded and turned away, heading up the passenger's side of the car.

When they were both inside, Shane started the car and began to turn it around. Christiana put her window down and looked out, up at the trees. "I thought you said Morrie was sending over his cousin or something?"

"I called him and told him to cancel that."

"You talked to him? On a Sunday?"

"Well, this morning, yes, but not when I called back. I left a message on his machine at the office. I have a feeling he checks that pretty regularly."

Christiana gave a little laugh. "He does. Calls in every few hours, even on weekends. His system's old as the hills, but he says he prefers it. I'm surprised it still works."

Shane piloted Christiana's Saturn down the gravelly drive, into the shadow of the trees. Reflections flickered on the hood like lace. As the Valley Road came into sight, peeking over the top of the next rise, Shane saw a semi truck there, unmoving. Its trailer caught the light blindingly, blocking the view beyond. *Haulin' ass is an important life skill,* Shane thought idly.

"Wait a minute," Christiana said in a different voice. "You left a message on his office machine? Not his cell phone?"

Shane shook his head. "No, not his cell. I thought that was for emergencies only. I called the office number. You think he didn't get the message?"

Christiana didn't reply. Shane glanced at her. Her face was tense, thoughtful. She blinked and looked at him, then smiled and waved a hand in front of her face. "It's nothing. Paranoia. Never mind."

Shane narrowed his eyes a little. "What is it? Paranoia may be a good thing right about now."

"It's irrational," she said, the smile dropping from her lips. "Like I said earlier. It was like when I worried that Randy might show up at the motel. There was no *way* he could know where I was, and yet I just couldn't shake the fear—the *certainty*—that the next set of footsteps I heard would be him. I'd worried that he might have made copies of my keys. If so, he'd have a key to the cabin, but he'd also have a key to the office. I was thinking... maybe he thought that's where I'd gone. Maybe he'd gone there himself, looking for me. Maybe..."

"Maybe he'd listened to Greenfeld's messages," Shane said, completing her thought. He found it an extremely likely possibility. And if he'd done that, he surely wouldn't have been above riffling through Greenfeld's rolodex in search of Shane's address. "So there's a chance he knows where you are. Do you think he would come here?"

Christiana shook her head, not in denial, but to say she didn't know. Shane believed she did. The Saturn reached the end of the gravel drive and Shane nosed it to the right, turning the car away from Bastion Falls. The semi truck had finally moved on, chugging and sending up a cloud of blue smoke from its side exhausts. Shane angled in behind it.

"Maybe it isn't safe for you to stay here after all," Shane said, reluctantly. "If he knows…"

Christiana shook her head again. "Look, he can't rule my life forever. I have to stop running."

Shane pushed the accelerator down slowly. There was a long line of traffic ahead, curving over into the left lane. A patrolman in a beige shirt with black pockets was directing traffic. His cheeks were red. Watching him, Shane felt a cold finger draw a line up his spine. He pulled ahead, following the truck as it angled over, passing by something in the right lane. Lights flashed beyond it, flickering red and blue. Something glittered on the gray asphalt, sparkling meanly in the sunlight.

"Besides," Christiana said, shaking her head. "If he knew… if Randy knew, he wouldn't waste any time. If he heard your message he'd have left immediately. He'd have been here before we even…"

Her voice trailed away as the truck sped up, passing the blockage in the road. Two patrol cars were pulled off onto the weedy shoulder, their light-bars flashing, illuminating the wreck where it lay in the ditch. Its wheels were up and its passenger's door was wrenched open, pointing at the sky like the wing of a dead bird. Christiana sucked in a long, whistling gasp and raised both of her hands to her mouth, not quite covering it. The car in the ditch was a white Corolla. Shane could see the nameplate on the rear end, although it was upside-down. His gaze travelled from the wreck to Christiana and back again. They passed it slowly, and she watched it go by, her head turning, unable to look away. Glass lay in the road like confetti. Bits of a shattered tail-light sparkled red, looking like candy left over from a parade… or like stumps of colored chalk left lying on a cellar floor.

Shane shuddered. He hadn't meant to do anything other than to sketch Christiana out of the chalk drawing. The best way he'd known how was to change the person behind the wheel of the silver car, to change it from Christiana to… someone else. *Anyone* else. He hadn't meant for it to be a specific person, but apparently that wasn't the way such things worked. He'd used his fingers to smudge out the unmistakable image of Christiana, and in its place he had drawn a man. The figure had been thin and sharp featured, with dark hair neatly parted on the right. He wore wire-framed glasses. A mild scowl of concentration had creased his forehead, pulled down the corners of his mouth. It had been Randy, of course. Shane just hadn't known it, anymore than he'd known when he was painting the footpath into the Riverhouse painting. Somehow, without intending to (at least consciously), Shane had spared Christiana the fate predicted by the chalk drawing only by passing it on to her tormenting boyfriend.

And he didn't feel the slightest bit bad about it.

Shane pulled ahead, accelerating slowly, following in the wake of the semi truck. An ambulance was parked beyond the patrol cars, its rear doors closed. An EMT paramedic was standing in the weeds nearby, watching and smoking a cigarette. Nobody seemed to be in any hurry. Shane noticed that there was only one vehicle involved in the accident. There was, however, a set of long, looping skid-marks on the road, glistening black in the bright sunlight. They looked fresh. Shane was quite certain that they'd been left by a pickup truck; one coming from the opposite direction, from Bastion Falls.

One with GMC stamped onto its huge, chrome grill.

Chapter Fourteen

Maybe it was another one of those things people understood instinctively, or maybe Shane had just picked it up somewhere along the way, perhaps from a magazine article or one of those awful afternoon talk shows: relationships that begin as a result of some outside adversity rarely last once the crisis is past.

At first, Shane told himself that it was silly to even think about it. He and Christiana didn't have a *relationship*, per se. At least not in the romantic sense. He'd just been the safe one. The good guy. That's how it had always been in high school. *I can't go out with you, Shane,* the girls would always say, *you're too nice. You're like my brother.* And they always smiled as they said it, crookedly, as if to say *silly rabbit, Trix are for kids; pretty girls are for bad boys. Nice guys just draw pictures and watch Star Trek, but that's enough, isn't it?* Shane knew that that was less true of grown-up romance than it was of the inbred world of high school dating, but it was a hard perception to shake. Sure, Christiana had come to him, had even called him first when she'd needed someone safe and solid in the midst of the awfulness with Randy. But that couldn't be because she felt anything meaningful for him. Shane was a *nice guy.* He was safe. What kind of woman chooses to be with the *safe* guy?

Of course, Steph had chosen him, but that had been different. Shane had pursued her, pursued her like he'd never pursued any other woman in his life. She had let him, but she had never fallen for him, at least not like he had for her. Her love for him had been a choice that she'd made, based on logic and practicality. It had not been something that consumed her, drove her, fueled her passions. Later, she *had* come to feel some passion for him—Shane was sure of it, in his deepest heart—but that had only come as a result of her initial clinical choice to be with him. She hadn't chosen to be with him because she couldn't be without him, but because he'd scored well enough on the checklist of good husband requirements. Shane had gotten lucky with Steph. She was beautiful, intelligent and rock solid, even if she had been a little clinical and pragmatic.

But Christiana was different. She'd never choose a man based on how he scored on any mental checklist. If that had been the case, frankly, she'd have never been with Randy. Somehow, Shane sensed that Christiana was a woman driven slightly more by her passions than she was by logic, despite her formidable intellect, and despite how she might appear to the casual observer. She was a closet romantic. She'd probably hate being called that, and yet Shane felt certain that it was true, nonetheless. After all, she'd given up a solid future law career, funded by her lawyer parents, to pursue a nebulous livelihood in the world of art representation. She had done so merely because she liked art and wanted to share it with the world, despite the fact that she herself couldn't create it. If that wasn't the choice of a heart-and-soul romantic, Shane didn't know what was. Women like that didn't fall for the *safe* guys. They fell for troublesome men with shady histories and dangerous demeanors. A woman like Christiana might fall in love with a starving artist, but never the trustworthy go-to commercial artist, the one who wore button-down shirts and khakis to his shift, who listened to the foreman in his head more than he did the muse. Things like that just didn't happen.

No matter how much he might want them to.

Randy had been killed in the accident. Shane knew that right from the beginning, from the moment he'd seen the paramedic standing next to the closed ambulance, smoking a cigarette. That afternoon, Christiana had gotten a call from Randy's mother. Shane had been with her at the time, at Greenfeld's office, having just unloaded the Florida painting. Christiana answered, and Shane could hear the woman's voice on the other end, shrill and nearly incoherent. Her baby was dead, poor Randy, poor sweet little man. Christiana listened and nodded and offered admirable condolences, and Shane thought he knew everything he needed to know about the woman on the phone. Randy had been the sort of boy who killed grasshoppers with a magnifying glass, burning their eyes out while they twitched on the sidewalk, and this woman had been the one who'd decided, from the very beginning, simply not to notice. Her perception of him had probably stopped developing around the time that he was five years old. To her, he was still a baby, still a sticky-faced toddler with skinned knees and tousled hair. After all, that was a far more pleasant image than that of the sullen, grown-up man with the cruel streak, the one who was just as likely to glower at her with murder in his eyes as he was to kiss her on the cheek.

Shane had been sitting at Greenfeld's desk while Christiana talked to the woman, and Shane had doodled on a yellow Post-it pad with a dull pencil. He'd doodled the woman's face, narrow and haggard, her eyes stunned wide, a phone clutched to her ear, her mouth hanging open, no teeth showing. As he did, the story grew in his mind, sending out tendrils of root, forming a disturbing scene. The woman knew her son had been dangerous, but had hidden that knowledge away, buried it, refused to look at it. Part of her had always been afraid—terrified, even—that her baby would someday take away someone else's baby. She'd expected him to show up at her house someday with a shapeless figure in his arms, wrapped in Glad garbage bags, or with blood all over his hands, telling her not to call the police, that he'd had a little accident, but that he could take care of it himself. And she knew that she would do whatever he told her to do. Because secrets have their own kind of inertia. At a certain point, you just can't stop them anymore. The weight of them will crush you. She would hide him, and protect him, and not ask any questions, no matter what. Even now, she had not called Christiana just to commiserate, to share her woe with the only other woman who had been close to her son. She had called Christiana to ensure that she, Christiana, was still alive, that her son had not murdered her before barreling off to kill himself, to plow his car into a tree on some nameless back road, grinning to himself and saying, *you aren't out of my reach yet, babe. Being dead won't save you. I'm coming. Just you wait...*

Shane stopped doodling. The scene in his head was fed by the picture on the paper, and that had been fed by the voice of the woman blathering incoherently on the phone (was it just grief that Shane heard in the woman's voice? Or was there a little secret relief, as well?) but it wasn't a nice picture, and he didn't want to think about it anymore. He dropped the pencil onto Greenfeld's desk, stripped the Post-it off the rest of the pad, and tore it in two. He balled the pieces up in his fist. Christiana looked at him, at his fist, then at his face, meeting his eyes. She shook her head sadly, listening to the woman on the phone.

"Uh-huh," she said. "I'm sure you're right. He's in a better place now."

But Shane could tell she didn't believe it. And neither did the woman on the phone.

Shane had invited Christiana to stay over at the cottage that night, but once they discovered that Randy was dead, there didn't seem to be any point anymore. To his surprise, however, she didn't seem to have any intentions of changing the plan. Without a word, she drove them from Greenfeld's office to her downtown apartment, a little duplex in a long narrow street, crowded with small, old houses and sweetgum trees. Shane followed her inside and mooned around the kitchen while she gathered a few things. Outside the little kitchen window he could see the corner of the rabbit hutch. He wondered if the rabbit inside was all right. He thought it would probably need watered and fed, but when he stepped out onto the back porch he found the hutch empty, its door neatly shut and clasped. The name painted over the door was "Winston". Shane couldn't know for sure, but he had a creeping certainty that "Winston" had been in the car with Randy when he'd crashed. He had probably been on the passenger's seat, inside a cardboard box with holes punched in the lid. Randy may not have succeeded in capturing Christiana, but he'd managed to take two rabbits with him before he punched his ticket. For a guy like him, that probably wasn't too bad a score. It was sad, but it could have been much worse. It *would* have been, if not for a few stumps of chalk and Shane's skilled fingers. He shuddered when he thought about it.

And yet, some part of him knew that the story wasn't completely over. Christiana wasn't safe yet. Not while Marlena was haunting the cottage, watching, filled with her inexplicable anger and misery. At first, the ghost had been pretty frightening, but she had also been sad, confused, even a little quaint. Now, all that was changing. She was no longer quaint. Now she was just frightening, especially because of her increasingly neurotic and frantic rage. Worst of all, Shane had a low, deep suspicion that Marlena was powerful, more so than she let on, maybe more so than even she knew. He thought of the last time he'd been out to the site of Riverhouse, thought of the way it had seemed to shimmer in the air over its dead foundation, faint, ghost-like in the twilight. Was she doing that? Or was he? Had he conjured the house again simply by painting it? Neither answer was a comforting one. Maybe he should destroy the Riverhouse painting. It would pain him to do so, but he thought he could. If it would diminish Marlena's power, if it would help keep Christiana safe, he'd do it. But not yet. There was still one more painting in his head, one more addition to the Shane Bellamy Insanity Stairs series. When that was finished, when the set was complete, then he would destroy the Riverhouse painting. Maybe he'd destroy them all. Not yet, though. His curiosity about the last painting was simply too great a force to deny.

Besides, Marlena had never shown any sign that she could affect things in the physical world. Even when she attempted to speak, the most she seemed capable of was that awful, rattling sigh. She could be rather frightening, but surely she couldn't pose any actual danger to himself or Christiana. Even the chalk drawing on the cellar floor—if, indeed, Marlena had been responsible for it— hadn't he thought that it might just as likely have been a warning as a threat?

He was rationalizing. He was aware of it, but that didn't change anything. It *had* occurred to him that it might be dangerous to allow Christiana to stay at the cottage, at least for any length of time. But surely not for one or two days. After all, Marlena listened to Shane. She had heeded him ever since that very first night, when she had first appeared and he had shown her the silver baby rattle. She watched him paint sometimes, and he sometimes watched her go on her nightly rounds, haunting through the library and kitchen, up the studio stairs, restlessly roaming, her black eyes solemn. She was his muse. She may not like Christiana, but he felt confident that he could keep Marlena mollified for a day or two.

Nobody intends to get into an abusive relationship, Christiana had said. *Some of us just don't intend* not *to.* Shane shuddered as he stood on the back porch of Christiana's apartment, looking into the empty hutch. He touched it, leaned on it with his right hand. The new rabbit's name had been painted over the previous one, but Shane could still read the original name, faint under a coat of white primer: Percy. *I kept thinking about how she'd died on my lap,* Christiana had told him in her calm, expressionless voice. *As I was stroking her fur. I hadn't been able to protect her...*

Shane shook his head, as if to dislodge his nagging, worrisome thoughts. *Ghosts can't hurt the living,* he told himself, *everybody knows that*. And then, a remnant of a nearly forgotten dream, a whisper: *boundary lands... rivers and valleys, shores and cliffs... here, the line is a lot deeper...*

Christiana poked her head out of the back door. She had a duffle bag slung over her shoulder. She was ready.

Later, at the cottage, she said she would sleep on the couch, but Shane refused. He insisted that she take his bed again, and that he would camp out in the sunroom. He told her that he had, in fact, slept the entire night away there, konked out on the big couch, on the night she had arrived. That was probably why he hadn't heard her pounding on the front door. She eventually agreed, reluctantly, and after a light dinner (pasta with olive oil and sautéed onions and garlic), a half glass of wine (a cheap Shiraz Shane had found in the basement), and an hour's worth of an old Hitchcock movie on AMC (Vertigo), Christiana had headed off to bed. Shane listened. When she went into the bathroom and closed the door, he ducked into the bedroom and changed into a pair of old sweats and a tee shirt. The bedroom was a safe place, Shane was sure of it. He'd never seen Marlena there, only in the doorway as she passed by, heading silently up the studio stairs. Christiana would be safe from her there in his bed, or so he truly believed. He finished dressing, and by the time she came out of the bathroom, he was sprawled on the big sunroom couch with one of his pillows and a spare blanket. Christiana stood in the opening of the French doors for a long moment, merely looking at him. Shane smiled wanly up at her.

"Are you going to be all right?"

She shrugged weakly. "I guess. Sure. It's all over, at least. I wouldn't have chosen for it to happen like this, but..."

"It's just the buffet of life," Shane said. "You can't control what the kitchen serves. You just have to take what comes."

Christiana shook her head slightly, wonderingly, and smiled. It was the first genuine smile Shane had seen on her face since her arrival. "That's one of the cheesiest things I've ever heard."

Shane laughed. "So cheesy it's true?"

She shrugged again, still smiling. "Maybe. Maybe all the truest things in life are like that. So common that they seem silly. Too obvious. Simplistic."

Shane nodded.

"Goodnight, Shane," she said, and behind her, a shadow swooped. It looked like a wing, or a shawl, tattered, billowing in a sudden gust. Shane gasped and sat up, but whatever it was, it was already gone.

"What?" Christiana said, frowning.

Shane shook his head, looking over her shoulder, into the darkness of the library beyond. It occurred to him that it might, in fact, have been a lot safer for Christiana to sleep in the sunroom. "Nothing," he answered, trying to keep his voice even. "Do you have everything you need?"

"I guess," she sighed. "I just wanted to say thank you. For letting me stay. You didn't have to, especially now. It feels better, though, just being around somebody. So, thanks."

"You're welcome," Shane replied, his heart still thumping hard in his chest. "Goodnight, Christiana. Sleep well. See you in the morning."

She nodded. A moment later, she was gone, the tail of her nightshirt swishing as she crossed into the dim glow of the kitchen.

Shane stood up, letting the blanket fall to the floor of the sunroom. Quietly, he approached the French doors and stood there, looking out into the dark library. Was Marlena there? It was cold, but that was probably simply due to the descending chill of autumn, seeping into the stone of the cottage, hinting at winter to come.

"She's just a friend," he whispered, barely audible. "She just needs a safe house for the night; to be around someone normal and sane. That's all. It's just for tonight. All right?"

Shane couldn't see anything in the darkness. There was no movement, no sound. He felt a little silly. Finally, he turned around, crept back to the couch, and lay down. It was, in fact, a surprisingly comfy couch. He reached and clicked off the light. He was worried about Christiana, but only a little. He wondered if it might be a good idea for him to stay awake, to watch over Christiana. Maybe he could creep up to the studio and paint. That might distract Marlena, if nothing else. *But what, really, could she do?* Shane reminded himself, beginning to doze. *She's only a ghost. Ghosts can't touch things. They can't hurt the living. Marlena's just confused and lonely. She doesn't understand what's going on. And besides, she's never been in the bedroom. It's just one of the places she doesn't go, for whatever reason. Christiana will be all right.* Thinking this, thinking that he'd wake and check on Christiana in a few hours, thinking of Percy the rabbit, and of flashing lights and glittering glass out on the River Road, Shane settled slowly into a deep doze.

Some hours later, in the silent core of the night, he awoke to find something heavy and warm pressed against him. Sleepily, he assumed it was Tom the cat, and then he heard her breathing, felt the tickle of her hair on his cheek. She was deeply asleep, squeezed onto the couch next to him, her face pressed into the crook of his neck. She had snuck out in the middle of the night and come to him. She seemed very small, pressed up against him. Her breath was so soft, so slow. It had been a long time since Shane had awoken to the sound of a woman's breathing. It was, to be sure, sweetly wonderful. He was glad that Christiana was there, glad that she had come to him. He slipped an arm under her and curled it around her shoulders. She snuggled in her sleep, moaned softly, and then resumed her deep, long breaths. Shane smiled, content, at least in the moment, his eyes blinking slowly in the dim blue shadows of the sunroom.

The French doors were open. There was nothing there, nothing floating in the darkness of the library beyond. Or maybe there was. Shane looked, already sinking back into sleep. There seemed to be two dark points in the air, hovering in the entry to the sunroom. They looked like blind spots, like the ghostly after-images burned onto one's eyes after you've inadvertently looked directly at the sun. He couldn't focus on them. Maybe they were the eyes of Marlena, her dead black stare, watching, simmering, calculating. But then again, maybe they weren't. Shane was too sleepy and too content to worry about it. It was too nice to have Christiana there with him, to hear her slow breathing, to feel the tickle of her hair. Shortly, without even realizing it, Shane drifted back to sleep.

Without moving, without blinking, the eyes in the doorway watched him. She watched them both.

Shane finally realized what was happening between him and Christiana on the day, a week later, when he found her in the cellar, scrubbing the chalk image off the floor.

She'd been around a lot in the days following the night she'd crept to join him on the sunroom couch. She'd gone back to sleeping at her apartment, but whenever she wasn't at work or managing her personal affairs, Shane could usually count on her to be there at the cottage, sitting on the back patio, or watching Mets games with him. They ate dinner together sometimes, and when they did, she helped him clean up afterwards. They didn't talk very much, at least at first. After her initial cathartic disclosure of the details of her relationship with Randy, Christiana seemed to need to be quiet for awhile. She needed time to think, to feel, to steep in the knowledge that it was all over. Shane could imagine it. All those pent up emotions and fears, harbored for so long, would take a while to go away, even if they had stopped being relevant. Watching her was like watching a block of ice melting in the sun; you couldn't rush it without breaking it. Shane would be patient. It was very nice having her there, no matter what it meant. He assumed that she was simply accepting the generosity of his hospitality, gratefully using the cottage and his presence as the backdrop for her slow rejuvenation. It couldn't be any more than that. Not yet, at least. Shane was the safe guy. He refused to take advantage of her vulnerability, or to assume that her presence meant anything more than friendship and the strange kinship of shared experiences. He was happy with that, even if it did mean that she'd eventually leave.

On Saturday afternoon, he'd returned from a bike ride to find Christiana's Saturn parked next to his truck. He peered in the car's windows as he pushed his bike toward the shed. She wasn't in the car, nor was she on the front porch. He expected to find her on the back patio, watching the river, bundled in a sweater, but she wasn't there either. He unlocked the sliding back door and entered, calling her name curiously. She was in the kitchen opening a can of tuna.

"I hope you don't mind," she said, smiling at him over her shoulder. "The door was unlocked. I thought you'd be hungry. I know I am. You like tuna salad?"

Shane nodded, happy to find her there, and yet puzzled. "The door was unlocked? The front door?"

"Yeah," she said, a note of scolding in her voice. "You should be careful about that. You may live in the boonies, but that doesn't mean bad guys might not try to steal your stuff. Your paintings alone are worth thousands. You know how mad at you I'd be if they got stolen before I had a chance to produce my next show?"

"I shudder to think," Shane replied smoothly. He walked to the front door and tried the knob. It rattled in his hand but didn't turn. She heard him.

"I locked it when I came in," she called. "Force of habit. Funny thing is, I was sure it was locked when I first tried it. It wouldn't turn. I started to go around to the back, but then I heard the knob click behind me. I assumed it was you, so I went back and tried again. The door opened, but you weren't here, so I knew you'd forgotten to lock it after all."

"Uh huh," Shane said, still looking down at the door knob. He always locked the door when he went on his bike rides. It was like Christiana had said: force of habit. He carried a house key zippered into the thigh pocket of his cargo shorts, even washed them with it inside, just so he wouldn't ever forget it. It had become so ingrained that he never even thought about it. He shook his head, thinking. Had Marlena let Christiana in? Could she do that? If so, why? No answers seemed to be forthcoming. Shane dismissed it.

Shane ate with her, showered, and then went up to his studio. He still hadn't started the new painting. He'd decided to wait until he finished the Florida series completely, fearing that once he got started on the new work, he'd find it hard to focus on his contract. The Florida paintings were done now, leaning against the short wall opposite the easel, underneath the low angle of the ceiling. They'd be dry by Monday morning, latest, and then they could go to Greenfeld for shipment. Christiana would probably take them herself, transporting them in the white Sprinter van he had first seen her in. Then he'd start the painting, the last one in the series. The portrait of Marlena was still there, sitting on the smaller easel in the corner. Shane looked at her, marveled at her. Her face was perfect, blank and stunned, her eyes shining, just beginning to widen as she studied the note in her hands. *Dear M...*

Something was wrong with the painting. Shane didn't know what it was, but it nagged him, tried to hook him. This time, however, he didn't allow himself to be hooked. Whatever it was, it could wait. Shane had other concerns now. He shook himself, tore his eyes away from Marlena and her note, and turned toward the stairs.

Christiana was nowhere in sight, and yet Shane could hear something, a sort of dull, repetitive scratching. It made him think of Christiana's story, of how she'd heard the new rabbit scratching in its hutch. Shane followed the sound. The cellar door was hanging open. The light was on. A thrill of worry shimmied down Shane's spine. He hadn't been down to the cellar since the day he'd gone down in search of wine, almost a week earlier. He'd forgotten all about the chalk drawing. How could that have happened? How could such a thing have slipped his mind?

He approached the stairs and descended them slowly, looking for her. Most of the drawing was gone already, reduced to very faint pastel smears on the old concrete, dark where it hadn't already dried. Christiana was kneeling in the corner by the front window, leaning on a large scrubbing brush with both hands, working it back and forth with swift, businesslike strokes. She saw him and stopped, leaning back on her haunches and blowing her hair out of her face. Her expression was calm, unreadable.

"You found it," Shane said. He didn't know what else there was to say.

She nodded, letting her eyes roam from him to the remains of the drawing on the floor. She sighed.

She thinks I drew this since he died, Shane thought. *She thinks this is how I deal with life's unexpected curve balls. She must. She couldn't know that that drawing was here before I even knew who Randy was, that it had predicted his death like some kind of chalk voodoo doll. She especially couldn't know that before it had been him in that picture, it had been her.*

But she looked up at him again, and he wondered. She knew *something*. After a moment, she set back to work again, scrubbing out the last of the markings, turning them into pale blurs, washing them away with soapy water from a red plastic bucket.

Shane went back up the cellar stairs. He sat at the desk in the living room, beneath the painting of the Riverhouse. He didn't turn the computer on. Instead, he simply looked out the window, watching the day fade, watching the sky turn red and pink, the colors brightening as the darkness pushed them downward, condensing them. Fifteen minutes later, Christiana came upstairs. Shane heard her dump the bucket out in the sink. Her footsteps approached him from behind and he didn't turn around. He was worried about what she might be thinking of him. Maybe she was going to leave him now and never come back. After all, it was bound to happen eventually. He felt her hands touch his shoulders from behind. She gripped him, turned him, swiveling the desk chair around so that he faced her. She sat down on his lap, leaned on him and put her arms around him. Her hair tickled his cheek again as she rested her head on his shoulder. She was warm, slightly sweaty from her work on the cellar floor.

"If you want to leave, I understand," he said quietly. "You don't need to stay here. It's all over now."

She shook on his lap, once, then twice. Shane thought she was laughing. He felt her breath, hot on his neck. She convulsed silently against him, breathing harshly out through her nose. And then, suddenly and monumentally, she sobbed. Shocked, Shane wrapped his arms around her, held her, and she cried on his shoulder, huge wracking spasms that seemed to come all the way from her toes. *This,* he realized, was what had been buried under all that ice, thawing for the last week. Somehow, finding the drawing on the cellar floor—and the subsequent effort of washing it away—had finally broken the vapor-lock on her heart. The years of abuse, the wasted time, the shame and fear and lies, all of it was finally crashing to the surface, letting go, bursting like a dam. Christiana sobbed on Shane's shoulder, her tears hot and wet on his neck, and he knew enough to simply hold her. He stroked her back, her hair, held her against him and waited. Her tears poured out like rain, like a summer storm. And like a summer storm, they eventually softened to a mist, and then to a sort of exhausted, humid stillness. Shane still held her. Eventually, some time later, she pushed back from him, sniffed, wiped her eyes, and looked at him. Her face was only a few inches from his. Her eyes were red, swollen, but bright in the dying embers of the sunset beyond the window.

"I don't want to leave," she said, not taking her eyes from his, studying him. She took a shuddering breath. "I don't want to leave, Shane. I want to stay."

And she did.

Chapter Fifteen

When Shane was eleven years old, his parents had taken him on a vacation to the Grand Canyon. He remembered it as one of those crystalline, Polaroid moments of youth. He remembered the long, hot car ride, with all the windows rolled down so that air roared through the back seat like a wind tunnel, riffling his hair, flapping his tee shirt, making him feel worn out and beaten by the time they got to the various motels along the way. He remembered breakfast at a crowded Waffle House adjacent to one of those motel parking lots, sitting across from his parents in the little booth, watching them drink black coffee while they waited for their pancakes and eggs, sipping orange juice from a miniature glass and listening to the hiss and clatter of the cook behind the counter. He remembered loving his parents very much in that moment, as they bantered about grown up things and studied the map unfolded on the table in front of them, remembered the warmth of that love, even though, being eleven years old, he himself felt awkward about showing it to them.

He remembered arriving at the Grand Canyon, suddenly and unexpectedly, after what seemed like weeks in the car, remembered everyone clambering out into the hot sun, blinking, stretching, groaning contentedly. They'd left their motel before dawn that morning, and by the time they'd gotten there a thick fog was just beginning to burn away as the sun climbed into the sky. Where the fog remained, it was dazzlingly white, seamless, like an enormous movie screen. Shane looked around, squinting in the brightness, wondering what the fog might do to the view. There was a low railing nearby, running in front of a line of parked cars. Shane stopped and looked at that railing, at the fog beyond it. In the warm morning air, he felt a sudden chill plait down his back. He'd never seen anything like it, never experienced such a sudden, delicious rush of mingled delight and fear. His parents' voices faded to silence as he drifted toward the railing, taking small, careful steps, reaching slowly out to touch the railing, as if to catch himself, as if he was running toward it rather than inching, mincing, feeling for the ground beneath his feet.

Shane had a thing about heights. Not a fear, necessarily, but a respect. An awe. The ground seemed to tilt beneath him, to tip him forward, toward that yawning, misty expanse beyond the railing. He looked, his eyes wide, his breath frozen in his chest. He touched the railing and leaned on it, gingerly, like a very old man leaning on a walker.

Beyond the railing was the end of the world.

Shane had heard tales of how people used to believe that the earth was flat, just a big Frisbee floating through space, with the sun going around it instead of the other way around. He'd been intrigued by the idea, entranced by the thought of how the world's oceans might spill over its edges, forming a constant, enormous waterfall, spreading and turning to mist, evaporating after some incalculable distance and being carried back up, up, pushed by the mysterious winds of the earth's underside. Eventually, that mist would condense into clouds, creeping back up around to the top of the plate of the world, where they'd finally rain down and start the process all over again. For the first time, however, standing there with his hands on the railing overlooking the fog-filled Grand Canyon, it occurred to Shane that if the world had been flat, surely there would have been continents somewhere along its edge, not just oceans. If there were, if there were land masses that bordered the lip of a flat earth, and if you travelled along them, heading to where the horizon lowered and lowered, aiming for the place where the earth dropped away to nothing, *this* was what you would find when you got there.

Dizzying, craggy terraces of earth, like giant's stair steps, dropped away before Shane, fading into white nothing. It was dreadful, apocalyptic, and intensely beautiful. It was one of those moments that etches immediately into the mind, becoming permanent and formative. In the months and years following, Shane tried repeatedly to capture that scene on paper, to recreate it with his skilled fingers using any medium at his disposal. He tried pencils, crayons and markers. He even made a halting attempt with watercolors, which were still new to him at that point. Nothing worked, nothing got even close. Eventually, he decided that the best picture of it was the one in his mind. Some things were simply too huge, too monumental and mysterious, to fit onto a piece of paper. If the scene had only been beautiful, he thought he could have done it. If it had been merely frightening, he suspected he could have captured that as well. But it had been both of those things, sublime and dreadful in equal parts, each in doses far greater than anything he'd ever experienced before. Such a thing could not be caged on paper, tamed with a pen or pencil or a paintbrush. It was humbling to know that, but also sort of nice. It was nice to know such things existed in the world, and that he could taste them, if only briefly, even if he couldn't tame them. Maybe even *because* he couldn't tame them.

Shane didn't think consciously of these things in the weeks after Christiana washed the chalk drawing off the cellar floor, but they were there, running underneath his thoughts like a subterranean river. Being with Christiana at the cottage was like standing on the ledge of the Grand Canyon on that morning so long ago, when fog filled the depths, pretending to be the end of the world. It was beautiful, because Shane loved being with her, loved the tapered grip of her hand when they walked together, and the casual delight of her weight across his lap as they lounged on the sunroom couch in the evenings, watching movies or just talking, comparing notes on life, on growing up, on family and dreams and the tentative soap bubble of the future. He wasn't quite willing to admit yet that he loved these things because he loved Christiana herself, but the knowledge of it was there, unspoken and patient, unavoidable.

But there was Marlena, as well. If Christiana was the natural beauty of the scene, then Marlena was the fog, the part that made it mysterious, capricious, and quietly dreadful. Shane couldn't know why Christiana's presence affected Marlena the way it did, but there was no mistaking it. Marlena hated Christiana, and wanted her gone. Thankfully, ever since his confrontation with the ghost on the stairs, when Marlena had shaken her hooked hand toward the sound of Christiana's breathing, Shane had not seen Marlena at all. She no longer drifted on her nighttime haunts through the library and kitchen, no longer floated silently up the stairs to watch him paint. Sometimes Shane thought this was a good thing. Maybe she'd gone completely. Part of him would be a little sad if that was the case, since he'd developed a sort of connection with her—a sympathy, if not an empathy. He thought he understood her, partly because they'd both lost their spouses and children, and partly because he'd painted her, shared that mysterious mind-meld of the artist and the subject. But another part of him, the larger part that loved Christiana and worried for her, was secretly glad at the idea that Marlena might be gone for good. Other times, however, he wondered. Maybe Marlena wasn't gone at all. Maybe she was merely hiding, biding her time, planning, simmering in her rage. She was the fog in the scene, secretive and erratic and potentially dangerous.

As the weeks progressed, Shane found himself frequently sitting in front of the painting of Marlena, the one he had begun to simply think of as "Dear M". He'd stare at her image on the canvas, at the white delicacy of her fingers where they held the note, or the calm dread on her face, or the subtle sparkle of the tear trembling in the corner of one bright, brown eye. He knew a lot more about Marlena now than he had when he'd first painted this picture. He knew the story of the candle in the mysterious, hidden window, knew the awful secret contained in the letter in her white hands. He'd heard her tale, and had begun to put all the pieces of her sad life together. Most of it had come from Earl Kirchenbauer's story, but not all of it. His retelling of Marlena's and Wilhelm's unhappy tale had filled in the blanks, but Shane had understood the essential framework of their marriage from the moment he'd begun the Riverhouse painting, maybe even from that first line etched in the dirt in front of the demolished house. Somehow, the art was a gateway. It connected him with the muse, and at least in this case, the muse had a very specific tale to tell. Earl had provided the fine points, but most of the story had come straight out of the canvas, from each individual brush stroke, even as Shane had painted them. It happened when he was fathoms deep in the creative process, in that strange limbo where the realities blended, where the canvas stopped being a flat surface and became a portal, a secret doorway. It was there that Shane had learned the story of the Riverhouse, and of Marlena. And yet, even here, he had encountered secrets. There was more to the story; Shane was sure of it. Marlena might be his muse but she wasn't telling him everything.

For one thing, there was the shadow in the corner of the Riverhouse painting, the approaching figure that Marlena was looking up at from her vantage point on the portico steps, shading her eyes and smiling enigmatically. It was crazy, of course, but Shane had become certain that that shadow was becoming longer, growing on a daily basis, preceding the figure. Someday, he'd look at the picture and see that the second person had finally come into view. *It's all just a stage,* Greenfeld had said on the day he'd first seen the Riverhouse painting. *The first act is about to begin, and she's going to be the main character... why's she sitting there, watching, waiting? Who's coming up the path, and what happens when they get there?* That was the question Shane kept returning to. Who is it? Whose shadow was spreading along the driveway, nearing the portico? And what would Marlena do when that person finally got there?

That was one of Marlena's secrets. The other one was the upstairs window with its mysterious white candle, the one he so often saw when he was returning from the old footpath, teasing and flickering beyond the limbs of the magnolia tree, begging him to paint, to come to the sordid embrace of the muse. He still hadn't gone into the attic to look for that window. He could lie to himself, pretending he simply hadn't had time, or had forgotten about it, but those things weren't the real truth. The *real* truth was that he was afraid of the answer. The shadow in the painting was a puzzle, but the mystery of the window and the beacon candle was a Pandora's box. Someday he *would* open that box, but not yet, and certainly not while Christiana was around. He was curious, but not yet curious enough.

Marlena had her secrets, and Shane had an idea that her painting was part of the map to revealing them, whether she liked it or not. Often, he'd tinker with the image on the canvas, dabbing at it with his brush, adding insignificant details, refining it, focusing it. One afternoon he added a vase of roses on the mantel behind Marlena, drooping in the darkness, leaving a small drift of petals in the shadow beneath the portrait of Woodrow Wilson. The next evening he added the upholstered arm of a sofa in the foreground, in the far right of the canvas, dark except for a fringe of light cast from the fireplace beyond. Finally, he added a small shape abandoned on the corner of the sofa, lost in its shadow.

When he finished the object on the sofa he looked at it, wondering why he'd painted it there. It wasn't that it didn't fit into the scene, exactly. On the contrary, it seemed perfectly essential, despite its position and apparent insignificance, lost in shadow. It was odd, but somehow exactly right. It hinted at meaning, like a keyhole, one that would unlock every mystery, if only Shane could find the right key. For the moment, however, the strange, inexplicable object on the painted sofa didn't make any sense at all.

Shane stared at, puzzling over it, not quite obsessed with it but certainly distracted by it, and maybe even a little disturbed. After all, he knew that shape very well. The last time he'd seen it, it had been sitting on a conference table, scuffed and torn, like an exhibit in a museum. It was Steph's purse, propped there in the shadow of the sofa, almost lost in the corner of the painting. It was unmistakable. Why had he painted it there? More importantly, why did it seem to belong there? Why did it seem like the axle upon which the entire scene turned?

Eventually, he would find the answer to that question. After all, there was still one more painting to complete, one final addition to the Shane Bellamy Insanity Stairs series. He'd barely begun it, but he had a sense of it already. The anchor on the end of this long chain was going to be huge indeed; the final painting was going to be amazing. He knew almost nothing about it so far except for one thing, one small detail that had popped into his head the moment he'd painted that first curving brush stroke: the title.

"Sleepwalker," he'd said aloud to himself, looking down at that first line, still wet on the canvas, glistening in the sunset light that streamed from the window over the stairs. That was going to be the title. It had just popped into his head. It didn't mean anything, but it would. And when the meaning to that one word came, he had a sense that the answer to every other question would also fall into place. After all, this last painting was his alone, even if it did come from the same mysterious well as the previous two. Marlena had opened the portal for him, but she couldn't completely control it. Not anymore. Because Shane was good at going to the well all by himself, good at dipping out whatever he needed, *without* the help of the muse.

Perhaps even in spite of her.

Christiana was in much better shape than Shane was, and this was no more evident than when they went on their first bike ride together.

"Come on, Bellamy," she called back over her shoulder, grinning. "Race you back home!"

He shook his head, breathing hard and coasting for a moment. She slowed as well, weaving gently side to side on the paved trail, standing on the pedals with her head thrown back, enjoying the stormlight. Leaves fell from the trees all around her like autumn snow, catching in the wind and fluttering across the path. Occasional gusts lifted whole rafts of them and swirled them like miniature cyclones. They crunched under Shane's front wheel as he caught up to Christiana.

"Not everything is a competition, sweetie-pie," he panted, a little sourly.

"It is if you keep on calling me sweetie-pie," she said happily, still looking up, watching the steely sky and the low clouds. "How else are you going to work off that piece of cherry cobbler?"

Shane had treated Christiana to lunch at the diner in Bastion Falls after riding their bikes there. He rolled his eyes theatrically. "Men don't think about working off their desserts. At least not straight men."

"Straight men don't worry about having clean finger nails or wearing clothes that match either," Christiana chided mildly.

"I guess it's a good thing gay men are gay," Shane replied, pedaling alongside her. "Otherwise us straight guys would never get a date."

"Damn right," she agreed, and sighed.

Shane squinted up at the low sky, following her gaze. After a moment, he asked, "So, is *this* a date?"

"Do you see any fabulous non-gay gay guys around?" she replied, pretending to peer around the woods as they coasted by.

"They're a little scarce around Bastion Falls, I guess."

"Hmm..." She glanced aside at Shane, smiling a little. The gray daylight was soft on her face, flickering dully in the shadow of the trees. "Then I guess I'm stuck with you."

"I could clean my finger nails, if you really want me to."

"Nah. Don't raise my expectations like that. Let me fall in love with you just as you are."

She was joking, but a mild thrill trickled down Shane's back. There was still a strange, almost deliberate ambiguity to their relationship. She came over to the cottage nearly every day now, and there was certainly a not-quite-platonic affection in the way they touched, the way they snuggled up on the couch sometimes, or even the way she looked at him across the patio when they sat outside and watched the twilight over the river. And yet, they had never kissed. They had talked about a lot of things, but never about the relationship that seemed to be growing up around them, like summer vines climbing a trellis. More than once, it had reminded Shane of Earl Kirchenbauer and his story, about how he'd come to work at the Riverhouse back in the spring of nineteen-forty. *I was never officially hired,* he'd recalled ruefully; *they just never told me to go home.* Shane smiled and shook his head as he pedaled, picking up speed.

"Hey," Christiana said. "Where do you think you're going?"

"I thought you said this was a race?"

"You bastard," she called delightedly, standing on her own pedals.

Shane grinned and pumped as hard as he could, driving his Trek forward, leaning over the handlebars. She caught up to him but didn't pass him. Together, they leaned into the curve as the path angled toward the Valley Road. She began to overtake him on the inside of the curve, but he pushed as hard as he could, grinning into the wind, and began to pull ahead of her again. She laughed with delight, her voice almost lost in the cool, rippling air.

"Last one back is a Stinky Pete!" she called.

Shane glanced back at her, glimpsed the corona of her black hair whipping around her face as she smiled grimly, her dark eyes twinkling. She was behind now, but she'd beat him in the end, and she knew it. Shane didn't mind. A very male part of him knew that coming in second behind Christiana, at least on a bike ride, was not such an unattractive prospect.

Something *popped* suddenly. It sounded like a pellet gun, or an inflated paper bag. Immediately, Christiana began to lose ground, and her bike began to wobble uncertainly beneath her.

"Damn!" she called, looking down at the flat tire on her rear wheel. "Damn, damn!" Shane was amused to realize that she was mostly angry about losing the race, rather than about blowing her bike tire. He braked his Trek gently, then swooped around on the path, heading back toward her. She hopped off her bike and held it by one handlebar, looking critically down at the rear tire.

"Must have hit a sharp stone on the path," Shane said, stopping his own bike next to her.

"I guess that makes me a Stinky Pete," she frowned.

"I guess it does," Shane agreed solemnly. "But there's always next time."

She sighed—her characteristic brisk exhale—and looked up at Shane. "So what should we do? You want to ride back while I walk?"

Shane was a little put off. "Of course not. I'll walk with you. We'll leave both bikes and I'll come back with the truck later and throw them in the bed."

"I'm a big girl, you know," she said, but Shane could tell she didn't mean it. She pushed her bike off the path and lay it in the tall grass on the side away from the Valley Road. It wasn't much of a hiding place, but it would do until Shane came back with the pickup.

"You could just ride on my handlebars, of course," Shane said.

"Just like when we were kids, right? I think my bum's a little too big for that nowadays."

"Shut your mouth," Shane said, scowling.

He ditched his own bike in the tall grass behind Christiana's and they began to walk along the path. After a minute, Christiana touched Shane's hand with her fingers. They held hands and walked together, following the path as it curved back toward the woods and the river beyond. Neither spoke. The silent snowfall of autumn leaves drifted down around them, making a sort of magical tableaux. Soon enough, Shane recognized the curve of the path ahead of them, saw the brightness of the clearing beyond the trees.

"So that's where it used to stand?" Christiana said, slowing, looking out over the weedy grass and concrete bunkers.

Shane nodded, stopping alongside but not letting go of her hand.

She shaded her eyes with her free hand. "Is there anything left of it?"

"Just a bunch of dirt where they filled in the cellar. And the front porch. I guess it was too heavy to carry away and too much work to break up. You can't see it from here. It's behind that big pile of mulch down there at the end."

"I want to see," Christiana said, and before Shane could respond she'd pulled her hand away from his and walked into the watery light of the yard. He followed her, looking around warily. If they had been on their bikes, this would have been much easier. She never would have been curious enough to interrupt their ride, especially if they were racing. Now, Shane felt a cold apprehension that had nothing to do with the gray stormy air. After all, if Marlena wasn't haunting the cottage anymore, then this was probably where she had retreated to. Shane caught up to Christiana and walked alongside her, watching the trees on either side of the yard, and especially watching the dead dirt of the Riverhouse's old foundation.

He was pleased to see that the strange, ghostly shadow of the house was not in sight. Even so, nothing had yet begun to grow in the dry dirt of the foundation, not so much as a single weed or splash of crabgrass. The yellow bulk of the front loader sat on the remains of the brick driveway, its bucket raised to the sky, a black stain of oil glistening on the weeds beneath it. They passed it slowly and Christiana broke away, angling toward the portico.

"I recognize this much of it, at least. From your painting. How did you know how to paint it?"

"Well, I'd seen it plenty of times before they tore it down, riding past on my bike."

"Maybe, but I bet it didn't look like it does in your work. Did you research it?"

Shane shrugged, but Christiana wasn't looking. "Yeah, sort of. Most of it just, sort of, came to me."

She glanced back at him, her brow slightly furrowed. She had one foot on the lowest step of the portico. "This place has a hold on you, doesn't it?"

Shane felt his blood cool. He began to follow her. He opened his mouth to answer, but she interrupted him, turning to climb the shallow stone steps.

"I guess that's how it is with all artists and their subjects. I can see how an artist's wife could get jealous of him and his work. Especially if he painted other women."

"I hardly ever use live models," Shane said inanely, following Christiana up the portico steps. The circular scars of the pillars looked up at the sky, two on either side of the long expanse, like the ghosts of gargoyles. "I use pictures, mostly, and my imagination. I find most of my resources online."

"But not all of them," Christiana said, turning back to Shane and smiling. "You painted this place. It's real, or at least it used to be. You're not above using real live models."

"Well, like I said, that was pretty unusual," Shane said, stopping on the gritty floor of the portico as Christiana approached him again. "Most of the time I—"

"Would you paint me?" she asked playfully, and struck a pose there on the stage of the portico, cocking her hips and raising both arms, clasping her hands behind her head. She looked out over the Riverhouse foundation, toward the river, her chin raised and her eyes sleepy, half-lidded. Shane couldn't help smiling.

"You've seen too many movies," he said, shaking his head. "It's not like that. Posing is hard work, believe it or not, especially for a painting. You have to maintain the pose for *hours*."

"I could do that," she said, dropping her arms. "I'm patient."

Shane nodded and shrugged, but before he could reply, she had stepped into his arms. A thrill of sudden delight welled up in him as she wrapped her arms around him, pressing herself against him. She rested her head against his shoulder and he curled his arms around her.

"I'm patient," she said again, more quietly.

Shane nodded. He knew what she was talking about. He was afraid to say anything in response, lest he say too much and spoil the moment. The fact was, they were *both* being patient, waiting to see what was really happening between them, unwilling to force it or even acknowledge it. After all, Randy had not even been dead for a month yet. It wasn't that Christiana needed to get over him or grieve for him, and yet *some* grief had seemed necessary— grief for all the lost time, for all the humiliations and shameful secrets. Shane knew that. He'd expected it to take months for Christiana to become ready to move on. And what about he, himself? It had only been a year since the loss of his pregnant wife. Could he possibly be ready to move on? Maybe this was a mistake, *whatever* this was that was happening between himself and Christiana. Maybe they were both simply clinging to each other because it was better to cling to someone—anyone—than to be alone with the memories. That was hardly a basis for a healthy relationship, was it? The responsible thing to do would be for him to end it before it even began.

He pushed Christiana away slightly and looked down at her. She raised her face to him, stood on tiptoes, and kissed him.

It wasn't a long kiss, but it wasn't a peck, either. Her lips were cool and soft, the breath from her nose warm on his cheek. With that kiss, all of his concerns suddenly vanished. It was as if a gust of wind had come and blown every thought clean out of Shane's head. He knew it was foolish. He was making the age-old mistake, believing the lie that because something felt good, it *was* good. But maybe sometimes it wasn't a lie at all. Maybe some things really were as simple as they seemed. It was good that Shane had found Christiana, and that she had found him. In the fleeting moment of that kiss, Shane realized something rather shocking. All of his fears and worries about them, about this secretly growing relationship, all came down to one simple thing: he was terrified of allowing himself to fall for her, because falling for her was the first step toward losing her. He'd already lost one woman he'd loved, her and the baby inside her. If something like that happened again...

But the kiss swept it all away. It didn't make the fears insignificant—just the opposite, in fact—but it made them inevitable. Shane could no more stop himself from falling in love with Christiana than he could stop the river from flowing along the bluff beneath his cottage. All he'd needed was to know that she felt the same way.

When their lips parted, Shane looked down at her. There were tears standing in her eyes. She swiped them away impatiently and pressed her face against his shoulder.

"Why the tears?" he asked curiously.

She shook her head against his shoulder. "I don't know." She sighed briskly, and her breath was hot against him. "I don't know. I didn't know if you..." Her voice trailed away.

"You didn't know if I what?"

She looked up at him again, smiled, and then looked away. "I didn't know if you felt the same way I did. I'm... I'm kind of damaged goods. You know? I wouldn't have blamed you for..."

"You're serious," Shane said, wonderingly.

"Of course I'm serious. I've been waiting and wondering. I mean, you've been so good to me, but maybe you're just, you know... the nice guy. Maybe I'm just the hurt little bird. Maybe when my wing heals up, you'll just put me out and expect me to fly away."

Shane studied her face. He wished this was a movie. If it was a movie, he'd have the ideal words to say, something that perfectly summed up his feelings for her, the ever expanding width and breadth of her in his heart. He had a feeling that if he tried to come up with something on his own, some pithy, romantic response that would explain everything to her and put all her fears to rest, it would come out sounding silly and contrived. Some things, he thought, were just too big to cage with words.

Christiana misunderstood his long gaze. She dropped her eyes and stepped back. "It's all right. I understand—"

Shane caught her this time, pulled her back to him. He cupped her face in his hands, tilting her head back, making her look into his eyes.

"What do you see?" he asked.

She looked. She shook her head slightly in his hands. "I don't... I see..."

Shane kissed her this time. It was a longer kiss, but softer. He'd been longing to do that for weeks, probably even from the moment he'd first met her, on the day she had arrived to pick up the matte painting. Slowly, she wrapped her arms around him again, clinging to him. When their lips parted this time, she was smiling slightly. She touched her forehead against his.

"What do you see now?" he asked.

"I don't know what I *see*," she replied, her smile turning to a grin. "But what I *feel* is a randy man pressed up against me."

Shane grinned back at her. "Actions speak louder than words, I guess."

She laughed with delight, and then stepped away from him, turning on the spot in a small, happy pirouette. "So what do we do now?"

Shane shook his head. "We finish our walk home, I guess. I'm getting hungry."

"Oh, you're hungry all right," she teased good-naturedly. Suddenly, she pranced away from Shane, out onto the dirt of the house's foundation. The grin evaporated from Shane's face as Christiana jumped into the middle of that dead, gray space, raising her hands like a girl waiting to be picked up by her daddy. She let out a girlish whoop of joy, and suddenly, noiselessly, lightning flickered over the river, illuminating the day like a flashbulb. It flashed on the trees bordering the yard, on the brown face of the river, on Christiana herself, standing in the middle of the Riverhouse's foundation with her arms raised over her head. To Shane's horror, the lightning also illuminated the Riverhouse itself. It surrounded Christiana, ghostly but complete, right down to the furniture. And worst of all, revealed in that flash, standing directly behind Christiana, was Marlena. She seemed unnaturally tall, her face pale and severe, filled with hate, her hands raised into hooks, looking down at the living young woman in front of her. Shane gasped and leaped forward, filling his lungs to shout a warning, but a moment later the flash—and the awful vision—was gone, leaving only its after-image burning greenly on Shane's retinas.

Christiana stood alone in the gray dirt, arms still raised. She hadn't seen the ghostly house, or the malignant specter standing over her. She hadn't even noticed Shane's startled response. He exhaled harshly, shakily, and she turned to look at him, her eyes still smiling.

She looked beautiful in the stormlight. Beautiful and naked, somehow. Vulnerable.

What have I done, Shane thought, fleetingly, a little hopelessly. *Oh God, what have I done?*

Whatever it was, it was too late now. He'd been thinking about it only a minute earlier, hadn't he? He could no longer stop himself from falling in love with Christiana than he could stop the course of the river that flowed even now behind her. The kiss had done it. There was no turning back now, even if he wanted to. And he didn't.

But I can protect her, he told himself, composing his face, straightening his back, forcing himself to smile back at her. *I can keep her safe. She's not a rabbit on my lap. She's the woman I am falling in love with. I can watch over her. Marlena... Marlena...* But that was where his thoughts stopped. He couldn't go on, because he just didn't know what she, Marlena, was planning, or what she was capable of. Christiana was the gorgeous canyon vista, but Marlena was the fog; secretive, silent, and capricious. There was just too much he didn't know about her, too much she wasn't telling him.

But Shane could find out, if he really wanted to. His smile hardened at the edges, turned brittle and determined. He *could* find out. Whether she wanted him to or not.

"What is it?" Christiana asked, coming back toward Shane, reaching to touch his hand.

He shook his head. "Nothing. It's nothing I can't handle. Come on. Let's go back before the storm gets here."

Lightning flickered again, and this time a grumble of distant thunder followed, rolling across the sky like a freight of cannonballs. Shane walked with Christiana down the porch steps, across the yard, past the front loader, and into the darkening stormlight.

When they got back to the cottage, the wind was picking up, switching violently, like the tail of a stalking cat. Shane walked around to the side yard to close the shed doors before the wind caught them and pulled them off their old hinges. Above him, he could see the candle burning in the circular window, almost hidden behind the swaying branches of the magnolia. It beckoned him, teased him, but this time he ignored it. He had a feeling that his love affair with the muse was very nearly over.

Worse, he was pretty sure that she knew it, too.

Part III: The Sleepwalker

Chapter Sixteen

That Friday, while Christiana was at work, Shane went for another bike ride into Bastion Falls. He wore an old green backpack, empty except for a scattering of ancient beach sand, a ticket stub from a Bonnie Rait concert, circa nineteen ninety-seven, and a twenty dollar bill stuffed into the front zipper pocket.

The day was cool, but bright with a hard diamond sun. It had been raining off and on all week, and the weather guys on KMOX were starting to talk potential flood in the coming few weeks. Shane's cottage would be fine if that happened, as high as it was on the bluff, but it wouldn't hurt to stock up on some groceries anyway, just in case the Valley Road got washed over. Maybe he'd take the truck down to the IGA this weekend. Maybe he'd even take Christiana with him. He'd enjoy introducing her to Brian, and maybe even old Earl Kirchenbauer over at Denny Acres. He smiled to himself. It was funny, because he knew he was acting a little like a teenager with a new girlfriend, wanting to tour the mall with her on his arm, showing her off to all of his friends and rivals. It was silly, but he decided to give himself a pass. After all, he hadn't had many chances to do that when he was in high school. And Christiana *was* attractive. Earl would probably flirt with her. He was just that kind of old man. Shane could imagine it, the little twinkle in Earl's eye, the knowing smile, the obvious double entendres. It would probably be Earl's way of stamping his approval on her. And then, on the way home, he and Christiana would chuckle about it. It would become a memory, the sort of thing they'd talk fondly about years later:

remember old Earl at Denny Acres? Remember the way he looked you up and down? Good old Earl...

But that was for later. Shane wouldn't be stopping in to see Earl or Brian today. For now, he had a different errand in mind.

At the end of the city's short main street was an old Revco drugstore. Shane parked his bike in the rack out front, clipped on the chain, and walked inside. It was cooler inside than outside, as if nobody had remembered to turn off the AC when summer had gotten over. Muzak wafted from hidden speakers, competing with the sound of a whining toddler hidden in one of the aisles.

"But I *waaant* it," the voice droned. "Pleeeeze?"

"I didn't bring enough money, Kyle. Come on, now."

Kyle ramped up his pleas, inching toward full-fledged tantrum status. Shane sympathized with the mother, but only a little. He had the minor luxury of believing that, if he'd had kids, they'd never have had tantrums in drugstores. He knew it was a foolish thing to think, but it was better than the thought that followed. He tried to shut it off, but it was too late. *If that was my son,* the voice in his head said wistfully, *I'd buy him whatever he wanted. Whatever stupid little plastic trinket he had his eye on. Why? As a thank you present. Thanks son, I'd say, thanks just for being alive. Thanks for not being dead, tiger. You wanna go get some ice cream?*

Shane wandered the aisles and finally found what he was looking for. Rows of pens and markers were hung on hooks. Shane passed these, scanning them idly, and stopped near the end of the aisle. He reached and plucked a small box off its metal hook. Big Crayons, the label on the front read, spelled with letters contrived to look like they'd been drawn by a child. The B was backwards. There were only eight of them, but Shane thought they would do. They were very nearly perfect, in fact. Below the racks of crayons and poster paints was a shelf crammed with notepads and sketchbooks. He squatted and picked one of them up. The front showed a drawing of fish and a mermaid, rendered in bright, primary colors. Above the picture, written in fat, balloon-like letters, were the words DOODLE BOOK. The paper inside was cheap, mere newsprint, gray and grainy. Shane nodded to himself and pressed his lips together.

On the way out, he picked up a Coke from the cooler by the registers.

"Gonna do some drawing?" the old woman manning the checkout counter said, swiping the notebook and crayons over her scanner. She was joking, of course.

"Indeed I am," he replied, grinning. She probably thought he was joking as well.

He drank the Coke while sitting on a bench in front of the store. Traffic tooled by sporadically on main street, mostly pickup trucks and minivans. When the can was empty, Shane belched on the back of his hand, tossed the can into a brown garbage bin by the front doors, unlocked his bike, and wheeled it out to the street. A minute later, he pedaled through the single stoplight on the corner by the IGA. He turned left and picked up speed, heading toward the open floodgates at the end of town. Those gates would probably have to be closed in the coming few weeks, he thought idly, looking up as he passed through them. It wouldn't matter to him, of course. He'd be high and dry in the cottage, his cupboards stocked, maybe even with Christiana there, flooded in, forced to stay over. He was fairly sure she wouldn't mind. Thinking that, he stood on the pedals, pushing forward, wanting to get back as soon as he could. He had things to do before she came over that night.

In the backpack, Shane's new notebook and crayons rocked back and forth, the crayons knocking hollowly in their box. Shane heard them as he pedaled. To him, it almost sounded like they were anxious.

Like they were waiting impatiently to be let out.

He parked the bike in the shed and closed the doors. He'd intended to go into the cottage, but for some reason he found himself walking around to the back patio. The stone floor was covered with leaves again, forming a thick carpet that crunched under his feet, releasing a dark, October scent. Shane pulled back one of the deck chairs and plopped onto it, slipping the backpack from his shoulders.

He stopped for a moment. His heart was thudding hard in his chest, so much so that his head sang and his spit tasted weird, like old pennies. The air seemed to have changed around him, become thick and electric, expectant. He looked around, without really knowing why. Tom the cat was watching him from a sunny spot on the low stone wall, his eyes half-lidded, bored.

"How you doing, buddy?" Shane said, a little too loudly. It sounded stupid and pathetic. Tom didn't blink.

It was crazy, what he was about to do. It had seemed perfectly sane and rational when he'd been planning it, thinking about the best way to do it. Even when he'd been buying the crayons and paper, it had seemed merely curious, like an experiment. Now, in the hard diamond light of the afternoon sun, it seemed more than simply irrational, it felt outright dangerous. It felt like he was getting ready to do the mental equivalent of sticking his finger into a light socket.

The art was, after all, a kind of conduit. That had become obvious. It had started with the Riverhouse painting. He'd tapped into something, or something had tapped into him, and the result was that he'd been granted a chance to step through the canvas, into the story behind the pictures. Shane had suspected that he could control the conduit if he really wanted to. He was that kind of artist. He was good at going down to the well all by himself, dipping out what he needed, completely bypassing the muse. Maybe he could control that conduit, manipulate it, possibly even use it to unearth Marlena's secrets.

He'd first tried it with his latest painting, the last installment in the Insanity Stairs series, the one he'd already dubbed "the Sleepwalker". He'd deliberately approached it with the intention of making it his own, of guiding the paint on the canvas, teasing it into showing him what he wanted to know. The result, however, had been mildly disastrous. He'd stayed up late the previous Wednesday, trying to force the picture to reveal itself, trying to dip out the answers to his questions about Marlena, but no matter how hard he tried, nothing came. It was almost as if the painting was fighting him, insisting on its own story. Eventually, Shane had grown frustrated, giving up in the small hours of the morning, exhausted and stupidly angry. The next day he'd gone up to the studio and found his paints strewn all over the floor and one of his brushes broken in half. Worst of all, the new painting had been tipped off its easel. It lay crookedly against his stool, one side of the wooden frame broken. Marlena had apparently been there, and had not been pleased with what she'd seen. Wearily, Shane had gathered up the scattered paint tubes, tossed the broken brush into the trash, and then set about replacing the broken piece of the painting's frame.

In the corner, Marlena's portrait looked down at the letter in her hands, stricken and miserable. Shane found himself glancing back at the portrait while he worked, each time expecting Marlena's painted eyes to be raised, glaring at him, smoldering with pained rage. Each time, however, her eyes remained just as he'd painted them, looking down, pointedly reading the letter: *Dear M.*

The problem, Shane had begun to suspect, was the medium. Both Marlena and Wilhelm had been artists. They'd both had very different styles, according to the few samples Shane had seen online, but for both of them, their primary medium had been oils. That was why Shane couldn't control the conduit when he was painting. The medium was too close to Marlena, too wedded to her. It may be that this last painting *would* tell him the secrets he needed to know, but it would only do so in its own time. He couldn't control it, couldn't make it give him just what he wanted, when he wanted it. It was like trying to water a garden with a fire hose. Unfortunately, Shane didn't think he could wait for the painting to tell him its secrets, not with Christiana there more often than not, living under the potentially malevolent shadow of Marlena. But maybe he could try something else, something more simple and basic, as far from oils as possible.

He had just finished fixing the wooden frame of "the Sleepwalker" and was replacing it on the easel when something on the floor caught his eye. It had rolled over into the corner by the stairs, knocked aside during Marlena's tantrum of the night before. It was a white wax pencil, mostly used up. That was when Shane had gotten the idea to try crayons. As soon as he'd thought it, it had seemed like just the thing. How many adult artists used crayons as their medium? None, of course. There was more to it than that, but Shane didn't know what it was. It didn't matter. All that mattered was that he had a plan, and he was fairly confident that it would work.

He'd waited until he'd known that Christiana would be gone. She was at work, and wouldn't be back to the cottage until that evening. He had at least two hours. He looked down at the backpack on his lap.

"I'm just going to draw some pictures," he said aloud, unzipping the backpack. "Nothing crazy about that, is there, Tom old boy?"

Tom pushed himself upright, stretched, and yawned luxuriously. He began to give himself a bath.

"Lotta help you are," Shane said, and pulled the crayons and notebook out of the backpack's pouch. He slipped open the lid of the box of crayons and dumped all eight of them out onto his lap. He picked up the black one, turned it over in his hands. It was indeed big and chunky. Still, something about it didn't feel quite right.

"Just going to draw me some pictures," he muttered, looking down at the black crayon, and then the rest of the colors on his lap. Idly, he jammed his fingernail under the paper label of the black crayon, tearing it. He began to pull it away, stripping the paper from the waxy black cylinder. "Just going down to the well with my bucket. Just going to dip out some art. Nothing crazy about that. I've been doing the same thing for almost ten years."

When the paper was stripped entirely off the black crayon, Shane held it in the palm of his hand. It felt exactly right, now. Of course it did. They might have had crayons in the forties, but they probably wouldn't have had printed labels on them. Why that should matter Shane didn't know, but he was beyond worrying about such things now. He was sailing into uncharted waters, dipping deeper into the well of creativity than he ever had before. If the muse saw, she would be unhappy with him, but Shane had to take that risk. There were things he needed to know. Things she was hiding from him.

He wrapped his fist around the black crayon, the way a kid might hold a spoon. With his other hand, he swept back the gaily colored cover of the sketch pad. The paper beneath was dirty gray, cheap and thin, speckled with black flecks. Shane drew a deep breath, inexplicably afraid to touch the crayon to that ugly, gray blankness. He felt like he was about to touch a copper wire to a battery, one whose voltage was uncertain and potentially deadly. His hand shook slightly.

"Just going to draw me some pictures," he muttered again. Nearby, unseen and forgotten, Tom the cat watched, his green eyes bright, alert, no longer bored.

Slowly, Shane lowered the crayon. The shadow of his hand darkened on the gray paper. He felt its cool, cheap surface with the heel of his fist, pressed down, bringing the crayon closer, closer.

The crayon touched the paper, made first a dimple, and then a mark. And with that mark, everything changed. The world retreated and Shane felt a preternatural calm descend over him. This was *right*. The crayons, the cheap newsprint, even the hard light of the diamond sun, casting his shadow over the paper, it was all exactly right.

Shane pulled the crayon along the paper. The dot became a line, and then a curve.

He began to draw.

He started with the cottage. He drew it slowly, haltingly, using lines so dark and firm that they pressed into the paper, wrinkling it slightly. He didn't look at the cottage as he drew it. Instead, he tapped into the well in his mind, dipping the picture out, forming it in his head. The cottage started as a square, and then grew a squat peak. He drew the back door, the kitchen window, the lines of the patio and the low stone wall. A rectangle formed the chimney of the barbecue, another formed the chimney on the house, crooked and leaning, as if drawn with a kid's simplistic perspective. He didn't draw the sunroom. It wasn't a deliberate omission; it simply wasn't part of the cottage in his mind, the one that came out of the well. His hand began to move faster, progressing from drawing to sketching. He shaded in the east side of the cottage, leaving a white circle for the upper window. There was no candle lit there, not now. He scribbled in the magnolia tree, but it was smaller, barely higher than the shed attached to the side of the cottage.

And then Shane's hand began to draw something else. He watched as the scribbles of the magnolia tree turned into cross hatching, forming a grid, and then a cube, something resting on the patio floor, taking up most of the space. It cast a long, dark shadow, pressed into the paper with repeated, horizontal strokes.

Shane stopped and stared at the drawing. He didn't know what the shape on the patio was. It was too rough, too primitive. He wanted to add details, but he didn't know where to start. The crayons prevented details, at any rate. The black crayon's tip was now reduced to a dull nub. The picture on the pad was like a cave drawing, or something tacked to an elementary school bulletin board. He shook his head and pushed back the page, revealing the next blank gray space. He picked an orange crayon this time and lowered it to the paper. It began to move immediately, easier this time, almost of its own accord. It was like some bizarre artist's version of a Ouija board. Shane watched as the new drawing took shape.

It was the Riverhouse, but changed somehow. It was taller, narrow and top-heavy, like a caricature. The round window beneath the peak was exaggerated, and a shape began to form there. Shane recognized it; it was Marlena. She was leaning, looking. Her eyes were primitive, barely two orange smudges, but they managed to speak volumes. She was looking, even though she knew there was nothing to see. This was much later, years after Wilhelm and Madeleine had gone, taking young Hector with them. Marlena still looked. She couldn't stop herself. She looked to see if the candle was lit again, glowing in the cottage window at the top of the bluff. The problem was that sometimes it *was* lit. Sometimes that candle flickered in the distance, teasing her. She never followed its beckoning call—after all, she knew it was just an illusion, that there was nothing there for her to find—but she couldn't help looking, hoping it *wouldn't* be there. And most of the time, it wasn't. But only most of the time.

Shane's hand stopped moving. The picture wasn't complete, but it was finished. Somehow, his hand knew it, even if his mind wanted more. He ripped the paper away and dropped it onto the leaves at his feet. The wind rustled it but didn't carry it away. Shane picked another color, green, and bore down on the paper once again.

Lines appeared, parallel and diminishing. They formed steps. There was a railing, descending toward a landing. Shane was drawing the interior of the Riverhouse now. He was drawing the Insanity Stairs. No single drawing could show their entirety, and yet the entire scene formed in Shane's mind. The stairs started on the main level, and then went up. They reached the next floor, but didn't open up onto it. They'd been sealed off, and new stairs added. The new stairs turned and went back down again, past the main floor, into the basement. And there, they stopped dead, meeting another wall, one made of brick. There was a window built into the wall, looking into the cellar. Shane could see the window in his drawing, a square pane with curtains hanging on both sides. On the right side of the curtains was a pull cord. Shane switched to the yellow crayon, scribbling the cord in gold. The cord operated the curtains, allowing them to be opened and closed over the strange window. Marlena stood at the window, her hand held out to the cord, not touching it, but poised, ready. She was watching, waiting. For what, Shane didn't know.

Another drawing pushed forward in Shane's head. He ripped the Insanity Stairs drawing from the pad and dropped it. The new picture formed in blue, quickly, roughly. Shane's hand could barely keep up with it. It seemed to be a hole, or some kind of well. It had a heavy metal grate on the top of it, forming a sort of sluice. Blue lines scribbled in all around it, implying darkness, perpetual night. This, Shane realized, was the view seen through the Insanity Stairs window. Brian had referred to it: the Bottomless Pit. It wasn't bottomless, of course, but it was very deep. Marlena had paid to have it excavated, boring right through the limestone bedrock of the valley floor. It looked like a well, but Shane knew that wasn't what it was, even if it did have water in the bottom of it. In a sense, it was just the opposite. This wasn't supposed to provide water; it was meant to take it away. Was it insurance against a future flood? A sort of primitive drainage mechanism? Somehow, that didn't seem exactly right. He looked at the grate embedded into the hole's top. It looked almost like a net, or a trap of some kind. But for what?

That picture ended as well. Shane stripped it away, letting it fall to join the others at his feet.

The next drawing showed a room. It was painted entirely black, including the floors and ceilings. There were windows in the room, but they were scribbled in, completely obscured. They'd been painted over as well, blinded. They were nailed shut.

Another drawing; a hallway. The doors were blank, closed and locked, their keys thrown into the river. The rooms beyond were all empty, their windows painted over, their walls and floors and ceilings covered with black paint. There was no rational reason for it. It just was. At the end of the hall was one open doorway. The door had been taken completely off its hinges, carted away, burned. Through that open doorway was nothing but a wall, but the wall had been painted to resemble a scene, a remarkably realistic vision, so true that it could fool the eye if you stood very still at the end of the hallway, looking past all those dead, locked doors. The painted scene showed more hallway, progressing past the end of the house. Lit windows on one side of the painted hall let in cheery sunlight. On the other side, open doors showed teasing glimpses of the happy rooms beyond. Standing before that false hallway, however, partly obscuring the skillfully painted windows and doors, was a family: a man and woman, with a young boy standing between them, posed as if for a portrait. It was like looking into a mirror at the end of the hall, a mirror showing an alternate universe. It would have been a pleasant scene if not for one detail: the faces were all entirely blank, mere flesh-colored ovals, as if the features had been seamlessly erased. Or were still waiting to be filled in.

More drawings came. Shane stripped each one from the pad as another followed. They collected around his feet like dead leaves, joining the autumn carpet that rustled and stirred in the breeze. His hand ached, but he barely noticed. The crayons grew shorter, shorter, dull as fingers. Individually, each drawing was a mere snapshot, but taken as a whole they formed an expanding story, like images on a roll of movie film. This was the tale of Marlena's madness, seen from the inside. It was confused and fragmented, and yet cruelly stubborn. Some of it he thought he understood, such as the phantom hallway, showing the life that Marlena had lost. More of it, however, seemed utterly inexplicable, deranged and obsessive. The Insanity Stairs, for instance, overlooking the grated pit in the cellar. It was more than a safeguard against another flood, of that Shane was certain. It was almost as if she had been waiting for the flood to bring something to her, something she'd wanted to capture, something she'd wanted some forewarning of. It was utterly insane. If such delusions had appeared in anyone else, that person would have surely been hospitalized, treated for whatever psychological disorder they were suffering from. Unfortunately for Marlena, though, she'd been too rich to be committed. She'd hired the workers to make her strange additions and modifications to the house, probably even stepping in and doing a lot of the work herself, and of course no one had deigned to stop her. After all, she had probably paid them very well. No one wanted to kill the Golden Goose, least of all Stambaugh, the Riverhouse's caretaker during those years of increasing madness. Stambaugh didn't appear in any of Shane's crayon drawings, but Shane sensed him in the background, playing along, doing the Missus' bidding, no matter how bizarre it might be. Maybe he'd even manipulated her deranged fetishes a little, sponging off more and more of her dwindling wealth, socking it away, maybe even convincing himself he was doing her a favor, saving the estate from her delusions. How easy it would be. And how would she know? She was too distracted, too obsessed with her nameless, irrational fears to pay attention to such banalities as the numbers on her bank statements.

Shane stopped drawing. He realized he'd been going forward on the timeline of Marlena's madness, following along as the years went by and she sank into incoherence, gradually transforming the Riverhouse into a twisted mirror of her dementia.

He was learning things, and yet he didn't seem to be finding what he really needed, the key to Marlena's dark obsession with Christiana. He dropped the nub of the blue crayon and shook out his fingers, looking down at the drawings scattered all around his feet. Finally, he looked at the pad on his lap again. The blank gray sheet stared up at him. He tapped the well in his mind again, tried to pull one more image out of it, but nothing came. The well was dry.

Frustrated, he flipped back to the first page of the notebook, the one showing the black drawing of the cottage. He looked at it. This was where it had all started, he thought. Not just his drawings, but the entire story. This was where all of Marlena's troubles traced back to. The cottage, where Wilhelm had first hidden his affairs with Madeleine, where he had summoned her, and where he had finally arranged to run off with her, taking Hector with them. This was the root of all of Marlena's madness.

Shane looked at the crayons on his lap. He found the black one again. It was worn dull, barely half the size that it had been when he'd first begun. He held it over the pad once more. Maybe this drawing was the key to what he needed to know after all. Maybe that was why he'd started there. Could the secret be in that odd shape on the patio? That strange gridded cube that he couldn't make any sense of?

Shane touched the shape with the crayon again. The crayon began to move. It made another shape, taller and more complicated: a man. Shane recognized the figure immediately, even though the head was barely a rough oval, topped with a rumpled cap. It was Earl Kirchenbauer.

"They're bricks," Shane said aloud, watching the figure take shape on the paper. "That's Earl, and that's a load of bricks next to him, all stacked and waiting. He's building something."

But that wasn't exactly right. Earl had brought the bricks there, had delivered them at some point in time before the day of this drawing, but they weren't for him to use. Now he was coming back. To check on the project? Was that it?

Shane drew, and as he did, the picture expanded. It swam up, filling his vision. It didn't take him away, swallowing him against his will, but he chose to walk into it. It was like a daydream, but like the strongest, most vivid daydream he'd ever experienced. He could smell the smell of the river, mossy and high, rotten with summer heat. He could hear a cicada burring away in the woods bordering the crayon cottage. And he heard Earl's footsteps scraping on the stones of the patio, grinding the grit that had accumulated around the stack of red bricks. The model A truck was parked out front, hidden by the cottage, but Shane could almost feel its heat, hear the ticks and pings of its engine as it cooled.

Earl reached out, touched the stack of bricks, and Shane saw how young he was. He was barely thirty, tall and tanned, a shadow of stubble on his jaw. He lay his hand on the bricks and looked at them. Shane could feel his thoughts; they came to him like signals on a short wave radio in the dead of night. Earl had assumed the bricks had been forgotten, that the delivery had just been another part of the Missus' strange new projects. She was doing a lot of such things lately, making odd changes to the house, closing off rooms, ripping up the rose garden; weird things, inexplicable things. Earl was worried about the Missus. She hadn't been the same in the previous months, not since Wilhelm had up and left, run off with that whore, Madeleine. After that had been the weeks of flood clean up, pumping the water out of the basement, scrubbing up layer after layer of mud, carrying buckets of silt out through the coal doors. The whole thing had taken a terrible toll on the lady of the house. It was a damn shame, that's what it was.

She'd asked Earl to deliver the load of bricks up to the cottage over a month earlier, saying she meant to make a few changes, but then she'd never arranged for anyone to go and do the work. Earl didn't even know what she wanted to do. Maybe she didn't either. The cottage had been Wilhelm's domain, but he'd left it, abandoned it along with his wife and his previous life. Now, the cottage was just an ugly reminder of his betrayal. Maybe the Missus had just wanted to put her stamp on it, somehow. Maybe she'd just wanted to change it enough to wipe his mark from it.

The funny thing was, some of the bricks were gone. An awful lot of them, in fact. Who had done the work? And what had it entailed? Was it possible that Earl could have been unaware that there was work being done on the cottage? He scoffed to himself. Nothing got done around the property that he didn't arrange, and always direct from the mouth of the Missus.

The river stank. It was hot and humid, and the river had been high of late. When it receded, it'd left stagnant pools all along the banks, covered with mosquitoes and stinking of rot. Earl was surprised at how pervasive the reek was, even up here on the bluff. He shook himself and took his hand off the remaining pile of bricks. He may as well poke inside, see what was going on. It was possible that the Missus herself had been up to something inside. She'd been out and about a lot in the previous months, and nobody really kept tabs on her, of course. She had the know-how, most likely, to do whatever she might choose to do with the cottage, even if she didn't necessarily have the brawn.

Earl approached the cottage, walking around the brick pile. The sliding doors weren't there, of course. Instead, there was a simple back door with a window set into the top half. Earl produced a key and socked it into the lock. A moment later, the door creaked open and Earl entered. He moved slowly, tentatively, almost as if he thought someone might be there, hiding in the darkness. He left the door open and moved to the left, heading into the kitchen.

Shane shifted his attention to the kitchen window, trying to focus, trying to follow Earl into the cottage. Unconsciously, he moved closer, ghostlike, floating over the patio, and then the breeze lifted, soughing in the trees. It caught the open back door, began to suck it slowly shut. Shane glanced toward it, and froze.

Marlena was there. She stood inside, ghostly and pale, looking out at Shane with piercing black eyes. It was impossible. She couldn't really be looking at him, because he wasn't really there. And yet Shane knew he was fooling himself. This wasn't the Marlena who was alive in the timeframe of this vision. This was *his* Marlena, his ghostly muse. She had discovered him, found him drawing his pictures, and invaded the scene he had conjured. The door swung slowly shut, closing off his view of her, but before it did, she shifted her gaze. She turned to the side, watching after Earl. Her face hardened.

Shane struggled to call out a warning to the young Earl of the vision, but he couldn't say anything, couldn't even draw a breath. Helplessly, he watched the kitchen window, straining. Shadows moved inside, but he couldn't make any sense of them.

A noise startled Shane, a dull slam, and he jerked upright. He was sitting on the deck chair, his right hand gripping the crayon over the notepad on his lap. He had scribbled over the drawing of the cottage, blotting it out, and the scribble looked like a words. They were barely legible, and yet Shane could easily read them. It was as if his hand remembered making their shapes: NOT THIS TIME. They were underlined repeatedly, furiously, making deep indentations on the cheap paper. The last line had torn the page.

Another noise came from inside the cottage. Shane jumped, dropping the notepad and scattering crayons all over the leaf-strewn patio. His heart hammered. Slowly, he stood up and began to move toward the sliding glass doors. He felt weak with fear, worn out from his experience with the crayon drawings. He reached for the back door handle and his hand trembled. He could see nothing but his own reflection in the glass. His fingers touched the wooden handle and the door shuttled open swiftly, as if of its own accord, swishing noisily on its track and releasing a gust of air. Marlena was there, pale and terrible. Shane stumbled backwards onto the patio, all the strength evaporating from his legs.

"Shane!" a voice cried out. Hands scrambled to catch him. He fought against them, and then looked up. It wasn't Marlena at all. It was Christiana, her eyes wide and frightened. "Shane, what's wrong? Are you hurt or something?"

She caught his arm and he grasped her, struggling to his feet. He was panting, sheened with sweat despite the cool breeze. When he spoke, his voice sounded unnaturally high and shaky. "What... what are you doing here already?"

"What do you mean," she replied, helping him up. "Why shouldn't I be here?"

Shane opened his mouth, and then stopped himself. Instead, he glanced down at his watch. It was five forty-seven. He'd been sitting on the back patio, drawing pictures and pursuing his strange vision of Earl and Marlena, for nearly three hours. He couldn't bring himself to believe it. He looked around and saw the twilight lowering over the river, felt the cold evening air pushing through the trees.

"Shane," Christiana said, her voice firm, worried. "What's going on? What's the matter?"

He glanced back at her, focused on her. He took a deep breath. "I think we need to go see Earl."

He pulled her back into the cottage, grabbing his keys from the hook in the kitchen as he went. Christiana trotted to keep up. As the two of them pushed through the front screen door, heading toward Shane's truck, she caught her breath enough to ask, "Who in the hell is Earl?"

He explained to Christiana on the way, but only a little. He told her how he'd met Earl, about how Earl and Brian, his grandson, had come to visit Shane in the cottage. He told her how Earl knew the place, and how he had told the story of its history. He didn't tell her any of that history, though. Nor did he tell her about Marlena, or the mysterious clairvoyant drawings he'd created on the patio. He didn't want to freak her out.

He was plenty freaked out for the both of them.

"I just have to see him," he told her as they drove. "I just have to see if he's all right. Do you ever get those kind of feelings?"

Christiana shrugged, her face noncommittal and grim, watching the road.

Ever since Shane had seen Marlena—*his* Marlena—appear in the vision of the cottage, he'd felt an increasingly urgent sense of foreboding. He kept telling himself that what he'd seen in the crayon drawing was only a vision, a memory, replayed through the small magic of recreating it on paper. He'd tapped into the story of the Riverhouse, deliberately, as he'd suspected he could if he really tried. Just because he'd seen Marlena in that vision didn't mean that she could act within it. She'd merely discovered what he was up to and invaded the moment. It had been frightening, but what could she do? Earl wasn't in any danger, no matter how the ghostly Marlena had looked at him. She could barely affect things in the present day (as far as Shane knew). Certainly, she couldn't pose a danger to some long gone version of Earl Kirchenbauer, buried in a forgotten summer day some seventy years past. Could she?

Shane pressed the accelerator of his old pickup to the floor, feeling the truck rattle and shimmy around him as it sped down the Valley Road. Christiana was pale on the bench seat next to him. She didn't speak, but she tightened her seat belt and held onto the dashboard with one hand.

It was mostly dark by the time Shane pulled into the parking lot next to Denny Acres, and his mind had concocted a variety of bizarre, utterly irrational suspicions. He imagined he'd go to the big round counter inside the front door of the retirement home and the orderly on duty would tell him that there was no one named Earl Kirchenbauer in residence there. They'd be so kind as to look him up in some kind of town database, only to discover that someone by that name had, in fact, lived in Bastion Falls at one time, but that they had died long ago, probably sometime around July of nineteen forty-five. Or worse, maybe Earl would still be there, but he'd be altered somehow, crazy and deranged, cursed with whatever madness had gripped Marlena herself. After all, crazy was contagious. Earl himself had said so.

It was all paranoia, of course. Twilight Zone stuff. Nothing like that ever happened in real life.

Shane and Christiana made their way through the breezeway, and Shane forced himself to walk normally, not to rush, not to seem at all alarmed or anxious, partly for Christiana's sake, and partly for his own. It was important not to let the old imagination get out of control. Earl would be fine, of course. After all, Earl had something to tell Shane; something he'd seen in the cottage all those decades ago, on one hot summer day in the year after Wilhelm had left. Maybe it hadn't seemed important at the time. Maybe it had slipped his mind during his retelling. Or maybe he had left it out on purpose, for reasons of his own. Whatever it was, though, it was the key to Shane's problems with the ghostly Marlena. That was why he'd drawn it. Marlena had interrupted Shane's conjured vision before he could follow Earl inside the cottage, before he could see what Earl had seen, but she couldn't stop Earl from recalling that day now. She couldn't stop Earl from telling Shane about it, not if he wanted to.

"Visiting hours are over at seven," the woman at the desk announced, shoving a clipboard at Shane and Christiana to sign. "Unless you have permission from the resident to stay later. Just have him call down to the desk, 'kay?"

Shane nodded, scribbling his name. Part of him was relieved that the woman hadn't blinked when he'd announced who he was there to see. Christiana matched his stride as he walked down the right hand hallway, past the gaily decorated bulletin boards. There were fewer wheelchairs and walkers in the hallways tonight, but there were more propped-open doors, more televisions warbling in dimly lit living rooms.

Shane knew he should be feeling better now. Obviously everything was fine. And yet, his sense of growing apprehension continued to cinch higher and higher. It was like a piano wire wrapped around his gut, tightening, constricting his breath, pushing him toward raw panic. He sped up, unable to stop himself, and Christiana matched his stride, almost jogging next to him. She had questions, Shane knew, but for now she wasn't asking them.

They rounded the corner, passed the cafeteria where a few stragglers still sat leaning over tables, staring at their plates. Dishes clanked and rattled in the kitchen beyond. Another corner, and Shane scanned the doorways on the left side. Earl's was the fifth one down. It was propped open with a rolled-up magazine, just as it had been the last time Shane had been there. The blue flicker of the television could be seen through the darkness of the cracked door. They reached the door and Shane peered in through the crack.

"Earl?" he called softly. "You home? It's me, Shane Bellamy."

No answer. Beyond the crack of the door, the television flickered and flashed.

"You might want to stay out here for a minute," Shane said, putting his hand on the doorknob. "He might not be, you know, decent."

"Nuts to that," Christiana said in a low voice. "You said he was almost a hundred years old, right? Guys like that aren't shy around the ladies. If something's wrong…"

Shane nodded and pressed his lips together. He pushed the door open slowly and stepped inside.

It was warmer in Earl's apartment. The only light in the main living space was the flash of the television and a dim table lamp next to his orange recliner. There was a stain in the middle of the carpet. Shane remembered it, remembered the broken coffee cup on the day he had come to visit the old man. There was a smell in the apartment, both medicinal and darkly organic. The mingled scents turned Shane's stomach.

"Where is he?" Christiana asked, her voice unconsciously hushed.

"Earl?" Shane called again.

There was a response this time. A shuffle and mutter. Shane whipped his head toward the sound and saw the mostly-closed bedroom door. Maybe Earl had simply gone to bed and forgotten to turn off the TV. Shane knew that that wasn't the case, but he told himself he *couldn't* know any such thing, reprimanding himself for being so paranoid. He inched toward the bedroom door, reaching out for the knob. It was very dark inside.

"Earl? I hate to wake you. I just want to make sure you're all right, okay? It's me, Shane. I brought a… a friend."

Another noise came from within the bedroom, a sort of rhythmic, chuffing hiss. Was Earl laughing? Shane felt his hair standing up on his head. Christiana was right behind him. He touched the doorknob, began to push the door open. Flickering light from the television leaked into the room, showing a narrow bed, a bedside table, an old Westclox wind-up alarm clock. It ticked loudly. Shane felt around for a light switch but couldn't find one in the darkness. He crept forward. The blankets on the bed were rumpled, covering a complicated shape. Earl was apparently in bed after all. Shane didn't feel the slightest sense of relief.

"Earl?" he said in a stage whisper. "Come on, Earl. You asleep, old buddy?"

Earl didn't move. The pillows were humped up at the top of the bed, hiding Earl's head in thick shadow. Shane moved closer, reaching out to nudge the old man. He hated to do it, but he couldn't stop himself.

"Shane, no," Christiana whispered from behind him. "Don't wake him, OK? Leave him be."

Shane touched the shape on the bed. He felt the figure under the covers, found Earl's elbow. He nudged it gently.

"Shane, quit it, come on," Christiana whispered, touching his shoulder. "Let him rest—"

She stopped as Shane's nudging altered the disarray of the bed's pillows. One of them leaned over and flopped aside, taking away the shadow that had hidden Earl's head. Instantly, Shane wished it hadn't done that. He wished that that shadow had remained. What it revealed was too sudden, too awful, too utterly unexpected. Earl was lying on his back in bed, but his face was gone. In its place was a huge, blocky shape, shiny and awkward and oddly geometric. Shane blinked at it, refusing to see it for what it was. All the blood fell out of his face and he swayed on his feet.

It was an iron, the kind Shane had seen in any number of laundry rooms, perched on the ends of any number of ironing boards. It's dull, flat bottom stared at Shane, shining in the blue television light, dotted with tear-drop shaped holes. The pointed end was buried in Earl's mouth, breaking his dentures, splitting his thin lips. The top half of his face had completely collapsed under the weight of the bludgeon. Blood welled out of Earl's mouth and the ruined remains of his face, black and wet, pooling in his ears and between the pillows. One pale blue eye peeked out of the gore, staring calmly up into the corner.

Shane tried to call out for help, but all he seemed able to produce was a series of breathy exhales. He backed up, retreating from the horrible sight, and bumped into Christiana.

"Don't look," he managed to rasp. "Turn around and go back. Don't loo—"

Behind him, Christiana screamed. The sound of it broke Shane's paralysis. He spun around, reaching for her, trying to block her view, but she wasn't looking at the bloody mess of Earl's face. She was looking to the side, toward the dark corner next to the door they had entered by. She clapped her hands over her mouth, stifling her own shriek. Shane turned, following her gaze.

Stambaugh sat on a small upholstered chair in the corner. He was bent forward, his shoulders hunched and his arms hanging between his knees, dangling and trembling, his bloody fingers flexing on nothing. His head bobbed upright as if on a string, wobbling obscenely, and his face was a mask of black glee. He chuffed laughter. It came out in rattling wheezes, and Shane recognized the sound he had heard when he'd called from the living room.

"Not *this* time!" Stambaugh cackled merrily, his voice high and tremulous. "Not *this* tiiiime!"

Christiana stumbled away, turning to bolt out of the bedroom, throwing the door wide as she went, but Shane couldn't move. Stambaugh grinned and giggled madly, his thin hair spraying from his head in white tufts, his eyes glittering, dancing in the darkness. He watched Shane closely as he cackled, as if the two of them were sharing the moment.

As if they were sharing some sort of delicious, mutual secret.

Chapter Seventeen

It was nearly ten o'clock by the time Shane steered his truck back up the gravel drive to the cottage. Christiana sat next to him and looked out the passenger's window, her face blank, her arms crossed over her chest, hugging herself. Shane was worried about her, about both of them. It had been a long night, a bizarre and terrible night, the kind that forms a pivot upon which the rest of one's life turns.

It had been like pandemonium in slow motion. Christiana's scream had alerted most of the retirement home's east wing that something terrible had happened. By the time Shane had followed her out into the antiseptic brightness of the corridor, people had begun to move cautiously out of their doorways, blinking owlishly behind thick glasses, leaning on canes, wearing nightdresses and robes. Most of them had been women, white haired and stooped, but with bright, alert eyes. Shane knew from his mother's career as a retirement home nurse that old men were a rarity in such places. Men just didn't live as long as their female counterparts. Earl had probably been fairly popular among the women congregating in the doorways. For most of them, sex was probably merely a quaint memory, but some things never got old, and being desired by a potential mate was surely one of them. Shane had seen it in the eyes of the woman across the hall from Earl's apartment. She'd apparently ignored Christiana, who stood some distance away, her back pressed to the wall with one hand over her mouth, breathing quickly. Instead, the old woman had looked up at Shane as he came out of Earl's door, her face merely politely inquisitive.

"Did something happen to Mr. Kichenbauer?"

Shane had stared at her, not quite hearing her, his thoughts racing, stumbling over each other. She'd looked into his eyes and pressed her lips together knowledgeably. She'd nodded. "Bad, was it?" she said, her voice almost a whisper. "Heart attack? Stroke? No, don't tell me. Come into my room and we'll call the desk, tell them that poor Mr. Kirchenbauer finally graduated."

Shane had startled and blinked at the old woman. She'd been short, with huge pink curlers in her hair. Her face was lined but soft and plump, her cheeks red enough that Shane had fleetingly wondered if she'd been wearing rouge. "Wh-What did you say?" he'd stammered.

"You've had a shock," she'd replied, taking Shane's elbow. "It'll be all right. You get used to it after awhile. I said we should call the front desk and tell them poor Mr. Kichenbauer's gone on. They'll know what to do. Bring your lady friend inside, why don't you."

The orderlies had come first, pushing a gurney, watched avidly by the still-living in their open doorways, their eyes flat, almost hypnotized. Shane thought morbidly that they looked like ghosts waiting to happen. He tried to explain to the orderlies, but they weren't really listening.

"He didn't just *die*," Shane had finally rasped, pulling the head orderly aside. "He was killed. And the murderer is still *in* there."

The head orderly's name had been Manny according to the tag on his chest. He'd looked aside at his partner, one eyebrow slightly raised. He had then patted Shane on the shoulder, almost heartily, as if to say *thanks for the heads-up, champ*. He and his partner had entered Earl's room then, rolling the gurney between them, one at either end.

A few minutes went by and the gurney had been rolled back out again, this time with a figure strapped onto it. It was Stambaugh. He'd still been giggling, his head lolling back and forth, a line of drool glistening on the side of his jaw. The orderlies looked decidedly paler.

"Wait here," Manny had said to Shane, his face hard under his sweaty forehead. Manny's partner, a much younger man with a red crew-cut, had been chewing his lips, his chin tucked toward his chest, as if struggling not to vomit.

Shane had waited. Christiana sat in the old woman's apartment across the hall, staring unseeingly at the television. CSI

Miami had been on. Shane had seen it flashing silently in the dimness. The old woman's name was Mary Ellen. She had offered Christiana some tea, which she had accepted but merely held without drinking.

The police had arrived shortly thereafter. Shane had had time to worry that maybe *he'd* be charged with Earl's murder. If this had been an episode of CSI Miami, that's surely what would have happened. After all, who would believe that the crazy old man with the scarecrow arms and toothless giggle was capable of such a thing? How could Stambaugh have even lifted the clothing iron, much less driven it home with enough force to collapse Earl's facial bones, shattering them like a chunk of old pottery? Perhaps if Christiana hadn't been there things might have been different, but she'd corroborated everything Shane told the police. She'd spoken with a sort of surreal coolness that almost looked like boredom. Shane had known it wasn't boredom, though. It was the serene calm of someone who, on many dark occasions, had mentally practiced telling her horrible story to the police, knowing that they may or may not believe her, knowing that everything rested on her composure. Randy had been dead for barely a month, but in that moment Shane could see that his effects still lingered. Probably they always would.

The police were polite, businesslike, and very thorough. Shane and Christiana had sat in the cafeteria with a middle-aged detective named Weekes, who'd worn a navy blue polo shirt stretched over his gut and drunk coffee out of a Styrofoam cup. He'd tapped a notebook with a small pencil, rereading his notes, grunting to himself.

"Awful thing to see," he'd said. "Sometimes the mind just cracks. The two of them used to know each other, I hear. Back before Mr. Stambaugh's dementia got the better of him. Used to be friends. I had a mother-in-law who got the Alzheimer's pretty bad. You know what the real ugliness of it is? It isn't like the Alzheimer's takes the brain away. It's that it just scrambles it all up, mixes everything together so that it's all still there, but you just can't get to the parts you need when you need them. Memories just pop up willy-nilly, and they seem like they're brand new, like they're happening right then and there. That's probably what happened tonight. Mr. Stambaugh probably remembered something from God knows how long ago, some old fistfight or gambling debt or argument, or whatnot. Maybe it even involved Mr. Kirchenbauer, who knows? And Mr. Stambaugh just went off and acted on that memory, like he was sleepwalking or something. A shame. An awful thing to see."

There had been a lot more questions, a lot of which seemed not to have anything to do with the events of the night. Weekes had asked about Shane's relationship with Earl, as well as with Christiana. Shane had had to tell the detective about his recent history—his divorce and the death of his wife, how he'd ended up living on the outskirts of Bastion Falls, what he did for a living, and on and on. Shane tried to answer patiently, although he couldn't imagine how any of it had to do with Earl's death. Weekes seemed sheepish about asking his questions, but he asked them anyway, jotting short notes on his little notepad and nodding. Finally, he asked the one question that Shane had been dreading.

"So what brought you out to see Mr. Kirchenbauer tonight, Mr. Bellamy?" the detective had asked, leaning back in his chair and sticking his little pencil behind his ear, as if Shane's answers from here on out were officially off the record.

"I wanted to introduce him to Christiana, I guess. And... I just thought maybe I should check on him. You know, guys Earl's age..." Shane's voice trailed off. Weekes stared at him and Shane resisted the urge to just keep on talking. After several seconds Weekes nodded.

"Yeah, by the time you get to be Mr. Kirchenbauer's age, every day is a gift, isn't it? You and he were close, then?"

Shane shrugged. "We hadn't really known each other long enough to be very close. He used to take care of the cottage I live in now. He told me stories about how the place was built, and what it was like back in his day. He and his grandson, Brian, they stopped in at my place."

"Lots of times, or just the once?"

"Just the once," Shane answered, avoiding Weekes' eyes.

"And that was enough to get you thinking you should come down and check on him? On the night he happens to get murdered in his bed?"

Shane glanced up at Weekes again. "Yeah. It did. I was thinking about him, thinking how I'd like to introduce him to Christiana. He once said that the cottage needed a woman's touch. Christiana's been there an awful lot lately, so I thought—" He stopped and shook his head, his face heating. "You think I have something to do with it, then? With Earl's death?"

Weekes held up both hands, palms out. "Not at all. For one thing, if you'll pardon me for saying so, if it was you who'd decided to do the poor old guy in, you'd probably not have brought your lovely friend here along for the ride. And if she *was* an accomplice, it'd be pretty stupid of you both to hang around afterward, answering all of my questions. Unless, of course, you're both evil geniuses, and frankly, I think the evil genius is pretty much an invention of the comic books. In my experience, most criminals are pretty stupid. So no, I don't think you're involved in what happened here tonight. I just think it's curious, that's all." He cocked his head and looked closely at Shane. "Don't you?"

Shane nodded slowly. "Yeah. It's pretty curious."

Weekes sighed. "These things happen," he said, standing up and stuffing his notepad into the pocket of his khakis. "Inklings. Little visions, stuff like that. Take my brother for instance. Lives in Arizona, but somehow I always know when he's gonna call me. I just start thinking about him out of the blue, start thinking I should give him a holler, and the next thing I know, bang, the phone rings and it's him. What do you say to stuff like that?"

Shane shook his head. "I wish I knew."

"Still," Weekes said, studying Shane and Christiana in turn. "If either of you think of anything else, anything you might have forgotten to mention, or just something that didn't seem important at the time, you'll give me a call, right? I'm at the city building most of the time. Just ask for me direct. All right?"

Both Shane and Christiana had nodded, but Shane knew he wouldn't be calling Detective Weekes. It wasn't that he didn't have any more information to give to Weekes, it was simply that the man wouldn't believe him if he did.

Before calling it a night, Weekes had told Shane a little of what he'd learned from the retirement home staff. According to them, Stambaugh hadn't taken a step out of his wheelchair in nearly a decade. This night, however, he had apparently traversed the entire length of the facility, from one wing to the other, entirely on foot and unseen by any of the second-shift workers. He'd stopped in at the laundry room along the way, collecting the iron and leaving behind a small puddle of urine. Normally, the laundry room door was always locked. As yet, no one knew how Stambaugh had gained entry. Shane thought he did know, even if he didn't say so. He thought that Stambaugh had tottered right up to the laundry room door and that the door had simply opened for him, unlocking and easing back on its pneumatic arm as if pushed open by an invisible hotel doorman. Stambaugh had probably giggled as he'd walked through it, heading right for the iron, peeing a little as he went, like an excited dog. Maybe that wasn't exactly how it had happened, but after tonight, Shane was beginning to feel spookily confident of such little visions—such "inklings", as Detective Weekes had called them.

As Shane parked the truck and flicked off the headlights, Christiana slid over on the bench seat, moving next to him. Shane thought at first, wildly, that she was trying to snuggle with him, like kids parked at Inspiration Point. He glanced at her and saw that she was merely getting out of the truck on his side, staying near him in the darkness. He didn't blame her.

"Sorry," he said lamely as they stepped up onto the porch. "What an awful night." He shook his head, turning back to her.

"I just want to know one thing," she said, moving very close but not looking into his eyes. She pressed her cheek to his shoulder and leaned against him. It was more a weary gesture than a romantic one. "Just one thing. How did you know?"

Shane drew a long, deep breath. He didn't know where to begin to answer that question, and yet he didn't want to lie. Not to her, and not tonight. "I knew because I saw it. I sensed it. I knew because... because I drew it."

She pulled her head away from his shoulder and looked up at him, her brow low and serious. He shook his head at her tiredly.

"I'll tell you everything. But not tonight. When it's daylight again, OK? Until then, I just can't. I don't have it in me."

She considered this, and then nodded slightly. She embraced him on the porch again, putting her arms around his neck and allowing him to support her. He did so, easily, marveling at how slight she was. A minute later, she let him go. Her hand found his and she led him inside, closing and locking the front door behind her.

Together, they walked to the bedroom. There were no words as she began to undress him. It was remarkably quiet in the cottage, and Shane could hear her breathing. It was a nice sound, a living sound. Tonight, those were just the kinds of sounds he needed. He listened, soaking in the moment. It felt odd, almost surreal, and yet somehow, it felt absolutely right. The horrors of the night needed some sort of balm, something to dull them and wash them off. It wouldn't last, Shane knew, but maybe it didn't need to. When he closed his eyes, he still saw the gruesome mess of Earl's head, the black pulp and single staring blue eye, the invading perversity of the iron shining dully. So instead, Shane kept his eyes open. He allowed his gaze to move over Christiana in the dimness of the bedroom, concentrated on the way the moonlight played over her skin as he revealed it. He tried to memorize the sound of her clothing slipping away from her, and the sensation of her body pressed against him for the first time, skin to skin, both warm and cool, soft and firm. Nothing they did could completely deny the horrors of the night, but it did succeed in pushing those horrors back a little, at least for the moment, at a point when those horrors would otherwise have been at their most potent and harrowing. He went to her like a shipwreck survivor thrashing to shore, burying himself in the vitality of her embrace, and she came to him in the same way.

Later, they lay silent in the moonlight that shone from the uncovered window, and Shane wondered if this was the real reason they had come together on this night—this tangle of arms and legs, warm under the sheets and blankets, quiet and close, cocoon-like. He concentrated on the sound of her breathing again as she drifted to sleep. As she did, he stared at the ceiling, and the horrors tried to come back. He'd have to deal with them sometime, but not now. He caressed her shoulder, focused on the warmth of her skin pressed up against him, on the rhythmic, slowing tide of her breathing. Maybe Marlena would come in the night. Maybe she would be irate, terrible with ghostly rage, but Shane didn't think so. She had spent her fury for the night. She, like him and Christiana, was done for awhile. He could sense it. The cottage was empty. Or at least, empty of her.

In the wee hours of the morning, however, Shane awoke to the sight of the bathroom light methodically turning itself on and off, slowly, almost thoughtfully. Shane watched it, snuggled up with Christiana, his arm curled around her as if she was a teddy bear. On and off went the light, and then on and off once more. Christiana was warm next to him. He felt her breath on his arm, and thought fleetingly of Steph, feeling a pang of stale guilt. Steph was the one who'd come up with the name for their light-switching, toilet-flushing mischievous spirit.

Smithy, he thought, drifting back to sleep. *Smithy's up to his old tricks again.*

And on the heels of that, already half-dreaming, he thought of Christiana opening the front door, letting the two of them back into the cottage, leading them to the bedroom. He'd been too distracted to notice it at the time, but that door had been locked. It was habit, pure and simple. He'd locked the front door as he had left with her earlier that night, in spite of his urgency. He remembered doing it. And yet Christiana had opened it easily, without a key, without even thinking about it.

Marlena hates her, Shane mused through a haze of sleep, *but Smithy likes her. How about that? He unlocks the door for her. Smithy likes her, and so do I. That helps things, a little. I guess two out of three ain't bad.*

The next morning, Shane got up and made coffee. Christiana put on one of his old NYU tee shirts and joined him in the kitchen, perching on the narrow counter and kicking her legs idly, squinting in the early sunlight that streamed through the kitchen window. Mist rose from the river in thick white clouds, burning bright as the sun climbed over the trees. It was cold outside; somehow Shane could tell it just by looking at the blinding whiteness drifting between the trees. The furnace thumped and kicked on and Shane could feel the warmth as it began to push up through the kitchen floor vent.

They sat in the sunroom, sipping coffee and eating melon slices, and Shane began to speak. He told Christiana everything. It was discombobulated, confused, with a lot of backtracking to fill in missed details, but he didn't spare anything. He started with Steph's final phone call, and her subsequent fateful collision with James Herk in his speeding GMC pickup truck. Of course, she'd heard a lot of it the night before, when Shane had been explaining his recent history to Detective Weekes, but that had been a sanitized version. It hadn't included Steph's doomed last meeting with Shane at the Spring Garden, for instance, or the bit about Steph's purse, unpacked on the law firm's conference table like a time capsule. Shane hadn't told Detective Weekes about the Paddington Bear rattle, but he told Christiana about it now. It probably wasn't really necessary—it didn't have anything specifically to do with the cottage and Earl's death—but it did seem relevant somehow, like a thread in a long tapestry, one that runs from one end to the other, connecting everything along the way.

Christiana showed surprising sympathy. For some reason Shane had expected her to simply listen, her face set in that grave, inscrutable expression she so often wore, but that face seemed to be absent today. She set her coffee down at one point and touched him, lightly, on the shoulder. *This, Shane thought, is the difference between having a cathartic conversation with one's psychologist and one's girlfriend. For one thing, the psychologist doesn't normally sit on the couch with you, touching your shoulder lightly, occasionally twisting a finger in your hair, nodding and sympathizing and occasionally saying commiserating phrases like "That's awful," or even "Poor baby."* Dr. Taylor had had his own way of empathizing, but he'd never once said "poor baby." In any case, Shane thought, it wouldn't have sounded the same coming from him.

Shane went on, then, and the story got decidedly weirder. He shied away from cleaning it up, or leaving out the most bizarre bits. He told Christiana about Smithy first, about how he and Steph had come to name the quirky personality of the cottage. He told her about the path, and the silver rattle, and the first appearance of Marlena, wraithlike and angry about the destruction of her home, the Riverhouse. Christiana still touched him, but she no longer stroked the back of his head or curled a finger into his hair. He continued, describing the process of painting the Riverhouse, how the imagery came to him as if from some source outside of himself, perhaps even from Marlena herself. She was acting as his muse, plugging into his creativity and feeding the pictures to him, giving him details he couldn't possibly have known otherwise.

He told Christiana about Marlena and Wilhelm, about Madeleine and baby Hector, retelling as much of Earl's tale as he could remember. Christiana listened now without touching him, her brow furrowed, interested but somewhat repulsed. It wasn't a very nice story, after all; the affairs and the insensitivity that Wilhelm had shown his wife, the mystery about who'd really born baby Hector, and the final betrayal on the night of the storm, when Wilhelm had run off with Madeleine, taking Hector and leaving Marlena with the house and the property—with everything and nothing.

Finally, he told Christiana about the Riverhouse, about how it seemed to be there again sometimes, ghostly and faint, as if conjured by his strange painting. He explained how the painting itself had been returned to him by Penn Oliver. Christiana had seen the painting on the mantel, of course, but had never asked about it. After all, many commercial artists painted multiple copies of their favorite works, adding them to their personal collections. When Shane told Christiana that the Riverhouse painting was the original, the one she had sold at her gallery show, Christiana surprised him by rolling her eyes derisively.

"And Penn told you to call her? Offered to send you an advance copy of her review?"

Shane nodded, mystified, and Christiana roller her eyes again, shaking her head. Finally, she flapped a hand at him, telling him to go on. Somewhat confused, Shane did so.

He described Marlena's increasing rage, specifically directed at Christiana, despite the fact that Smithy himself—if there really was such an entity—seemed to like her, going so far as to unlock the doors for her, letting her into the cottage. He tried to explain his fears for her safety, his suspicion that Marlena meant to harm her somehow, for her own nameless reasons.

Finally, he stood and led Christiana to the corner of the sunroom that overlooked the patio. He pointed toward the leaf-strewn stone floor outside, and she looked, her brow furrowed, thoughtful, obviously struggling to keep up with Shane's fantastic tale. The leaves of the patio floor were peppered with dingy white sheets of paper, blown hither and thither, now damp with cold dew. Each page was covered with a crayon drawing. The newsprint doodle pad was still laying in the leaves beneath one of the deck chairs, surrounded by a scattering of fat, half-used crayons. Shane saw the drawing of the Insanity Stairs. It was stuck to a leg of one of deck chairs, flapping wetly in the breeze. He shuddered.

"Marlena saw me," he finally said. "She found me tapping into the story, and it made her mad. I was about to find something out about her, something Earl had seen, but she shut it down. And then she went after Earl, using Stambaugh. It's just like Earl told me: crazy is contagious. Somehow Marlena planted the suggestion in Stambaugh's mind, sending him after Earl before I could get there, before he could tell me whatever it was that he'd seen on that day, decades ago."

Christiana had that hard, grim look on her face now. "So I'm trying to understand all of this," she said, still looking out at the patio floor. "You thought you could use your drawings as a... a sort of doorway. That you'd be able to look into the past through what you drew. Right?"

Shane nodded, sighing. It sounded unutterably stupid when she said it.

She went on. "Because you wanted to find out why the woman who used to live here—Marlena—why her ghost might have it in for me? But she saw you, knew what you were doing, and then she sent her old caretaker off to kill the only other person who might have known her secrets."

Shane nodded again, looking aside at her.

She raised her eyebrows and met his gaze. "If you want to know if I believe you, I'd have to say I'm about fifty-fifty at this point. I'm not going to say things like this don't ever happen, I'm just saying that none of them have ever happened to *me*. I've had enough problems with the living. I've never really had the luxury of worrying about the dead."

"I wouldn't call it a *luxury*," Shane began, feeling that she was missing the point, but she raised a hand and shook her head.

"Sorry. Strike that remark from the record."

"I don't think that that works outside of the courtroom, counselor," Shane replied, perturbed.

"The point is," Christiana said, plowing on. "You did this because you were worried about me, right? And you were worried because you didn't know why this woman's ghost might hate me. Is that it?"

Shane exhaled wearily and nodded again.

"You can't be this dense, can you?" she said, not meanly. "You're a sweet man, Shane, but you're pretty naïve about women. You know that?"

"Rub it in, why don't you," Shane said, turning and heading back to the sofa. He plopped down onto it and picked up his coffee mug. It was cold.

"Sorry, babe," Christiana said, and smiled a little. The smile didn't reach her eyes, however. "The Riverhouse painting, for instance. You totally missed that one, didn't you? I mean, talk about a softball."

"What are you talking about?"

"Penn Oliver wanted you to call her. Didn't she spell it out for you pretty plainly? She *likes* you. She collects artist boyfriends like trophies. You're the flavor of the month, as far she's concerned. She sent the painting back to you to get your attention, because you didn't take her up on her offer of an advance copy of her review. She's not used to getting blown off like that. It probably drove her completely crazy."

Shane frowned at her, incredulous. "How can you possibly know that?"

"Well, the *man's* answer to that question is that Morrie told me all about her. Like I said, they used to date, and Morrie gossips like a school girl. But the *woman's* answer is that I just know. Come on, you expect me to believe that this place is haunted by two ghosts—a woman and some weird little sneaky imp—and that your painting of that damned house somehow brought the house itself back to life, but you yourself doubt something as simple and obvious as woman's intuition?" She shook her head, smiling ruefully.

"All right, all right, I get it," Shane said, patting the sofa next to him, summoning her to rejoin him there. "So what's the point?"

"The *point* is, you completely missed Penn Oliver's hints, and that tells me everything I need to know about how it is you don't understand what might be going on right here in the cottage. *If* everything you say is true, which I am not quite ready to accept. Yet. Sorry."

"That's fine," Shane said as she settled down next to him again, "just so long as you don't think I'm crazy."

"You may *be* crazy," she said lightly, but not quite jokingly, "but that won't change how I feel about you, and that's what your real concern is. Don't worry."

Shane relaxed. She was right. "So what am I missing?"

"You are a sweet man," she said, leaning close to him and looking him in the eye. "But you are a bit clueless in some ways. Frankly, I like that about you. You risked everything—in your own mind, at least—trying to find out what it is that this Marlena spook might hate about me, why she might have it in for me, when the answer was right there in front of you."

"What?" Shane said, not really sure that Christiana knew what she was talking about, but willing to indulge her anyway. "What am I missing?"

She raised her eyebrows again. "It's us, silly," she said, shrugging and gesturing between them. "Our relationship."

Shane frowned, thinking. Christiana went on.

"She thought she had you all to herself. You see that, right? You were the replacement for the husband she lost. Crazy as it sounds, she fell for you. I mean, look at you. You're about the right age, I'd guess. You're an artist. You live in the cottage where her husband did all of his painting. And you yourself were alone, recently abandoned by your own wife. It was perfect. It was a match made in hell. Sorry," she said, smiling crookedly, "couldn't resist."

"You're serious," Shane said, narrowing his eyes.

She nodded, a little patronizingly. "She fell for you, Shane, you old dog. She thought you were hers. And then I showed up, and everything changed. It's the story of her cruddy, faithless husband all over again. Her man's sleeping with another woman. My presence is just rubbing salt in some very old wounds. Let me lay it out for you. If this ghost of yours really exists, she's *jealous*."

Jealous, Shane thought, narrowing his eyes, trying it out to see if it fit. *Marlena is jealous.* Now that Christiana had said it openly, he was amazed that it hadn't occurred to him before. But then that wasn't really true, was it? He remembered painting the bikini-clad girl in the Florida illustration, using the woman in the Flickr photo as a reference. He'd felt like the portrait of Marlena was watching him, judging his intentions. He'd even turned to the portrait afterwards, telling Marlena that she didn't have anything to worry about. *You're still my main squeeze,* he remembered saying. *Marlena is jealous,* he thought again, and this time it felt true. It felt as obvious as the sun in the sky. *She hates Christiana because Christiana is taking away what she thought was hers. Christiana is taking me away from her.* Maybe there was more to it than that, some specific that he was missing, but that was certainly the core of it. It was so simple that he'd completely overlooked it.

"So," Shane said slowly. "What *do* you do with a jealous ghost?"

Christiana shrugged and shook her head. "Move away?"

Shane stared at her blankly, wondering if she was joking. She merely looked back at him, her eyebrows raised inquisitively, as if to say *why the hell not? What's keeping you here anyway?*

It was a good question, a sane question, and yet it was a question Shane didn't have a meaningful answer to. Moving out of the cottage had never even occurred to him. It was his cottage, damn it, despite its long and interesting history. He wasn't about to abandon it just because some dead woman had gotten herself into some kind of neurotic, jealous snit.

But there was more to it than that, and Shane knew it. He just couldn't put his finger on it. It was all mixed up with his curiosity about the new painting, The Sleepwalker, the one sitting unfinished on the easel upstairs, and the candle that still flickered sometimes on the windowsill of the mysterious, room-less window, and the Riverhouse painting itself, with its haunting, approaching shadow, growing longer everyday in the bottom right of the picture. Shane wasn't going to go anywhere. Not until all of that was resolved. He was curious, yes, but more than that, he was a *part* of it. He couldn't abandon it anymore than he could will himself to stop breathing. Surely Christiana understood that. Later, when the questions had been answered, then maybe he'd move. Maybe he'd propose to Christiana, ask her to marry him, and they'd pick out a place together. Maybe he'd even convince her to move back to New York with him, leave all this ugliness behind them once and for all. Maybe she'd even say yes. On both counts.

But not yet. Not for a little while longer. Marlena was dangerous—Shane knew that now, knew it very well—and yet he still believed that he could hold her off if he really wanted to. And he *did* want to. Of course he did. Christiana was the rabbit on his lap, and Marlena was the jealous lover, crouched in front of him, reaching for her as if to pet her, but Shane was no fool. He could protect Christiana. For a little while longer. Just long enough to finish the last painting. When that happened... everything would be different.

"So," Christiana said, leaning back on the couch with a crooked smile on her face. "Since you *obviously* aren't planning on moving away from this lovely little joint, should I start wearing garlic around my neck when I'm here? Or am I supposed to carry a wooden stake and mallet wherever I go? I can never remember which kills what."

Shane smiled back at her and shook his head. He was glad that she could laugh about it. After all, there was nothing Christiana could do on her own to protect herself from Marlena. Nothing at all.

That was his job.

Chapter Eighteen

Earl's funeral turned out to be a crowded and boisterous affair. The funeral home was packed with people of all ages, all chattering loudly, as if it was a family reunion. Children chased each other through the throng of legs, followed by the stern calls of their mothers. Shane had been to funerals like it before. Earl had been very old. Even though he'd been rudely pushed into the afterlife, no one doubted that the Reaper had had Earl's name on his short list anyway. Shane moved through the crowd, brushing past a dozen conversations, and stopped in front of the closed wooden lid of Earl's casket. He touched it lightly, and said in a low voice, "Sorry, Earl. I didn't know what I was stirring up. I should've taken your advice after all. I should've stopped asking questions when I could."

"How did you know Mr. Kirchenbauer?" a voice asked. Shane turned to see a man in a prim black suit standing nearby, the look on his face a carefully tailored mask of polite sympathy— obviously the director of the funeral home.

"He was a friend," Shane replied, taking his hand off the casket lid. "I hadn't known him for very long. But he made an… impression on me."

The director nodded, smiling meaningfully. Shane glanced away, unable to look at the man's practiced sincerity any longer. Brian was standing near the doorway, looking red-faced and uncomfortable in an ill-fitting suit jacket and tie. Shane made his way toward him.

"Thanks for coming, Mr. Bellamy," Brian said somberly. "Especially since it was you who… you know."

Shane nodded. "I know. I'm sorry it turned out this way. What a mess."

"A goddamn mess," Brian agreed in a low voice. "But it's all over now. You know they took Mr. Stambaugh away? He's in a psychiatric home up in New Haven now, doped all to hell and back. I'd guess that's how they'll keep him until he finally kicks the damn bucket. None too soon, if you ask me."

Shane didn't want to talk about it, but he felt drawn into the topic. "Will there be a murder trial or anything?"

Brian shrugged as if he didn't care. "What's the point? Everybody knows he did it. What are they gonna do? Give him life in prison?" He laughed darkly. "Or the death penalty? That's a joke. It'd probably be a relief to the old coot. If it was me, you know what I'd do? I'd make him young again, just so he had a long, long life to live, knowing what he'd done." He nodded to himself, looking askance at the closed casket. He cleared his throat and swiped once at his eyes with the heel of his hand. "That's what I'd do," he said again, and sighed.

Shane left shortly thereafter, taking off his tie as he climbed into his pickup. He didn't go to the graveyard for the burial. He didn't figure Earl would mind.

On the Monday before Halloween, Shane delivered the final painting in the Florida series to Greenfeld. Christiana took it in the white Sprinter van and Greenfeld called once she arrived at his office.

"I've already got the check in hand," he told Shane. "You want me to send it back with your girlfriend here?"

Shane smiled. "Sure, thanks. You aren't jealous are you, old boy?" If it had been anyone else, he'd never have been so bold as to mention it, but in Greenfeld's case it was hard not to.

"Bite me," Greenfeld replied amiably. "She'll get tired of you as soon as that old Bohemian artist shtick wears off. Besides, I've got my cats and my afternoon stories."

"That's the spirit."

"So are you ready for some more work? Or are you going to take a little lover's vacay or something?"

"No lover's vacay. I think I am going to take a short break, though."

"You sure? I have some more studio work on the table, based on the success of your matte painting. Sony needs something for a kid's movie. Sort of a martial arts fantasy thing, with dragons and anime princesses with eyes the size of softballs, that sort of thing. Straight to video, but it's got some big name voice talent in it, not that it matters to you. They need a whole series of background plates. You could do it in your sleep."

"What's the deadline?"

"End of November. No problem for a machine like you. What do you say?"

Shane considered it, looking out the kitchen window at the dim afternoon light. The sky was low and dark, churning slowly. "I think I'm going to pass this time, Morrie. The machine needs a breather."

Greenfeld was a sharp guy. He asked, "You got another project in the works, maybe?"

Shane smiled again. "Yeah, I guess I do. One more, just for me."

"For you and maybe your artsy girlfriend?" Greenfeld said.

"You just can't let that one go, can you?"

"Behold, your Morrie is a jealous Morrie," Greenfeld said, sighing loudly into the phone. "I care a lot less about you taking her away from me than I do about *her* taking *you* away from me. Twisted, isn't it? Come to think of it, that's probably the biggest reason I'm still in the place I am. But what can I say? As the Chairman of the Board used to say, I gotta be me. Go ahead and finish up whatever you've got going. Good luck with it. But don't expect me to stop calling, eh?"

"I wouldn't have it any other way," Shane said, still smiling. It was hard not to like Greenfeld, in spite of his rough edges. A moment later, Shane hung up the cordless and stuck it in the charger in the library. He'd been planning on going out for a short bike ride, but the darkening sky made him think otherwise. He peered out the front window. Wind switched and flicked over the yard, whipping the grass and swirling dust eddies on the gravel drive. The weather guys on KMOX had been predicting storms off and on all through the week, issuing flood warnings for most of Jefferson and St. Louis counties, but Shane took it all with a grain of salt. He'd lived in the flood valley long enough now to know that the news people tended to cry flood at the slightest warning, apparently believing it was better to err on the side of alarmism than to be caught with their pants down by a sudden deluge.

Shane opened the front door and stepped out onto the porch. Wind sucked at the door as he closed it, making it slam behind him.

It was hot outside, but gray and dark, the air humid and thick with electricity. Shane guessed that today, at least, the weather guys had it right on. Even if it didn't rain, the gusting wind would make for a challenging bike ride, carrying the trail grit and dead leaves in its arms, flinging it all into Shane's face like a playground bully. He walked around to the shed anyway, peering at the trees along the edge of the yard, eyeing the entrance to the footpath. He hadn't been along the path for a few weeks. Not, in fact, since the day he and Christiana had kissed on the portico of the Riverhouse. Once, before that, Shane had taken Christiana for a short walk along the path. They hadn't gone the entire way, but Shane had told her where it ended up, about the angel statue and the stepping stones across the stream, about how it had once connected both properties. She hadn't seemed particularly interested, and Shane had been secretly glad. They'd sat on the wrought iron bench for a while, with that careful, deliberate distance between them, watching the river where it peeked through the trees at the edge of the gully. She'd never mentioned it since.

The path could be seen now, dark, full of shadows, like a tunnel mouth in the corner of the yard.

Shane touched the doors of the shed but didn't pull them open. It really wasn't good bike-riding weather. Maybe he'd go for a walk along the path instead. It'd been awhile, after all. Maybe he should check to see if any weeds were growing up again, undoing all of his careful work. He started toward the path, dreamily, as if drawn to it by something outside himself, and then stopped. He turned and looked back over his shoulder. The little window above the shed was mostly obscured by the swaying leaves of the magnolia tree. Shane squinted, watching. Sure enough, he could see it. The candle flame was tiny but bright, unmoving despite the switching wind. Beyond it was seamless dark. *Go on,* the flame seemed to say. *Walk the path. Keep it clear. Go all the way to the end and visit the Riverhouse. It's lonely. It misses you. It* loves *you.*

Shane squinted up at the candle. Like the flame, its voice was tiny but bright, pervasive. Its suggestion was very hard to ignore. Hard, but not *impossible.* Shane turned around and walked back toward the front of the cottage. The footpath could wait, and so could the Riverhouse. He'd decided to go upstairs instead.

He'd decided to paint.

The painting was going to be called the Sleepwalker, but that was about the only thing Shane knew for sure about it. He didn't know what the subject matter would be, or what style it might be in. Both the Riverhouse painting and the Marlena portrait had been done in a sort of weird fusion, mixing photo-realism with a sort of tortured abstract-cubism that looked like something out of Picasso's nightmares. He assumed this final painting would be of the same style, and sure enough, as he held the brush over the canvas, he could feel that strange compulsion coming over him again, that weird mix of calculating angles and hot scribbles, all welding together, forming a bizarre stylistic alloy that seemed to both complement and contradict itself. The brush strokes nearly vibrated as they began to come, slowly this time, but confidently. This time, the painting had nothing to do with the muse. She wasn't directing the brush strokes, or dictating the final image on the canvas. She had shown Shane the way to this particular well of creativity, and he'd remembered it. Now, just like he had with the newsprint sketch pad and the crayons, he was tapping into the well all by himself, independent of her. The crayons had been a shortcut, of course, giving him a greater degree of control over the portal, but the images he had created with them had been imperfect; cloudy and incomplete, rushed to the point of childishness, skipping over the story like flat stones on the river. The Sleepwalker, however, was not going to be rushed. It was going to go deep into the story, just as Shane had originally suspected; maybe deeper than he was truthfully comfortable with, and certainly deeper than Marlena wished. The knowledge of that—of her stern, ghostly disapproval, perhaps even her fury—gave him a sort of dizzying dread every time he settled the brush to the canvas.

The image began to form, sketchy but certain, and yet Shane could make very little sense of it. He painted in drab browns, blacks and mossy greens—storm colors, he thought, probably influenced by the churning sky outside the studio window. Indian summer had descended with typical Missouri suddenness, turning the autumn air hot and still, making the remaining leaves hang from the trees like washcloths dried out on the kitchen faucet. Shane had opened the window over the stairs, but the thin curtains hung dead, with barely a breath of breeze to push them. Shane's forehead was beaded with sweat as he painted. He could feel the story coiling in his chest, pushing through his arm, straining at the feeble medium of the brush, suddenly anxious to get out onto the canvas. He remembered when he'd first begun the Sleepwalker, weeks earlier. It had been a slow, frustrating process. The image had been like a deer at the edge of the woods, timid and tensed, ready to flee at the slightest false move. He'd been forcing it then, trying to make it show him what he wanted to know. Now, however, he thought he finally had his answers, or at least enough to make sense of Marlena's malevolent moodiness. She was jealous. It was as simple as that. She'd thought Shane was hers, the replacement for the husband who had abandoned her and taken away everything that mattered to her. But then Christiana had come along, threatening to steal Shane away from her. And worse, she had succeeded. Shane was indeed in love with Christiana. He hadn't said those words to her yet—nor had she to him—and yet they were there, waiting just offstage, listening for just the right cue. That cue would come, and the tension of waiting for it was both frightening and delicious. Shane felt it. He thought Christiana probably felt it, too. But most importantly, he thought Marlena felt it as well. It was probably like a knife in her dead heart, waiting to be twisted. That was her secret misery, the source of her rage and pain, the spearhead of her hatred for Christiana. It was Madeleine and Wilhelm all over again. Some stories, Shane thought as he painted, were cyclical; some histories just couldn't help repeating themselves. Now that he knew the source of Marlena's torment, he approached the Sleepwalker with a calm patience, ready to let it tell its own story, in its own time. And somehow, the painting responded to that, turning from a trickle into a pipeline, pushing the story through him, out onto the canvas, with sudden, almost startling urgency.

Even still, the image that was forming, sketchy and frantic, didn't make any sense. The first line, the up-stroke with the gentle, feminine curves, had indeed become a sort of figure, but then the story had leapt away from that shape, filling in the sides of the wide canvas. A large, blocky shape had constructed on the right side, complicated and busy, making Shane think of the uneven stack of bricks from his crayon drawing vision. This shape was flatter, though, and softer, somehow. A piece of upholstered furniture? Or maybe a bed? He tried to focus on the shape, to force his hand to produce the necessary details, but the story refused, impatient, brushing off his questions and moving to the opposite side of the canvas, taking his hand with it. There, he painted a jumble of blocky shapes, apparently thick with shadows. He thought he could recognize these—trunks and crates, mostly empty, merely stage dressing. A large cloth seemed to be draped over them, turning them into an abstract backdrop, but Shane knew that these were unimportant details. The focus of this side of the canvas was an upholstered chair, high-backed, with dainty wooden legs, each represented by one quick slash of curve. There was something sitting on the chair. Not a figure, but another shape, smaller and indistinct, and yet familiar. Shane squinted at it, wondering, but then the focus of the story darted away again, moving back to the central figure. A shape formed around it, a sort of halo, perfectly round, framing the head and shoulders. The halo quickly became the centerpiece of the scene, partly because it was, in fact, in the exact center, but also because it was the only light-colored object in the scene, formed of a pale, dusty blue. *Baby blue*, Shane thought idly as his arm arced around, tracing the curves, making them perfect.

Wind suddenly switched outside the window, lifting the curtains out over the stairs and singing a high note in the screen. Downstairs, startling Shane badly, a dull slam suddenly reverberated. It shook the cottage, and Shane nearly dropped his brush. He sat back, his heart thudding, and drew a deep breath. He knew what had caused that slam—the changing air pressure had merely pulled a door shut downstairs, slamming it—but it had still unsettled him, broken his mental link with the story on the canvas. After a moment, he glanced down at his watch and saw that he'd been at it for nearly two hours. His shoulder was tired, but not quite sore. He could paint more, if he wanted to. The story was still there, hovering in the air, crackling like electricity, waiting to find life on the canvas. First, however, he should go downstairs and close some of the windows, just in case it did storm and the wind blew the rain in. As he passed the window over the stairs he felt the sudden cool of the air outside. It chilled the sweat on his brow and made him shiver slightly.

Shadows filled the downstairs as he moved through the rooms, pushing the windows down, rattling the handles of the front door and the door over the basement, making sure that they were securely latched and wouldn't swing wide again with any more gusts of air. Even with the windows closed, it was an old cottage, and there were plenty of leaks all around the place, letting the air pressure push through the walls like a sieve. Satisfied, he retreated down the short hall and pounded back up the stairs to the studio. The air from the window was much colder all of a sudden. Shane stopped at the top of the stairs, his hair prickling and his breath puffing out in a white fog.

The Sleepwalker was no longer on its easel. It was hovering in the air in the middle of the studio, facing him directly, its image looking stark and naked in the light of the window. Shane stared at it, his eyes wide, his hand gripping the top knob of the banister hard enough to turn his knuckles white. Was it Marlena? Smithy? Somehow, he didn't think so. This was both of them somehow, or neither of them. This was something larger, more pervasive, less human—almost like the ghost of the Riverhouse itself. It filled the studio with its cold presence, packing the space, making the air feel crowded and dense, almost too thick to inhale. Shane forced his lungs to fill and when he tried to speak, to ask who was there, nothing came out but a thin rasp. The Sleepwalker began to drift slowly toward him, and as it did, it grew brighter, gathering the stormlight, focusing it, making the rough brush strokes leap off the canvas. The image loomed over Shane, but he could barely focus on it. Dimly, he realized he wasn't breathing. His vision began to darken at the edges, spiked with angry pulses as his heart pounded. Still, the Sleepwalker pushed toward him, demanding that he look, that he make sense of the images. And suddenly, vaguely, he thought he did. The shape on the right was indeed a bed. Someone was lying in it, covered roughly with a mass of blankets, their head buried in the pillows. The red slashes weren't the light of a sunset, as Shane had originally thought. They were spatters of blood on the pillows, hiding the ruin of the figure's head. Shane felt dismay sink its claws into him, making him sway on his feet. And yet it was the object on the left side, the object sitting on the cushion of the high-backed chair, that followed him down into unconsciousness. He should have recognized it right away—and part of him had. After all, he'd already painted it once. It was a purse. It sat open, its inside full of black shadow, its secrets already revealed. None of it made any sense. It was pathetic and frustrating and terrifying, all at the same time. As the Sleepwalker drifted toward him, suspended in the grip of that awful, nameless force, Shane began to black out. He fell forward, collapsing as if in slow motion, all the strength evaporating from his arms and legs, and as he did, a gust of cold wind pushed through the open window, belling the curtains over him, sighing in the window screen. The sigh of the wind sounded almost like a word, and that word followed Shane down into oblivion, echoing, tolling like a bell. *Riverhouse,* it said, over and over, backwards and forwards, beckoning and warning, teasing and threatening. *Riverhouse... Riverhouse...*

He awoke some time later, startling to the sound of a door slamming again somewhere in the cottage. His ribs hurt and he rolled over pressing his hand to them, remembering everything in a rush—the Sleepwalker floating in the air, looming over him, the air going dense and poisonous, the revelation of the images on the canvas, and finally himself falling forward, collapsing onto the top few steps, bruising his ribs. He jerked upright, suddenly sure the painting was still hovering over him, descending on him like a set of gaping jaws. The painting wasn't there, however. Neither were the stairs, or the rest of the studio. He blinked in the darkness, looking around. He was in his bedroom, on his own bed. It was rumpled, the pillows damp with sweat, as if he'd just awoken from a very restless nap. He drew a shaking breath and felt another pang of pain in his ribs. It hadn't been a dream, of course. Had it? He frowned, squinting into the muddy twilight of his bedroom, staring toward his dresser. The antique silver baby rattle sat on top, next to his wallet and a wooden bowl filled with loose change. The rattle caught the waning light, condensing it into watery glimmers.

He remembered the sound that had awoken him, the sound of a door slamming somewhere in the cottage. He listened: footsteps, light but purposeful, and then a dull thunk. Shane knew what that sound was, and smiled to himself, in spite of everything. Christiana was home. She'd just put her bag on the kitchen counter. Another thump; the refrigerator closing. She liked a Diet Coke when she got back from work. It was nice to know someone's habits like that, and nice to be known by them as well.

"I'm in here," he called, his voice thick and raspy. "Just took a little nap. Apparently."

Nothing. Shane listened for another moment, and then climbed off the bed. His legs felt weak beneath him, nearly geriatric. He leaned on the bedroom door for a moment. "Chris?" he called again, but no answer came. The cottage was suddenly perfectly silent. The hallway into the kitchen was packed with shadows. He walked slowly along it, his hair prickling. Christiana's bag sat on the kitchen counter. An open can of Diet Coke sat next to it, already beading in the humid evening stillness.

"Chris?" he said, his voice faltering. Where could she be? A surge of frustrated hopelessness welled up in him. It was his job to protect her, wasn't it? It had only been a few minutes. Surely Marlena couldn't have gotten to Christiana in such short a period of time. Could she have? Worse, what if it wasn't Marlena at all? What if it was that nameless, pervasive force—the inhuman spirit of the Riverhouse itself—he'd felt (or dreamed he'd felt) in the studio? Panic tried to shimmy up Shane's spine like a monkey, but he fought it back. She had been here only a moment earlier; she couldn't have gone far. He moved through the kitchen, into the library, and then stopped.

The sunroom was the brightest room in the cottage, filled with diffuse twilight from the low sky outside. Something was standing in the center of the room, blocky, silhouetted against the dim blue light. Shane sucked in a breath, his heart pounding, but the figure didn't move. It wasn't a figure at all. It was a painting on an easel. He recognized it. It was the portrait of Marlena, the one he thought of as "Dear M". It stood on the smaller of his two easels, looking incongruous in front of the cushioned ottoman. A flicker of heat lightning lit the painting, illuminating it brilliantly—Marlena's shocked eyes, her white fingers gripping the letter, the blood red fireplace behind her. And the purse in the shadow of the sofa, of course; Steph's purse, its mouth open and dark. Shane continued forward, drawn to the painting, his eyes widening. It was almost magnetic. The paintings were portals, after all.

"Chris?" Shane said one more time, his voice barely a hoarse whisper.

"What?" she said, from directly behind him.

Shane startled violently, barking a hoarse bellow of shock and spinning so quickly on his heels that he nearly fell on top of her. She screamed in surprise at *his* surprise, dancing backwards away from him and nearly dropping the bottle of wine in her hands.

"What the hell!" she cried, her eyes wide but already beginning to laugh. "Don't *do* that! What's wrong with you?"

Shane moved forward, taking the bottle from her hands and touching her shoulder, flush with relief. He drew her into his arms and began to laugh weakly. "Sorry, Chris. I didn't know where you'd gone. You just disappeared. I was... worried, I guess."

"I was in the basement, you big dope," she said against his shoulder. "Getting a bottle of wine. Excuse me for living. Do I need to get a permission slip next time?"

"Maybe you do," he said, letting her go and looking down at her. Her cheeks were red. She seemed caught between annoyance and amusement.

"So why so jumpy?" she asked, looking up at him critically. "I mean, apart from the usual?"

Shane shrugged and shook his head. "What's the occasion?" he asked, raising the wine bottle in his hand and nodding toward it.

Christiana sighed her characteristic businesslike sigh, taking the bottle away from him. "Well, I'll have you know that your girlfriend has been asked to host a new gallery showing, this time on the main floor of the Art Museum, not in some little side hall. I got a call today from an organization called the American Aesthetic Underground. They want me to host their annual Women in the Arts exhibit. It's bigger than anything I've ever done so far, but I didn't tell them that, of course. Apparently, they read Penn Oliver's review of my last show and figured I had the know-how and connections to make it happen. I'm sure it doesn't hurt that I wear a skirt to work, but I'm willing to take every break I can get."

"*I've* never seen you wear a skirt to work," Shane said, following her into the kitchen. She ignored him, flipping on the overhead light.

"So tell: what's got you so antsy?" she asked, setting the wine bottle on the counter and picking up her Coke. "Besides the obvious, of course. Something to do with that painting in the sunroom? Is that why you moved it?"

Shane shook his head and leaned against the counter. He didn't want to worry Christiana any more than she already was, and he didn't want to taint her good fortune with more otherworldly weirdness. He shrugged. "I don't know," he said a little lamely. "I just... I like it in there. It was... in the way upstairs."

To Shane's surprise and dismay, Christiana shuddered. "'Riverhouse' I can deal with," she said, "But that Marlena painting creeps me out. Sorry. Maybe it's just the story you told me about her, but I don't think that's it entirely." She shook herself and looked up at him. "Whatever. Time to talk dinner. If it was up to me, I'd just drink your wine all night—my stomach's already in knots about this new show—but I think I used up all my 'get out of a hangover free' cards when I was in college. You got any more of those pork steaks in the freezer?"

Shane nodded, smiled, and crossed to the refrigerator.

Behind him, Christiana took a sip of her Coke and then said, "You know what I first thought when I got here and saw that painting in the sunroom?"

"What's that?" Shane said, opening the freezer compartment and peering inside.

"I thought you'd moved her into there because of what you said about the sunroom, about how her ghost seems unable to go in there. I had this crazy notion that you were trying to... sort of, put her to sleep or something. Like maybe the sunroom was some kind of dead zone for her."

Shane nodded as he closed the freezer. "I guess that would make sense, wouldn't it?" He was thinking of the Sleepwalker, thinking about how he'd worried that if Marlena found him painting it, she'd be upset—maybe even dangerously furious. He thought of the weird force that had held the Sleepwalker up in front of him, forcing him to really *look* at it. Maybe Christiana's theory was partly right. Maybe locking Marlena's portrait up in the sunroom, instead of leaving it upstairs, in sight of the Sleepwalker, was a way to keep the secret just a bit longer, a way to keep her from interfering, just long enough to finish the new painting. It did make a certain, strange kind of sense. Moving Marlena into the sunroom was a pretty good idea.

It just hadn't been his.

Three hours later, the two of them were sitting on the patio, him in one of the deck chairs, her on his lap. A thick blanket was wrapped around both of them, warming them against the October cool. Wind sang a whispering chorus in the trees. Lost in the darkness below the bluff, frogs called to each other over the river.

Christiana sighed deeply and pulled the blanket tighter around her. "So you think I can pull it off?"

"What? The gallery show? The Women in the Arts thing?"

"Mm-hmm."

Shane thought about it, and then nodded. "I think so. It's what you've been waiting for."

"But there will be so much more to manage this time. And without any help from Morrie. I mean, I'm glad to do it on my own. I just didn't expect it to happen this soon."

"Will Morrie be mad?"

Christiana arched her eyebrows in the darkness, as if she hadn't even considered such a thing. After a moment, she shook her head. "No. Morrie's not like that. He may try to angle his way in somehow, but more out of habit than anything else. He'll be fine."

"So what are you worried about?"

She shrugged. "It's just going to be a lot to manage. All those artists vying for space, but waiting until the last possible moment to send me their bios and titles. Getting the right kind of museum space so that it feels cozy and roomy at the same time. Making sure all the art gets safely delivered and set up, especially the heavy stuff, the sculptures. And what about the installment pieces? One of them is comprised almost entirely of broken glass. Do I need insurance? What if somebody gets hurt? What if Dolores Grand shows up and scoffs at the whole thing, says it's all just a bunch of pretentious, melodramatic claptrap? Penn Oliver will probably quote her in her review. Worst of all, what if they're right?"

Shane shook his head, blinking. "So what if all of that happens? You can manage it. You're smart and quick-witted, and most of all, you love this. You love art. What's the worst that can happen?"

Christiana slumped on his lap. She extricated her hand from the blanket and reached for her wine glass on the nearby table. It was nearly empty. She stared into it disconsolately, and then set it back down on the table. "I have a cousin who wrote a book," she said, laughing a little. "I bet you didn't know that about me. One of my cousins is an author. Sounds impressive, doesn't it?"

Shane shrugged and nodded a little. "I suppose. Your cousin's not John Grisham is he?"

She laughed. "Not quite. It was just a computer book, one of those Idiot's Guide type of things. It was all about how to sell stuff on eBay. And it's a she, actually. My cousin Rachel. She lives in Alaska with her Air Force husband. She had a lot of time to hone her computer skills, him being gone so much and it being dark there so much of the year. The point is, the book was all about what she loves doing. She got really good at online auctions, at selling this, buying that, and selling it all over again. She started doing it for her friends, and found out it was a real talent. It's all about how she takes the pictures, and writes the descriptions, and sets the initial price. For some reason or other, she's totally into it, and better yet, she's a natural at it. So she wrote her book, got it published through one of those Complete Dummy's Guide publishing houses, and the next thing she knew she was seeing her name on a cover at Barnes and Nobles."

Shane shook his head wonderingly. "That's pretty amazing. Good for cousin Rachel."

"It *is* good for her," Christiana agreed. "But that's not the reason I brought it up. I only mention it because I saw her last year, at a family reunion over in Chicago. Rachel came with her husband, and she had a copy of the book with her. Everybody passed it around, ooh-ing and ahh-ing over it, but otherwise not really knowing what to say about it. When it finally got to the end of the table where my parents were sitting, my dad just held it in his hands, glanced at the cover, flipped it over, and then hefted it, as if its worth was based on how much it weighed. And he said to my cousin, 'Not bad. So what do you get, two, three bucks per copy?'" Christiana stopped and shook her head curtly. "That's it. That's all that mattered to him. It didn't matter that Rachel had found a way to make a living doing something that she loved to do, or that she'd even *found* something she loved to do. You know how rare that is? To find that one thing that lights you up inside, that thrills you and inspires you? Let me tell you, it's pretty damn rare. But that didn't matter to dad. All that mattered to him was the bottom line. How much money did it make? If it made her a lot, it was a worthwhile thing for her to do. If it didn't... well, then what was the point? And you could tell by the way he barely glanced at the cover—just flipped it over to look for the price—you could tell that he thought there wasn't any point in it otherwise."

"Sounds a bit like my dad, I guess," Shane said thoughtfully. "Maybe a bit like everybody's dad."

Christiana leaned back against him, her lips pressed together tightly. After a moment she went on. "My parents were paying for my college. They were paying for my apartment, for my car, my insurance, everything. But the point is, what they were really paying for was a lawyer daughter. That's what they wanted. That's what they still want. Dad especially. When I told him I was quitting school to get into art representation, it was like telling him I was getting into making lesbian pornos. Frankly he probably would have preferred that. I mean, at least lesbian porn makes money."

"You can't really mean that," Shane said.

She sighed. "I wish I was joking. Maybe I am, but only a little." She stopped, shaking her head slowly. They sat together in silence for several minutes, listening to the gusts of wind in the trees, the throbbing calls of the frogs down by the river. It still hadn't rained, although Shane could feel it in the air, cool and misty, smelling of moss. Finally, Christiana went on.

"My dad is waiting for me to fail. And he's patient, damn him. It isn't enough that I've found the thing I love. It isn't enough that it makes me happy. Those things don't even come into the equation for him. All that matters is that I'm not yet a success at it. Do you know why you were the first person I thought of calling when I got off the phone with the people at the AAU? Because deep down I know that if I call my parents to share that kind of news, they won't celebrate with me. They won't even say congratulations. They'll ask how much the event pays. And I'll have to tell them that it pays virtually nothing. I'll have to spend all my time explaining to them that it's all about getting my name out there, developing a reputation, making contacts. You'd think they'd understand that, because that's how one gets started as a lawyer, too, doing pro-bono work in the hope of getting attached to something big, something noteworthy. But they won't understand it in terms of what I've chosen to do, the life I've decided to live. But that's not even the main point. That's not the biggest reason it didn't even occur to me to call my parents. The biggest reason is that if I call and tell them about it, then they'll *know* about it. And if they know about it, and it turns out to be a failure, they'll never let me forget it. They'll use it as a lever on me, pushing me back into the world they designed for me, patiently and constantly, one little comment at a time, like Chinese water torture. You asked me what's the worst that can happen? That's the worst that can happen."

Shane frowned. "What, that your parents use one little failure as a lever on you, trying to force you back into what they want you to do?"

She shook her head. "No, not just that. The worst that can happen is that they'll succeed. The worst is that they might be right. Maybe I *am* going to be a failure at this. Then what?"

Shane laughed, softly at first, and then a bit louder. Christiana sat up and looked at him suspiciously, one eyebrow raised. "Are you laughing at me?"

"No," Shane said, shaking his head, still smiling. "Not at all. But is that it? Is that what this is all about?"

"What?"

"Fear of being a failure. Is that what's at the bottom of all of this?"

She lowered her brow. "You make it sound like it's no big deal. This is only my life I'm talking about."

"No," Shane replied, growing serious. "It's only your life as an art representative we're talking about. What, you think that's all you are in the whole world?"

"Go on," she said, her eyes narrowed.

"I think you are very good at what you do. I think you have a passion for it, and your passion makes you a perfectionist, which can stress you out and make your life pretty hard every now and then, but it also makes you very good at your work. In short, *I* think you will be a smashing success. But just for the sake of argument, let's say you aren't. Let's say you fail spectacularly and discover—who'd a-thunk it?—that art representation is a terrible fit for you. Does that mean the only road left for you is going back to law school?"

Christiana merely stared at him, her expression tense, but listening. He went on. "There's value in learning what you *don't* want to do, you know. More importantly, there are a thousand more—a *million* more roads you can try out afterward. You can live your entire life and never run out of options, never fail so many times at the things you *like* to do that you have to turn back to the one you hate. And most important of all, none of those things that you choose to do with yourself, whether it be art representation, or becoming an agent like Morrie, or, I don't know, going to truck driving school and hitting the open road in a big rig, none of those things are *you*. They are just what you do. Failing at them doesn't make you a failure. It just makes you bold enough to try, and to be willing to try again."

Christiana was still frowning at him, her face only inches from his in the chilly darkness. Shane considered kissing her, but decided it might not be exactly appropriate in the moment. Finally, she looked away and leaned against him again.

"So if I'm not what I do," she asked slowly, "then what am I? Don't answer that."

"Why not?"

"Because even though you might think you have the answer, I think it'll just be a bunch of flattering happy crappy. No offense. It may even all be true, and some other time I'll really want to hear all of it, so keep it in mind, all right? But if the things you say are true at all, then I think I need to figure out the answer to that question on my own. Would you agree?"

Shane nodded thoughtfully. "And what about your dad?"

"The less he has to do with that question, the better."

Shane shifted slightly on the deck chair, wrapping his arms around her on his lap. "Maybe," he said tentatively, "just *maybe* it's time you at least considered setting your compass by someone other than your father."

She nodded. "Like myself, you mean?"

He bobbed his head noncommittally. "Yeeaah... I was actually thinking of me. But that works, too."

She grinned and poked him in the stomach with her elbow. "You think you're up to that kind if task? You planning on being around long enough to make it worth my while?"

"I'm not going anywhere," he said, stroking the hair at her temple. "And if I do, I'm planning on asking you to come along with me. What do you say to that?"

She nodded playfully, her eyes twinkling as she looked back at him. After a moment she turned and settled against him once more, leaning her head back onto his shoulder. It was a very dark night, with low clouds obscuring the stars, blotting out the moon. The tops of the trees across the river were barely visible against the sky.

"I have an idea." Christiana said quietly. "For our little problem. Your 'other woman'."

Shane blinked up at the clouds. "Marlena? I thought you didn't really believe all of that?"

She shrugged lightly. "I didn't say I didn't believe your story. I said I was fifty-fifty. The point is, *you* believe in her. That makes her something that we have to deal with before... well, before we go anywhere else together. If you know what I mean."

Shane knew what she meant. He nodded. She felt it and went on. "You asked me what you do with a jealous ghost. I thought you were joking at first, but then I gave it some thought. I mean, if she's real, then she's a woman, and if she's a woman—especially the kind of woman you described to me—then maybe you deal with her the way you'd deal with any jealous ex. Maybe we just go talk to her. More importantly, maybe *I* go talk to her. I'm the one she has the problem with, after all. We could go down to the site of the old Riverhouse and just, sort of, make a statement. Maybe I'd tell her that I respect her, and don't mean to take anything away from her. Maybe if I talk to her, woman to woman…"

Shane felt a chill falling over him. He shook his head, firmly. "We can't do that, Chris."

"Why not? I mean, whether she's real or just in your head, maybe that's the best way to mollify her. Jealousy is really only about feeling slighted, about being rejected for someone else. But if we talk to her, we could tell her that none of those things even come into it. She's a ghost, right? It has nothing to do with who's better or more desirable. Frankly, I probably wouldn't have held a candle to her in her prime. It just has to do with who's still alive. Right? She'd understand that, I bet. Maybe she'd even, you know, give us her blessing."

Shane pushed Christiana upright, turning her to look at him. "Look, I can't explain it, but I just don't think it would work. I don't know how I know, I just do. She's not… rational, anymore. I mean, no matter how you look at it, how can a ghost be sane? I don't think she realizes the difference between what's happening now and what happened back then. I don't think time means anything to you once you're dead. I appreciate that you thought about it, and I am amazed and impressed that you'd even consider it. But no. I can handle it. I don't want you any more involved than you already are. I don't want you going down there. All right?"

Christiana was looking at him curiously, studying his face. "You think it's because I'm a skeptic? I can't help that, Shane. It's just my nature. I didn't grow up reading Nancy Drew mysteries or telling ghost stories around the campfire. I grew up with Habeas Corpus and Matlock. Is that it?"

Shane exhaled and sat back. "No. Maybe. I don't know. I just know that it'd be a mistake. A bad one. Besides, it'll all be over soon. I'm… working on it."

"You're painting it, you mean?"

Shane looked at her sharply, but she didn't blink. "That's where it all came from, isn't it?" she asked. "The paintings, starting with 'the Riverhouse'. There's one more to go, right? And then it's all over?"

Shane looked away. "Maybe. That's a little simplistic, but maybe that's what it comes down to."

"What makes you think that'll put an end to it?"

Shane didn't have an answer to that question. He couldn't even begin to articulate his feeling about it. It was the final painting in the series, yes, but there was more to it than that. Somehow, he just knew that it had to be, that the Sleepwalker was the key to everything. When it was done, it would all be over. One way or another. After that, he and Christiana would be free. After that, they could leave together, and never look back.

Christiana seemed to see all of this on his face. She nodded to herself, smiling a little. "All right, then. If it means that much to you, I'll leave it to you. You handle it. Finish it off. I'll stay out of it. We won't go down to the Riverhouse to fix things up with your 'other woman'. You find a way to tell her on your own. Fair enough?"

Shane looked at her closely, thinking. "Fair enough," he answered finally, smiling a little. The truth was, he was secretly glad of Christiana's skepticism. The less she became enmeshed in the whole affair with Marlena, the better. The easier it would be to eventually forget. Maybe Christiana's doubt was her best defense against whatever plans Marlena might make against her. Maybe it was like in the movies; maybe the ghost could only hurt you if you *believed* it could hurt you. It was a thin hope, but it was persistent, and Shane held onto it. He clung to it, not knowing that Christiana's doubt, helpful or not, was soon to be completely shattered.

Chapter Nineteen

It stormed for three days straight, beating the river into a brown lather, swelling it dangerously in its banks, and turning the cottage's gravel driveway into an obstacle course of deep ruts and mini mudslides. On the third day, Christiana had to abandon her car at the base of the first hill, having mired it hopelessly in the soggy marsh that bordered the Valley Road. She walked the rest of the way to the cottage, fuming and drenched, her shoes caked with thick brown mud, arriving in a seamlessly black mood, flinging off her wet clothes in the doorway and demanding Shane's robe. For his own part, Shane struggled not to laugh, with little success. She saw his suppressed smile and rolled her eyes.

"I swear," she said, shrugging into his red terrycloth robe, "if this is turning you on, I'll punch you right in the nose."

They dried her clothes while she sat at the little computer desk beneath the Riverhouse painting, sending emails and researching details for her upcoming show. Later, Shane talked her into joining him for a ride into town.

"We'll get some groceries, just in case we get stuck here for a few days. At this rate, the floodgates are sure to close soon, if they haven't already. We can check on your car, too. Maybe it's not as stuck as you think it is."

"You're such a man," she replied, but without any real conviction.

Shane navigated the truck gamely along the drive, feeling the jerk and slew of the uneven surface, gripping the steering wheel as it rolled, trying to spin out of his grasp. The rain was a constant blatter, transforming the gray evening into a watercolor abstract, swished gamely by the squeaky windshield wipers.

"I'm over there," Christiana said, pointing suddenly.

Shane saw her green Saturn, tilted partly off the drive, nose-down into the muddy weeds on the right side. The rear quarter panel was covered with a fan of thick mud.

"You really dug it in good," he said admiringly. "Good to know you don't give up without a fight."

She sighed tersely. "So what do you think, oh Master of the Universe. You think it's as stuck as I thought it was?"

"I swear I'll never doubt you again," he answered, steering carefully around the Saturn.

"Famous last words," she said. Shane glanced at her, glad to see the small smile on her face.

The ride into town was uneventful, and Shane was happy to find that the floodgates were, in fact, still open when they got there. The IGA sign glowed like a beacon over the broken parking lot, sparkling in the millions of rain droplets that coated the parked cars. Inside, the aisles were more crowded than he'd ever seen them, packed with shoppers obviously doing the same as he and Christiana. Shane avoided using a cart, opting instead for one of the red plastic hand baskets, which he filled quickly. Christiana picked out another bottle of wine from the meager supply along the far right wall, next to the cheeses and below a huge red banner proclaiming WEDNESDAY IS SUPER SAVER DAY! Together, they waited in line, and Shane found himself quietly enjoying the mundane pleasures of shopping with someone else, someone who would likely be sharing the assorted goods in the red plastic basket. It had been awhile since that had happened, and he assumed that, before too long, he would once again take it for granted, but for now he soaked in the moment. He put his free arm around Christiana's shoulder as they waited in the long line, listening to the muzak and the babble of voices and the persistent beep of the checkout scanner. She leaned into him, reaching up to lace her fingers into his. She seemed tired, but content. She didn't always spend the night at the cottage, and on the nights she did, they didn't always sleep together—Shane's quazi-Baptist upbringing reared its guilty head whenever they did—but there was no question that tonight she would stay over. For the first time, his primary feeling was not physical desire for her, but a deep, simple happiness in her presence, in her having chosen him, in the fleeting comfort that this might be a glimpse of what the rest of their lives might look like—she and him together, content and unselfconscious, sharing a mutual life the way two travelers might share a narrow path.

Brian wasn't manning the checkouts that night, but Shane wasn't particularly disappointed. Christiana would meet Brian eventually. He could tell her all about his grandfather Earl. For some reason, Shane thought it was important that she know him, at least as more than the mangled shape they had discovered in his bed on that horrible night. Thinking of Earl dead in his bed reminded Shane of the Sleepwalker painting, of course. He had worked on it consistently over the past few days, filling in minor details, not rushing, even feeling a strange reluctance to push ahead. The truth was that, suddenly, the painting seemed to want to exist even more than he wanted to paint it. The removal of Marlena's portrait from the studio had apparently freed it. In her absence, the story's eagerness frightened Shane a little. His curiosity about it hadn't diminished, exactly; it was just offset by a growing sense of quiet dread, a creeping conviction that soon the story would be over, and that he might not exactly like the way it ends. Part of him—a small, timid part in the very back of his mind—told him he should stop painting the Sleepwalker, stop before it was too late. *This isn't your story,* the voice said, whispering, as if afraid of being overheard. *This story belongs to someone else—some thing else—something scary and dangerous. It's a mistake to dig it up. Some things should just stay buried. Let it go. Escape before it's too late. Take Christiana with you. You can stop this still, but not for much longer. Time is running out. Go while you can.* Shane knew there was sanity in that voice, and yet he didn't heed it. It may well have been the voice of reason, but it was such a tiny voice, such a timid voice, and the pull of the Sleepwalker—of the end of the Riverhouse's dark story—was simply too huge and pervasive. He *couldn't* turn away from it, not really. Or so he told himself. Thus, he continued to paint, slowly but ceaselessly, filling in, defining that strange perplexity of artistic styles, adding depth and detail, making it come alive on the canvas. He was just over halfway done. Soon, in no more than a few days, it would be complete. Shane honestly didn't know if he looked forward to that completion, or if he dreaded it.

The two of them were silent on the drive back from town. Christiana held Shane's hand across the truck's big bench seat, but he had to let it go as he braked, preparing to downshift and turn into the drive. It was nearly dark now, with only a narrow fringe of sunset rimming the horizon, peeking from beneath the caul of gray clouds. The headlights lit Christiana's Saturn brightly as Shane swung the truck around, accelerating slowly up the incline. The wheels tried to slew away from him, and Shane clenched his jaw, working to keep the truck in the center of the wet gravel. The hill was steep, slick with oozing mud, and the dark trees seemed to encroach ominously over the drive, reaching with their bare branches, trying to scratch at the windows as the truck inched along. Shane leaned forward, peering past the streaked glass, but the night sucked at the headlights, making them nearly useless. Something glinted at the top of the hill and Shane couldn't help taking his foot off the accelerator for a moment. There was something blocking the drive, something large and black, something that hadn't been there before. The truck quickly lost momentum on the incline and Shane strained his eyes, squinting to see through the streaked, watery glass. A flash of silent lightning flickered across the sky, illuminating the road and the woods for one bright second, and Shane nearly bit his tongue in surprise. For a split second, the object blocking the drive was a large black pickup truck, its wheels huge and spoked, its bed squat, dripping rainwater. Shane didn't know much about antique cars, but he was filled with a sick certainty that the truck revealed in that bony flash was a model A Ford, the one Gus Wilhelm had once provided for his grounds crew. A moment later, however, the lightning was gone and the scene had changed. The shape blocking the road was a tree, dripping blackly in the glow of the headlights.

"Oh no," Christiana said, leaning forward as Shane braked the truck. "Ah, damn."

"Give me a minute," Shane said, wrenching the driver's door open. "I think I can move it. It's not that big, especially with all the leaves off it."

"You want some help?"

Shane glanced aside at her, one leg already out the door, pattering with dark raindrops. "Maybe. Let me take a look. You already did your tramp through the rain today. I'll wave if I need you, kay?"

She nodded. "Don't strain anything. We can carry the groceries from here if we need to."

Shane grunted and climbed out, slamming the door behind him. The sight of the phantom model A truck had unnerved him, but he'd already determined that it had only been his imagination. He'd tried not to let it get out of control, but he was beginning to learn that it was a much harder dog to leash than he'd originally expected. He approached the tree, peering over it toward the cottage beyond. If the leaves had still been on the trees, he wouldn't have been able to see it at all, It looked small and quaint on its knob of hill. There were no lights on inside, except maybe for the candle in the upper east window, which he couldn't see from this angle. Shane sighed and shook his head, flinging rainwater from his hair. He reached out and touched the fallen tree. The trunk was barely six inches thick where he gripped it, wet and rough with ragged bark. Its bare branches had cushioned it, keeping it from falling flat onto the drive. Shane thought he could probably pull it out of the way, and some small part of him was still keen on impressing Christiana. After all, artists might be known for a lot, but rugged strength wasn't usually one of them. He climbed over the tree carefully, meaning to pull it away from the truck, angling it from the root where it was still half embedded in the mud. He gripped it and pulled, but his first attempt was useless. His feet slipped on the wet drive and he nearly fell underneath the tree. He spread his legs, squatted to give himself better leverage, and gripped the trunk with both hands.

Suddenly, silently, the lights of the pickup truck blinked out. Seamless darkness fell over Shane, reducing the world to a black tableau of pattering rain and creaking trees.

"Chris?" he called. "What are you doing? I need those."

No answer came from the truck. Shane leaned forward over the tree, trying to see the pickup in the dark. All he could make out was a blocky shape, slightly darker than the trees beyond.

"Chris! Turn the lights back on, all right? It's too damn dark out here to see anythi—"

Another flash of silent lightning flickered across the clouds overhead. In it, the pickup truck lit up like pale daylight. Christiana could be seen inside, her face a white circle of surprise, her mouth open and her eyes wide. She wasn't looking at Shane. She was looking at something next to her, something in the driver's seat. Shane glanced at it, but darkness fell too quickly, blinding him again.

"Chris!" Shane called again, his voice splintering. He made to clamber over the tree, but the branches seemed to snag at him, catching his jeans, hooking his foot. He tripped and stumbled over the tree, falling onto the gravel on the other side. His sleeve was still caught on the tree, hooked by a splintered branch. He pulled, ripping his shirt and breaking the branch. He called Christiana's name again, struggling to get his feet beneath him, slipping on the muddy slope.

The pickup truck began to roll slowly backward. It matched his speed, moving ponderously, rocking slightly on its springs. The windshield was a black mirror of the clouds above. Shane lunged forward, his heart pounding up into his throat. The ground was like ice beneath him and he slipped again, falling onto his right hip and sliding. The truck continued to move backwards, rolling silently, its headlights looking like tarnished pennies in the darkness.

Shane struggled to his feet once more and bolted forward, lunging for the truck. He ran into the grill, bracing himself with his hands, and then lurched around to the passenger's side door. The truck suddenly stopped moving, squeaking to a halt, and Shane could see Christiana pressed against the passenger's window, turned away from him. Shane gripped the door handle and pressed the thumb button, but the door was locked. He could see the knob of the lock just inside the window. It rattled as he rammed the button with his thumb.

"Chris!" he barked. "Unlock it! Unlock the door!"

Slowly, almost dreamily, Christiana turned inside the truck. She peered out, and her eyes were unfocussed, as if she couldn't quite see Shane standing on the other side of the glass.

"Unlock the door!" he cried desperately, thumbing the handle again, yanking helplessly. "Let me in! Unlock the door!"

Christiana finally met Shane's eyes. Her gaze was glassy, her mouth slack. A dark shape loomed behind her, moving on the driver's seat, and Shane finally recognized it. It was Marlena, of course. Her eyes were black and huge, eating into her face. Her mouth was turned down into a grimace of hate and frustration, but she wasn't looking at Christiana. She was looking past her, toward Shane, her empty gaze boring into him. Her brow lowered, as if in resignation, and Shane felt a deep, inexplicable weight of horror settle onto him, pressing him down into the mud, chilling him to the bone.

Slowly, Marlena reached forward, as if to caress Christiana's cheek. Her fingernails were very long on her skeletal hands, sharpened to talon-like points. Christiana was still looking at Shane through the glass of the passenger's window, and she didn't flinch when Marlena touched her. Shane thumbed the door latch again, pulling so hard on the handle that it made a metallic ping, popping slightly loose in his hand. He groaned desperately, thinking that he could simply break the glass with a rock, but unwilling to take his eyes away from the scene inside the truck.

Marlena extended her index finger and traced a line on Christiana's left cheek, scratching it. The cut immediately welled beads of blood. They looked black in the darkness. Shane cried out and smacked his hands on the wet glass, but neither Marlena nor Christiana responded. Christiana stared out, her eyes blank and dazed, as Marlena drew her nail over her cheek, drawing a shape in thin, bloody scratches. The shape was small, but meticulously clear. It was a letter M. When she was finished, Marlena leaned forward, arising from the driver's seat and turning phantasmic. Her face loomed over Christiana's shoulder, becoming huge and pale, her black eyes deep as wells. Shane suddenly took his hands from the glass and stumbled backwards as Marlena streamed through the window, towering over him in the rain, her face terrible, glaring down at him. She opened her mouth and turned her hands inward, clawing at her own face now, as if tortured with anguish and frustration.

"I'm sorry," Shane heard himself rasp, not even knowing why he was saying it. "I didn't mean to hurt you. I'm sorry, M."

The specter suddenly arched her back, as if burned by Shane's words. She shrieked pathetically up at the falling rain, and the sound was a thin screech, like nails on a chalkboard. It seemed to rip out of her, emptying her, and when it was over, she collapsed forward, falling onto Shane. He threw up his hands, either to catch her or ward her off, but she shredded away into the night, tattering like paper and vanishing through the trees all around.

Shane lay half collapsed in the marshy weeds on the side of the driveway, boggling up at the sky and the empty wood all around. There was a dull thump as the doors of the truck unlocked. He glanced toward the sound, and then scrambled to his feet. The passenger's door opened easily and Christiana lolled out into his arms, as if she'd been leaning on it. Her eyes were still unfocussed, but the rain seemed to revive her slightly. Shane held her up, helping her to her feet next to the truck. Lightning pulsed overhead, and the mark on her cheek looked very clear, very red, the blood smearing and diluting in the rain.

"Marlena," Christiana said, her voice hauntingly clear and firm, despite her blank gaze. "Goodbye, Shane. She says... she says... she says to tell you goodbye." And then in an awful, childish voice she sang the word over and over, "*Good*bye... *good*bye..."

Shane held Christiana in the darkness, tears of frustration and anger welling in his eyes, mixing with the rain. He shook her in his arms.

"Chris, wake up! It's me! It's over. Come on, wake up!"

She blinked, and then shook her head, clearing it. Her brow furrowed and her mouth turned down into a grimace of perfect disgust, as if she'd just tasted something horrible. Her eyes flickered and locked onto his face.

"It was her," she said thickly. "I saw her. She... she talked to me. She was... oh God Shane, she was awful. So awful."

She shuddered violently in his arms and he hugged her to him. "She's gone now. It's all over. She's gone."

She looked up at him then, apparently unsure whether to believe him or not. Her eyes were clear now, but the bloody scratch on her cheek remained, livid on her pale skin. She seemed unaware of the mark Marlena had made, at least for now. The shape of the scratch was unmistakable. It burned on Shane's vision like an accusing finger, like an omen whose warning had come one decision too late, one step beyond the point of no return.

M, the mark said, red in the occasional glare of the lightning. *Dear M.*

"So what will you tell Morrie and the people at the office?"

Christiana didn't answer right away. She was standing in the bathroom, brushing her hair, dressed for work except for her blouse. Shane sat on the end of the bed, staring gloomily toward the window. It was just past dawn. The light outside was a mesmerizing combination of pink and gold, lighting the tattered clouds like stage props.

"I'll tell them I scratched my cheek on some thorns when I was walking back from my car, after I got stuck in the mud."

Shane glanced toward the bathroom. He was about to admit that that was an extremely plausible explanation, and then stopped, reminding himself that she'd had plenty of opportunities to hone that particular skill. He felt a vague, but pervasive, sense of guilt. It spread like poison, seeming to take up far more space inside him than should be possible. Instead, he asked, "Does it hurt?"

She shook her head, still looking at herself in the mirror as she put on her earrings. "No. I don't remember it hurting at all. I didn't even know she was doing it."

"What *do* you remember about it?"

Christiana put her hairbrush in the drawer below the sink. Shane watched her from his vantage point on the end of the bed. The rest of the cottage was morning-dim, but the bathroom overheads lit Christiana brightly, highlighting the tan skin of her shoulders, shining on her black hair. Apparently satisfied, she took her blouse off the hanger hooked over the shower curtain rod and slipped into it. She either hadn't heard his question, or didn't intend to answer it. She came out of the bathroom, clicking off the light, and sat down next to him on the bed. Silently, she began to put on her shoes.

"I'm sorry," he said. The words sounded stupid to him; meaningless and tiny.

"Sorry for what?" she asked, not looking at him as she buckled the strap on her right shoe. "Did you summon her, somehow?"

Shane shrugged. "I think maybe I did. Somehow."

"By painting her?"

"I think so," he said, nodding slowly. "But maybe just by being here. Maybe by not leaving."

She finished putting on her shoes and turned on the bed, looking directly at him. She studied him for a moment in the dawn light. "You warned me about her. I didn't really believe you then, but I do now. It's pretty hard to deny at this point. I'm still here, aren't I? You aren't the only one making a choice, Shane."

"Maybe it's the wrong choice."

"Maybe, but we're making it together, all right? You've chosen to stay, and I've made my own choice. I've chosen to trust you. You can see that, can't you?"

Shane looked at her. He could see it. He nodded again.

She pressed her lips together, and then leaned forward, kissing him lightly on the lips. Her own lips were warm, soft, but distracted. He could tell that she was already thinking about her day, about the phone calls she had to make, the details she had to arrange. Shane was amazed at how quickly she had bounced back to the mundane sanity of the everyday after her harrowing experience in the truck the previous night. Then again, he thought to himself, what was the alternative? He'd seen the same tendency in himself, when Marlena had first appeared in the cottage. The mind seemed to rebel against the bizarre, burying it away, latching onto the normal and rational like a life buoy. Christiana didn't want to talk about it, or even think about it, and Shane didn't blame her. He wouldn't force it on her. In some small way, he was envious of her.

He followed her into the kitchen and gave her the keys to his truck.

"It's touchy," he said as she opened the front door. "First gear especially. It'll try to stall on you if you aren't really easy on the clutch."

"I learned on a stick shift, sweetie," she said, kissing him on the cheek. "I'll manage."

A minute later, Shane watched his truck dip down the gravel drive, swaying in the muddy ruts. The fallen tree still lay in the ditch on the left side where he'd eventually hauled it, its root ball half ripped out of the earth. Christiana beeped the horn once and was gone. Shane peered up at the sky. It was no longer raining, and the clouds were breaking apart, showing glimpses of a deep blue morning sky. The air was wet but warm, pushing through the trees and swishing in the grass of the yard. It was probably only a short reprieve—the weathermen on the radio were predicting more, and worse, storms in the coming days, but for now, the break in the weather was a welcome relief. Shane went back inside, closing the screen door but leaving the main door open, letting in the fresh air.

He got dressed for the day, made himself some coffee, and stepped out onto the back patio to drink it. The river below the bluff rode high in its banks, brown and fast, dotted with sticks, logs, even the occasional uprooted tree. It wasn't at flood levels yet, but it soon would be. The cottage would be safe, high on the rocky bluff that overlooked the river bend, but Bastion Falls would surely close down. The Valley Road would be impassable. Nature would do its thing, as it always did, but the cottage would survive, as *it* always did. Shane found that he didn't care anymore. He almost wished the flood would come all the way up, that it would wash away the cottage and everything inside, including his paintings of the Riverhouse, and Marlena, and even the Sleepwalker. He didn't care about finishing it. Not anymore. All that mattered was that Marlena had hurt Christiana. Not much, of course, at least not yet. But Shane had been working under the assumption that Marlena was not capable of physically touching a living person, that if he was vigilant, and watched over Christiana carefully, he could protect her. Now, he knew that that had all been a mistake. Marlena had indeed touched Christiana, had made her mark on her. It was a warning, in much the same way that the chalk drawing on the cellar floor might have been a warning. *Next time,* Marlena seemed to be saying, *next time I won't stop at a scratch on the cheek. Next time I'll finish what needs to be finished...*

Shane remembered sitting on the patio with the newsprint sketchpad on his lap, drawing furiously, making crayon snapshots of Marlena's fractured, final days. The Insanity Stairs, overlooking the strange sieve drain in the basement of the Riverhouse, the hall of empty rooms, their windows painted over, their doors forever locked and nailed shut. Mostly, however, he remembered the clever image painted on the wall at the opposite end of the hallway, the one that showed Marlena's family as if in a sort of magic mirror—herself with Wilhelm and baby Hector, but with the faces all left blank, smooth and featureless, like white balloons.

Shane put his coffee down on the stone wall next to the barbecue. He felt vaguely sick. He turned to go back into the cottage, and then couldn't quite bring himself to do it. The place had a hold on him, a sort of mental death grip. He could feel the pull of it, and yet he resisted, simultaneously captivated and revolted. It was like waking up after a night of hard drinking, finding yourself in bed with someone you've never met before, someone horrible, disgusting, someone with whom you might have done almost anything in the stupor of drunkenness. Shane backed away from the cottage, staring up at it wide eyed. He'd believed that the Riverhouse was the real danger, the source of Marlena's contagious madness—and that might even have been true. But the cottage was the sister of the Riverhouse, the older one, the very first. The two structures beat with the same blood, shared the same legacy. Why else had Marlena fled there when the Riverhouse, the site of her original haunting, had been torn down? How could Shane not have realized that the same madness that tainted the Riverhouse also flowed through the cottage, pulsing darkly, making its own numbing gravity?

Finally, slowly, he went back inside, leaving the sliding door open behind him. He looked around, as if seeing the place for the first time. Everything was different. He could almost believe that everything he thought of as home, everything that made the cottage feel like his, was just a thin mask, stage dressing over something far older, something that didn't belong to him at all. He moved through the kitchen, feeling the silent pull of the place, pushing back on it, trying to keep his new awareness alive. Christiana's car keys sat on the counter next to an empty Coke can. He picked them up and slipped them into the pocket of his jeans. A moment later, he stopped at the base of the staircase, looking up toward the studio, the place where he had created all three of the paintings in the Shane Bellamy Insanity Stairs series. The third one was as yet unfinished, its power still only half formed, but he could feel it up there, lit in the morning sunlight that streamed in from the window over the stairs. It called to him, demanding his touch. It wanted to be finished, wanted the story to be complete, for the circle to be closed. Shane shuddered, violently, as if someone had poured a pitcher of ice water down his back. He backed away from the stairs, his eyes wide, and turned toward the hallway. He passed the cellar door. It was open, and he glanced down. Christiana had washed the chalk drawing off the floor, but she hadn't erased it completely. Vague discolorings on the concrete floor still picked out the main shapes. They looked different, somehow, as if the drawing had changed, cycling over to some new destiny, something possibly worse than the one that had first appeared there. Shane thought the shapes now showed the Riverhouse, pale and looming against a stormy gray background. He tore his gaze away, not wishing to see anymore, not wanting to know.

He was sure he had left the front door open, letting the morning breeze in, drawing some of the rainy mustiness out of the front rooms, but it was closed now. Closed and locked. Shane moved toward it, gripped the handle and unlatched the bolt. He glanced aside as he pulled the door open, and then stopped, his hand still on the cold metal of the doorknob. The Riverhouse painting had changed again. Marlena was no longer sitting on the steps of the portico, shielding her eyes against the sun, looking up at her approaching visitor. Now she was standing, one foot on the bottom step, the other on the brick drive. On her face was a smile of heartbreaking happiness, as if she'd finally recognized the person who was coming to meet her, and was delighted at their arrival. Shane stared at the painting, expecting it to begin moving right before his eyes, the figures coming alive like characters in a movie. They didn't, of course, but that didn't make the scene any less frightening. The painting was very much alive, moving only when he wasn't looking, approaching an irreversible climax. The shadow in the lower right of the painting, the one stretching out onto the brick drive, was very dark and long now. Whoever it was, they were almost inside the scope of the painting. Once more, he forced himself to look away. He didn't want to know, didn't want to see any more. He'd seen too much already. The voice in his head—the quiet, timid one, the Voice of Reason—had been right all along. This wasn't his story. It belonged to someone else—some*thing* else. Something powerful, and frightening.

Shane walked out the front door, moving like a man in a dream. He thought about packing some of his things, some clothes and toiletries, but that was silly. He couldn't go back inside, not now, not once he had begun to walk away. He should have done this weeks ago, maybe even months ago. He stepped out of the shadow of the porch, into the bright haze of the morning sun, and squinted. The grass was wet. It soaked through his canvas shoes almost immediately but he didn't slow down. The driveway sloped toward the hill in front of him, cutting through the trees, looking like a highway. He angled toward it, stepping onto the muddy gravel. The cottage was behind him, pulling at him, trying to draw him back. He resisted, and was shocked to realize that it was very hard to do. His resolve was hardly rock solid. It was flimsy, weak, but for the moment, it held. He thought again of Marlena reaching forward with her skeletal right hand, her nails grown to obscene talons, scratching lines on Christiana's living cheek. Lines were the language Marlena understood. She was an artist, after all, like her husband. She had spoken to Shane in the best way she knew how. She had drawn him a picture. That time it had been a warning, he thought to himself. But not the next time.

Not this time, he thought, remembering the words scrawled on the bottom of the last crayon drawing, embedded in the cheap paper so deeply that they had torn it. *Not this time,* Stambaugh had said, cackling in the chair next to Earl's bed, his hands wet with the old man's blood. Shane quickened his pace, descending the hill. The sun was over the tree line now, sparkling brightly on the wet weeds and the bare branches of the trees. Christiana's Saturn sat crooked on the side of the driveway far below, barely ten yards from the mailbox and the River Road. Shane could see the rutted tracks where she had slipped off the drive, the front left wheel bogging down in the soft earth that bordered the trees. The mud had already begun to dry around it, lightening in color, turning thick. Shane thought he could push the car back up onto the gravel, at least enough to give the front wheels the traction to back out. He'd drive Christiana's car into downtown St. Louis, meet her at Greenfeld's office, maybe take her to lunch. She'd told him she trusted him, and that was a responsibility he meant to take seriously. The first part of that responsibility was never bringing her back to the cottage again. Not after last night. Not after that final, warning mark, drawn in Christiana's own blood.

Shane looked up. Someone else was walking along the driveway, coming up the hill, halfway between him and the Saturn. The figure was wearing a pair of old green coveralls with a handkerchief hanging limply from the front pocket. A pair of worn work boots gritted on the gravel as the figure plodded toward him. Shane's feet continued to carry him forward, but his brain seemed to have shut down, revolting against what he was seeing. It couldn't be who it seemed to be. This wasn't his imagination. This wasn't some flashbulb vision revealed in a flicker of lightning. Shane could hear the scrape of the boots, hear the puff of the man's breathing as he climbed the hill.

They both stopped walking at the same time, and the figure raised its head, looking up at Shane.

"Earl," Shane said weakly.

He wasn't an old man, but he was still plainly recognizable. His face was grim, hopeless, but resolved.

"It's too late," Earl said, and his voice was just as old as Shane remembered, despite the younger features, despite the pate of thick black hair. "It's too late now. You have to finish it. Understand?" He stopped, still looking up at Shane, his eyes piercing. He drew a long, deep breath and shook his head slowly. "I'm sorry."

Shane felt rooted to the spot. Distantly, he heard himself ask, "Sorry for what, Earl?"

"Sorry I didn't tell you everything when I had the chance," Earl said, and he began to turn away, as if his job was done and he meant to go back. As Earl turned, however, Shane saw that there was something wrong with his profile, something strange about the back of his head. It was horribly lumpy, and bald. It wasn't the back of his head at all. As he finished turning, Shane saw, and his breath stalled in his chest: the back of Earl's head was another face, grinning up at him madly, full of manic glee. Stambaugh stood on the driveway now, watching, his eyes dancing, daring Shane to come down the hill and meet him. Behind Stambaugh, the Saturn sat in the sun. Shane heard something, a wheezy lilt, and realized Stambaugh was singing to himself. He was singing "the Good Ship Lollipop."

Hopelessness filled Shane. It welled up in him and poured out of him, spreading away like a ripple, covering everything in sight. The sun seemed to dim, as if a cold cloud had passed in front of it. Maybe it even had. Shane didn't look to see.

He turned around. Slowly, he began to trudge back to the cottage. Stambaugh's singing voice, horribly cracked and off-key, followed him. He thought he could still hear it even when he got back inside, even when he went up to the studio and stood in front of the unfinished face of the Sleepwalker. He only stopped hearing it when he finally dipped the brush, reached forward, and began to paint.

When he began to paint, he stopped hearing everything.

Chapter Twenty

By the time Christiana returned that evening, driving Shane's truck up the driveway and squeaking to a halt in front of the porch, the sky had turned ominously dark again. The low clouds moved sluggishly, groaning with distant thunder. Shane heard the screech of the truck's old emergency brake from the studio. He stopped painting and put down the brush without taking his eyes from the canvas. He'd been painting feverishly for nearly six hours, not bothering to stop to eat or to even turn on the overhead light as the afternoon dimmed outside, casting the studio into a pall of shadows. The Sleepwalker was nearly finished, and yet it didn't make any more sense to him now than it had that morning. The three main images remained the same: the bed on the right, covered with rumpled sheets, hiding the bloody form that lay on it; the upholstered chair on the left, empty except for the purse, its mouth dark and somehow damning; and the figure in the center, silhouetted against the brightness of a round, bluish halo. The picture had refined much over the past few hours, but no new details had emerged, save for one: there was something in the central figure's hand, held loosely, but purposely. It was long and thin, tapered to a point. Shane had a suspicion that it was a knife, but he didn't know for sure. He couldn't even tell the gender of the figure, since any defining features were lost in the depths of the silhouette. The hair was matted flat to the head and the lower half of the body was lost in darkness, hiding its shape. Apart from the three main elements, the whole picture was thick with shadows, all represented with layers of green and blue, so dark that they were nearly black.

Shane drew a deep breath, shuddering a little, his back aching, and climbed slowly off the stool. Downstairs, he heard the front door open and close, slamming. The curtains over the stairs billowed as a gust of air moved through the cottage, bringing in the cool scent of the river and the approaching storm. It was going to be a proper deluge, Shane sensed. If there was going to be a flood, it would probably happen tonight. The floodgates down at Bastion Falls would close as the Valley Road submerged, sinking into the river as it swelled to overtake it. The lower woods would turn into a swamp and the cottage would suddenly become a virtual island, perched on its rocky bluff. It would probably only last a few days, and there would be a mess of sandy sludge on the roads and the trail for weeks afterwards, but that was all right. It was simply the price one paid for living near something so unpredictable and capricious. It was the price one paid for living on the boundary land.

"Hey, you up there?" Christiana called from the kitchen. "I brought back some sandwiches from the office. Gotta eat quick. I'm meeting some people tonight. Can I use the truck again?"

Shane met her at the base of the stairs and gave her a quick hug. She handed him a half a Subway sandwich, wrapped in paper. "Leftovers from some client wingding Morrie hosted today. Hope you don't mind."

"Free food is always nice," Shane said, taking the sandwich but not unwrapping it. "I'll grab a bite later. Not really hungry now. And yes, you can use the truck again. We'll pull your car out tomorrow, assuming it isn't windows deep by then."

"Yeah," Christiana said, moving into the kitchen ahead of him. "They're predicting it to rain buckets tonight. Said it'll start getting really heavy by midnight. I hope I'm back by then. Otherwise I'll have to go back to my place. I'll call if I do."

Shane leaned on the kitchen entryway, watching Christiana open the fridge and reach for her customary can of Diet Coke. He asked, "So what's going on?"

"Preliminary meet and greet with the show organizers," she said. She sounded tired and harried, but Shane could tell that she was excited about it. "I'm meeting them for drinks downtown. I've got a few hours to kill, but I've got plenty to do in the meantime. I'll probably leave again pretty quick. Wish me luck."

"Luck," Shane said, inclining his head.

"What's going on with you," she asked, approaching him and looking closely at his face. She reached up and touched his chin, raising his head again. "You seem... subdued. More so than usual."

He sighed and looked toward the window. "I've been painting all day. Buried pretty deep. Sorry. It's hard to come up out of it sometimes, especially when I've been at it so long."

She nodded. "You working on that last painting?"

He grunted and shrugged.

"Get it out of the way," she said firmly, turning away again. "Wrap the whole thing up, all right? And then, if you'll pardon me for being a little bossy, let's get the hell out of here. What do you say to that?"

Shane sighed deeply. "I say that sounds wonderful."

"This place is no good for you, Shane," she said, rummaging in her purse, producing her cell phone. "Maybe it's the ghost and all the weirdness that goes along with it, but there's probably more to it than that. I mean, this was you and your ex-wife's place. It's got to be full of memories and reminders of her. In a way, this place was haunted before you ever saw Marlena here. You know?"

Shane nodded again, slowly, still looking out the kitchen window.

"Snap out of it," she said, closing her phone and putting it on the counter. She moved close to him again and laid her hand on his cheek. "You're acting like all those tortured starving artist types you told me about. It's almost over, isn't it? So what's riding you?" She frowned up at him, and then, in a different voice, she asked, "Did you see her today?"

Shane looked at her. After a moment he shook his head. "No," he answered honestly. "I didn't see her today. I don't think she's in the cottage. Not since her portrait was moved into the sunroom."

Christiana nodded grimly. "Leave it there then. Finish what you have to finish, and, God help us, Shane, let's just get out of here. 'Kay? I know I'm not showing it much, but last night..." she paused, chewing her words, still looking up at him. "That was hard to handle. I've never seen anything like that before. Never felt anything so... so cold and awful. It makes the whole world seem a little off-kilter. It's like everything I thought I ever knew was just a sham, just a prop in some kind of crazy play. Seeing something like that... it pushes reality aside like a curtain. I didn't like what I saw behind that curtain. Maybe some people can get used to it. Maybe some people don't have a choice. But we do, right? We can live the rest of our lives on this side of the curtain of reality and never look back. I need to know you are with me on that, Shane. Are you?"

Shane nodded again. He softened his features, smiled at her. "I'm with you, Chris. No matter what. I have to finish this, but when it's done, it's *all* done. I promise."

She moved a half step closer to him, so that her front pressed lightly against him. Shane thought she meant to kiss him, but she didn't. She merely looked up at him, her eyes searching his, her brow slightly furrowed.

"I love you, Shane," she said. She said it as a statement, a mere declaration of fact. Her expression didn't change as she looked up at him. "Your mess is my mess. And vice versa. From now on. That's just what love does to us. I don't regret it at all, either. So finish it, as soon as you can. Capiche?"

"Capiche," Shane agreed. He kissed her, lightly, as if sealing an agreement.

"That's better," she said, as if dismissing him. She turned away and grabbed her sandwich off the counter. "Now go finish that damn painting. I can tell you're still two-thirds buried in it. I've got a few phone calls to make and then I'll be heading out. Don't wait up."

Shane smiled again, more genuinely this time. "I think I'll do that. Both of them."

"What's that?"

"Finish the painting. *And* wait up for you."

She rolled her eyes and smiled.

Shane turned and headed back down the short hall, passing the closed basement door. He stopped at the base of the staircase and turned back.

"And Chris?"

She looked at him from the kitchen, her mouth full and her cell phone open in her hand.

"I love you, too."

She smiled at him and allowed the phone to lower in her hand. Her eyes sparkled. It was hardly a romance novel moment, but it was meaningful. People don't forget the first time they profess their love, Shane thought, even if it's unplanned and mundane. Even if one of them has a mouthful of hoagie and the other is distracted and cranky. People don't forget something like that because it only happens once. After that, it turns into a novelty, and then a routine.

It may never mean any less—and hopefully, over time, it'll mean more—but the first time is always special. The first time has its own small magic.

Shane felt it, and it was good. Despite everything—despite the painting and the approaching storm and the scratch that still shone on Christiana's otherwise perfect cheek—it was very good

Shane still didn't turn on the light in the studio. He sat in front of the Sleepwalker, leaning forward with his chin resting on one hand, simply staring at it. The paintbrush lay abandoned on the little work table. The painting itself sat in a wash of stormy light, looking drab and blue, frustratingly mysterious. It was almost all there now, and yet it still didn't make any sense. The previous two—the Riverhouse and the portrait of Marlena, Dear M—had been obvious. They had created their own portals, telling their stories, defining the scenes and giving them meaning. That hadn't happened with the painting of the Sleepwalker, however. Shane's hand had moved over the canvas as if in the grip of some alien force, like he was merely a tool, the necessary means for bringing the image to life. He'd expected this final image to be the last piece of the puzzle, the key that would unlock everything and bring the entire story into focus. He had hoped that that would be all it took to break Marlena's hold on him, to deconstruct her mysterious hatred of Christiana. This painting, however, didn't seem to be a key to anything. It was merely a weird still life, showing apparently disconnected scenes— Steph's purse, Earl dead in his bed, and the faceless figure silhouetted against that inexplicable blue halo. Shane drew a deep breath and let it out slowly, frustrated and worried. He didn't know what to do next. He had at least finished the final painting, just as the ghostly vision of Earl had instructed him. Would the Riverhouse let him leave now? Or was there still more to come? He had a vague, creeping sense that *something* had been set in motion with the completion of the Sleepwalker, but he couldn't put his finger on it. It was both subtle and huge, like destinies cycling behind the curtain of reality, hidden and foreboding.

Christiana had left a little while earlier. Shane had heard the front door open and close again, slamming as the wind caught it. He was glad she was gone for the night, and hoped that, when she returned, he'd be able to keep his promise to her. It was time to leave now. His work was finished. There was nothing left for him here. Outside, the sky was dimming as night fell, bringing a constant, shifty wind in from the west. It twitched the curtains and sang in the window screen, gusting randomly. There was still no rain, but Shane could feel it in the air. He could nearly taste it.

Christiana had been right about more than one thing. The cottage had been haunted before Marlena had ever showed up. There had been Smithy, of course, but that wasn't what she had meant. The cottage was haunted by Stephanie. Not by her living ghost, but by Shane's memories of her, by the constant, low grade reminders of her that popped up in every corner, every forgotten nook and cranny: a tea bag in the back of a cupboard, a half used bag of potting soil behind the door of the shed, a hair barrette in the bottom bathroom drawer, a few of her hairs still caught in its tiny hinge. Every one of them was a pang of loss, even after all this time, even after finding Christiana and falling in love with her. Death lag, Dr. Taylor had called it. Death lag, he'd explained, was that awful moment between being reminded of a dear one and remembering, with a sudden sinking lurch, that they are no more. All Shane had left was the memory of Steph's last phone call, the one that had left everything perpetually unfinished, ringing in the stillness of his heart like the toll of a silver bell, or like a child's lost rattle.

Downstairs, the telephone rang, and Shane wasn't surprised. Part of him, he realized, had even been expecting it. He got off the stool and tromped slowly down the steps. The staircase was very cool, misty with the air that had come in from the open window. It seemed to pour down the steps like a slow river, chilling the downstairs. The cordless phone continued to ring, burring senselessly on the bottom step of the staircase. Shane sat down on the step with a sigh and collected the phone, thumbing the Call button as he did.

"Hello," he said blandly.

There was a long moment of silence. Shane could hear a thin shushing sound in the earpiece. Finally, there was a shuffling sound and a man's voice said, "Is this Shane Bellamy?"

"Yeah," Shane answered, cradling his forehead in his free hand.

"Shane? Sorry. This is Detective Weekes. Bastion Falls P.D."

"Detective...?" Shane said, raising his head and furrowing his brow. "Oh, yes. What was... what can I do for you?"

"Mr. Bellamy, are you all right?"

"I'm fine," Shane lied. "I was... napping. I'm feeling a little fuzzy, that's all."

Weekes seemed to accept this. "Sorry to bother you, Mr. Bellamy, but I came across something. It's probably nothing, but... well, the thing is, I can't imagine how it *could* be connected to anything. It just struck me as a pretty strange coincidence, and I thought it'd be best for me to ask you about it. You have a minute?"

"I have all the minutes you need." Shane replied. He was staring very hard into the open door of his bedroom, not really seeing anything, listening intently as Weekes drew a deep breath. Shane realized, with some degree of wonder, that the shushing sound he heard in the background of the phone call was rain. It was raining in Bastion Falls, five miles away, but the rain had not yet reached the cottage.

"All right," Weekes said, sounding either weary or strained, as if he was trying to maintain his patience. "You told me when I interviewed you—and I'm going to try to quote you here—that you had 'never had any contact with Walter Stambaugh'. Is that right?"

"Yeah," Shane said slowly. He was thinking of Stambaugh standing inexplicably on his driveway earlier that day, grinning up at him, singing to himself in his thin, wheezy voice. "That's true. I'd seen him once before, across the cafeteria, when Earl pointed him out to me. But that was it. I didn't know him at all."

"OK," Weekes said. "All right, then. So you are telling me now that you didn't know that Walter Stambaugh has a daughter named Jennie, and that she moved to New York City with her husband when they got married? They lived there at the same time that you were living there, although they have since moved to Atlanta, Georgia, after their son got into some trouble with the law. Mostly minor stuff, possession with intent, solicitation, truancy. Ring a bell?"

"Detective Weekes," Shane said, getting a little annoyed. "You must have some idea of how big New York City is. You can't possibly think I knew them just because I lived there."

"I don't think that," Weekes said mildly. "But I still thought that you would know them. Or at least know *of* them."

"What, are they famous? I don't see the point, and if you don't mind—"

"Jennie Stambaugh married a man she met in college. Name of Matthew Herk. Unfortunate name, if you ask me. Herk. Not the sort of name you're likely to forget. Their son, he's about twenty-three now. His name's James. James Herk. So, I say again: ring a bell?"

Shane's mouth dropped open. His head swam as he stared unseeingly into his bedroom. *James Herk*. Weekes was right. It wasn't the sort of name you tended to forget. It sounded like the noise you make right before you're going to throw up. It was a singularly ugly name.

"Mr. Bellamy? You still there?"

"I'm here," Shane said, his voice high and thin. Weakness stole over him and he had to struggle to hold the phone to his ear.

"James Herk was driving a vehicle that struck your wife's car on Interstate ninety-five on August tenth of last year, isn't that right? You told me about the accident. You told me she was hit by a truck while driving to meet you. You didn't mention that that truck was driven by Walter Stambaugh's grandson. Did you not know that at the time?"

A small part of Shane's mind tried to reply, but it was overwhelmed by this sudden, incredible new reality. His mouth moved slightly but nothing came out. His fingers gripped the phone tightly, pushing it against the side of his head. His eyes were wide, stunned with disbelief.

"Mr. Bellamy?" Weekes said again, more sharply this time. "Did you know about that? Because if you did, I can't imagine why you didn't bring it up. And if you didn't, well that's just one more whopper of a coincidence. You can add that to the one about how you suddenly decided to go and check on Mr. Kirchenbauer on the night he happened to be murdered. One coincidence is just a coincidence, Mr. Bellamy, but two coincidences, especially big, weird one like that... well, that's what the people at the Police Academy call 'circumstantial evidence'. You've watched enough TV to know what that means, right?"

"I didn't..." Shane said, his voice shaking.

"I'd like you to think about coming in to my office to discuss this, Mr. Bellamy. Nothing official, at least for the moment. Just you and me. Can you do that?"

The strength finally leaked out of Shane's arm and he lowered the phone. It fell out of his hand and clattered to the floor at the bottom of the steps. He stared into the darkness of the bedroom, his eyes bulging, his breath shallow. He shuddered. Had it been Marlena? Was it possible? Could she have actually reached out and killed Stephanie? Earl had said that crazy was contagious, and maybe that was true, but could Marlena's madness truly be that far reaching and deadly? Weekes was right. It was certainly more than a coincidence. Whatever was at work here in the cottage, whatever mad design was unfolding even now under the cover of the growing storm, it had begun long before Shane had started painting the Riverhouse, long before the Riverhouse itself had even been torn down. Maybe it had somehow been set in motion on the very first night that he and Stephanie had stayed in the cottage, sleeping in zipped-together sleeping bags in front of the cold fireplace. Something had marked them. It had marked Stephanie for death, and had marked Shane for... for what? What part was he meant to play? Had he played it? He had a terrible, harrowing suspicion that he had done exactly what had been expected of him, willingly and with wild abandon. He had painted. He had brought the Riverhouse back to life, given it back its story and made it new again. Now, it was too late. The circle was very nearly complete. The Sleepwalker was the key that had brought it all finally together.

Shane leapt to his feet and turned. He flung himself back up the steps, his heart hammering in his chest. Outside the upstairs window, it was finally beginning to rain. Cool droplets blew in through the window screen, belling the curtains and making them damp. Shane shoved them aside and reached for the wall switch. It clicked on and the room flooded with light. Shane stopped and boggled at the painting on its easel.

He had meant to come upstairs and destroy it. If it was the key to everything, the keystone bringing the entire ugly story together, then he would simply undo it. Perhaps it wasn't too late. He could burn it, or rip it to shreds, or even douse it with turpentine and watch as the thick paint bled away into chaos, obliterating the image. He didn't do any of those things, however. Suddenly, astonishingly, the painting *made sense*. In the sterile light of the studio overheads, he saw it, saw all of it, and it shook him right down to his heels. It was like finally reaching to scratch a nagging itch, forgetting everything else in the bliss of relief.

Shane walked slowly toward the painting, his eyes wide, soaking in the image, wondering how he could have missed it all before. The purse was the keyhole, just as he had always known it would be. The reason he'd never seen it before was simple: it wasn't *Steph's* purse. It never had been.

It was Madeleine's.

Shane thought of the portrait of Marlena, the one currently sequestered in the sunroom. "Dear M" the letter in her white hands had begun. Suddenly, he remembered painting that salutation, even though he had been sleep when he'd done it. He remembered drawing the letters carefully with brown paint and a number two sable brush, mimicking Wilhelm's neat cursive handwriting. But Wilhelm had never called his wife M. He hadn't even called her Marlena. He'd called her Lena, always and without fail, ever since the first time he had met her. Lena. The letter in Marlena's hands, the one that had caused her so much anguish and endless misery, the one that had sent her off into decades of madness—it hadn't been addressed to her. It had been written to the other M in his life— Madeleine, Wilhelm's lover.

"You discovered it in Madeleine's purse," Shane said aloud, speaking to Marlena's ghost. She wasn't there, of course, but he spoke to her anyway, or maybe just to her memory. "You were snooping. You couldn't help yourself. Gus seemed so suddenly happy with you, with you and baby Hector, but you were worried that it was too good to be true. You found Madeleine's purse on the sofa, and you thought it couldn't hurt to peek. If it had been any other day, things might have ended differently. But you looked on *that* day, the day he'd planned to run off with her, telling her in that letter when and where to join him. Telling her to bring her things along to the cottage that night, and to bring the baby as well, the one that she was paid to nanny, the one that everyone believed was hers anyway. Baby Hector."

The realization was like a floodgate, opening and letting everything through. It came with perfect clarity, shockingly bright and brilliant. Shane continued to step forward, approaching the painting, drawn toward it.

"Everyone thought Hector was Madeleine's baby," he said wonderingly. "They didn't know the truth, and wouldn't have believed it if they did. Hector really *was* your baby. You had born him for your husband, believing it would make him finally love you. But now you knew that he didn't. He loved Madeleine instead. He allowed people to believe that the baby was hers. And when they ran off together, he meant to forget the truth himself. He meant to pretend the baby was theirs completely. He meant to convince himself that you had never even been."

Wet wind pushed through the screen, more insistently this time. It rattled in the pictures tacked on the wall, made the M. C.

Escher quote knock and sway. It riffled Shane's hair as he reached for the painting, his fingers trembling, curling around the edges of the canvas. He touched the painting, and the cottage seemed to sigh around him. At the same time, as if from some distance away, carried along on the stormy wind, another sigh sounded. It came from the Riverhouse itself. When Shane touched the painting, when he heard those twin sighs, he knew everything. He held the painting a moment longer, not lifting it from its easel but just cradling it between his palms, steeping in it.

The note had not been meant for Marlena. It was not Wilhelm's announcement to his wife that he was leaving her. It was an explanation of his plan for Madeleine, telling her what to do and where to go. Marlena had found it after Madeleine had read it, but before she had carried out its instruction. Marlena had found the note *before they had even left*.

Shane finally let go of the painting. He turned and went downstairs again, quickly and purposefully. In the hallway, he approached and opened the cellar door. He clumped down the wooden steps into the darkness, not needing the light to find his way. It flipped on of its own accord, and then flipped off again. Shane ignored it, moving toward a set of old shelves attached to the far wall. The light flicked on and off again, almost like a warning.

"Ding dong," Shane muttered to himself, scanning the shelves. "The show's about to start. Everyone find their seats."

The light flicked on and off once more, and then on again. This time it stayed on. Shane found what he was looking for. He wrapped his hand around it, hefted it, and carried it back across the cellar floor. The faded drawing beneath his feet seemed to move with his passing, like a movie seen through a curtain of gray fog. "Ding dong," Shane said again, huffing as he tramped up the steps, carrying the long object in his hand. He rested the heavy end on his shoulder.

He climbed the stairs back up to the studio and stopped again, looking at the painting of the Sleepwalker. No wonder he hadn't recognized the picture of Marlena in the center. Her hair had been matted with rain at that point, plastering it to her head. Her wet dress clung to her, hiding her shape. He could recognize her now, however. Now, he understood everything.

Shane lowered the head of the sledgehammer from his shoulder, plopping it into his free left hand with a meaty smack. He moved toward the painting of the Sleepwalker, and then past it. He positioned himself in front of the wall behind the easel, spreading his feet and bending his knees a little. Finally, somewhat reluctantly, he raised the head of the sledgehammer again, heaving it back over his right shoulder, both hands gripping the haft of the handle. He coiled his strength, took a deep breath, and swung.

There were bricks underneath the old plaster. Shane wasn't at all surprised.

Chapter Twenty One

The plaster cracked and shattered away easily, sending up puffs of thick white dust, but the bricks were remarkably solid. Shane struck them repeatedly, aiming low, trying to hit the same spot. On the ninth hit, one of the bricks broke away. It knocked sideways in its old bed of mortar, pushing partly through into the space beyond. Shane aimed for the same brick and struck it squarely. It shot through the hole and clattered into darkness, thumping distantly. Shane listened to the sound, his hair prickling at the base of his neck. He'd known that there had to be some forgotten, sealed-off upstairs space—the secret round window on the east side of the cottage demanded it—and yet somehow he'd never fully believed it. Hearing the brick hit the floor of that forgotten room made it suddenly very real. He didn't want to see what was there, and yet he knew he had to. Grimly, pressing his lips into a thin line of resolve, Shane raised the sledge hammer again.

The bricks around the small, rectangular hole gave way much more easily. Each hit loosened a few more. Shane worked as quickly as he could, and as he swung, breathing in the thick plaster dust and listening to the somehow satisfying sound of the bricks cracking beneath his blows, the story came fully alive in his mind.

When Marlena found the letter in Madeleine's purse, Madeleine herself had, of course, still been in the house. Wilhelm's plans had not yet been carried out. Marlena took the letter—and Madeleine's purse as well—and fled the Riverhouse, running out into the rain, without coat or umbrella, intent on confronting her husband at the cottage.

Marlena was a strong woman. Earl had been right about that. She had only one weakness: she believed in the power of her love for her husband. She believed it had the ability to soften him, to transform him, to make him see the mistake he had very nearly made. She ran along the path, and Shane watched her, watched the vision of her in his mind as he swung the sledgehammer, shattering the brick wall one blow at a time. He saw the rain as it sheeted through the trees, beating the grass and weeds into submission and turning the path slippery with a thin coat of mud. He watched Marlena as she reached the stream that cut through the clearing nearest the Riverhouse. The water had risen enough to make the stepping stones appear insubstantial, like lily pads that would collapse immediately under her weight. She didn't pause, however, but ran nimbly over them, holding her wet skirts up to keep them out of the way.

The angel statue loomed over her, its arm raised in benediction. Marlena ran past it, Madeleine's purse clutched in her hand, the letter rammed back inside, growing damp as rain leaked in. A stitch formed in Marlena's side. She pressed her free hand to it but didn't slow. The sky was growing very dark, even though it was barely five o'clock. Up ahead, a point of light flickered—a candle, high in the east window of her husband's studio. Marlena moaned to herself, a pathetic, aching sound of abject betrayal. She slogged forward on the path, slipping once, going down on one knee and dropping the damn purse. She collected it again, righted herself, and went on.

Finally, the trees opened before her. The meticulously neat yard of the cottage welcomed her, but coldly. This was not her place. She had barely set foot here before, and had only been inside the cottage on a handful of occasions. Never without her husband, of course, and *never* uninvited. She went around to the back of the cottage, her boots clacking on the flagstone patio, and reached for the door. The knob was slippery with rain: locked. Gus had apparently given Madeleine a key, yet he had never given one to his own wife. She pounded on the door, rattling the glass and crying out incoherently. She glanced around, eyes wide. There was a small pile of river rocks in the corner of the patio, smooth and round, collected probably by her husband. She lunged for them, grabbed one that fit easily in her right hand, and turned back to the cottage. She brought her hand up and then down again, ramming the large rock against the window set into the back door. The pane over the door knob shattered, cutting her fingers. She barely noticed. With her left hand, she reached in through the jagged glass, found the bolt latch, turned it. A moment later, she was inside the cottage, breathing hard, leaving the back door hanging open. Rain and leaves blew in behind her.

"Gus!" she screamed, her voice cracking.

His voice came almost immediately, echoing in the stillness of the cottage. "Up here, dearheart," he called. The sarcasm was unmistakable.

She followed the sound of his voice, her eyes wild, her fingers welling blood where she had cut them. Madeleine's purse was in her left hand now. As Marlena climbed the stairs into her husband's large, airy studio, she held the purse out, open, knowing she didn't need to say anything.

He was packing when she found him. A small suitcase was open on the narrow bed, filled with neatly folded clothes. Paintings cluttered the studio, canvases of all sizes leaning against the walls, often three or four deep. Very few of them had sold. Few people seemed to be enthralled with Wilhelm's more esoteric works, the nymphlike naked people, the gods and goddesses lounging indolently, looking like angels with consumption. The only works people seemed to be interested in were the portraits, the kings and queens, the presidents, the super wealthy elite who formed the backbone of the unofficial American aristocracy. Wilhelm had done fewer and fewer of the portraits in recent years, however. He wanted to prove to the world that his art was more important than the mere notoriety of its subjects, and yet the world hadn't agreed. Marlena had known how this galled her husband, and had tried to comfort him, to commiserate with him. As a fellow artist, she understood, perhaps even more so than he did, the fickleness of the art buying public. After all, she painted in the abstract. She loved the simple ballet of color and shape, relieved of the draconian demands of the literal. Wilhelm had rejected her comfort, however, perhaps because he didn't feel it was necessary. He simply could not accept that people did not care for his own works, despite the evidence of the unsold canvases all around him. He persisted in believing that he would eventually be recognized for the genius that he was, like Michelangelo, and Da Vinci, and that "drunken Spaniard", Pablo Picasso, whom Wilhelm had never met but hated tacitly. Picasso's works, after all, were a lot more like Marlena's than his own. Was it possible that he resented her comfort because he was jealous of her?

Marlena refused to consider such things. As temperamental as he was, as occasionally spiteful, cold and self centered as he was, she loved him. She always had, ever since he had first won her heart, even if it was often—as it had been then—against her own better judgment.

Besides the narrow bed and the small suitcase, the studio was cluttered, crowded with props: trunks and boxes covered with huge hanks of muslin, a few upholstered chairs and lounges, a pile of easels looking like dried skeletons, and Wilhelm's huge paint table, covered with paint pots, brushes, palettes, jugs of thinner and wads of rags. Wilhelm himself was standing in front of a low dresser. He looked up as Marlena stood at top of the steps, holding the purse with its damning letter inside. He slid a drawer shut and shook his head.

"Don't act surprised, my dear," he said, approaching the suitcase on the end of the bed. "You should have known something like this was inevitable. You did, didn't you? Otherwise you never would have been sneaking around, spying us out."

"You made me believe you were happy," Marlena said simply. In the vision, Shane could see that her face was still wet with rain, but there were tears there, too; tears of frustration and anger as well as sadness.

"And you believed me," Wilhelm said, shaking his head and smiling a little. "I hope those are good memories. Those were the memories I wished to leave you with. Grant me that, at least. I wanted you to remember us as happy."

"It was a lie."

"So many of the beautiful things in life are lies, Lena," Wilhelm said airily, not looking at her. "Happy little lies. Useful lies. We tell them to ourselves to make life bearable. And this is as it should be. I tell myself the happy lie that Madeleine loves me, and yet, deep down, I cannot know this. It is, of course, far more likely that she loves my money, and my fame, and the egotistical thrill of believing that she has won me. And yet I persist in my belief that she truly does love me. Why? Because it pleases me. I need to be loved. I need to be adored, Lena. You know this, of course."

"*I* love you," Marlena said, but weakly. "*I* adore you. Why is that not enough?"

"It's not you," Wilhelm said, smiling indulgently. "Comfort yourself with that. It doesn't matter who it is. Madeleine is who I love now. Will I love her forever?" He stopped, and looked aside, as if seriously considering the prospect. "I was about to say 'probably not', but do you want to know something amusing? Maybe I am simply getting old and sentimental, but I think I very well might. I truly do love her, you see. Unlike I have ever loved anyone. She is... different. She is special. You, my dear, are common. I'm sorry to say it, but it is not a bad thing. Nearly everyone in the world is common. That's what gives the word its meaning. I am *not* common, of course, thus we were never a good match. New wine in old wine skins and all that. You see that, don't you?"

"I bore you a son!" Marlena said, advancing on him now, tossing the purse onto one of the nearby chairs. "After the doctors said I would never be able to. After you yourself had sought out that damned whore to give you what you believed I couldn't. *I* did it, not her."

Wilhelm nodded, his face reddening a little at the word "whore". He drew a deep breath. "This is why I am leaving all of this to you, Lena dear," he said, spreading his arms wide. "I will be taking a substantial share of the money, of course, but all of this, the cottage and the Riverhouse, it is my debt of gratitude to you. Hector is indeed the desire of my heart, and you gave him to me." It seemed to gall him to admit it. His face had grown hard, his eyes dark. Outside, the storm grew, bringing a fresh torrent of rain with it. Thunder grumbled and banged in the distance. Lightning flickered, highlighting the side of Wilhelm's stern features.

"Don't do this," Marlena said. Her voice was calm now.

"It is already done," Wilhelm said, turning away from her, approaching the bed again.

"It isn't. Your lover is not here yet. She comes, but it isn't too late. You can keep her as your lover if you wish, if you truly love her. But don't leave. Please, Gus."

He ignored her as she followed him across the room. He bent to shut the suitcase.

"Gus," Marlena said, but he interrupted her, wheeling on her, towering over her.

"You damn, stupid woman," he said, his voice low and terrible. "You don't understand anything. You believe you know what is best? You believe that the world is on your side and that I am the bad one? You are a simple-minded fool; a mere sheep, responding only to some primitive, instinctive concept of morality. This is why I cannot abide you. This is why you are unfit to be my wife. And this, more than anything, is why you are unfit to raise my son. I won't have him growing up believing he must be constrained by your pathetic concepts of obligation, your stupid notion of *blind duty*. He is meant for greatness. That which I have only tapped, he will master. I will see to it. He will tame the world and make it his own if he so wishes, but only because he will not be hobbled by *your* weakness. He will be untainted by your commonness. Do you recall when those idiots threw stones at the Riverhouse because they believed I was a Nazi sympathizer? I may not have been so then, but now I am not so sure. Maybe Herr Hitler was right after all. Maybe we *should* winnow out the weaknesses of our ancestry, and of the lesser races. Of course, someone like you will not even consider such a thing. But Madeleine, she understands this, despite her own lesser heritage. She shares in the hope for our son. Together, we have already begun to teach him the way of strength and pride. I thank you for bearing him to me, my dear Lena, but I will tell you now—and only because you force me to—that that is a fact I will forget as soon as I can. A fact he, himself, will never realize. The boy you bore will cease to know you. He will not even remember your name."

Marlena's eyes had grown glassy, but it was not his last words, his final hateful salvo, that had pierced her. It was his claim about Madeleine, and their plans for Hector. *Together, we have already begun to teach him the way of strength and pride*, he'd said. Hector, her sweet boy, her sensitive boy, the one who refused to step on an ant for fear that its ghost would come and haunt him at night, who loved music and, although barely two years old, already drew constantly—happy mermaids on the banks of the river, smiling suns, dancing kitty cats—they were taking him away from her, changing him, had in fact already begun their work, and right under her nose. He was being taught to subdue that beautiful nature of his, to seek power, to cultivate pride. They were tainting him, molding him into something contrary to who he was, something cold and selfish, a mirror-image of Gustav Wilhelm himself, but exaggerated, honed to a dagger's point. Her husband, the father of her child, didn't see her motherhood as something valuable, a balancing force to counteract his own hedonism and pride. He saw her motherhood of Hector as a poison, a weed to be systematically rooted out, burned, and forgotten. And he had already begun that work, with Madeleine's help.

"No..." Marlena whispered, her voice quiet, strangely calm.

"Yes," he said quickly, still looking at her piercingly, wanting to be sure she fully understood, wanting to break her. "She comes even now, and my son comes with her, carried in her arms. They are arms that he already knows more than yours, arms that have held him since birth, cradled him, fed him. From this day on she will not be his nanny. From now on, she will be his mother, in name as well as deed."

None of it was true. Marlena had nursed Hector, and had only recently weaned him. She had held him far more than Madeleine, and had even slept with him on many occasions. She had bought him his favorite toy, the silver rattle that he carried with him everywhere he went. Wilhelm would not know this, of course, nor would he believe her if she tried to tell him. It didn't matter. Marlena could not allow them to take Hector away from her. She couldn't allow them to change her sweet son, to pervert him into something he wasn't. It was too horrible even to consider.

"No," she said again, more firmly this time.

"It is not your choice to make," Wilhelm said, dismissing her, turning away again. He began to snap the buckles of the suitcase. "The deed is as done. You may stay and watch, but I forbid you from interfering. You will only embarrass yourself."

"You will forbid nothing," Marlena said calmly.

Wilhelm's hand swung out, almost casually, and struck Marlena, back-handed, on the cheek. She reeled to the side, but kept her footing. Her expression did not change. He turned on her one more time, raising his hand again.

"I have never struck you before," he said. "But I am not above it. Heed me or be prepared to receive the consequences."

Marlena swung her own arm, barely aware that she had meant to do it. She had never hit anyone in her life, had never had the need to. She meant to smack him, to shame him, to show him the full weight of her pain and rage. She had forgotten that she still had the river rock in her hand.

The smooth rock smashed into the side of Wilhelm's cheek, shattering it and throwing him off his feet. He collapsed sideways and backwards, falling like a tree and landing partly on the bed. The suitcase was knocked aside. It popped open and spilled the neatly folded shirts and socks onto the wooden floor. Marlena looked down at her hand, at the smooth brown rock gripped in her fingers, as if mildly surprised to see it there. Smears of blood marred its surface, and she noticed, for the first time, that she had cut her hand on the glass of the door. Not all of the blood on the rock was hers, however. She looked down at her husband again.

He tried to speak, but his jaw seemed to be stuck. The left side of his face was already swelling, turning purple. Blood ran from his ear and the corner of his mouth. He rolled over onto his back, his legs still sticking off the end of the bed, his heels knocking on the floor. Marlena saw him as if he was a figure in a dream, a bogeyman that had threatened her, threatened to take away her son, to eat him perhaps; a bogeyman that would still do it, if she allowed him the chance. She moved forward, feeling the weight of the river rock in her hand, hefting it.

"No," Wilhelm tried to say, but the word came out as merely a mushy bark. He coughed and blood sprayed from his lips, staining his teeth.

Marlena shook her head slowly, lifting the rock. Wilhelm struggled backwards onto the bed, raising his hands, but it was no use. Marlena was not herself. She moved like a woman sleepwalking, barely aware of what she was doing, responding to some basic, primordial instinct. She gripped the rock in her white, bloody fingers, raised it, and brought it down again. The sound of the impact was like the sound of Clara's rolling pin striking a slab of dough in the kitchen of the Riverhouse. She repeated the action and Wilhelm collapsed backwards, making the bed squeak. Marlena climbed up onto the bed, straddling the now motionless form of her husband. If someone had glimpsed the two of them at that moment, in the stormy dimness of the studio, they might have believed that this was a moment of intimacy, even tenderness. Marlena had not descended upon her husband in order to be close to him, however. Nor had she done it because she felt any pity for him, or any remorse at the memory of the years they had spent together, the many times they had shared a bed, just as they were now. She'd done it simply because he was tall, and he had fallen backwards on the bed.

She'd done it to give herself a better angle to keep hitting him from. She raised the stone in her hand.

Shane brought the sledgehammer down on the fractured wall and a large portion of it caved in, falling to the floor with a heavy, resounding crash. Brick dust, plaster and mortar choked the space, obscuring the view through the broken hole. Shane coughed and covered his mouth and nose with his hand, breathing through his cupped fingers. He dropped the sledgehammer and hunkered over, peering into the darkness of the hidden room. The first thing he saw was the round window. It hung in the darkness, glowing blue, showing the black branches of the Magnolia tree and the peak of the forest beyond. Wind and rain tore at the bare trees, making them wave up at the gray sky as if in a panic. A small narrow shape stuck up from the bottom of the window, peaked with a bright tongue of flame. The candle burned, casting its reflection on the old glass. Shane could smell the scent of its hot wax, could see a bead of it dripping down into the brass base. He stepped gingerly through the hole, careful not to twist his ankle on the broken bricks that lay beneath it. The space was very small; the same length as his studio, but barely four feet deep. Cobwebs and dust cocooned everything, turning the scene into a gray photograph. It looked almost exactly like his final painting, except for a few minor details. The purse on the chair to the left was made of some sort of brocade fabric. Its mouth was framed in brass, with tiny hinges at the sides. On Shane's right, the bed was shoved against the wall, obscure with shadows, but not enough to hide the shape sprawled beneath the loose sheet. One skeletal foot stuck out from beneath the covering, canted toward the window, still shod in a black leather shoe. Shane understood why his own version of the scene, shown in the Sleepwalker painting, was different than what he saw here. He had, of course, allowed his own story to mix with the vision. He had painted Steph's purse instead of Madeleine's. He had painted Earl dead in his bed instead of Gustav Wilhelm. They were small differences, but they had been just enough to hide the true story from him, to keep it just out of his grasp until now. Until it was too late.

The candle at the bottom of the round window burned, and Shane understood the centerpiece of the painting now as well, the element that gave it its name: the Sleepwalker. Marlena had stood there once her husband was dead, looking out at the stormy night, watching, a woman somehow disconnected from herself, as if in a dream. Shane could all too easily envision her there even now, framed in silhouette against that round blue shape, haloed against it. She had gone downstairs, into the rudimentary kitchen, and found a knife. She didn't mean to kill Madeleine with it, or so she vaguely believed. She only meant to scare her, to make her give over her son, and then to leave, forever. Marlena stood there in the window, behind that single glowing candle, just outside the reach of its light, and watched the path. She knew Madeleine would come. She might have realized by now that Marlena knew about the plan, but she would come anyway. Madeleine would believe that Gus Wilhelm had the situation in his control, no matter what. She would come even if she knew that Marlena was there with him. All Marlena had to do was wait.

Shane watched as the vision played out in his mind, almost as if it was a memory, as if the crypt of this room had saved it up, collected it, and was now feeding it to him. Just like now, it was storming on the night that Marlena had stood there, the blood of her husband on her hands, his body haphazardly covered on the bed nearby. Marlena watched through the storm, unmoving, unthinking, and eventually, when it had grown fully dark outside, she saw them. Madeleine came quickly along the path, almost invisible in the darkness. She had a small suitcase in one hand. The other was wrapped around young Hector. She carried him on her hip, and he clung to her neck, sopping wet with rain, crying. Marlena could hear him, hear his simple, alarmed words under the roar of the rain.

"Wet, Nanna," he said, clinging to her, his feet dangling. "Rattle! I dropped my rattle, Nanna! it's wet!" He was pointing back toward the path, his little hand seeming very white in the darkness.

Madeleine didn't reply. She shushed him as soothingly as she could, bouncing him gamely against her shoulder as she began to cross the yard. Her own face was dripping with rainwater, since her hands were too full to carry an umbrella. Marlena saw Madeleine glance up toward the cottage, looking toward the window, toward the pinprick of white flame that burned inside it. A flash of lightning lit the world outside, making everything jump into sharp focus, causing every branch and blade of grass to leap into view. A moment later darkness engulfed the scene again. Marlena's eyes were dazzled. She lost sight of Madeleine and Hector. Taking a step closer to the window, she forced her gaze to readjust to the darkness. Madeleine was no longer walking across the yard. She was merely standing there in the rain, staring up at the window, her own eyes wide and blank.

A slow realization spread over Marlena, chilling her. Madeleine had seen her, had glimpsed her in that sudden flash of lightning. It was evident in the sudden wariness on her face, the way she stood there and watched the window, uncertain and hesitant. Marlena fingered the knife in her hand and slowly backed away from the window, away from the glow of the candle. In the yard below, Madeleine backed away as well, slowly, one step. Then two.

"Rattle!" Hector cried, reaching over Madeleine's shoulder, reaching toward the path. "Rattle, Nanna. Go back!"

Marlena turned swiftly. She bolted for the stairs, clambered down them at a near run, taking two at a time. She spun through the hall and kitchen, grabbing the frame of the open back door with her left hand. The rain was coming harder now, drenching her almost immediately. Wind tore through the trees, gusting so hard that it was like a hand on her chest, pushing her backwards. Underneath the roar of the storm, Marlena could still hear the insistent voice of her son, crying, calling for his rattle. She ran.

The side yard was empty. Madeleine and Hector were nowhere in sight. Marlena bolted toward the path, following the sound of her son's voice. She saw them as she came into the first clearing, the one that rounded the knob of the bluff that overlooked the river. Madeleine was on the far side, following the path back into the woods. Hector was leaning over her shoulder, still reaching, calling for his rattle. He saw Marlena and his face transformed in the darkness. He lit up, smiling with delight and surprise.

"Mama!" he called out, waving.

Madeleine stopped. Slowly, she turned around. Hector scrambled in her arms, trying to slip out of her grip, trying to keep Marlena in view. "Mama all wet!" he cried, laughing suddenly.

Madeleine made eye contact with Marlena across the clearing. In the distance between them, the wrought iron bench sat in its drift of hydrangeas, now void of their blooms. Marlena shook her head, slowly, begging the other woman with her eyes. Wind tore at Madeleine's dress. It stuck to her legs and flapped wetly. It was very dark, and yet Marlena could see Madeleine's eyes. They looked into her own eyes, and then dropped to the knife in Marlena's hand. It was all the confirmation Madeleine needed. Somehow, she seemed to know everything. Her lover was dead. And for all she knew, she soon would be as well. Her eyes met Marlena's again, full of grim understanding, and then she turned. She hugged Hector against her, and she ran.

"Wait!" Marlena called across the clearing, but it was too late. Madeleine was gone. Marlena dropped the knife into the weeds and gave chase.

She passed the angel statue again. It glistened with rain, its face calm and benign. When she entered the second clearing, she saw that the stream had now swollen to the point of being impassable. Water coursed over the stepping stones, rendering them useless. They must have been very nearly submerged when Madeleine had first crossed over them, carrying Hector in her arms. Marlena shuddered to think about it. She looked around, knowing that Madeleine would never attempt such a crossing now, but neither she nor Hector were anywhere in sight. Marlena voiced a moan of fear and worry. As if in response, a thin cry suddenly sounded, carrying on the wet wind. Marlena turned toward it, gasping, her eyes wide. Madeleine and Hector were just visible in the dark distance on the river side of the clearing. They were descending toward the bank, toward the rickety wooden dock below.

"No," she said to herself, shaking her head in helpless negation. "She wouldn't..."

Marlena lifted her skirt again and ran.

The dock had been built three summers ago, meant to be used for fishing and for mooring the little rowboat that visitors sometimes enjoyed taking out on the river when the current allowed it. Hector loved the boat, loved being out on the rocking waves, even though Marlena herself had never taken him out in it. Under the best of conditions, she didn't like the idea of him being out on such a big river in such a little craft, but he talked about it constantly, and even featured it in his drawings. He'd draw himself in the little rowboat, sometimes with his father, sometimes all by himself, usually waving to the viewer, or to the mermaids that poked their heads happily from the waves. He had a name for the little rowboat, one he had picked up from the songs that Gus had played for him on the Victrola. He called it the Good Ship Lollipop.

As Marlena crested the low hill that overlooked the bank, she saw them again. They stood on the end of the dock, which was nearly submerged in the swift current. Madeleine was lowering Hector into the boat, but he was clinging to her in the darkness, unwilling to go. It was pure madness to go out on the river now, with the current so high and fast, and the rain beating it in sheets, turning it into a brown cauldron.

"Madeleine, no!" Marlena screamed, cupping her hands to her mouth, but it was useless. Thunder barreled across the sky overhead, drowning her out. She tried again, but the wind tore her words away. She gave up and ran down the short hillside, heading toward the dock.

Madeleine looked up and saw her coming. Her eyes were wide with terror. She gave up trying to set Hector in the little boat.

Instead, she clambered down into it herself, still carrying him. It rocked precariously.

"Stop!" Marlena cried, her voice cracking. "Don't take him out there! Please!"

Hector was crying, still clinging to Madeleine. She turned away from Marlena and reached for the ropes that anchored the boat to the dock. Her hands moved quickly, undoing the simple knots.

Marlena screamed again, this time a wordless exclamation of terror. She reached the dock and began to pound along it. It was wet, slippery, and seemed to rock with the force of the current and the rushing waves. Hector finally looked up. He saw her just as Madeleine finished untying the ropes. The boat immediately began to drift, sucked out into the current.

"Mama!" Hector cried, suddenly letting go of Madeleine. "Rattle fell, Mama! All wet in the woods!" He pointed with one hand, reached for her with the other.

Marlena ran to the end of the dock, almost forgetting to stop. She threw both of her arms out toward the receding boat.

"My baby!" she screamed. "Bring him back to me! Row! Bring him back!"

Madeleine looked at her, her face growing quickly smaller as the boat became locked in the rushing current. She saw that Marlena no longer had the knife. She glanced around, as if surprised to see where she was. She scrambled toward the middle of the small boat and reached for the oars.

"Mama!" Hector cried, clutching the stern gunwale with his little hands.

"*Hector!*" she called back to him, still reaching, her hands opening and closing, willing the distance between them to disappear. It grew instead. The boat rocked precipitously as Madeleine tried to row. It was no use. The current was far too strong. Lightning flickered across the low sky and thunder roared. Something large was moving along the center of the river. In the flash of the lightning, it looked monstrous and dark, like the back of some mythical sea beast. Marlena clutched her face helplessly as the object bore down on the tiny boat. Madeleine looked up and saw it coming, but Hector never looked. His eyes stayed locked on his mother where she stood on the dock, growing smaller, screaming his name.

It was a tree, huge and black, still festooned with a canopy of spring leaves. The uprooted end preceded it down the river, pulled along under the inertia of its own weight. It towered over the tiny boat, pushing a froth of splashing water in front of it. Madeleine let go of the oars and reached for Hector. Marlena saw no more, because the tree blocked her view at that point. She didn't hear the sound of the tree striking the boat, but she saw the prow of the little craft suddenly jerk to the side. It plowed under the mass of roots, dragging at the water. An instant later it was gone.

Marlena screamed. She clutched at her face, pulling furrows into the smooth skin of her cheeks, her eyes bulging and wild, unbelieving. In the torrential darkness, she screamed, and screamed, and screamed.

Shane felt weak under the weight of such loss and grief. It plugged all too neatly into the loss and grief he himself had experienced. He stepped backwards, away from the round window and the storm that raged beyond it. His heel bumped the pile of bricks and he nearly fell backwards. Instead, he half turned and caught himself on the ragged edge of the hole in the wall. The bricks were brittle and dry under his grip. The last hands to touch them, he realized with dull horror, had been Marlena's. She had built this wall herself, closing off this little corner of the world, hoping she'd never have to think of it again. Had Earl known? Had he seen the wall when it was only half finished, seen what it was meant to hide? Maybe he had, and had kept Marlena's secret. He had loved her, after all. He might not have known the whole story, but he'd have figured out enough. Maybe he had even helped her finish it.

And yet it hadn't been enough. Like the classic Edgar Allen Poe story that Shane had read in college, the tell-tale heart had continued to beat, haunting Marlena, driving her slowly into the embrace of madness. She'd watched the cottage through the window in the attic of the Riverhouse, sometimes seeing the light of that damning candle, teasing and mocking her. She'd built the Insanity Stairs, with their bizarre window, overlooking the huge sieve drain installed in the basement floor. And Shane now knew why. In Marlena's tortured mind, another flood could bring back to her that which she had lost. Maybe it would return her beloved sweet boy to her. But if it did, it might also return Madeleine. Marlena knew that she had to be wary, to watch with vigilance. If Madeleine came back with Hector, she might not be as easy to get rid of as Marlena's husband had been. Madeleine might be less willing to die this time around.

Shane climbed back through the hole, into the light of his own version of the studio, smaller than Wilhelm's, but otherwise very similar. He felt dazed, sick, horrified with what he had seen. Aimlessly, he moved toward the stairs.

Christiana had said that Marlena hated her because she, Marlena, loved Shane, and had wanted him for herself. But was that all there was to it? In the light of what he now knew, he wondered. It had made sense when he'd believed that Wilhelm had betrayed and abandoned Marlena, running off with his lover. That was the story that the world had believed, and why not? It fit perfectly with what everyone knew of the hedonistic, arrogant painter. Now, however, Shane knew that it was all a lie. A happy lie, as Wilhelm himself might have called it, covering up a much uglier truth. In light of that, did it make sense that Marlena might love Shane as a replacement for the husband who had betrayed her?

The stairs leading down into the lower half of the cottage were wet with rain. Shane's feet squeaked on the wooden steps as he descended, hanging onto the banister, his thoughts reeling.

Earlier, he had asked himself what part he had been meant to play in the unfolding story of the Riverhouse. Even then, he had partly doubted Christiana's simple take on the tale. Marlena's jealousy was just too seamless, her rage too vehement for it to be mere romantic jealousy. But what was it? What was he missing?

Shane turned the corner at the bottom of the stairs, stepping into his bedroom. He stopped, swaying slightly on his feet, and stared into the stormy darkness. Lightning flickered outside the window, painting stark shapes onto the walls, throwing his dresser into relief. Something glittered on the dresser, shining in that bright, silvery glow. Shane looked at it.

Rattle fell, Mama, he thought.

A hard shiver coursed down his spine, shaking him. He moved toward the dresser, reached, wrapped his fingers around the silver rattle. It jingled merrily as he picked it up.

She doesn't love me as a husband, he thought, his eyes slowly widening with revelation. *She loves me as a son. She loves me as her sweet boy.*

"She loves me as Hector," he said to himself, his voice thin with wonder.

The Riverhouse

Lightning flickered again and thunder followed it, booming and rolling across the sky. Shane held the rattle, remembering the first time he had seen Marlena, remembering how he'd held the silver rattle up in front of him, as if to ward her off with it.

All she'd ever wanted was her son back. She'd ended her days wishing only to live with him, to watch him grow, to hear his happy laugh and rambunctious play fill the rooms of the Riverhouse. And then, long after her ghost had grown mad with loss and regret, a man showed up, a man with artistic skills, a man who himself had lost the ones he loved, a man whose heart was ready to be filled again. It was as if they'd been meant for each other—a match made in hell. And as the final perfect touch, he'd had the silver rattle, the favorite toy of her long dead son, to prove it.

He thought of the paintings he had created, the ones he thought of as belonging to the Shane Bellamy Insanity Stairs series. They were all of a unique style, a strange blend of realism and modernism, each overlaying the other, sometimes complementing, sometimes warring. He'd never painted anything like it before, and now he understood why. It was simply a part of the role he had been meant to play. His art was now a mix of both Gustav Wilhelm's haunting realism and Marlena's free-form abstraction, both blended together and reborn at the hand of their would-be son. Shane had indeed played along. Without even realizing it, he had played his part exceptionally well.

Even in his visions of Marlena, she had never appeared as his lover or wife. She had seemed huge, towering, sometimes indulgent and sometimes commanding, but always, as he could now see, imminently maternal. She didn't want to punish him. She loved him. But even the best mothers sometimes had to discipline their children. It was for their own good.

He kept the rattle in his hand as he walked back into the light of the hallway. It all made so much sense now, and yet there was no comfort in it. When Shane had believed that Marlena's passion for him was that of a jealous lover, it had seemed frightening, but somehow manageable. Lovers may be passionate, but they could also be fickle, or sullen, or maybe even reasoned with. A mother's love, however, completely superseded reason. A mother's love was instinctive, powerful, and ultimately undeniable. A mother would do anything to protect her children. Anything at all.

Shane leaned on the kitchen entry. His half of the sandwich still sat on the counter, still wrapped in paper. He stared at it, and then beyond it. Christiana's empty Coke can sat next to the sink, near a small stack of papers and folders that she had brought with her from the office. Shane rested his gaze on her things, thinking. Something about the sight nagged him, set off little warning bells in the back of his mind, but he was too distracted to pay any attention to it.

How did Christiana fit into it all? If Shane was meant to play the role of Marlena's lost son, what role did Christiana have to play? Was there a role for her at all?

Shane stopped. He finally looked at the collection of Christiana's things, taking them all in: the Coke can, the small sheaf of folders and papers, a Post-it pad with a series of phone numbers scribbled onto it.

Two sets of keys lay on the counter next to the Post-it pad. The set with the leather key fob was Christiana's. The other was Shane's. They were the keys to his pickup truck.

Shane's eyes widened as his thoughts sped up to a blur. He pushed himself away from the kitchen entryway, his eyes still nailed on the keys. He had heard her leave, hadn't he? He had heard the front door open and close from his seat up in the studio. It had slammed shut because the wind had caught it. But he hadn't heard the truck start. He hadn't heard the squeak as she released the emergency brake.

He hadn't heard those things because she hadn't taken the truck. She had walked to her first appointment.

I've got a few hours to kill, she had told him, *but I've got plenty to do in the meantime. I'll probably leave again pretty quick. Wish me luck.*

Shane walked slowly, dazedly, around the corner of the hallway, heading toward the front room. He didn't want to see, but couldn't stop himself.

The painting of the Riverhouse had changed once more. Marlena was still standing, smiling, one hand held out in greeting, but the shadow in the lower right of the canvas had finally revealed its owner. Shane had always suspected it would be him, but of course it wasn't. Christiana stood in the foreground, dressed exactly as Shane had seen her an hour earlier. Her back was to Shane, but he could clearly see her shape, the tanned curve of her calf below her skirt, the curled fingers of one hand, the glossy black of her hair. Christiana had gone to the Riverhouse after all. Shane should have known that she would, especially after her own encounter with the reality of Marlena's specter. She had gone to settle things, to talk reason with her ghostly nemesis. She believed she was going to meet merely a jealous rival. Instead, she was walking into the vengeance of a bereft mother, one bent on preventing her loss from happening all over again.

Shane drifted helplessly toward the painting, cold to the bone. Terror sank over him, settling onto him like a lead weight. The mark Marlena had made on Christiana's cheek wasn't a warning, he suddenly realized. It was a mark of identification. Perhaps Marlena had meant it as a final hint, a clue to help him understand what was really happening between them all, and what was truly at stake. *M,* the mark had read. It didn't stand for Marlena.

It stood for Madeleine.

Chapter Twenty Two

Shane didn't think. He was out the front door and running across the soggy lawn almost before he realized it. Of course he could never catch up to Christiana—she could have easily made it to the Riverhouse and back by now—but he was beyond the reach of such rational thoughts. All he knew was that the woman he loved was walking into a deadly trap, and he had to get to her. It was already too late, but that didn't change anything. If only he had known. If only he'd paid more attention. The signs of Christiana's intentions had to have been there, if only he hadn't been so distracted. After all, the Riverhouse painting had known all along. Perhaps, in some unknowable way, the painting had even *caused* it to happen.

Shane dashed through the storm, so blinded by the darkness that he was forced to navigate almost entirely on instinct, relying on his memories of the yard and the mouth of the path. He sensed the trees closing around him as he entered the woods. A flash of lightning lit the world for one bright second, revealing the footpath ahead of him, and even in his distress, Shane saw the changes. The stones that formed the path were no longer partially obscured by decades of moss and weeds. They were utterly pristine, as if they had been laid only yesterday. They shone in the brilliance of the lightning like a highway cutting through the forest. Shane ran on, his feet kicking up splashes and his breath coming in harsh bursts. Shortly he came to the first clearing, the one that overlooked the bench where it leaned amongst the overgrown hydrangeas. The bench didn't lean, however, nor were the hydrangeas overgrown. Now, they grew in a neatly cropped arc around the back of the bench, which sat straight and clean, without a speck of rust. Shane stumbled to a stop, bewildered and disoriented.

"Chris!" he called, cupping his hands to his mouth. There was no answer, of course, but for the steady roar of the rain and the low creak of the trees. A glimmer of light caught his eye alongside the path. He looked down and saw something reflecting dully. It was a knife. Its blade was clean, spotless; its handle polished black. Shane considered picking it up, and then decided against it. If it hadn't worked for Marlena, it wasn't going to work for him. He threw himself forward and ran on.

The entire forest seemed to be subtly changed all around. At first, Shane couldn't figure out what it was. Some trees seemed to be in slightly different places. Others seemed noticeably smaller. Even the landscape was vaguely different; steeper in some places, more level in others. With a sinking dread, Shane began to grasp that the woods had transformed back to what they'd been on that fateful night so many decades ago, the one during which Marlena had run this same path. With that realization, something else occurred to him: Marlena had changed the circumstances this time around, subtly but meaningfully. She had realized her fatal mistake—that of waiting at the cottage for Madeleine and Hector. Surely, she had spent years replaying that night in her mind, examining every detail, weighing every consequence. She would have realized that it had been an error to simply wait at the cottage once her husband was dead. If, instead, she had gone directly back to the Riverhouse, she might have been able to meet Madeleine there, might have been able to confront her even before she, Madeleine, had learned of her missing purse, before she had realized that her lover's plan had been found out. If Marlena had done that, she could have saved her Hector. Tonight, she meant to rectify that one mistake. This time, she'd waited at the Riverhouse, waited for Christiana—the new Madeleine—to come to her. It had been Marlena's plan all along. *Not this time*, she had said. If only Shane had known what she'd meant. If only he hadn't been so distracted, so hopelessly enthralled by the story as it unfolded before him, coming out of the end of his paintbrush like a genie coming out of a lamp. He tried to convince himself that he'd been bewitched by the Riverhouse, and yet he knew that he had not been *completely* duped by it. He had allowed himself to be entranced, had willingly embraced it, almost from the beginning. He'd thought he could control it, firmly believed that he could walk right up to the cliff's edge and look out at that awesome, awful chasm of the world's end, and not fall off. Little had he known that someone had been sneaking up behind him the whole time, arms outstretched, waiting for him to get right up to the ledge—waiting to give him a push.

He ran, and as he did, things moved in the woods all around. They weren't real, and yet they didn't appear ghostly or insubstantial. Most of the things were people. They moved throughout the wood randomly, with no reference to one another. Some laughed raucously, ran, capered amongst the trees. Others walked with their heads down, their mouths moving as if in deep conversation, their hands gesturing vaguely. All of them were dressed in the clothes of a dead era, complete with straw hats, watch chains, and even a few monocles. They drifted aimlessly through the trees, mostly far off, but some near to hand, close enough to touch. None of them seemed the slightest bit wet, and none of them noticed Shane as he ran past, his breath rasping, his eyes wild, searching. Some of the strange things in the woods weren't people. The Model A truck sat on a rocky rise that overlooked the footpath, its engine idling roughly, looking like a brooding beast. Further on, an antique record player, a Victrola, sat on a tall table right in the middle of the path. A black funnel poked from the top of the player, shaped like an enormous lily. Shane slowed as he approached, sidling to get past the inexplicable machine. The record was turning quickly, so fast that Shane couldn't read the label, but as he passed it, he could hear the music it was playing, dimly, almost like a memory. It was "the Good Ship Lollipop", of course, sung by the irrepressibly happy Shirley Temple. The last thing Shane saw on the path was a tall and imposing figure, towering over the flagstones like a vengeful spirit. It was the angel statue, but somehow larger, its upraised hand now looking like a command rather than a benediction. Its face looked terrible in the shadows, full of grim purpose. Shane passed it, still running, his shoes soaked and smacking wetly. His feet slipped on the steps as they led down, around the gully, and emptied onto the grassy plain below. Shane stumbled into the clearing and almost ran head first into Christiana.

"Chris!" he cried, reaching for her, his voice caught between a laugh and a sob.

"Shane," she said dazedly, looking up at him. "What are you doing here?"

"I came looking for you!" he answered, grabbing her shoulders and holding her. "I came to find you! When I realized you'd come here..." he stopped and looked at her more closely. "Why are you still here? You left so long ago!"

"Did I?" she replied, looking around. "Seems like it's only been a little while. I got kind of turned around, I think."

"Why did you come here, Chris?" Shane asked, and then shook his head. He knew the answer already. "We have to get out of here. We have to go back."

"I'm trying," Christiana said, finally seeming to rouse. "But I can't. I'm stuck on this side. The stream..."

Shane blinked at her, bewildered. "What are you talking about?" he said, raising his voice over the roar of the rain. "You really are lost, aren't you? We have to go back *that* way!" He pointed behind him, not taking his eyes from Christiana's face. She looked very pale in the dim storm light.

"No. No, that's where I just came from," she said, but uncertainly. "It's all wrong. We need to cross the stream, like I did on the way here, but it's all flooded now. The stepping stones are underwater. Look!"

"Chris, the stream is over there, between us and the rest of the path. *That's* the Riverhouse side. The cottage is back that wa—"

Shane turned, pointing, and the word stuck in his throat. The stream was behind him now, running high and furious in its banks. The stepping stones were nowhere in sight. He stared, his eyes wide and wild, rain running down his face.

"Shane," Christiana said, her voice strangely calm. "How did *you* get over here?"

Shane swallowed past a large lump in his throat. "I don't know," he said.

"I don't know either. But, somehow, I think we have to go on. At least a little way. Don't you?"

Shane turned back to Christiana. He looked at her again, studied her face. She looked up at him openly. Finally, hopelessly, he nodded. They began to walk together, heading toward the rest of the footpath, the shorter length that led up to the site of the Riverhouse.

"Did you see her?" Shane asked as they walked.

Christiana was next to him, holding his hand. "No, of course not. I didn't even get to the end of the path. I got... lost, I think."

"But how, Chris? The footpath only goes one place. Did you walk off it, into the woods?" He thought of the spectral people he'd seen drifting silently through the trees. Were they the remains of Wilhelm's gaggle of artist friends? The ones who'd come to stay for weeks at a time back during the Riverhouse's heyday? *The Wanderers*, they'd called themselves. He shuddered.

"No. I mean, I don't think so. Time seems weird out here. How long ago did you say I left?"

"At least an hour. Probably an hour and a half."

Christiana was silent for a long moment. All around them the wood seemed suddenly very still except for the endlessly falling rain. She stopped on the path. A moment later, Shane did too.

"Something's very wrong," she said in a quiet, thoughtful voice.

"Yeah," he agreed. "Everything's wrong here. That's why we need to get out of here. We should have gotten out weeks ago. I'm sorry, Chris."

She was shaking her head, and when she looked up at him again, her eyes sparkled with tears. "That's not what I mean, Shane. I don't... I don't *know* what I mean."

"Come on," he said, pulling her hand to him, beckoning for her to follow, but she remained rooted to the spot. A sudden thrill of worry shook him and he looked at her, truly looked her up and down. All the expression went out of his face.

"Chris," he said, his voice suddenly small and weak. "Why... why aren't you wet?"

She looked at him, and then looked up at the dark sky. "Why?" she asked. "Is it raining or something?"

Shane stepped toward her again. Her hair was perfectly dry. Her face was clean and smooth, without a drop of rain on it. He looked closer and his knees went weak, making him sway on his feet. Christiana reached for him, her own face turning pale and dreadfully alarmed.

"Shane!" she cried, holding his hand tightly, making him look at her. "What is it? What's wrong?"

He pointed toward her cheek with one trembling finger. He touched it, feeling the smoothness of her skin. It felt cold. "The scratch," he said hoarsely. "The M. It's gone. It's... just gone."

Dreamily, Christiana reached up. She touched her cheek, felt the unmarked skin. Her eyes met Shane's again. She nodded very slowly.

"I know things," she said.

"Christiana, no," Shane said quickly, moving his hand from her cheek to her lips. "No! Let's just go back. It isn't too late. It can't be. When I came out to find you, I knew it was no use. But I ran anyway. Someone—" he stopped, laughed a little wildly. "Someone told me recently that hauling ass is a valuable life skill. I hauled ass, Chris, even though I thought I'd be too late. But I found you!"

She was shaking her head sadly. She took his hand away from her lips, lowered it. "No, Shane. No, I... I don't think you did."

"That's crazy!" he exclaimed, his voice cracking. "You're right here! You're all right. You *must* be. Why would I have... why would you still be..." his voice trailed away as he looked at her face. Her words didn't convince him, but her expression did.

"I know things, Shane" she said, almost whispering. "I know things I couldn't know. I think you were too late. I'm... I'm sorry."

Shane looked away, screwing his face up in denial and shaking his head vehemently. He looked back again. "This is crazy! It can't be this way! I *love* you!"

She nodded once more, her eyes glistening with tears. "I loved you, too."

"But how?" he demanded. "She's a ghost! Ghosts can't hurt the living!"

Christiana blinked at him. "What makes you think that?"

Shane shook his head again, refusing to acknowledge the undeniable truth. "Walk with me, Chris. Come with me. We can go around and up to the road. Everything will be fine then." He began to move along the path again, drawing her forward with him. She came, but slowly.

"She met me at the steps," Christiana said, as if the memory was just coming back to her.

"No," Shane protested, not looking at her, simply walking forward, pulling her with him.

"She stood up, like she meant to greet me. The storm was coming, but it hadn't yet started. There was still some light in the sky, and I saw her face. She looked so... so reasonable. So understanding. And I thought to myself, 'Chris, you did the right thing. I'm really majorly creeped out here, but I think this is going to turn out all right after all'..."

Shane could see the trees opening as the woods thinned. He drew Christiana forward, his face grim, turned down in a frown of persistent denial. "Chris, please—"

"She came forward and held out her hand. Her other hand was behind her, but I didn't think anything of it. I went to shake her hand. It's what we're trained to do, isn't it? And she looked so pleasant, so… beautiful. It wasn't just habit. I *wanted* to shake her hand. I wanted to be friends with her. When I got close to her, I could see that she was sad underneath her smile. Her eyes had tears in them. She reached out to me before I could ask her about it, though, and she did more than shake my hand. She drew me into a sort of half embrace. Something hit me in the back. It felt like a baseball, thrown really hard, hard enough to sting. I took a breath to ask what in the hell it was, but the breath… it *hurt*. Hurt like I was inhaling broken glass,"

"Chris, stop!" Shane said, nearly moaning.

"Marlena sort of grunted then, still embracing me," she said, ignoring him. "And I felt something tug inside me. Marlena grunted again, as if she was working at some tough job, and the tug came again, only this time it didn't just tug, it *ripped*. It felt like it took most of my chest out with it, right out of my back. The world keeled beneath me, came up to meet me, and I was grateful for that. I felt so tired all of a sudden. I just wanted to lay there. Marlena stood over me, and the tears were running down her face now. She looked so miserable, so sad. For some reason she had a big set of gardening shears in her left hand. They were wet with something. It glistened in the darkness. She knelt over me and lifted the shears again, opening them with both hands…"

"Stop, Chris! Stop!" Shane cried, turning to her, grabbing her and hugging her to him. "Stop this! Please don't! Please! I can't hear anymore!"

"I know things, Shane," she said, not hugging him back. "I know you could have stopped this. I know you chose to stay. I was the rabbit on your lap. You were supposed to protect me."

"I know!" he cried desperately, hugging her tighter. "I know! I'm so sorry! I failed!"

She hugged him back then, gently but sincerely. "I know," she whispered. "And I was partly responsible too. It's like I told you earlier. Your mess is my mess now. I meant that. I chose it. I could have walked away. Maybe I should have, but I didn't. And you know what? I'm not sorry. In spite of everything, I'm glad I stayed. I loved you. But still. You needed to know."

"Why?" he demanded, his face buried in her shoulder.

He felt her shrug, and then she said, "Because it's part of the view. The part you couldn't see until you were standing right on the edge of the cliff."

"But how could this happen, Chris," he asked again, begging an answer from her.

Christiana shook her head. "I don't know, but I have a sort of inkling. A shadow of an idea. I think it takes a lot to make a ghost, a lot of unresolved business. But that's not the only thing that's going on here. Ghosts alone can't explain it."

Shane ran a hand helplessly through his hair, flinging water from it. "Then what does?"

Christiana sighed deeply and furrowed her brow, looking around at the dark, dripping trees, and suddenly Shane thought he knew what she was going to say. After all, somehow, he'd already dreamed it. "There's a reason why Gus Wilhelm chose this spot to build the Riverhouse, a reason why people all over the world settle in places like this," she said in a low voice. "It's a boundary land. It's where water meets earth. We're drawn to the boundary lands of life, the shores and valleys, the foothills and cliffs. Instinctively, we know such places have power. But this one is unusual. There are other places like it, but not many. Here, the boundary line is a lot deeper. The river forms a boundary between land and water, but also between the present and the past, even between life and death. This is one of the thin spots, where reality is worn almost all the way through to the other side. You can sense it, can't you? I'd bet that everyone who ever came here could. It's like an echo in a room you can't quite see. Here, the line between the dead and the living blurs. Tonight especially. Probably because of the flood, because of the way it brings two points in history together, folded together like pages in a book. Tonight, here at the boundary line, I think the difference between the living and the dead is completely erased."

Shane took both of her hands, drawing her to him. "Then maybe it can be undone," he said urgently. "Maybe what happens here isn't really real!"

She smiled sadly at him. "I don't think it works that way, Shane. I wish it did. Just because nothing that happens here is exactly real, that doesn't mean it's a dream. It just means we can't quite understand it. It just means the normal rules don't apply. Not even the normal ghostly rules."

"But you're *real*," Shane insisted desperately, touching her face. "I can *feel* you."

She didn't say anything; merely looked at him, letting the truth sink in. He hugged her to him. "I'm so sorry, Chris," he said, his voice tight, strained. She nodded. After a moment, she pushed him gently away.

"It's not over," she said. "I know that now. After Marlena was through with me, I was confused for awhile. I was down in the clearing again, just moving around, looking. I saw a dock down by the river, on the other side of the stream. There was a little boat tied to it. The Good Ship Lollipop. I didn't go near it. It scared me. I wandered around, following the stream. I think I was looking for you, waiting for you, although I didn't remember why. I do now. I know things. I need to tell you what I know."

Shane drew a deep breath. It hitched in his chest, but he held it. Slowly, he nodded.

"The first thing," Christiana said, moving toward Shane again, touching his arm. "Is that Stephanie says hello. She misses you. She says you were right about that day at the Spring Garden. Right about everything. She says she is sorry. And she says your child was a girl."

Shane sobbed suddenly, helplessly, and turned away. He reached up and swiped at his tears with the heels of his hands. "A girl," he said, his voice shaking. He laughed a little. "Steph wanted a girl. I think I did, too. A little girl. I wonder what her name was going to be."

"I don't know," Christiana whispered apologetically. "But I saw her. She has her mother's eyes. They're two different colors. Blue and green. But I didn't get her name."

Shane laughed again, and cried again. He turned on the spot, looking blindly around the dark woods. Lightning flashed. He drew another breath and let it out shakily, steeling himself. "All right," he said. "What else? What else do you have to tell me?"

Christiana came close to him. She leaned towards him, as if she meant to kiss him one last time. Shane knew it was too much to hope for, and he was right. She cupped a hand to her lips and leaned close to his ear. He could feel her breath on the side of his neck. Like her cheek, her breath was cold. In a tiny, whisper, almost like a child's secret, she told him.

Chapter Twenty Three

Shane walked on, approaching the end of the footpath. Christiana followed behind him, but she spoke no more. She would be gone soon. He knew it somehow, instinctively. He didn't want to see it happen. The woods opened up before him finally, and he saw the second statue, the one that had appeared in his painting, the one guarding the Riverhouse entrance of the footpath. It was the twin of the one on the other side of the stream, except that this one was male. Its lips were turned up in a gentle smile. Its eyes were blank white orbs in the darkness.

Shane stopped in the shadow of the statue and stared up at the sight that loomed over him, his face draining of color. The clouds were low, moving slowly, massively, like an inverted ocean. Lightning played through them, illuminating them from within. Beneath that sky, towering like a dark sentinel, stood the Riverhouse. It was no longer a half-transparent ghost, or merely a teasing flicker in the lightning. It was as solid as the ground it stood on, but dark, with no lights shining from its tall windows. The chimney was a black monolith, stretching up into the cauldron of the clouds. Rain fell from the awnings and gutters in steady curtains. The rose garden stretched neatly down the slope of the yard, reaching for the river beyond. Shane drew a deep breath and began to walk towards the house, simultaneously repulsed and enthralled. He wanted to run away. He wanted to go inside and never come out again. He warred with himself at every step.

"It's so... tall," he breathed. "I didn't get that part right in the painting. I don't think I could have. There wouldn't have been enough room."

There was no answer. Christiana was gone now. Maybe she had never even been there. A deep sense of loneliness filled him as he approached the house, moving along its side. The chimney rose next to him, complete with its wrought iron W bolted halfway up its height. The metal shimmered in the lightning as water coursed down it. He supposed he could have gone in through the back door, by way of the rose garden, but that didn't seem right. The portico was where he had first met the Riverhouse, at least the version of it that Gus Wilhelm had built, rather than the rambling monstrosity that it had later become. He had only come to know the real house, to taste its silent magic, once that later version had been destroyed. Now, thanks to him, the original Riverhouse had been reborn, returned to its original shadowy splendor. If Shane was going to enter it at all, he would go in through the front door, the one that he had painted, the one below that high round window that looked so much like the one on the east side of his cottage.

He turned the corner and saw the driveway stretching off into the far woods. It was purple in the darkness, each brick straight and crisp, looking sharp enough to cut his finger on. He continued to turn, to move around the front of the house, and saw the portico steps, and the tall pillars on either end, framing the face of the Riverhouse. And he saw Christiana. She lay on her back, her legs tangled on the steps, her shoulders on the bricks of the curved driveway.

Shane stumbled towards her body, his vision doubling with tears. She'd been stabbed in the chest as well as the back. The wounds formed two ragged holes in the fabric of her blouse, dark with blood. Her face looked calmly up at the storm, her eyes open but dull, unblinking as the rain spattered into them. Blood ran in rivulets along the seams of the bricks, spreading away from her corpse in a dim fan. Shane fell on his knees next to the pathetic, diminished figure. He touched her hand, her wet cheek, and then fell on her, laying his head on her cold breast, wrapping his arms around her. She felt horribly light, sodden with rain. He cried against her, delirious with grief.

"This isn't you," he sobbed, repeating the phrase over and over. "This isn't you. You're gone now. I saw you in the woods. You weren't like this. You were better. You were whole. You didn't even have the scratch on your cheek. You weren't even wet. This… isn't… you…"

He tried to convince himself, and yet the vision of Christiana he'd seen in the woods already seemed ghostly, faint, like a mirage. The body that lay on the bricks, broken and bloody, seemed all too real now. All too final. It was his fault. It had been his job to protect her, and he had failed.

Christiana had had her role to play. She was Madeleine. Marlena had always known that Madeleine would come back, had even known that it would happen during a flood. She had watched and waited for that moment, aware that when the time came, she'd have a job to do. A difficult, grisly job, but Marlena was a strong woman. This time around, Marlena knew that Madeleine might not die so easily.

This time around, she hadn't taken any chances.

A rhythmic noise attracted Shane's attention, a dull scuffling sound, and he realized that it had been going on since his arrival on the portico steps. He looked up, following the sound, and saw a figure some distance away, on the other side of the driveway. The figure was dressed in a black raincoat, but wore no hat. It was Earl. He was digging a hole in the shadow of the woods. Shane thought he understood now. The Riverhouse was like a beacon. It was built on the portal, on the boundary line between life and death, between then and now. It drew those who had dwelled in it, brought them back across the gulf, blessed them or cursed them with the task of reliving their roles over and over. Earl had gotten caught in that tide, and now here he was again, still performing his chosen part, even beyond death. After all, he had known, or at least suspected, what had happened between Marlena and her husband. He might even have helped her to cover it up. Now, he was doomed to continue that work, covering up one more murder, burying the evidence. Maybe he knew the truth, and tried to fight it. Maybe he didn't. Maybe for him it was all just a bad dream, like the most vivid nightmare ever.

Shane thought he could understand that feeling.

He climbed slowly to his feet, too weak to raise his voice, to attempt to stop Earl. What good would it do anyway? It was too late. Christiana was gone. He stood swaying on his feet in the rain, Christiana's blood staining his shirt. Slowly, he turned toward the dark house. Marlena's garden shears lay open on the portico, slick with blood. Shane remembered painting those garden shears, placing them in the shadow of the porch next to Marlena's hand. In the painting, she had just finished pruning the rose garden and was resting, her face turned up, one arm raised to shield her eyes from the sun. He had given her those shears, placed them into her hands.

But it was she that had killed with them.

For the first time, Shane felt a spark of anger welling deep inside him. It was small, but persistent. As he looked down at the bloody shears, the anger swelled. His face was still stained with tears, his eyes red and swollen, but the anger emboldened him. The murderer of his love was inside that house, waiting for him. Marlena might end up killing him, too, but somehow Shane didn't think so. She loved him. For the first time, he was glad of that. After all, love is a two-edged sword. Shane knew that now as well as anyone. Maybe, just maybe, he could use that sword himself.

He walked slowly up the portico steps, stepping over the bloody garden shears. He reached for the door but before he could touch it the handle turned by itself. The door swung open silently, revealing a mass of dark shadows, deep and still, waiting for him.

Shane didn't pause. He entered the house, feeling the silent warmth of its rooms engulf him, welcome him, draw him in. Behind him, the door closed. He didn't look back.

The house seemed larger inside than it had appeared from the yard. The rooms felt twenty feet high, dim and silent, thick with shadows. He moved through the hall and crossed into the main parlor. The fireplace was there, but it was dark and cold, filled with gray ash. The curtains were pulled back from the high windows, letting in the glow of the stormy evening. Shadows rippled in that light, cast by the sheeting rainwater, and the shadows gave subtle motion to the entire room. The portrait of Woodrow Wilson stood on the mantel, towering over Shane. The old rejection note was still pinned to the top right corner, now yellowed and brittle with age.

"I'm here," Shane said to the room. "You got what you wanted. Here I am." He hadn't raised his voice, but the silence of the rooms magnified it. He sensed his words echoing throughout the Riverhouse. "I'm here, but not because I want to be. I'm only here because you took away everything that mattered to me. I'd rather be dead. I don't love you. I hate you. I hate everything about you."

The Riverhouse seemed not to care. His words echoed through the rooms and came back to him, sounding small and weak, meaningless. And then, attached to his words, trailing behind them, another voice spoke.

"Five, ten, fifteen, twenty," the voice sang. It was a smiling, female voice. It was the voice of his mother. "Twenty-five, thirty… thirty-five, forty…"

It wasn't his mother. It was Marlena. Her voice came from all around, disjointed, echoes of echoes.

"I don't love you," he said again, but he didn't sound like he meant it. He sounded like a petulant little boy who'd been denied a treat. He tried to remember the bloody gardening shears, the pitiful, diminished shape of Christiana's body, but the memory was slippery. It was hard to concentrate on. And Marlena sounded so pleasant, so warm and comforting. The echo of her voice continued.

"Forty-five, fifty… ready or not, here I come… I hope you didn't hide too well, sweet boy. I'm going to find you, and when I do, I'm going to tickle you! I'm going to tickle you and hug you and never let you go…" She was happy. Shane had never seen or heard Marlena happy. He realized, with some dismay, that it was a wonderful sound. An entrancing sound. He would do almost anything to keep that smile in her voice. Not because he was afraid of her, but because… because he loved her. He always had. Almost from the moment he had first seen her, pathetic and lost in the shadows of the cottage. He had pitied her, and he had wanted to make her happy. He still did, despite everything. Of course he did. She was his mother.

"But you took away what I loved," he moaned, trying to cling to the vision of Christiana's lifeless body. "You ruined everything. I loved her, and you killed her."

"I know it doesn't seem fair," Marlena's voice came, echoing distantly through the rooms, sourceless and directionless, full of sympathy. "I'm sorry it hurt you, my dear son. What hurts you, hurts me. But it was necessary. Someday you'll understand. Someday when you get a little older. Sometimes, grown-ups have to do things that they don't want to do."

Shane nodded. He wanted to believe her. And yet, deep down, he couldn't. Something was wrong. Something about the echoing words was like sweet poison. Marlena wasn't his mother.

But perhaps she could be, a voice whispered from the back of his mind. Shane recognized it. It was the voice of the entity he had first met in his studio, the one that had held the Sleepwalker painting in its invisible grip and squeezed all the air out of the room with its suffocating weight. It was the voice of the Riverhouse itself. *Perhaps she could be your mother. After all, what do you have left? Is this not pleasant? Is it not comforting? What more does a heartbroken boy want than the unconditional embrace of a mother's arms?*

Shane nodded again. It was true.

"I'm going to *fiiind* you," Marlena sang. Her voice was delightful, like silver bells, like birdsong on a spring morning. "And then it will be my turn to hide, and you can find me. We can play together forever, you and I. Oh, I've been looking for you for so long, sweet boy. It's so nice to have you home again. So nice to be back together again, here in the Riverhouse."

It *was* nice to be home, Shane thought dreamily. He stopped and shook himself in the darkness, trying to break the hold of her words, of her smiling, comforting voice. This *wasn't* his home. It wasn't a home at all. It was a tomb, full of restless ghosts. It was the grave of his would-be fiancée. He heard Christiana in his memory. *Something is very wrong*, she had said. He clung to those words, repeating them in his thoughts like a wake-up call. No matter how it feels here, he reminded himself, no matter how it feels in these haunting, silent rooms, it isn't right. It is horribly, poisonously wrong.

Go to her, the whispering voice of the Riverhouse prodded. *Forget what you think you know. What does it matter, now? Go to her. Let her find you. You can't be so cruel as to deny her, can you?*

Shane blinked in the darkness. He looked around, at the looming furniture, the gaping, dark fireplace, the unnaturally tall windows with their streaming, watery glass. It all seemed so huge because he was so small. He was just a boy, barely a toddler. This was a grown-up's world, a world that didn't make a lot of sense to him. His mother would help. As long as he had her, none of it would seem strange or scary. He would go to her. He would climb into her arms, and everything would be all right. He began to move, to walk, to seek her singing, happy voice.

I know things, a voice said in his memory. The voice belonged to someone he used to know, someone named Christiana. Who was she? A playmate? Where was she now? Tears welled in his eyes, because he knew he loved her, but knew he would never see her again. Had she moved away? Had she gotten hurt somehow? Or lost? *I know things*, she'd said to him, and then she'd told him what she knew. Shane thought of her words. They seemed a little funny, but pointless. Christiana had told him a secret. It was about the woman who was singing even now, happily moving through the Riverhouse, looking for him, calling for him.

"I'm going to tickle you..." she called, teasing. "I'm going to tickle you and hug you..."

The spell broke and an overwhelming sense of pity came over Shane, and with it came a realization. Marlena had killed Christiana, but Marlena was also a victim. She was a prisoner and a slave of the Riverhouse itself. Shane looked around. The room still seemed unnaturally tall, but it no longer loomed over him as if he were a child. He walked, crossing the room and passing in front of the portrait of Woodrow Wilson. He passed through the entryway into the kitchen. It was dense with shadows, stacked with cupboards and glass-fronted cabinets, all painted the color of green apples. There was an alcove in the back of the kitchen, between the sink and the huge ice box. He moved toward it, knowing what he'd find hidden around the corner. After all, he had painted the Riverhouse. It existed in his mind. He knew where to go.

"Where are you, you silly boy," Marlena called again. Her voice sounded a bit more distant. "I hope you aren't hiding anyplace you know you aren't allowed to be..." There was a hint of worry in her voice. It pained Shane to hear it.

Go to her, the voice of the Riverhouse soothed. *Comfort her. She is worried. She is afraid. She has waited so very long...*

Shane ignored the pull of Marlena's echoing words. It was very hard. Instead, he turned the corner into the alcove and found what he'd expected. A flight of narrow stairs climbed up into darkness. They were very steep, uncarpeted; the servant's stairs. He began to ascend them.

"I hear you," Marlena called. "Don't be a naughty boy, now. Come to your mama. Come to my arms. Let me tickle you. Let me hug you. I've missed you so much..." Her voice was even more distant now. Shane climbed slowly into the darkness at the top of the stairs. There was a small landing, and then two more stairs to the left. They led to a long hallway, layered with shadows. Doors lined both sides. Shane knew without touching them that they were locked, nailed shut, their keys thrown into the river. He knew that the rooms beyond those locked doors were painted black, from floor to ceiling, covering even their windows. He began to walk down the hall. It was cold. His breath puffed ahead of him. He began to shiver.

Go to your mother. She is heartbroken without you. Don't be so cruel. She loves you. And you love her.

It was the voice of the Riverhouse, and it was louder. It came out of the darkness like chimes from a broken bell. Shane was getting closer to it, nearing what passed for its brain. After all, the house was only as strong as the hands that had built it. Shane was nearing its center, approaching its secret, pulsing core. He walked on, his eyes straining at the darkness. At the end of the hall, barely visible in the shadows, was a painting. It was life sized, rendered with painstaking realism. Shane had seen it before, but only dimly, represented in a child's crayon drawing on cheap newsprint paper. The painting showed a family, a mother and father, and a young child between them. Their faces were perfectly blank, like white balloons. Shane approached the image, not knowing what to expect. The Riverhouse ended beyond that image. There was no place left to go. Marlena's voice echoed to him still, but very distantly. He couldn't make out her words, but he could sense her tone. She was worried, bordering on outright alarm. Her boy had gone where he wasn't supposed to go, where *no one* was allowed to go. He had gone to the place of danger, to the cold dead heart of the Riverhouse itself. She herself didn't even go there, but she would go there now if she had to. She would go there to save him. She was coming even now, her panic driving her faster and faster, despite her own fears. Shane sensed her approach.

He got to the end of the hallway. Even close to, the painting was utterly perfect. He couldn't see as much as a single brush stroke in the meticulously painted figures.

They began to move. They parted, the woman moving to the left, the man to the right. The boy stayed by his mother, held her pale hand. As they moved aside, Shane saw the room beyond. It was Gustav Wilhelm's studio. He stepped forward, entering the portal of the painting, and as he passed through it, the coldness of the hallway fell behind him. The wooden floor of the studio met his feet and he looked back. The painting stood on a tall canvas now, leaning against the wall next to the stairs. It looked exactly as it had at the end of the hall of the Riverhouse, but inverted. The figures had moved back together again, blocking the way back. Shane turned around slowly.

Gustav Wilhelm stood at the work table, leaning against it, his arms folded over his narrow chest.

"Welcome, son," he said. The tone of his voice didn't seem particularly welcoming, however. He seemed to be angry, in fact, but Shane sensed that this was the kind of man who was very practiced at holding his anger in, honing it, sharpening it to a point. "You're a stubborn young man, but I guess I shouldn't be surprised, should I? Like father... like son."

"I'm not your son," Shane said weakly. The force of the man's black gaze was like a weight, pushing him down into the floor.

"You are very naughty not to go to your mother," Wilhelm said, his eyes locked on Shane. "But it does not matter. She comes here to meet you. Perhaps it is best this way. Perhaps it is best that it end this time with all three of us together. It will allow me to see the look in her eyes when it happens. It will be so much more... satisfying."

Shane recognized the man's voice. He'd been hearing it in the back of his head ever since he'd entered the Riverhouse. "You," he said.

"You must think me mad," Wilhelm said, turning now and waving a hand dismissively. He walked toward a back corner of the studio. "Being murdered by your wife will do that to you. Being forced to occupy the scene of your death, to watch your body rot and molder before your eyes, caged for decades in your own crypt, it does have its effects. You couldn't possibly comprehend it. Under the circumstances, I think I've held up remarkably well. In many respects, in fact, I think I've gotten rather better." As he spoke, he moved some of his leaning canvases, looking for something. He nodded to himself, and lifted a particularly large painting from the stack. He turned it around and placed it in the front, showing it to Shane.

"See? Much more evocative than my previous works. Don't you think?"

The painting was meticulously detailed. It showed a complicated mangle of metal glinting in the sunlight. Shane recognized it immediately. It was Stephanie's Honda, lying upside-down next to a stretch of highway. A starburst of broken glass had turned the windshield milky white, but Shane could see the shape of her head behind it. Blood had stained some of the glass pink. It glimmered in the sunlight.

"Breathtaking, isn't it?" Wilhelm said, admiring his work. "There are more. Some of them feature Mr. Stambaugh. Useful man, once I'd gotten my will into him, pried his mind open a bit. Amazing how that sort of crack can be passed on through generations. I liked Mr. Stambaugh a lot more than I do his grandson, but a tool is a tool. Both of them at least know how to get a job done, wouldn't you agree?"

Shane shook his head, unable to take his eyes away from the horrible painting. He'd thought it had been Marlena who'd marked Stephanie, orchestrated her death, but he'd been wrong. He should have known. He remembered the dream he'd had, months earlier, after he had first found Marlena's ghost haunting the cottage. The dream had ended with Shane lost on the footpath, caught in the shadow of something huge and horrible, something that towered over the trees, watching him, studying him like a butterfly pinned to a corkboard. It had been the Riverhouse, grown massive and bloated. But even that had only been a disguise. It had been Wilhelm all along. He had been behind it all, moving beneath the surface like a disease, manipulating and coaxing, weaving his own master plan of revenge.

"I knew she would take a fancy to you," Wilhelm said, as if reading Shane's thoughts. "I knew she would see the similarities in you, the ways you were so like our son. And I knew you would not reject her. You both needed each other, albeit in different ways. I hardly had to do anything. I knew she would inspire you to paint. And I knew you would want to please her. All I had to do was influence and suggest, hint and whisper. It was very simple: take away your wife, give you the silver rattle. Always secretly. Never seen. It was remarkably easy to keep my secrets. Marlena built the wall, closing me off, so she would never again have to look at what she'd done. And it worked. She never saw me here, never sensed me, because she never dared to *look*." He sighed contentedly to himself, shaking his head slowly. "But now she comes, of course. Your 'mother'. She will know the truth, yes, but it will be too late. She always feared I'd return, you see, even when she'd been alive. She lived in terror of it. If only she'd understood the truth. I wasn't going to return. How could I, when I'd never even left?"

"You hate her," Shane said, merely giving voice to his own realization.

"Of course," Wilhelm said, laughing a little. "Wouldn't you? She took everything from me. And now I will return the favor."

Shane stood rooted to the spot by the studio stairs, unable to move, almost unable to breath. *I will return the favor.* Marlena wouldn't kill the man she believed to be her son, but Wilhelm would. It had been his plan from the beginning.

"You understand now, don't you?" Wilhelm said. He stepped toward the round window and sat on the end of the bed. It squeaked slightly, and Shane was chilled by the sight of the skeletal figure cocooned in the sheets. Wilhelm's ghost rested its hand on the shoe of its corpse's skeletal foot. "She denied me everything. My lover, my son, and my life. You can relate, I think. At least in part." He smiled crookedly at Shane.

Shane said, "But she lost all those things, too."

"Once, yes. But that's simply not enough. I'll take those things from her again, tonight. And again and again, if I have my way. Another flood, another replay of her crime, and her just punishment. I'll do it for the rest of eternity. I admit, it is the only thing that gives me pleasure. Besides, what else have I to do?"

"I'm not going to die here," Shane said, but his voice was weak, pathetic.

Wilhelm laughed. "I love your spirit, boy. I'd expect nothing less from you. You do your 'father' proud."

Shane heard the thunder, felt the rumble beneath his feet. He could hear the rush of the river below the bluff. It sounded unusually close.

Wilhelm brightened suddenly. "She comes," he said, glancing toward the stairs.

Shane heard the slam of the door below. A moment later, footsteps sounded on the stairs leading up to the studio. A figure came into view, and Shane turned to look. It was Marlena, of course. There was nothing ghostly about her. For the first time Shane saw her actual eyes, rather than mere empty black holes. They were brown, just like in his painting. She looked around the studio, and saw her husband. Her face went instantly pale, but she didn't seem surprised, exactly. Shane saw that she had always secretly suspected this. She tore her gaze away from Wilhelm, saw Shane, and her face lit with a smile of pure relief. She moved to him, throwing her arms out.

She embraced him. Shane stood there, feeling the warmth of her body, the perfect humanness of her touch. Slowly, helplessly, he put his arms around her. She was shorter than him, nearly the same height that Christiana had been.

"My boy," she whispered harshly. "My naughty boy. Why did you come here? But it doesn't matter now. I have you. I've found you."

Shane drew a breath, trying to remember what this woman had done to Christiana. It was extremely difficult. "I'm not Hector," he said, gritting his teeth. "I'm not your son."

"Shh," Marlena shushed. Shane felt her breath on his chest, felt her tears soaking through his shirt. And he realized something awful. She already knew the truth of his words. She knew it, and was simply denying it. Shane looked over her head, meeting Wilhelm's eyes.

"Of course," Wilhelm said, shrugging languidly. "Of course she knows. But what else does she have? Give her what she wants while you still can. Don't be cruel."

There was another rumble as thunder rolled across the sky outside. The rumble shivered the floor, shook dust from the ceiling. The painting of Steph's mangled Honda keeled forward and fell to the floor with a dull clunk. Wilhelm didn't look down at it.

"What's happening?" Shane asked.

"Shh," Marlena said again, still embracing him. "Hush, son. It's all right now. Hush little baby, don't you cry..." She began to sing.

"What have you done?" Shane demanded roughly, looking at Wilhelm.

"I've done nothing," the man said, still sitting on the end of the bed that bore his own corpse. "Just as I have already said, I've merely watched and waited, suggested and hinted. Nothing lasts forever. Credit me for simply having impeccable timing."

The rumble beneath Shane's feet hadn't stopped. It vibrated in his heels, carried up into his guts. The world seemed to be suddenly full of hidden, subtle motion. He turned his head and looked out the window over the stairs. The trees that bordered the river were inexplicably missing. Shane could see nothing but falling rain and darkness. Slowly, horribly, he began to understand.

Marlena had already lost her son once to the river. Wilhelm meant to see it happen again.

The window cracked suddenly. It shattered as the frame bent out of plumb. Shards of glass fell inside, breaking on the stairs. Wind and rain blew in, billowing the curtains. Shane felt the mist on his face, heard the roar of the advancing river. The rumble beneath his feet grew, became more pronounced. The floor suddenly seemed to be tilted very slightly. It leaned toward the broken window. Paintbrushes rolled off Wilhelm's work desk and clattered to the floor.

"Marlena," Shane said, struggling to control his voice. "You have to let me go. The river is rising. It's broken through the bluff. Do you understand?"

She looked up at him then. Her eyes were beautiful, haunted but clear, adoring. "My boy," she said. "My sweet boy."

"He means to make it happen again," Shane said. "Your husband. He's been planning this all along. It's his revenge. He wants to make you live through your loss all over again. Starting tonight. Starting *now*, Marlena."

A pang of pain swept over her face and a tear spilled onto her cheek. "Call me mama," she said, looking up at him, her voice broken, miserable. "Call me mama. Please. Just once."

She knew it all. None of it surprised her. It was unstoppable.

There was a long, ominous creak. Something crashed downstairs, long and loud, shaking the floor. The cottage leaned. In the distance, a deep, rumbling tremor shook the air. The bluff was falling away into the river, worn away by the decades of floods, finally letting loose. It was just as Wilhelm had said: nothing lasts forever.

"I'm not your son," Shane said, his own eyes welling with tears. "I'm sorry. I'm not him. Your son is dead."

Marlena's lips trembled, turned downwards. Her face filled slowly with anguish, but she still looked up at him, pleading at him with her eyes, begging him not to go on. Shane struggled against the urge to give in to her, to give her what she so desperately wanted.

"I'm sorry," he said, and swallowed thickly, fighting back tears. "I wish I *was* your son. I wish I could give you what you want. But I can't. I'm Shane. Your son's name was Hector. Hector Wilhelm. Hector…"

Shane stopped. His eyes grew unfocussed as his thoughts aligned, clicking suddenly into place. In his memory, he saw Christiana leaning toward him, as if to kiss him. He saw her cup her hand to her lips, felt her breath on the side of his neck as she whispered.

Marlena's maiden name was Smythe, she'd said, cupping the words as if to keep them from escaping. He'd understood the words, but hadn't understood their significance. Now, suddenly, he thought he did.

"Your son's name..." he said, his voice growing firm, grimly certain. "Your son's name was Hector Smythe Wilhelm. In honor of your dead father."

Marlena nodded up at him slowly, miserably.

Across the room, Wilhelm's voice came low and dark. He was standing slowly. "How can you know that?"

"Your husband resisted you on that decision, didn't he?" Shane said, meeting Marlena's gaze. "He wanted to name the boy after himself. Hector Gustav. But you insisted. And he let you win. At least for the moment. Later, when he'd taken your son away from you, he knew he could change it. He could name the boy whatever he wanted. But for the moment, he'd let you win. Your son's name... was Hector *Smythe* Wilhelm."

"Quiet, boy," Wilhelm said menacingly, advancing on Shane and Marlena, his face terrible. "Children should be seen and not heard."

Shane almost laughed out loud. "He hid the truth from you," he said, ignoring the advancing specter. Marlena's brow was furrowed, worried but curious. Maybe even a little hopeful. Shane went on. "It must have taken him so much effort. I can't even imagine. But he did it."

Marlena shook her head slowly, not understanding. Of course she didn't. She didn't know what Shane knew.

He disengaged from her, and she let him go, reluctantly, watching. Shane reached into his pocket. The silver rattle was still there. It jingled as he pulled it out. Marlena watched it, her lips trembling.

"This isn't mine," Shane said, holding it up. Lightning played on its shiny bells, flickered on the smiling cherub's face. "But I know who it belongs to."

"Be *still!*" Wilhelm roared, raising his hands, his face crumpling into a mask of rage. Shane ignored him. He had a strong sense that, unlike Marlena, Wilhelm's ghost really couldn't touch anyone. As Wilhelm watched, Shane raised the rattle and shook it playfully, making the bells jingle and chime.

"Smithy?" he called, but not very loudly. He didn't have to. "Smithy, I have something that's yours. Come on out. You can have it back now."

There was a tiny scuffle on the stairs. Shane looked, and so did Marlena. A figure moved in the shadows. A set of small fingers curled over the banister. A moment later, very slowly and tentatively, a face rose behind the fingers, peering over.

"Rattle," the face said, and then. "Mama."

Shane turned back to Marlena. She was staring at the staircase, her eyes wide, her mouth open in a small O of complete shock.

"Rattle!" the little face said again, and then, with happy excitement: "Mama!"

Marlena moved in a rush, in one single, balletic movement. She swooped to the stairs and swept the small figure into her arms, hugging him to her and calling his name, weeping his name, saying it over and over. They had both been there the whole time, throughout all the decades, and yet somehow, they hadn't known it. Wilhelm had kept them apart, hidden them from each other. It had probably been easier when Marlena had haunted the Riverhouse, and Hector had stayed in the cottage, flushing its toilets and clicking the basement lights. Once the Riverhouse had been destroyed, however, and Marlena had been forced to flee to the cottage, it must have taken Wilhelm an enormous effort to blind them to one another, to stand between them in the darkness like a curtain, hidden himself, and yet separating them from each other. Surely, it had weakened him. Perhaps that was why Wilhelm seemed so powerless now.

"Hector!" Marlena cried, holding her son up, laughing with joy. "Oh, my sweet boy, my wonderful boy! Hector... Hector!"

Hector laughed and squealed in her arms as she spun him around. Shane couldn't help smiling, even as tears ran down his own cheeks. He cried for their reunion, but he also cried for his own lost daughter, the daughter whose name he would never know. He cried for Christiana, dead, sacrificed for this moment. He was sad, but strangely, what he felt most was a sort of bitter joy. Marlena had killed. She had taken away everything that he had loved. And still, in the end, he'd pitied her. And now, helplessly, he rejoiced for her.

Marlena stopped turning Hector in her arms. She looked at him, hugged him, covered his ghostly face with her kisses. Hector grew serious, however. He reached over Marlena's shoulder, his fingers working, opening and closing. "Rattle," he said meaningfully.

Shane approached them. He held the rattle up and Hector smiled. He took the rattle, looked at it in his hand, and then shook it vigorously. In his hand, the sound it made was like fairy music. It sounded like a hundred pixies banging tiny cymbals. The boy laughed happily.

"Do you know who I am?" Shane asked him.

Hector looked at him. He nodded slowly, shyly, still smiling.

"You like to flush toilets, don't you?" Shane asked him, matching the boy's smile. "And to turn on and off the lights?"

The boy nodded again, slowly, as if he thought he might be scolded for his playfulness. Marlena was looking at Shane now, smiling thoughtfully, happily, as she held her son.

"You like to draw, too," Shane whispered. "Don't you, Hector? You like to draw, and you're pretty good at it, just like your mother and father. But you like to use crayons. And chalks."

Hector nodded once again, and then leaned closer to Shane. In a loud, conspiratorial whisper, he said, "I drawed for Nanna Chris. I like Nanna Chris. I open the doors for her. I drawed for her, too. On the floor in the cellar. I didn't like Nanna Chris to get hurt. I helped. You helped, too."

Shane nodded, barely trusting himself to speak. "The drawing on the cellar floor," he whispered. "It was a warning. You knew somehow, didn't you?"

"I *saw* it," Hector said soberly, struggling with his words. "I… dreamed it. I didn't want it to happen. I drawed it to tell you. To help you make it go away."

"It worked," Shane said, tears doubling his vision. "At least for a little while."

Hector stirred in his mother's arms. "Mama and me go home, now," he said, no longer whispering. "Home to the Riverhouse. We can take the Good Ship Lollipop. OK, Mama?" He looked at her earnestly. She smiled at him, laughed, and nodded.

"I suppose, sweetheart," she said. "I suppose we can, just this one time."

She looked at Shane then. There might have been an apology in her eyes, but Shane couldn't be sure. He couldn't even be sure that she saw him. She seemed thinner, somehow. There was less of her there. She turned with Hector in her arms. Slowly, she began to descend the staircase. She hummed to her son as she went, and Hector leaned on her shoulder, one arm around her neck, the other clutching the silver rattle. He shook it as they went. Shane heard them—her melodic humming and his happy jingling—for several moments after they had faded from view.

The cottage shook. It no longer merely vibrated. Now, its motion was a ratcheting, lurching grind, as if the entire structure were rolling slowly downhill on a bed of boulders. For all Shane knew, it was. He struggled to stay on his feet, but it was suddenly a very hard task. He grabbed for the banister with both hands, supporting himself with it. He knew he had to get out, but also knew it was probably too late. Besides, he still had Wilhelm to deal with. He glanced back towards the tilting, rattling studio. Wilhelm was nowhere in sight. He scanned the room, eyes wide. Had it been that simple? Had the mere act of reuniting Marlena and Smithy defeated him? Shane didn't believe it. And then he noticed the bed. The moldy sheets had been thrown back. They lay crumpled half on the floor, stiff with dust and cobwebs. A single leather shoe lay nearby. There was no sign of Wilhelm's corpse.

"You've made a rather large mistake, boy," Wilhelm said. His voice seemed to come from everywhere, from every brick and floorboard, every creaking bone of the shuddering cottage. "I was merely going to kill you. You were meant either to drown in the Riverhouse, or be crushed in the grave of this cottage. Was that so bad? Now, though, I'm going to kill you, and *keep* you. It's only fair, isn't it? You've managed to send away my family. Now, you'll just have to take their place."

Shane looked around wildly, trying to pinpoint the sound of the voice. It was no use. And then, for the second time that night, he thought of the words of the trucker, the one he had met at the diner in Bastion Falls. *Haulin' ass is a valuable life skill,* he'd said, *you never know when it'll come in handy.*

Shane bent his knees and tried to steady his balance on the creaking, tilting floor. Holding onto the banister, he worked his way around to the stairs. Glass gritted and cracked under his feet. The cottage creaked ominously and Shane couldn't resist looking out the shattered remains of the window. All he could see was rain falling into darkness. The sound of the river was loud and hungry, busy, going about its destructive work.

"Stay here, why don't you?" Wilhelm said, his voice calm, almost playful. "Stay with me. What's the point of trying to escape?"

"I don't think you can even hurt me," Shane called out as he worked his way down the steps, leaning hard on the exterior wall. "If you could, you would have done it when I called out for Smithy, your son. You'd have stopped me. I think you wasted all your strength keeping Marlena and Hector apart all those years. She was the stronger one. That's why she was able to touch us, and to kill Chris."

"Her strength was my strength," Wilhelm replied casually. "She did what I allowed her to do. What the Riverhouse allowed her to do. But you were right about one thing. I couldn't stop you. Not then. I was too divided. It's hard work, revenge. But things are different now, as you can see."

Shane reached the bottom of the steps. His bedroom was already mostly gone. Rain and wind tore at the remains of the bedroom floor, which jutted, naked and shattered, out over darkness. Vertigo tried to grip him, to freeze him in his tracks, but he resisted it, turning away, toward the hall. He began to work his way along it, fighting the disorienting lean and rumble of the walls all around him.

"I don't believe you," Shane called out, gritting his teeth, steadying himself on the frame of the basement door. He could tell by the sounds from below that the basement was already gone, ground away into the guts of the collapsing bluff. "I think the thing you're best at is lying."

"I have watched my body all these years," Wilhelm mused, ignoring Shane. "I watched it molder away to bones and dust. I knew that if I ever entered it again, I would be doomed to inhabit it again forever. As a spirit, one simply understands these things. The use of my corpse would be futile to me in the long term, but what does it matter now? My time here is nearly done. It was worth it to rejoin my bones in order to stop you, to imprison you here with me, to keep you with me forever. *You* will be my son now, since you succeeded in taking mine from me. Perhaps it is even better this way. He never wanted me, once he learned the truth. But you will accept me. You will love me. In time."

"You're crazy," Shane called, moving now across the floor of the living room, toward the front door. It hung open on one hinge, swinging like a broken bat's wing. Beyond it, the night boomed and flashed, beckoning.

Wilhelm laughed then, long and loud. "I am indeed crazy. We discussed that, already, if you recall. Death does it to you. You'll find out soon enough."

"Not if I can help it," Shane said, gripping the frame of the door, pulling himself toward it.

"But you can't," Wilhelm's voice whispered in his right ear. A skeletal hand wrapped around Shane's neck. It was surprisingly strong. Wilhelm's other hand clutched Shane's head, covering the top half of his face like a bony spider. Wilhelm laughed again, pulling, dragging Shane backward into the collapsing cottage. Shane smelled the rancid puff of the corpse's breath. He was still holding the frame of the door with one hand, but his fingers were slipping, one by one. He beat at the skeletal arms with his free hand, but it was no use. The skeleton drug him backwards, breaking Shane's grip on the doorframe. The darkness of the cottage surrounded him, and Shane panicked. He coiled his strength and lunged with his legs, heaving forward. The skeleton was strong, but it was light. Shane carried it forward with him now, and it clung to him, squeezed him in its unforgiving grip. Shane felt the jaws snap at him, clacking together next to his ear. He reached for the doorframe again, caught it, and began to pull himself forward once more. The cottage groaned suddenly, enormously, and began to slide beneath him. It juddered and rammed into something buried in the bluff, slamming again to a halt. Windows shattered all around and the chimney disintegrated, falling ponderously apart and leaving a gaping black hole in the side wall. The Riverhouse painting fell into the darkness. Shane slipped on the wet floor and collapsed, falling full length with his fingers on the doorstep, gripping it. He struggled to pull himself forward, fighting the tilt of the floor.

"Come with me, son," the corpse of Wilhelm rasped in his ear. It was grinning, although Shane wasn't sure that it had much of a choice. Cold rain ran into the house in splattering rivulets, soaking him and making the floor slippery. Shane bared his teeth and moaned, straining his arms, inching forward. He got one elbow over the edge of the doorstep. The porch had folded down, away from the door. Its roof was entirely gone, pulled away and to the side, leaving nothing but booming clouds overhead. Shane could see out over the yard. Its angle looked all wrong. It seemed to slope precipitously away from him, and yet Shane knew that it was actually level. It was the cottage that was falling away, sliding, grinding, disintegrating into the river behind it. It wouldn't last much longer. His arms revolted against him. They trembled, strained to the limit. The skeleton pulled him, breathing its rotten breath into his ear, laughing.

Movement caught Shane's eye. He glanced toward it and saw something small and dark, moving stealthily, approaching the cottage. A flicker of lightning revealed it, lit in its bright, green eyes. It was a cat; Tom the cat. Shane felt a giggle of madness bubble inside him. And then, he heard the cat's strange, high voice. It was yowling.

"RRooooowwwwwww!" it cried, long and thin under the roar of the storm.

Wilhelm's corpse stopped pulling Shane. It went still on his back, the bony hands loosening their grip ever so slightly.

"RRRROOOooooowww!" the cat howled, as if it were in heat. It crept slowly across the yard, closing the gap between them slowly, lifting its feet stealthily above the wet grass and putting them down without disturbing a single green blade. "Yooooowwww," it said. "YOOOooowwwww!" It sounded almost human.

Wilhelm's corpse shuddered. It began to push away, not taking its gaze from the advancing cat. Shane took the opportunity to scramble upright. He gripped the doorframe and pulled himself out onto the remains of the porch. The skeleton had gotten tangled in Shane's clothing, however, and it came as well, suddenly scrambling, trying to disengage itself.

"No," Wilhelm said. "How...?"

"YOOooowww!" the cat cried, and it sounded like a word. It sounded like it was saying the word "you", over and over, accusingly. Another series of lightning flashes barraged across the sky, and in the flashes, Shane saw more than a cat. A human figure seemed to be crawling across the yard, its head raised, glaring at Wilhelm. It was rotten and wasted, bent over in a deformed parody of the cat's stealthy creep. It looked vaguely, perversely female. Shane suddenly recalled something Steph had said a long time ago, as if in a different life. *When I was a little girl,* she'd told him, *I thought all cats were girls.*

"Yooouuuu!" the cat-thing howled, its voice no less damning than an accusing finger. *"You!!!"*

"No!" Wilhelm's corpse cried, its bony joints still caught in the fabric of Shane's shirt. It ripped and pulled, tearing itself away from him, its ghastly face still locked onto the approaching creature. Shane finally saw Wilhelm's dead body in its entirety. Tufts of black hair still clung to the cracked skull, along with the partial remains of a face, dried and leathery. Its clothing was rotted and threadbare, pocked with moth holes. Amazingly, the corpse no longer seemed to be smiling. The jaw creaked open and Wilhelm's voice rasped, "You're dead!"

"Ssso are *yoooouuu,* lover," the cat-thing hissed. In the lightning, it had begun to stand, to pull itself into a slightly more human posture. But still it stalked, creeping forward. It was horrible. Long sheets of black hair hung from its skull like seaweed. The eyes were blank holes. The grin was more giddy than Wilhelm's had been. It was still vaguely catlike. "But I *knewww* you'd never leave me... I *knewww* if I only *waited...*"

"I meant to," Wilhelm's corpse said, still trying to clamber away, not noticing that it had gotten its skeletal foot lodged in the crack between the porch and the leaning cottage. "I always... you know that..."

"I spent nearly all of my lives waiting," the cat-thing said. "But you caaaaame baaaack... just like I *kneeeeww* you would. I thought you would be only a ghost... a wisp of a memory, useless to me, but you put on your *best* for meeee... you put on your *body,* so I could *touch* you... so I could *loooove* you. Just like we *planned.* Don't you remember?"

Wilhelm began to flail, to clamber backwards, and yet his distraction made him reckless. He was caught in the jaws of the broken porch. His hand broke away between two planks. His jaw clacked and jibbered. Shane could've sworn that his remaining hair was sticking up in terror.

The cat-thing was nearly upon them. It paid Shane no attention at all. It scooped Wilhelm up into its horrible arms, and lightning lit it brightly, revealing it in all its rotten horror. It looked a little like the cat, and a little like Christiana. It was neither.

"Mad!" Wilhelm shrieked, throwing up the remains of his hands, beating uselessly at the thing as it embraced him, pulled him upright. "Madeleine! I didn't mean for it to happen like this...!"

"*Yoooouuu promisssed,*" the thing hissed. "You *promised* to take me *away* from all thissss... but it isn't too late. Yoooouuu came *back...* Kissss me, lover... kiss me like you *used* to..."

The thing opened its mouth, revealing a set of long, yellow fangs. The mouth unhinged, yawned wider and wider, distorting the face. It looked like a cat hissing, and still the mouth grew, eating into the face, exhaling with rapture. The Madeleine-thing gripped Wilhelm's head. It drew him forward, into its yawning jaws, and it bit the front half of his skull off. His head shattered, exploding with bits of rotten flesh and tendon. Wilhelm's hair was caught in his lover's teeth, and still he screamed, beating weakly at the thing's head and shoulders. The Madeleine-thing moaned with ecstasy. It opened its jaws again, and pushed Wilhelm's corpse further inside.

Shane could watch no more. He lunged forward, forgetting his spent muscles and overworked lungs. He threw himself up onto the yard and grabbed fistfuls of the wet grass, using them as handholds, pulling himself forward. With maddening lethargy, he struggled to get his feet beneath him. Rain pelted him in sheets, chilling him to the bone, but he barely noticed. Behind him, both the cottage and Wilhelm seemed to scream. Their mingled shrieks filled the air, rising, rising, until they passed right out of the range of Shane's hearing. He pelted across the grass, stumbling and slipping, but managing to stay upright. Finally, as he reached the perimeter of the woods and felt the blissfully hard surface of the packed driveway beneath his feet, he turned, panting, leaning with his hands on his knees.

The pickup truck had rolled sideways as the gravel pull-off caved in beneath it. The cottage itself was keeled backwards, half crushed and nearly unrecognizable. Its broken windows were like black eyes, staring up at the sky in shock. Gradually, accompanied by a deep, guttural groan, it began to slide. It moved as if in slow motion, turning on its foundation, the stonework disintegrating and popping loose in chunks. It swiveled and slid backwards, imploding in on itself as it went. The shed came into view as it splintered into sticks. For one second, Shane saw his bicycle inside, glinting in the lightning, tumbling backwards. And then, just before the structure slid away entirely, Shane saw the round window on the upper side of the east wall. Its glass was shattered and gaping, leaving glittering fangs all around. In the lower arc of the window, a tiny shaft of pale white still stood. Shane glimpsed it for less than a second, but it was long enough for him to see, and to remember. The candle's flame was dark. It had finally, and forever, gone out.

The crash of the cottage was almost entirely lost in the grating rumble of the rest of the bluff as it finally gave way. The death rattle of its destruction carried down the driveway as a sustained tremor, a dull roar that Shane felt as much as he heard. And then, finally, it was over.

Rain fell all around. It shushed among the trees, which stood strangely still now, without any wind to move them. It was as if the storm had finally spent itself. Shane shivered, both with cold and with a sense of debilitating, morbid exhaustion. He felt as if he could lay down right there on the gravel of the driveway and go straight to sleep. He didn't dare, of course. The Madeleine-thing had probably gone with the cottage, but he couldn't be sure. It was simply too dreadful even to think about.

He turned and began to shuffle down the hill toward the Valley Road.

Lightning flashed among the distant clouds. In its white flicker, Shane saw the glint of metal and glass at the foot of the driveway; Christiana's car, of course. He angled toward it, knowing that it was no use. The Valley Road would be flooded and impassable. And besides, Christiana's keys had been on the kitchen counter in the cottage. They were at the bottom of the river now, buried in a grave of brick and stone.

Shane reached the car, sloshing through the mud on the driver's side, and tried the door. It was unlocked. He plopped inside and pulled the door shut after him, finally shutting out the persistent roar of the storm. He reached instinctively for the ignition and his fingers struck something, producing a low, musical jingle. He thought of Hector's rattle, but that wasn't it, of course. It was Christiana's keys. He looked and saw them hanging from the ignition, glinting darkly. He wasn't all that surprised, considering.

He turned the key and the car started right up. The radio sprang to life, loud, shocking him for a moment. For a split second, he was convinced that it was playing "The Good Ship Lollipop" at him at full volume, but of course it wasn't. Christiana had had a soft spot for oldies. For now, the local golden age station was playing an old Anne Murray song. Shane thought it was called "You Needed Me". He turned it down, but let it play on. For the moment, he was simply too tired to do anything but sit there.

The car was probably still too stuck in the mud to move, especially after all the rain of the night. The Valley Road was probably impassable, although it was slightly possible that the northbound lane, the length that ran away from Bastion Falls, might still only be covered by a half foot or so of water. Maybe it didn't even matter what he did. He sighed, exhausted and numb, bereft and shocked at everything he had seen. What could possibly matter after all of that?

On the radio, Anne Murray sang, "You held my hand when it was cold. When I was lost, you took me home. You gave me hope when I was at the end..."

Shane drew a deep, shaking breath and turned, peering out of the car's rear window. The road seemed mostly clear at the end of the driveway. Maybe he should give it a try. Maybe he'd make it. Maybe he wouldn't. But he could at least give it a shot. He owed that much to Christiana. It was too much to think about moving on after everything that had happened, too much to comprehend the enormity of living life in the wake of the Riverhouse. But he could maybe handle shifting the car into reverse and pushing the gas a little. Just to see what might happen. The next steps could handle themselves.

He exhaled. He shifted the car into reverse. Slowly, he pushed the accelerator.

Somehow, the car moved. Maybe the tires had settled enough into the mud, adhered enough to it to form a tentative grip. Maybe. Or maybe somebody had given the car a little push. Shane didn't think it mattered.

He backed slowly out onto the Valley Road, leaving long, muddy tire tracks on the wet pavement. A moment later, he shifted into Drive. Slowly, he pressed the accelerator and the car rolled forward. Shane steered weakly, and let the car pick up speed. Water splashed up into the wheel wells, but it was manageable. He thought he'd probably make it to the top of the hill. After that, he didn't know what would happen next. Neither did he care.

On the radio, Anne Murray continued to sing. Shane let her.

Chapter Twenty Four

From *the Bastion Falls Monitor*, November 5, 2009

Historic Local Landmark Destroyed in Mudslide; Potential Victim Still Missing

The building that once housed painter Gustav Wilhelm's art studio, famed for his portraits of presidents and royalty, was lost to a mudslide yesterday which destroyed it and most of the bluff it had been built upon. Current owner of the structure, Shane Bellamy, 35, escaped the destruction with minor injuries, although a friend, Christiana V. Corsica, 30, who had been hiking nearby at the time, is still missing.

"It's never a good idea to take nature for granted," Franklin Sherman, head of the Jefferson County Department of Parks and Recreation, said in an interview this morning. "Erosion is a serious threat to any riverfront property, no matter how long it seems to have stood the test of time. We can only hope that Ms. Corsica wasn't in the area when the slide took place, although we should be careful not to be too optimistic at this point."

Citizens familiar with the history of the river valley will recall that the studio's sister property, the official Wilhelm residence once known as the Riverhouse, was torn down in August of this year, after decades of water damage and deteriorating conditions.

Gustav Ferdinand Wilhelm moved to the Missouri River valley from New Hampshire in the spring of 1933, bringing with him both a worldwide distinction and a unique culture of the arts that has remained in the area to this day. While Wilhelm himself was only known to occupy the properties until the mid-nineteen forties, his artistic impression, and the mystery of his life after Bastion Falls, has left a lasting mark on the culture of the town. Thus, while the properties had long since been broken up and resold, the demolition of both the studio and the Riverhouse in such close proximity seems to mark a particularly poignant end to a decades' long era.

From *the St. Louis Post Dispatch*, November 7, 2009

Jefferson County sheriff's deputies are investigating a death Wednesday near the River Valley Road seven miles north of Bastion Falls. Col. Jay Sappington said 30-year-old Christiana V. Corsica of St. Louis was found dead Wednesday morning, having apparently drowned during a flash flood while hiking.

"It appears the female died sometime during the recent flood and was discovered in the woods this morning by parks workers sent to clean up an outdoor storage facility," he reported.

Sappington said officers are unsure of the circumstances surrounding the death at this time, since the body seems to have suffered at least two puncture wounds, either before or after the time of death. The body has been sent to the state crime lab for an autopsy.

"Floods can move very quickly, carrying debris with an awful lot of force. The body could very well have been damaged by broken tree branches, or thrown against some sharp objects during the deluge." Sappington said. "At this point, we are operating under the assumption that this was an accidental death. We'll know for sure once we get the results of the autopsy, but I'm not expecting any surprises."

He said the autopsy is scheduled for 10 a.m. Thursday.

Chapter Twenty Five

On the one year anniversary of the night that the cottage fell into the river, Shane went for a bike ride along the river trail. It was a crisp, cool day, but bright, without a single cloud in the hard sapphire sky. He parked the Saturn in the gravel lot at the end of the park, two miles north of where he used to live. It wasn't Christiana's Saturn, but it was similar. Hers had gone to her parents, along with the rest of her worldly goods. Shane knew how such things worked, of course. His Saturn was a similar model, but dark silver in color, with four doors and a new Thule bike rack attached to the trunk. Shane climbed out, unhooked his bike (no longer a Trek, but a perfectly serviceable used Giant) and straddled it, squinting around at the park and the trail. The ball diamond was empty, with a carpet of leaves covering most of the outfield. The tiny cinder block building that housed the restrooms was locked for the season. Beyond a line of ancient trees, the river moved serenely, fat and lazy, brown in the sunlight. Apart from the wind, nothing moved. No one was in sight. Shane stood on the pedals, pushing the bike forward and angling onto the trail connected to the gravel lot.

It was the first time that Shane had been back on the trail since that fateful night. It wasn't that he'd stayed away on purpose, exactly, or so he thought. It was just that there was too much associated with the area, too much loss and sadness, too much ugliness. Worse, not all of it was his own. The river valley collected such things, hoarded its occupants' horrors like teeth on a necklace. It wasn't that the river valley was evil, necessarily. It just couldn't help being what it was. It was a boundary land, and a particularly powerful one. *This is one of the thin spots,* Christiana had told him, or maybe that had only a dream. After all, she'd been dead by then. *One of the thin spots, where reality is worn almost all the way through to the other side. You can sense it, can't you?* Shane could. He guessed that, deep down, everyone that came here sensed it. It was the very thing that drew them, like moths to a flame. Everyone is fascinated with the cliff edges of life. Everybody thinks they can creep up to the edge and peek over and not fall off. Nobody remembers that there are other things out there, unseen and sneaky, waiting to give a little push at just the right moment. Shane knew that now, but he'd paid a very high price to learn it. When he was honest with himself, he knew he was still paying it.

It's part of the view, the ghost of Christiana had told him, her voice hollow, resigned, *the part you couldn't see until you were standing right on the edge of the cliff.*

Shane rode, and soon enough he came to the gravel drive. It cut through the trees, leading up the first hill toward his old property. It had never really been his, though, even if the insurance people had sent him a decent check in the wake of its destruction. The cottage had never really stopped belonging to Gustav Wilhelm. It belonged to him still, wherever it was. He'd bound himself to his corpse, after all. Wherever the cottage was, he was there too, broken and smashed, half-devoured by the crazed thing that had once been his lover, Madeleine. Shane shuddered, thinking of it. He turned the bike's wheel onto the gravel and pedaled it up the hill, shifting into first gear.

The yard was there, but overgrown, dominated by weeds and tall, swishing grass, now mostly yellow. Part of the porch remained, reminding Shane of the portico of the Riverhouse, left like a headstone, a reminder of what once was. Beyond the remains of the porch, however, the ground fell away. Shane stood on the broken planks and looked down. The formerly steep angle of the river bluff had been reduced to a ragged jumble of boulders and scree, descending toward the river below. There were bits of the cottage buried in that chaotic slope, Shane knew. Not all of it had ended up in the river. He sighed, and the sigh turned into a shudder. Without another thought, he turned and walked back to the gravel drive, where his bike leaned on its kickstand, casting a hard, skeletal shadow.

He pressed on, pedaling swiftly, feeling the cool wind push past him, listening to the crunch of the leaves under the bike's tires.

He stopped once more, at the end of the old brick driveway. The parks crews still used the lot as a storage facility, so it was hard to see the site of the old house, hard to make out the shape of the stone portico. He stood on tiptoes, still straddling his bike, and squinted toward the back of the lot. What he saw made him smile grimly. The portico was still there. The reason he hadn't been able to see it was that weeds had grown up all around it, obscuring it. Beyond it, the dirt-filled cellar was completely buried in wild grass. It swished in the breeze, singing its own senseless tune. The boundary land could collect, but it couldn't hold onto anything permanently. *Nothing lasts forever,* Wilhelm had said. Perhaps even he hadn't fully understood the truth of those words.

"Nothing lasts forever," Shane said aloud, looking at the portico in its grave of weeds, looking at the spot where he had found Christiana's broken body. He'd wanted to go back himself to find her, once the storm was over, once the water had receded enough for him to return to the river valley. The parks workers had beaten him to it, however. Maybe that had been for the best. Detective Weekes, at the Bastion Falls Police Department, had been suspicious of Shane to begin with. If he had showed up with Christiana's lifeless body, things probably would have gotten a lot more complicated.

Shane hadn't spoken to Detective Weekes since that night. For his own part, Weekes seemed to have let the matter go. Maybe he'd decided that, strange as it all seemed, there was nothing specifically incriminating about any of it. Or maybe he'd decided that some questions were simply best left unanswered, and some stories were best left untold. If that was the case, Shane gave him credit. If that was the case, then Weekes was a very smart man indeed.

Shane pedaled on. He rode all the way to Bastion Falls and back. On the way back, he passed both the Riverhouse and the old gravel drive again without so much as a backwards glance.

Shane's new life, what he thought of as his second do-over, had started with taking a class at the university in nearby Webster Groves. He couldn't bring himself to paint again, at least not yet, so he'd decided to learn Photoshop. He took an evening class, and was surprised to see how many other middle-aged men and women were sharing the class with him. The instructor was a tall guy, about Shane's own age, and he'd explained to them that most college-agers had grown up using graphics programs like Photoshop. It was the people who'd entered the industry before the "digital revolution" who were coming back to classes like his, looking to pick up some new skills and "enhance their productivity". He'd told them not to worry, that they'd catch up quickly, and soon enough be running rings around their younger counterparts, since they brought with them an old school sense of design and experience, rather than merely the ability to draw with a mouse and a love of video games. And to Shane's delight, the instructor had been right. What had seemed utterly clumsy and incomprehensible on the first day of class had quickly become not only manageable, but inspirational. Shane began to tentatively envision how the mix of traditional art and digital enhancement could open up interesting new horizons for his own art. He started to experiment with it. He scanned some of his charcoal drawings and colored them in Photoshop, clumsily at first, but with a giddy sense of excitement at the possibilities. His instructor seemed impressed, not only with Shane's curious fusion of styles, but with his drawings.

"Have you ever considered teaching?" the instructor had asked him one evening after class.

"Teaching? No," Shane had said, shaking his head dismissively. "I'm not a teacher. What would I teach, anyway? I can barely keep up with all this stuff."

"That's not true and you know it," the instructor smiled. "But I'm not talking about teaching Photoshop. I'm talking about teaching drawing. You have an instinctive understanding of how it works, and why it's important, especially in digital media. Most of the kids here don't get that. They come in here thinking they can just grab a mouse and start creating. They don't understand that art rarely starts that way. It can't go straight from the head to the screen. It needs a halfway house, and that halfway house has to be something concrete, something real. Something as simple as a piece of paper and a pencil. I was just telling this to the head of the department, telling him we need a new class, something like 'drawing for the digital age'. Something to show these kids how important that step is, and to give them the basics of how to get started with it, the simple building blocks of perspective and contrast, balance, conceptualization, all of that."

Shane shook his head, flattered but skeptical. "I see what you're saying, but... you can't mean me. I wouldn't even know where to start."

The instructor shrugged. "Just think about it. I think you'd be surprised at yourself. I think you might even enjoy it."

Shane *had* thought about it. A few weeks later, he had approached the instructor and told him he was willing to give it a shot, *if,* that was, they were willing to take the risk that he might be awful at it. They were more than willing, and Shane suddenly found himself walking into a classroom as a teacher instead of a student. He was petrified on his first day, and spent most of the first twenty minutes standing behind his desk, reading verbatim from a sheaf of notes he'd prepared the night before. The students merely stared at him, dead-eyed and bored, until he'd finally sighed, dropped his notes on his desk, and told them he didn't know what the hell he was doing.

This had, of course, brought a smile and a trickle of laughter from the students. Shane moved to the front of his desk, leaned on it, and simply asked them what they wanted from the class. Once he got them talking, he found it easier to relax, to step out of his own insecurities and into the role he had been hired for. He realized, with a small shock of surprise, that he really did have something he could teach these students. Further, he realized that they wanted to learn it. Slowly, tentatively, he developed a rapport with his students. They liked him, and Shane was pleasantly stupefied to realize, halfway through the semester, that they were, in fact, benefitting from his instruction. By the end of the fall term, Shane had signed a contract to teach full time the next year. It wasn't great money, but it was enough. Shane had learned to live much more simply. In the wake of the previous few years, living simply had become a relatively easy choice.

When he wasn't teaching, Shane had begun to experiment with painting again. Not oils, of course. Shane had a feeling that he'd never paint with oils again. Instead, he tinkered with watercolors. One day, he had gone into the college art store and bought a set of cheap watercolors and a handful of brushes. He'd gone back to his apartment, feeling simultaneously hesitant and excited, and determined that he would paint the first thing he saw. As it turned out, the first thing he'd seen had been an old chair that he'd picked up at a junk shop downtown, a place called Burris Trader. He'd drug the chair out into his apartment's tiny back yard, sat down on the rear stoop with a pad of watercolor paper on his lap, and painted the chair where it sat in the sun. The result had surprised him. The watercolor was light, messy, bleeding slightly where the colors touched, and yet Shane had sort of liked it. The image was pleasantly surreal, with the chair gleaming in the brightness, set against the backdrop of the alley and a chain link fence. It probably wasn't what anyone else would call art, but Shane had been almost absurdly pleased with it. He liked it a lot, no matter what anyone else might think of it. He'd waited for it to dry, then placed it in an old frame and hung it in his kitchen, where the light from the window could play on it.

The next weekend, he had gone down to Burris Trader and bought another chair. This one had been an antique dining room chair with a ratty velvet cushion. He paid twelve dollars for it, placed it on the back seat of his Saturn, and drove it out to the edge of town. He found an old, black train bridge that spanned a side road. Parking on the shoulder in the shadow of the bridge, he collected his paints from the trunk, hefted the chair in his other hand, and lugged it up the slope of the weedy hill. He set the chair in the middle of the tracks, sat down himself on one of the rails, and began to paint. He had to jump up and move the chair twice, making room for the occasional freight train, but that was all right. He smiled up at the engineers as they rumbled past, tipping a finger to his forehead. One of the engineers tipped a salute back at him, unsmiling.

When the painting was done, Shane simply looked at it. He took it home, framed it, and hung it next to the first one. Together, they formed an interesting series, part whimsical, part bizarre. Shane thought, with some satisfaction, that they were delightful. It was a new series, and it was entirely his own, created independent of both the muse and the foreman in his head. Looking at the two paintings, he felt like he had rediscovered some small part of himself. It filled a hole. Not completely, but a little. Maybe that was the best he could hope for.

He donated the old kitchen chair to Goodwill. The next weekend, he went back to Burris Trader and bought another chair. It became his hobby. He gave one of the paintings to his old Photoshop instructor, who was far more impressed with it than Shane had expected. He'd hung it in his office and suggested that Shane sell his works, maybe at the coffee shop near the campus. Shane thought it was a good idea, mainly because he had quickly run out of room for the paintings on his own walls. The manager of the coffee shop, a twenty-something girl with a nose ring and a half dozen short pony-tails jutting from her head at all angles, had agreed easily, especially since Shane insisted on selling them very cheaply.

"Cheap enough for college students," he'd told her, smiling. "I don't want them hanging around here gathering dust. If I'm going to sell them, I want them sold."

They did sell. As they did, Shane painted more. The students that frequented the coffee shop called them Crazy Chairs, with that strange mixture of affection and sarcasm that seemed to be the hallmark of their generation. Shane didn't mind, but he didn't call them that himself. He didn't really call them anything, but what he thought of them was just the opposite. He thought of the paintings as his Sanity Chairs series.

He supposed that didn't have quite the same ring to it, though.

At night, Shane thought sometimes about Christiana. He thought about how much he missed her, and what their life together might have been like, had he done things just a little bit differently. He tried not to dwell on it, but in the long sleepless hours after the lights went off and the world shut off its distractions, it was hard not to. He sort of thought he owed it to her. It was his penance, maybe. It was just part of the view, the part he hadn't been able to see until he'd stood right on the edge.

He thought about Stephanie, too. He thought about the daughter he'd never know, the one who had two different colored eyes, just like her mother. He wondered what her name was, and where she was, if she was with Stephanie. And he wondered if he'd ever find them, someday, when it was all over. He hoped so, but he couldn't know for sure. For now, hope was good enough, even if, in those long nighttime hours, the hope felt tiny and flimsy, and reality felt hard and cold, more like a stone than a curtain, separating them from him, maybe forever.

The day after Shane went on his last bike ride along the river trail, he slept in late. It was Sunday, and he knew that Burris Trader wouldn't open until eleven, if that. The owner, Henry Burris, was an old guy who kept fairly sporadic hours. Henry had asked Shane what in the world he bought all those chairs for, and Shane had told him about his paintings, even showing him one of his most recent examples, which had been in the back of the Saturn, on its way to the coffee shop. Henry had studied it critically, apparently unimpressed. From then on, however, Henry had taken it upon himself to point out any new chairs that came into his junk shop, even suggesting which ones he thought would make the best subjects for Shane's "pitchers".

"Got a new one in for ya," Henry said when Shane entered the store that day, jingling the bell over the door. He stood up from the wooden chair behind the front counter, peering over his reading glasses and nodding toward the far corner of the crowded showroom. "Over there in the back, under the window. Came in with a whole truckload of salvaged junk from one of my dealers. Water damaged, I'd guess, based on the condition of the upholstery. I'll give you a good deal on it. Go take a look."

Shane went and took a look. As he approached the far end of the store, weaving through the precariously stacked antiques and shelves of forgotten miscellany, the musty showroom brightened. The sun had come out from behind a cloud, spearing through the big, dirty window and lightening the entire place, transforming it from a drab junk shop into a whimsical attic, packed with unknown treasures. The sunbeam landed on the chair, lighting it like a diamond in a jeweler's display case. Shane stopped, blinking at it. It was upholstered in a dull embroidered fabric that had probably once been very colorful. The legs were wooden, crafted into tapering curves.

Shane approached it slowly. He recognized it, of course. He'd already painted it once. The only thing missing was the purse, sitting open on its cushion. He touched it, felt its threadbare upholstery. It smelled musty and old.

And then he turned, slowly, looking behind him, sweeping his gaze over the rest of the recent salvage. It was piled haphazardly, not quite ready for display. None of it had price tags on it yet. Shane stopped. His expression didn't change. The truth was, he wasn't really surprised at what he saw. He crossed the aisle, moving to the dark corner beneath the window.

The Riverhouse painting sat atop an old roll-top desk, leaning in the shadow of a pile of old shutters.

Shane approached it. It was frameless, filthy, bent out of true so that the canvas bulged slightly, loose in its struts. It looked far older than Shane knew it was. He squinted at it, and then reached to touch it. He felt the texture of the paint, ran his fingers gently over it, over the lower right corner, where Christiana's shadow had once appeared. It wasn't there now. The image looked exactly as he had originally painted it. Marlena sat on the portico, leaning back on one hand, her other raised to her brow, shielding her eyes from the sun. She looked like she was peering right out of the painting, right at the viewer. It was just a trick of perspective, however. She wasn't looking at anything. She was only paint on canvas. Marlena was gone.

Shane raised his eyes, looking toward the top of the painting, and blinked in surprise. Penn Oliver's note card was still there, pinned to the upper right corner. It had gotten wet and adhered itself to the canvas. It looked like an old receipt that had accidentally gone through the wash. He reached for it, tentatively, and plucked at it. It came away easily, leaving a lighter patch on the canvas beneath it.

He looked at in his hands. It had bent over onto itself, obscuring the handwriting. He unfolded it gently, careful not to tear it. He remembered what Penn Oliver had written, but for some reason he was curious. He had a suspicion, an inkling, and as he opened the note, he saw just what he expected. The handwriting was different now. Christiana was a lefty, after all. Her backward slanting cursive was immediately recognizable. Shane read it several times.

Her name is Amelia. After your mother.

Shane didn't buy the painting, or the chair that had come with it. But he did keep the note. Henry Burris didn't mind one bit.

The end

Made in the USA
Coppell, TX
30 November 2019

12180563R00226